P9-EKE-819

The Invisible Library

Genevieve Cogman started on Tolkien and Sherlock Holmes at an early age, and has never looked back. But on a perhaps more prosaic note, she has an M.Sc. in Statistics with Medical Applications and has wielded this in an assortment of jobs: clinical coder, data analyst and classifications specialist. She has also previously worked as a freelance roleplaying game writer. Her hobbies include patchwork, beading, knitting and gaming, and she lives in the north of England. *The Invisible Library* is the first novel in her Invisible Library series.

By Genevieve Cogman

The Invisible Library
The Masked City
The Burning Page

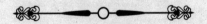

THE
INVISIBLE
LIBRARY

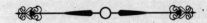

GENEVIEVE COGMAN

TOR

First published 2015 by Tor,
an imprint of Pan Macmillan
The Smithson, 6 Briset Street, London EC1M 5NR
EU representative: Macmillan Publishers Ireland Ltd, 1st Floor,
The Liffey Trust Centre, 117–126 Sheriff Street Upper,
Dublin 1, DO1 YC43
Associated companies throughout the world
www.panmacmillan.com

ISBN 978-1-4472-5623-6

18

A CIP catalogue record for this book is available from the British Library.

Typeset by Ellipsis Digital, Glasgow
Printed and bound by CPI Group (UK) Ltd, Croydon, CR0 4YY

Visit **www.panmacmillan.com** to read more about all our books
and to buy them. You will also find features, author interviews and
news of any author events, and you can sign up for e-newsletters
so that you're always first to hear about our new releases.

ACKNOWLEDGEMENTS

Thank you to everyone who helped with this book. Thank you to my agent, Lucienne Diver, who is awesome and whom I still can't quite believe I got as an agent, and my editor, Bella Pagan, who is fantastic and turned this into a much better book than it was originally.

Thank you to all my readers, supporters, and friends, including but not limited to: Beth, Jeanne, April, Anne, Phyllis, Nora, Walter, Em, Jennifer, Stuart, Elaine, Lisa, Hazel, and Noelle. You are all cool and awesome.

And thank you, now and always, to my parents.

CHAPTER ONE

Irene passed the mop across the stone floor in smooth, careful strokes, idly admiring the gleam of wet flagstones in the lantern-light. Her back was complaining, but that was only normal after an evening's work cleaning. The cleaning was certainly necessary. The pupils at Prince Mordred's Private Academy for Boys managed to get just as much mud and muck on the floor as any other teenagers would. Clean indoor studies in the dark arts, military history and alchemy didn't preclude messy outdoor classes in strategic combat, duelling, open-field assassination and rugby.

The clock in the study struck the quarter-hour. That gave her forty-five minutes before the midnight orisons and chants. She knew from weeks of experience – and, to be honest, her own memories of boarding school – that the boys wouldn't be getting up a moment earlier than necessary. This meant most would be dragging themselves out of bed at eleven forty-five, before heading to the chapel with hastily thrown-on clothes and barely brushed hair. So that gave her thirty minutes before any of them started moving.

Thirty minutes to steal a book and to escape.

She propped the mop in her bucket, straightened, and took a moment to rub her knuckles into the small of her

1

back. Sometimes undercover work as a Librarian involved posing as a rich socialite, and the Librarian in question got to stay at expensive hotels and country houses. All while wearing appropriately high fashion and dining off *haute cuisine*, probably on gold-edged plates. At other times, it involved spending months building an identity as a hard-working menial, sleeping in attics, wearing a plain grey woollen dress, and eating the same food as the boys. She could only hope that her next assignment wouldn't involve endless porridge for breakfast.

Two doors down along the corridor was Irene's destination: the House Trophy Room. It was full of silver cups, all embossed with variations on *Turquine House*, as well as trophy pieces of art and presentation manuscripts.

One of those manuscripts was her goal.

Irene had been sent by the Library to this alternate world to obtain *Midnight Requiems*, the famous necromancer Balan Pestifer's first published book. It was by all accounts a fascinating, deeply informative, and highly unread piece of writing. She'd spent a month looking for a copy of it – as the Library didn't actually require an *original* version of the text, just an accurate one. Unfortunately, not only had she been unable to track down a copy, but her enquiries had caught the interest of other people (necromancers, biblio-philes and ghouls). She'd had to burn that cover identity and go on the run before they caught up with her.

It had been pure chance (or, as she liked to think of it, finely honed instinct) that had prompted her to notice a casual reference in some correspondence to 'Sire Pestifer's fond memories of his old school' and more, 'his donations to the school'. Now at the time that Pestifer had *written* this early piece, he'd still been young and unrecognized. It was not beyond the bounds of possibility that in his desper-ation for attention, or simply out of the urge to brag, he'd donated a copy of his writings to the school. (And she'd exhausted all her other leads. It was worth a try.)

Irene had taken a few weeks to establish a new identity as a young woman in her mid-twenties with a poor but honest background, suitable for skivvying, then found herself a job as a cleaning maid. The main school library hadn't held any copies of *Midnight Requiems*, and in desperation she'd resorted to checking the necromancer's original boarding house. Beyond all expectation, she'd been lucky.

She abandoned her cleaning equipment, and opened the window at the end of the hall. The leaded glass swung easily under her hand: she'd taken care to oil it earlier. A cool breeze drifted in, with a hint of oncoming rain. Hopefully this bit of misdirection wouldn't be necessary, but one of the Library's mottos was borrowed directly from the great military thinker Clausewitz: no strategy ever survived contact with the enemy. Or, in the vernacular, Things Will Go Wrong. Be Prepared.

She quickly trotted back down the corridor to the trophy room, and pushed the door open. The light from the corridor gleamed on the silver cups and glass display cabinets. Without bothering to kindle the room's central lantern, she crossed to the second cupboard on the right. She could still smell the polish she'd used on the wood two days ago. Opening its door, she withdrew the pile of books stacked at the back, and pulled out a battered volume in dark purple leather.

(When Pestifer sent the book to the school, had he fretted and paced the floor, hoping to get some sort of acknowledgement back from the teachers, praising his research, wishing him future success? Or had they sent him a bare form letter to say that they'd received it – and then dropped his work into a pile of other self-published vanity books sent by ex-pupils and forgotten all about it?)

Fortunately it was a fairly small volume. She tucked it into a hidden pocket, returned the other books to cover her tracks, and then hesitated.

This was, after all, a school that taught magic. And as a Librarian she had one big advantage that nobody else had – not necromancers, Fae, dragons, ordinary humans or anyone. It was called the *Language*. Only Librarians could read it. Only Librarians could use it. It could affect certain aspects of reality. It was extremely useful, even if the vocabulary needed constant revision. Unfortunately, it didn't work on pure magic. If the masters at the school had set some sort of alarm spell to prevent anyone stealing the cups, and if that worked on *anything* that was taken out of the room, then she might be in for a nasty surprise. And it would be hideously embarrassing to be hunted down by a mob of teenagers.

Irene mentally shook herself. She'd planned for this. There was no point in delaying any longer, and standing around reconsidering possibilities would only result in her running short on time.

She stepped across the threshold.

Sudden raucous noise broke the silence. The stone arch above the doorway rippled, lips forming from the stone to howl, 'Thief! Thief!'

Irene didn't bother pausing to curse fate. There would be people here within seconds. With a loud scream she threw herself down on top of her mop and bucket, deliberately sprawling in the inevitable puddle of dirty water. She also managed to crack her shin on the side of the bucket, which brought genuine tears to her eyes.

A couple of senior boys got there first, scurrying round the corner in nightshirts and slippers. Far too awake to have only just risen from sleep, they'd probably been busy with some illicit hobby or other.

'Where's the thief?' the dark-haired one shouted.

'There she is!' the blond one declared, pointing a finger at Irene.

'Don't be stupid, that's one of the servants,' the dark-haired one said, demonstrating the advantage of stealing books while dressed as a servant. 'You! Wench! Where's the thief?'

Irene pointed a shaking hand in the direction of the open window. It chose that moment to swing conveniently in the rising wind. 'He – he knocked me down—'

'What's this?' One of the masters had arrived on the scene. Fully dressed and trailing a drift of tobacco smoke, he cleared a path through the gathering mob of junior boys with a few snaps of his fingers. 'Has one of you boys set off the alarm?'

'No, sir!' the blond senior said quickly. 'We just got here as he was escaping. He went out through the window! Can we pursue him?'

The master's gaze shifted to Irene. 'You, woman!'

Irene hastily dragged herself to her feet, leaning artistically on the mop, and pushed back a straggle of loose hair. (She was looking forward to being out of this place, so she could have hot showers and put her hair up in a proper bun.) 'Yes, sir?' she snivelled. The book in her skirt pocket pressed against her leg.

'What did you see?' he demanded.

'Oh, sir,' Irene began, letting her lower lip quiver suitably. 'I was just mopping the corridor, and when I came to the door of the trophy room here,' she pointed it out needlessly, 'there was a light inside. So I thought that one of the young gentlemen might be studying . . . and I knocked on the door to ask if I might come in to clean the floor. But nobody answered, sir. So I began to open the door, and then all of a sudden someone pushes it open from inside, and it knocks me down as he runs out of the room.'

The audience of boys, ranging from eleven to seventeen years old, hung on her every word. A couple of juniors set their chins pugnaciously, clearly imagining that they themselves would have been ready for such an event. They would undoubtedly have knocked the intruder unconscious then and there.

'He was a very tall man,' Irene said helpfully. 'And he was all dressed in black, but something was muffled round his face so that I couldn't see it properly. And he had something under one arm, all wrapped in canvas. And then the alarm went off, and I screamed for help, but he went running down the corridor and escaped through the window.' She pointed at the clearly open window, an obvious – perhaps too obvious? – escape route for any hypothetical thief. 'And then these young gentlemen came along, just after he'd escaped.' She nodded to the first two arrivals, who looked smug.

The master nodded. He stroked his chin thoughtfully. 'Jenkins! Palmwaite! Take charge of the House and have everyone get back to preparing for chapel. Salter, Bryce, come and inventory the room with me. We must establish what was taken.'

There were muffled noises of protest from the milling crowd of boys, who clearly wanted to leap out of the window and pursue the thief – or, possibly, go down to the ground floor and *then* pursue the thief without leaping out of a second-floor window. But nobody actually tried that.

Irene cursed inwardly. A large-scale attempted pursuit of a non-existent intruder would have confused matters nicely.

'You,' the master said, turning to Irene. 'Go downstairs to the kitchen and have some tea, woman. It must have been an unpleasant experience for you.' Was that a flash of genuine concern in his eyes? Or was it something more suspicious? She'd done her best to leave a false trail, but the fact remained that she *was* the only person in the vicinity, and something had just been stolen. Most of the masters round here ignored the servants, but this one might be the unfortunate exception to the rule. 'Hold yourself ready in case we need to question you further.'

'Of course, sir,' Irene said, bobbing a little curtsey. She picked up the mop and bucket, and pushed through the crowd of boys, heading for the stairs, taking care not to walk suspiciously fast.

She'd need two minutes to get to the kitchen to dump the mop and bucket. Another minute to get out of the House. Five more minutes – three minutes at a run – to get to the school library. She would be cutting it fine.

The kitchen was already bustling when she got there, with the house maids preparing kettles of post-chapel porridge. The housekeeper, butler and cook were playing cards, and no one had bothered to investigate the alarms from upstairs.

'Something the matter, Meredith?' the housekeeper enquired as Irene entered.

'Just the young gentlemen being their usual selves, ma'am,' Irene answered. 'I think it's one of the other Houses playing some sort of prank on them. With your permission, may I step out to the washroom to get myself cleaned up?' She indicated the dirty wash-water stains on her grey uniform dress and her apron.

'Be sure not to take too long,' the housekeeper said. 'You'll be sweeping out the dormitories while the young gentlemen are in chapel.'

Irene nodded humbly, and left the kitchen. Still no alarm from upstairs. Good. She quietly opened the boarding house door, stepping outside.

The boarding houses were in a row along the main

avenue, with a central quadrangle holding the chapel, the assembly hall and – most importantly to her purposes – the school library. Turquine House was the second along, which meant there was just one house to pass, preferably without drawing attention. Not run. She mustn't run yet. If anyone saw her running, it would only attract suspicion. Just walk, nice and calmly, as if she were simply running an errand.

She managed a whole ten yards.

A window flew up behind her in Turquine House, and the master who'd spoken to her earlier leaned out. He pointed at her. 'Thief! *Thief!*'

Irene picked up her skirts and ran. Gravel crunched under her feet, and the first drops of rain slapped against her face. She came level with the next boarding house, Bruce House, and for a moment she considered abandoning her arranged escape plan and simply ducking into there in order to break her trail and slow down pursuit. But common sense pointed out that it wouldn't work for more than a few minutes –

The whistling screech from behind warned her just in time. She dived to the ground, throwing herself into a roll, as the gargoyle came screaming down, its stone claws extended and clutching for her. It missed, and struggled to pull out of its dive, its heavy wings sawing at the air as it laboured to gain height. Another one had swooped from the roof of Turquine's, and was circling to reach a suitable angle of attack.

This was one of those moments, Irene reflected bitterly, when it would be wonderful to be a necromancer, or a wizard, or someone who could manipulate the magical forces of the world and *blast annoying gargoyles out of the sky*. She'd done her best to avoid attention, keep her cover, and not endanger bratty little boys who left mud all over the floor and didn't bother to hang up their cloaks. What had it got her? A swarm of attacking gargoyles – well, only two gargoyles so far, but still – and probably a mass assault by pupils and masters within a few minutes. So much for the rewards of virtue.

She quickly reviewed what she knew about the gargoyles. There was one on the roof of each boarding house. They were even listed in the boarding school prospectus as a guarantee of student safety – ANY KIDNAPPERS WILL BE TORN TO BLOODY RAGS BY OUR PROFESSIONALLY MAINTAINED HISTORICAL ARTEFACTS! Though after working here for several months, she thought the pupils themselves were much more lethal to possible kidnappers.

On the positive side (one must always look for the positive side) the gargoyles were extremely showy, but not actually that *effective* over a short space of ground. On the negative side, running in a straight line to escape would make her a beautiful moving target. But getting back to the positives, the gargoyles were made of granite, as lovingly described in the prospectus, unlike anything else within earshot.

This would need careful timing. Luckily the gargoyles weren't particularly intelligent so they would be focused on capturing her, not on wondering why she was standing conveniently still.

She took a deep breath.

The first gargoyle reached suitable swooping altitude. It called to the other gargoyle in a carrying screech, and then the two of them dropped towards her together, their wings spread in wide, dark traceries against the sky.

Irene screamed, at the top of her voice, '**Granite, be stone and lie still!**'

The Language always worked well when it was

instructing things to be what they naturally were, or to do what they naturally wanted to do. Stone *wanted* to be inert and solid. Her command only reinforced the natural order of things. It was therefore the perfect antidote to the unnatural magic keeping stone gargoyles in flight.

The gargoyles stiffened mid-stoop, their wings freezing in place, and overshot her easily. One thumped squarely into the ground, pounding out a crater for itself, while the other came in at more of an angle. It ploughed a wide groove along the nicely smoothed gravel path, before colliding with one of the stately lime trees bordering the avenue. Leaves rained down on it.

There was no time for her to pause and feel smug, so she ran.

Then the howling started. It was either hellhounds or teenagers, and she suspected the former. They'd been in the prospectus, too. The prospectus had been very helpful about the school's security precautions. If she ever had to come back here again, perhaps she could sell her services as a security consultant. Under a pseudonym, of course.

A sudden burst of red light sent her shadow leaping down the avenue ahead of her, and proved the hellhound theory. Right. She'd planned for hellhounds. She could plan for *organized* magic, even if she couldn't perform it. She just had to stay calm and cool and collected *and get to the fire hydrant ahead before they caught up with her*.

Among its modern conveniences, the school included running water and precautions against fire. Which meant fire hydrants spaced along the main avenue. The one that lay between her and the school library was twenty yards away.

Ten yards. She could hear pounding paws behind her, throwing up gravel in a rattle of ferocious speed. She didn't look.

Five yards. Something panted *just behind her*.

She threw herself at the hydrant, an unimpressive black stub of metal barely two feet high. But as she did, a heavy scorching weight collided with her back, slamming her to the ground and pinning her there. She wrenched her head round enough to see the huge dog-like creature crouching on top of her. It wasn't quite burning her, not yet, but its body was as hot as a banked stove. And she knew, if it wanted to, it could get much, *much* hotter. Its eyes were vicious coals in its flaming head, and when it opened its mouth, baring ragged teeth, a line of searing drool dripped across the back of her neck. *Go on, try it,* it seemed to be saying. *Just try something. Give me an excuse.*

'Hydrant, burst!' Irene screamed.

The hellhound opened its jaws wider in lazy warning.

The hydrant exploded at approximately knee level. Fragments of twisted iron went spraying out in all directions with the first intense burst of water. Irene was torn between thinking *Thank goodness I'm on the ground* and *That's what comes of sloppy vocabulary and word choice.* A bit of metal sheared through the air a few inches above her nose and slapped into the hellhound almost casually, sending it cartwheeling backwards with a howl of pain.

It took Irene a moment to pull her wits together and scramble to her feet. The water should slow the hellhounds and douse their fires for a while, but she didn't have any other backup plans. And she still had to get to the school library. Her dress wet and her shoes soaked through, she broke into a stagger, then into a run.

The library doors were made of heavy studded wood, and when she yanked them open, warm lantern-light spilled out over her. *Making you a target for anyone looking in your direction*, her sense of self-preservation pointed out. She stumbled into the vestibule and swung the heavy door closed, but there was only one large lock on the door, and no key. But then again, she didn't need one.

She leaned over and murmured in the Language, '**Lock on the library door, lock yourself shut.**'

The sound of tumblers moving into the locked position was very satisfying. Especially when the next noise, a couple of seconds later, was the heavy thud of hellhound hitting the door on the other side.

'What's going on there?' an annoyed voice called from deeper inside the library.

Irene had scouted out the place earlier, with a duster and wax polish as an alibi. Directly ahead were the non-fiction stacks, shelves full of books on everything from astrology to Zoroastrianism. And to the right, there was a small office where books were stored for mending. More importantly, the office had a *door* she could use to get out of here and that was what she needed.

There was another thump from behind her. The main door shivered slightly under attack, but stood firm.

She didn't bother replying to the voice she'd heard. Instead she brushed the gravel from her clothing, forcing herself to calmness. The atmosphere of the place soothed her automatically; the rich lantern lights, the sheer *scent* of paper and leather, and the fact that everywhere she looked, there were books, books, beautiful books.

Another thump from the outer door, and the sound of raised angry voices. All right, perhaps she shouldn't relax *too* much.

She stood in front of the closed office door, taking a deep breath.

'**Open to the Library,**' she said, giving the word *Library* its full value in the Language, and felt the tattoo scrawled across her back shift and writhe as the link was established. There was the usual flurrying moment of awareness and pressure, as though something huge and unimaginable was riffling through the pages of her mind. It always lasted just that little bit too long to bear, and then the door shuddered under her hand and opened.

A sudden burst of noise indicated that her pursuers had managed to enter. She spared a moment to regret that she hadn't had time to grab any other books, and quickly stepped through. As the latch clicked shut behind her, it re-established itself as part of the world she'd left behind. However many times they might open it now, it would only ever reveal the office to which it originally belonged. They would never be able to follow her here.

She was in the Library. Not just any library, but THE Library.

High shelves rose on either side, too high and full of books for her to see what lay beyond. The narrow gap in front of her was barely wide enough to squeeze through. Her shoes left wet prints in the dust behind her, and she stepped over three sets of abandoned notes as she edged towards the lit area in the distance. The only sounds were a vague, half-audible creaking somewhere to her left, irregular and uncertain as the slow oscillations of a child's swing.

The cramped space abruptly opened out into a wider wood-panelled room, with a wooden floor. She glanced around, but couldn't identify it offhand. The books on the shelves were printed, and some of them looked more modern than any from the alternate that she had just left, but that in itself proved nothing. The large centre table and chairs were covered with dust, just like the floor, and the computer sitting on the table was silent. A single lantern hung from the ceiling, with a white crystal burning brilliantly in the centre. In the far wall, a bow window looked out over a gaslamp-lit night-time street, and a wind tugged at the tree branches, making them silently bend and sway.

With a sigh of relief, Irene sat down in one of the chairs, brushed loose gravel out of her hair, and drew the stolen book out of her hidden pocket. It was safe and dry. Another job done, even if she had been forced to abandon her cover identity. And she'd even given the school a legend. The thought made her smile. She could imagine new boys being told the story of The Night Turquine House Got Burgled. The details would expand over time. She'd eventually become a world-famous master thief that had infiltrated the place in disguise, seduced half the teachers, and summoned demons to aid her escape.

Thoughtfully she looked down at the book in her hands. After all this trouble to get hold of it, she was just a little curious about what great secrets of necromancy might be revealed within. Raising armies of the dead? Invoking ghosts? How to unnaturally extend your life for thousands of years?

She opened it at the beginning. The page read:

It is my theory that the greater truths underlying life and death can best be understood as a parable — that is, as a fiction. There is no way that the human mind can understand, let alone accept, any of the fundamental principles that govern the transmission and return of souls, or the flux of energies which can bind a body on the line between life and death, in practical terms: the laws which other people have discussed, proposed, or even affirmed, in higher texts on the subject, slip past the boundaries of that level of understanding which would allow true inherent cognisance and manipulation of those necessities.

Too many commas and overly long phrases, she decided.

I have therefore decided to describe my work and my experiments, and the understanding which I have derived from it, in the form of a story. Those who wish to do so may take what they can from it. My sole desire is to explain and to enlighten.

And, Irene hoped, to entertain. She turned the page.

It was on the morning of Peredur's birthday that the ravens came to him one last time. He had been three weeks at the house of the witches, and they had taught him much, but he had long been absent from the court of Arthur. The first raven stooped down, and took on the form of a woman. When the morning light struck her, she showed the form he knew: a withered old hag, scarcely able to bear the helm and armour she wore. But when she stood in shadow, then she was young and comely: never had hair been so black or skin so pale, or eyes so piercing sweet.

'Peredur,' she said, 'in the name of the Ladies of Orkney, I ask that you remain here one day longer. For my sisters and I have searched the stars, and I tell you that if you leave us now, then you will perish before your time, and that in a fool's quest: but if you stay one day more with us, then your path will be steady and your sister will meet you before all is done.'

'I have no sister,' said Peredur.

'Aye,' the raven witch said. 'None that you have met . . .'

Irene shut the book reluctantly. Of course she had to send it to Coppelia first, for inspection and evaluation, but perhaps after that she could get her hands on it again.

There was nothing wrong with being curious about how a story turned out, after all. She was a Librarian. It went with the job. And she didn't want great secrets of necromancy, or any other sort of magic. She just wanted – had always wanted – a good book to read. The being chased by hellhounds and blowing things up was a comparatively unimportant part of the job. Getting the books, now that was what *really* mattered to her.

That was the whole point of the Library: as far as she'd been taught, anyway. It wasn't about a higher mission to save worlds. It was about finding unique works of fiction, and saving them in a place out of time and space. Perhaps some people might think that was a petty way to spend eternity, but Irene was happy with her choice. Anyone who really loved a good story would understand.

And if there were rumours that the Library did have a deeper purpose – well, there were always so many rumours, and she had missions to complete. She could wait for more answers. She had time.

CHAPTER TWO

Irene focused on the next steps. The sooner she handed in this book and filed a report, the sooner she could get herself clean and dry, and sit down with a good book of her own. And she should be able to expect a few weeks off for her own projects, which quite frankly she lusted after at the moment.

The computer in front of her hummed to life as she flicked the on switch. She wiped the screen with her sleeve, and blew dust off the keyboard. It was a pity that nobody could control the re-entry point of forced passages back to the Library from alternate worlds. All you knew was that you'd end up in the Library – although there were horror stories about people who'd spent years finding their way back up from some of the catacombs where the really old data was stored.

The screen flared with the Library logo: a closed book, with login and password windows. She typed quickly, hit return, and the book slowly opened, pages riffling to show her inbox.

At least nobody had figured out how to spam the Library computer system yet.

She called up a local map. It blurred into existence on the

screen in a three-dimensional diagram, and an arrow in red pointed out her current room. She wasn't too far out, only a couple of hours' walk from Central. Reassured, she sent a quick email to Coppelia, her direct supervisor and mentor.

Irene here. Have secured the required material. Request appointment to deliver. Currently in A-254 Latin American Literature 20th century, about two and a half hours from your office.

The beep as she sent the email broke the room's silence.

It was a pity that mobile phones, or wi-fi, or any similar technologies, all failed in the Library. Any sort of transmission not based on strictly physical links failed, or malfunctioned, or spouted static in bright warbling tones. Research had been done, research was being done, and, Irene suspected, research would still be being done in a hundred years. Technology wasn't the only failure, either. Magical forms of communication were useless too and the side-effects tended to be even more painful. Or so she'd heard. She hadn't tried. She liked her brains inside her skull where they belonged.

While she was waiting for an answer, she caught up on her email. The usual stuff; mass-mailed requests for books on particular topics of research, comparisons of Victorian pornography across alternative Victorian worlds, someone touting their new thesis on stimulant abuse and associative poetry. She deleted a plaintive begging letter looking for suggestions on how to improve penicillin usage in Dark Age era alternates. But she highlighted a dozen Language updates, which she put aside to check later.

The only personal email in the whole batch was from her mother. A quick note, as quick and brief as Irene's own email to her supervisor, to let Irene know that she and her father would be in Alternate G-337 for the next few months. They were in Russia, looking for ikons and psalm settings. The note expressed hopes that Irene was well and enjoying herself, and asked vaguely what she might like for her birthday.

As usual, the note was unsigned. Irene was expected to read the name on the email address and not ask for more.

She rested her chin on her hands and stared at the screen. She hadn't actually seen her parents for a couple of years now. The Library kept them all busy, and to be honest she never knew what to say to them these days. One could always discuss work, but beyond that was a whole minefield of social interaction. Her parents would probably be retiring to the Library in a few decades, and hopefully by then she'd have worked out how to make polite conversation with them. It had been so much easier when she was younger.

I'd love some amber,

she replied to the email. That should be safe enough.

The Language updates were what she might have expected, given three months' absence. No new grammar, but some new vocabulary, most of it world-specific and dealing with concepts or items that hadn't come to the Library before. A few adjectival redefinitions. A collected set of adverbs on the action of sleeping.

Irene scanned through them as quickly as she could. The problem with an evolving language that could be used to express things precisely was that, well, it evolved. The more contributory material agents like Irene brought into the Library, the more the Language changed. She wondered morosely if her recent prize would inspire a new word or two, or just change an old one. Perhaps it would help define a particular shade of black.

Still. There were compensations. Like being able to give orders to the world around you. But when she'd signed up for eternity, she hadn't quite expected to spend most of it revising vocabulary lists.

The computer beeped again. It was a reply from Coppelia, and it had arrived surprisingly fast. Irene opened it, and blinked at the size of the response.

My dear Irene,

What a pleasure to see you back here again! Though of course, when I say see, I mean to be aware of your presence in the Library. It's been several weeks now, and you wouldn't believe how glad I am to have you back . . .

Irene frowned. This looked like something that had been prepared ahead of time. She had a bad feeling about it.

. . . and I have a little job for you to do.

Right.

Your frequent work out there in the alternates has left you behind on the required curriculum of mentoring new students, but fortunately I have been able to find a way round that.

Irene snorted. Coppelia had certainly assured her that it'd all be sorted out. But she'd given the impression of managing to sidetrack it and get round it, rather than having to make it up later via some unpleasant duty.

It just so happens . . .

She was just so totally screwed.

. . . that we have a new recruit on our hands who's up for his first fieldwork, and naturally I thought of you as the ideal person to mentor him! You'll be able to give him all the benefits of your experience, while at the same time getting some credits on your record for handling him.

Handling him? What was he, an unexploded bomb? She'd had quite enough of pupils in the last few weeks.

It's quite a short assignment, and shouldn't take you more than a few days, maybe a week. You should be operating near a fixed exit point into the nominated world, so if there are any problems or delays you can send me a report.

It sounded, Irene reflected, as if Coppelia really wanted to cover her own back on this one.

My dear Irene, I have the utmost confidence in you. I know that I can rely on you to live up to the Library's traditions and expectations, while providing a valuable example to this new recruit.

It also sounded as if Coppelia had been reading too many bad recruitment brochures and codes of practice.

I've authorized Kai (that's his name) to take one of the rapid shifts to where you are, so you can expect him any moment.

Irene paused to listen nervously. If that was true, then Kai had been allowed to use one of the most closely restricted methods of transport in the entire Library. This either meant that Coppelia didn't want any argument and just wanted her out of the way and on the job, or that the mission was very urgent, or that there was something about Kai so dubious that he shouldn't be seen in public. Perhaps Kai simply couldn't handle normal Library navigation, which was bad news in itself . . . and that was multiple clauses based on an either/or, which was bad grammar. She hated bad grammar.

He's got all the details on the mission.

Now that was really bad. That could mean that Coppelia wasn't prepared to put it in an email. Irene could smell politics, and she didn't want to get involved with that at all. She'd always thought that Coppelia was a more reasonable, research-oriented, only-Machiavellian-once-in-a-while sort of supervisor. Not the sort of supervisor who'd dump her with an unprintable mission, an inexperienced trainee, and a rapid push out through the nearest Traverse exit point.

Do leave your latest input material with the nearest Desk; tag it with my name, and I'll see that it gets processed.

Well, that was something, at least . . .

From the corridor outside came a sudden gust of wind and a thud. It was reminiscent of a pneumatic pressure tube delivering papers.

A pause. A knock on a nearby door.

'Come in,' Irene called, turning her chair to face it.

The door swung open to reveal a young man.

'You must be Kai,' Irene said, rising to her feet. 'Do come in.'

He had the sort of beauty that instantly shifted him from

a possible romance object to an absolute impossibility. Nobody got to spend time with people who looked like that, outside the front pages of newspapers and glossy magazines. His skin was so pale that she could see blue veins at his wrists and throat. And his hair was a shade of black that looked almost steely blue in the dim lights, braided down the back of his neck. His eyebrows were the same shade, like lines of ink on his face, and his cheekbones could have been used to cut diamonds, let alone cheese. He was wearing a battered black leather jacket and jeans that quite failed to play down his startling good looks, and his white T-shirt was not only spotlessly laundered, it was ironed and starched.

'Yeah,' he said. 'I am. You're Irene, right?'

Even his voice deserved admirers: low, precise, husky. His casual choice of words seemed more like affectation than actual carelessness. 'I am,' Irene acknowledged. 'And you're my new trainee.'

'Uh-huh.' He strode into the room, letting the door close behind him. 'And I'm finally getting out of this place.'

'I see. Please sit down. I haven't finished reading Coppelia's email yet.'

He blinked at her, then strode across to the nearest chair and flung himself down into it, triggering a choking cloud of dust.

Handle matters smoothly and efficiently, and you may expect some spare time for private research when this is over. I regret having to send you out again this fast, but needs must, my dear Irene, and we must all make do with the resources available to us.

Yours affectionately,

Coppelia

Irene sat back and frowned at the screen. She was no conspiracy theorist, but if she had been, she could have constructed whole volumes based on that paragraph. 'Coppelia says that you've got all the details on the mission,' she said over her shoulder.

'Yeah. Madame Coppelia,' he stressed the honorific slightly, 'gave me the stuff. Didn't look like much.'

Irene turned to face him. 'If you wouldn't mind?' she said, extending her hand.

Kai reached inside his jacket, and pulled out a thin blue envelope. He handed it to her carefully, making the gesture courteous rather than a simple transfer. 'There you go. Boss? Madame? Sir?'

'Irene will do,' she said. She hesitated for a moment, wishing she had a paperknife, but there wasn't one to hand and she didn't feel like showing Kai where she kept her hidden blade. With a slight wince at the inelegance, she ripped it open and slid out a single piece of paper.

Kai didn't actually lean forward to peer at the letter, but he did tilt his head curiously.

'Objective,' Irene read out obligingly. 'Original Grimm manuscript, volume 1, 1812, currently in London, parallel B-395: closest Traverse exit within the British Library, located inside British Museum, further details available from on-site Librarian in Residence.'

'Grimm?'

'Fairy tales, I imagine.' Irene tapped a finger against the edge of the paper. 'Not one of my areas. I'm not sure why I've – why we've been assigned it. Unless it's something you've experience in?'

Kai shook his head. 'I'm not well up on the European stuff. Don't even know which alternate that is. Do you think it's something that's unique to that world?'

That was a reasonable question. There were three basic

reasons why Librarians were sent out to alternates to find specific books: because the book was important to a senior Librarian, because the book would have an effect on the Language, or because the book was specific and unique to that alternate world. In this last case, the Library's ownership of it would reinforce the Library's links to the world from which the book originated. (Irene wasn't sure into which of the three categories her latest acquisition fell, though she suspected a case of 'effect on the Language'. She should probably try to find out at some point.)

If this Grimm manuscript was the sort of book that occurred in multiple different alternate worlds, then it wouldn't have warranted a specific mission from Coppelia. By the time that senior Librarians had become senior Librarians, they weren't interested in anything less than rarities. An ordinary book existing in multiple worlds would simply have shown up in someone's regular shopping list, probably along with the complete works of Nick Carter, the complete cases of Judge Dee, and the complete biographies, true and false, of Prester John. The question of *why* some books were unique and occurred only in specific worlds was one of the great imponderables, and hopefully Irene would actually get an answer to it some day. When she was a senior Librarian herself, perhaps. Decades in the future. Maybe even centuries.

In any case, there was no point standing around guessing. Irene tried to phrase her answer to make it seem sensible, rather than simply shutting Kai down in the first ten minutes of their acquaintance.

'Probably best to find out from the on-site Librarian, when we reach the alternate destination. If Coppelia hasn't told you, and hasn't told me . . .'

Kai shrugged. 'As long as it gets me out of here, I'm not going to complain.'

'How long have you been here?' Irene asked curiously.

'Five years.' His tone was smoothed to careful politeness, like sea-worn stones. 'I know it's the policy to keep new people here till they've studied the basics and they're sure we're not going to do a runner, but it's been five sodding years.'

'I'm sorry,' Irene said flatly as she tapped in a quick response to Coppelia's email.

'Sorry?'

'Yes. I was born into the job. My parents are both Librarians. It probably made things easier. I always knew what was expected of me.' It was quite true; it had made things easier. She'd always known what she was being brought up to do. The years in the Library were rotated with years in alternates, and they'd gone by one after another, with study, practice and effort and long silent aisles of books.

'Oh.'

'I don't expect that waiting has been . . . fun.'

'Fun.' He snorted. 'No. Not fun. It was kinda interesting, but it wasn't fun.'

'Did you like Coppelia?' She dispatched the email, then logged out neatly.

'I've only been studying under her for the last few months.'

'She's one of the more . . .' Irene paused, considering what words she could use that wouldn't get her into trouble later if repeated elsewhere. She personally liked Coppelia, but words such as *Machiavellian*, *efficiently unprincipled*, and *ice-hearted* didn't always go down well in conversations.

'Oh, I liked her,' Kai said hastily, and Irene turned to look at him, surprised at the warmth in his voice. 'She's a strong woman. Very organized. Commanding personality. My mother would like – would have liked her. If. You know. They never take people to work here with close living relatives, right?'

'No,' Irene agreed. 'It's in the rules. It'd be unfair to them.'

'And, um . . .' He looked at her from under his long eyelashes. 'About those rumours that sometimes they make sure that there aren't any close living relatives? Or any living relatives at all?'

Irene swallowed. She leaned across to turn off the computer, hoping that it'd hide the nervous gesture. 'There are always rumours.'

'Are they true?'

Sometimes I think they are. She wasn't naive. She knew that the Library didn't always stick to its own rules. 'It wouldn't help either of us for me to tell you they were,' she said flatly.

'Oh.' He leaned back in his chair again.

'You've been here five years. What do you expect me to say?'

'I was kinda expecting you to give me the official line.' He was looking at her with more interest now. His eyes glittered in the dim light. 'Didn't expect you to hint it might be true.'

'I didn't,' she said quickly. She slid the paper back into the envelope, and slipped it into the pocket of her dress. 'Here's my first suggestion to you as your new mentor, Kai. The Library runs on conspiracy theory. Admit nothing, deny everything, then find out what's going on and publish a paper on the subject. It's not as if they can stop you doing that.'

He tilted his head. 'Oh, they could always get rid of the paper.'

'Get rid of the paper?' She laughed. 'Kai, this is the Library. We never get rid of anything here. Ever.'

He shrugged, clearly giving up on the enquiry. 'Okay. If you don't want to be serious about it, I won't push it. Shall we get going?'

'Certainly,' Irene said, rising to her feet. 'Please follow me. We can talk on the way.'

It was half an hour before he began speaking again, apart from casual grunts of acknowledgement or disagreement. She was leading the way down a spiral staircase of dark oak and black iron; it was too narrow for the two of them to walk side by side, and he was a few paces behind her. Narrow slit windows in the thick walls looked out over a sea of roofs. The occasional television aerial stood out among classic brickwork edifices and faux-Oriental domes. Finally Kai said, 'Can I ask some questions?'

'Of course.' She reached the bottom of the staircase, and stepped aside so he could catch up. The wide corridor ahead was crammed with doors on either side, some better polished and dusted than others. The lantern-light glinted on their brass plates.

'Ah, if we're going by foot to the exit point, isn't this going to take a while?'

'Fair point,' Irene said. 'It's in B-395, you remember?'

'Of course,' he said, and looked down his nose at her. He was several inches taller than her, so that allowed for a fair amount of condescension.

'Right.' She started off down the corridor. 'Now, I had a look at the map before you came in, and the closest access to B Wing is down this way and then up two floors. We can check a terminal when we get there and find the fastest way from there to 395. Hopefully it won't be more than a day or so from where we are.'

'A day or so . . . Can't we just take a rapid shift to get there?'

'No, afraid not. I don't have the authority to requisition one.' She couldn't help thinking how much easier it would have made things. 'You need to be at Coppelia's level to order one of those.'

'Oh.' He walked in silence for a few steps. 'Okay. So what do you know about B-395?'

'Well, obviously it's a magic-dominant alternate.'

'Because it's a B, or Beta-type world, right?'

'Yes. Which sort were you from, by the way?'

'Oh, one of the Gammas. So there was both tech and magic. High-tech, medium magic. They had problems getting them to work together, though – anyone who was too cyborged couldn't get magic to work.'

'Mm,' Irene said neutrally. 'I'm assuming you don't have any machine augmentation yourself.'

'No. Good thing too. They told me it wouldn't work here.'

'Not exactly,' Irene said punctiliously. 'It's more that no powered device can cross into or out of the Library while still functioning. Devices would work perfectly well if you could turn them off while you were traversing, and then on again once you were in here . . .'

Kai shook his head. 'Not my gig. What's the use of it if I'd have to keep on turning it on and off? I wasn't really into the magic either. I was more heavy on real world stuff, like physical combat, martial arts, things like that.'

'How did you get picked up for the Library, then?' she asked.

Kai shrugged. 'Well, everyone did research using online tools where I was. But from time to time I used to get jobs hunting down old books for this researcher. Some of them were, you know, not legal – and real big-time not legal too . . . So I started looking into his background, thought I might find something interesting. And I think I sort of looked a bit too hard. Because next thing I was getting a visit from some real hardline people, and they told me I needed to come and work for them.'

'Or?'

Kai glanced at her icily. 'The "or" would have been bad news for me.'

Irene was silent for the time it took to walk past several doors. Eventually she said, 'So here you are then. Are you unhappy?'

'Not so much,' he said, surprising her. 'You play the game, you take the risks. It was a better offer than some people would have given me, right? One of the people teaching me here, Master Grimaldi, he said that if I'd had a family they'd never have made the offer. They'd just have warned me off some other way. So I can't complain about that.'

'Then what can you complain about?'

'Five years.' They turned a corner. 'It's been five fricking years I've been here studying. I know about the time continuity thing. It'll have been five years since I dropped out of my own world. All the guys I used to run with, they'll have moved on or be dead. It was that sort of place. There was this girl. She'll have moved on to someone else. There'll be new fashions. New styles. New tech and magic. Maybe some countries will have gone and blown themselves up. And I won't have been there for any of it. How can I call it my own world if I keep on missing parts of it?'

'You can't,' Irene answered.

'How do you cope?'

Irene gestured at the corridor. 'This *is* my world.'

'Seriously?'

Irene's hand tightened on her book. 'Remember I told you that my parents were both Librarians? I wasn't born in the Library, but I might as well have been. They brought me in here when I was still a baby. They used to take me on jobs. Mother said I was the best prop she'd ever had.' She smiled faintly at the memory. 'Father used to tell me a bed-time story about how they smuggled a manuscript in my nappy bag.'

'No.' Kai came to a stop. '*Seriously.*'

Irene blinked. 'I am serious. I used to ask him to tell it every night.'

'They took you on missions like that?'

'Oh.' Irene could see what was bothering him now. 'Not *dangerous* ones, just safe ones where I was useful. They left me behind on the dangerous ones. And then later on, when I needed proper teaching and social acclimatization, they put me in a boarding school. The only problem was that I had to be careful how much holiday time I spent in the Library, or it'd have thrown me out of time-sync with the world I was schooling in. They did talk about moving me between worlds to different schools so that I could have years at the Library in between, but we didn't think it would work.' She'd been so proud to have had them talk it over with her, to have them treat her as an adult and ask her opinion.

'And you had . . . friends at boarding school, right?' Kai put the question tentatively, as though she was going to bite his head off for asking it.

'Of course.'

'Still in contact with any of them?'

'The time factor counts against it.' Irene shrugged. 'With the amount of time I had to spend in dedicated study in the Library, or in other worlds, it's been hard . . . I did stay in contact with some of them for a while. I dropped off letters whenever I could, but ultimately it didn't work. It was a school in Switzerland. A nice place. Very good on lan-guages.'

They turned another corner. Ahead of them, the corridor narrowed dramatically, and began to slope upwards. The floor, walls and ceiling were all made of the same creaking boards, worn and aged. Panel windows in the left wall looked out over an empty street lit by flaring torches, where muddy wheeltracks marked the passage of traffic, but there was no sign of anyone there.

'Straight ahead?' Kai asked.

Irene nodded. The floor creaked under their feet as they began the climb.

'This is like a bridge,' Kai said.

'Passageways between the Wings are always a little strange. I went through one once that you had to crawl through.'

'How did they move books through that?'

'They didn't, usually. They routed them round some other way. But it was useful if you were in a hurry.'

He jerked a thumb at the window. 'Have *you* ever seen anyone out there?'

'No. Nor has anyone.' The passageway levelled out, then began to slope downwards again. 'Now if only we could find a Traverse that accessed onto that, wouldn't it be interesting.'

'Yeah. That was one of the big topics of conversation among the students.' Kai sighed.

Irene had been looking around, and she saw what she wanted on the left. 'Just a moment,' she said, indicating a slot in the wall. 'Let me drop this book off for Coppelia.'

Kai nodded, and slouched against the wall, leaving Irene to take an envelope from the stack by the wall slot and slide her book into it. He did lean over just a little bit as she scribbled Coppelia's name on the envelope, just enough to see the title of the book, and his eyes narrowed in curiosity. 'You could always take it to her in person,' he suggested.

'Say you wanted to make sure she got it, and ask her a bit more about the assignment while you were there.'

Irene dropped the envelope into the slot and raised an eyebrow at him. 'Yes, and I could also get myself called an ignorant buffoon who didn't know how to read orders, let alone follow them. Someone who clearly didn't deserve any sort of mission, if I was just going to come running back to her for more details when she'd given me everything I needed.'

'Oh.' Kai sighed. 'Oh well.'

'Did you think I hadn't heard that speech from her?'

'I know I have. I was kind of hoping you hadn't.'

'Yes.' Irene gave him a brief smile before starting to walk again. 'Good try, though. So, 395.' The corridor turned and they walked into a room containing two terminals on a glossy ceramic table. One was being used by a young man, who didn't bother looking up, keeping his focus on the monitor's screen. His brown suit was scruffy and battered at the elbows and knees, and lace cuffs framed his bony wrists. It was probably appropriate for whatever alternate he'd just come from, or was about to go to. And it was still better than Irene's current battered grey dress.

'See,' Irene said, and took a seat at the other terminal. 'Give me a moment and I'll find the best route to get to the Traverse point for this mission.' *And pick up anything else I can about that world*, she added to herself. She'd been too flustered by Kai's arrival to do the sort of research she'd normally put in on a mission. Also, even if they were briefed by the alternate's Librarian-in-Residence, it'd be useful to have some idea of where they were going.

Kai looked around pointedly at the lack of other chairs, then sank down to sit cross-legged with his back to the wall, with an air of saintly patience.

Irene quickly logged in and pulled up the map. The

Traverse to B-395 was within half an hour's walk. Better than she'd hoped. No wonder Coppelia had sent Kai to her, rather than have Irene come to meet her. She reached for the usual pen and notepad, and jotted down directions, before looking for more information on the alternate itself.

Her reaction must have shown on her face, because Kai straightened and frowned at her. 'What is it—'

Irene hastily pointed at the other young man, and mouthed *Shhh*, putting her finger to her lips in as obvious a manner as she could.

Kai glared at her, then relaxed again, looking away.

She scribbled down the few facts hastily, then folded the paper and logged off the computer. With a vague nod to the young man, she got to her feet and strode for the door. 'Come on, Kai,' she said briskly.

Kai rose elegantly to his feet and strolled after her, his hands in his pockets.

Some way down the corridor on the far side, once out of earshot, she said, 'I apologize for that.'

'Oh, don't worry,' Kai replied. He twitched a shoulder in casual dismissal, seemingly fascinated by the beech-panelling and decorated plaster ceiling. His voice was arctic in tone. 'You're quite right, I shouldn't have made a noise and disturbed other students at work. I apologize for offending against the Library rules—'

'Look,' Irene said before he could get any more sarcastic, 'don't get me wrong. I'm not apologizing for being rule-orientated.'

'Oh?'

'No. I'm apologizing for snapping at you to shut you up, because I couldn't discuss classified information with someone else in the room.'

Kai took a few more paces. 'Oh,' he said. 'Right.'

Irene decided that was the closest to an apology *she* was

going to get for the moment. 'Our destination is quarantined,' she said briskly. 'It's listed as having a high chaos infestation.' Which meant its risk factor went way beyond simply dangerous, she thought furiously. What was Coppelia thinking, sending them there? If a magically active world was quarantined, that meant it had been corrupted by chaotic forces. Its magic had tipped just too far the wrong way in the balance between order and disorder. As Kai would have been told, chaos corrupting ordered worlds was an age-old and potentially lethal hazard for Library operatives. And it went against everything that the Library represented, as an institution upholding order. A high level of chaos would mean that they could expect to meet the Fae, creatures of chaos and magic, who were able to take form and cause disorder on such a corrupted world. And that was never good news.

'And there's no balancing element that's trying to bring the world from chaos back to order?'

'No. Either the dragons don't know about that alternate, or they're just staying well out of it.' And what she didn't say, as she was struggling to calm her own fears, was that without a balancing element, a corrupted world could tip all the way over into primal chaos. Nobody could be sure where the dividing line between chaos infestation and total absorption might lie. And she sure didn't want to find out.

Kai frowned. 'I thought – that is, we got told in basic orientation that the dragons always interfere if there's a high chaos level. That they could bring a world back into line. That the worse it got, the more likely they were to interfere.'

'Well, according to the records, there's no sign of them there.' It might be true that the dragons disliked chaos, being creatures of law and structure. Irene had received the same basic briefing as Kai. But that didn't necessarily mean they were going to interfere wherever it was found. From her own personal experience with alternate worlds, Irene had come to the conclusion that dragons preferred to choose their battles carefully. 'Perhaps the world's Librarian will know a bit more. His name's Dominic Aubrey. He's got a cover job on the British Library staff. Head of the Classical Manuscripts section.' She tilted her head to look at Kai. 'Is something the matter?'

Kai shoved his hands further into his pockets. 'Look, I know they tell us students the worst possible scenarios in orientation so that we won't try anything stupid. And they probably make them seem even worse than they actually are, but a world with a high chaos infestation with no dragons to even start balancing it . . . sounds kind of risky for a first assignment for me and for . . .'

'For a junior grade like me?'

'You said it,' Kai muttered. 'I didn't.'

Irene sighed. 'For what it's worth, I'm not happy either.'

'So how bad is it?'

She considered running her hands through her hair, having a hysterical fit, and sitting down and not doing anything for the next few hours while she tried to figure out a way to avoid the job. 'They have steam-level technology, though there was a side-note that recent "innovative advances" had been made. The chaos infestation is taking the form of folklore-related supernatural manifestations, with occasional scientific aberrancy.'

'What does that mean?'

'You can expect to find vampires. Werewolves. Fictional creations that go bump in the night. You might also find their technology working in unexpected ways.'

'Oh well,' Kai said with jaunty enthusiasm. 'No problem there.'

'What?'

'I'm from a Gamma, remember? I'm used to figuring out magic. Even if I didn't do it myself, we had to know how to work the system if we wanted to stay out of trouble. Magic always seems to involve taboos and prohibitions too. So all we have to do is work out what these are and then avoid them while we pick up the document or book. No problemo.'

Irene nodded. 'So, high chaos infestation.' The thought clearly worried her far more than it did Kai. Possibly because she'd had experience with a chaos infestation before and hadn't enjoyed it at all.

Chaos made worlds act unreasonably. Things outside the natural order infested those worlds as a direct result. Vampires, werewolves, faerie, mutations, superheroes, impossible devices . . . She could cope with some spirits and magic, where both operated by a set of rules and were natural phenomena within their worlds. The alternate she'd just come from had very organized magic, and while she hadn't actually practised it, it had at least made *sense*. She hoped that she could cope with dragons too. Again, they were natural to the order of all the linked worlds, a part of their structure rather than actively working to break down order.

She had no idea where to start coping with chaos. No one knew exactly how or why chaos broke through into an alternate – or maybe that knowledge was above her paygrade. But it was never natural to that world and seemed drawn to order so it could break it down, warping what it touched. It created things that worked by irrational laws. It infected worlds and it broke down natural principles. It wasn't good for any world it entered, and it wasn't good for the humanity in that world.

Even if it did make for good literature.

The Library had a whole set of quarantines for chaos

infestations. But the one on this particular alternate was one of the most extreme she'd ever seen, while still permitting entrance. She wasn't happy about taking a student along on the job, however well he thought he could handle things.

'Pity Madame Coppelia didn't give us more information,' Kai remarked. 'And don't look at me like that. We're both thinking the same thing, right? I'm just saying it so that you don't have to.'

Irene nearly laughed. 'Okay,' she said. 'We agree on that one. And we both agree it's going to be bad, and neither of us really knows each other either. So it's probably going to be messy, nasty and dangerous. Then if we do manage to get the manuscript, I'm sure it'll be top-secret and we'll be lucky to get any sort of mention of it on our records at all because everything will be buried in the files.'

'Remind me why I took this job,' Kai muttered.

'People pointed guns at you. Right?'

'Yeah. Something like that.'

'And you like books.' She glanced sidelong at him.

He flashed a quick, genuine smile at her. 'Yeah. That would be it.'

They exited their latest corridor to find themselves overlooking a large hall. Their route continued along a wrought-iron bridge with ornate railings, which arced grandly from side to side above the open book-lined space, staircases winding up the walls to meet it at various points.

'Hey,' Kai said in pleased tones, 'I've been in this one before. There were a load of Faust variants down there.' He pointed over to the lower right corner of the room. 'I was cross-correlating versions from different alternates for Master Legis. It was a training exercise, but it was one of the better ones, you know?'

Irene nodded. 'Could've been worse. Schalken had us looking up illustrations of mosaics when we were doing training. Far too much time spent sitting with a magnifying glass and a scanner trying to work out if there was a difference or if there was, um,' she tried to remember the turn of phrase and tone of voice, '"a comprehensible yet tolerable deviation from the norm, as expressed in the chosen world, given natural variations in the availability of minerals and colour . . ."'

A soft round of applause made her break off. Both she and Kai turned to look at the far end of the bridge. A woman in light robes was leaning against the railings, skin pale as ice and hair like a dark cap.

She smiled.

Irene didn't.

CHAPTER THREE

'You've captured him exactly,' the woman said. 'Not surprising, given how often *you* had to listen to him say it until you got it right.'

'Bradamant,' Irene said calmly. The back of her mind noted that her stomach was twisting, and that she felt sick, and that she was *not* going to show it. 'How nice to see you. To what do we owe the pleasure of your company?'

'You can always tell when she gets annoyed,' Bradamant said confidingly in Kai's direction. 'She gets so very correct.'

'I don't think that we've met,' Kai said. Irene was conscious of him at her elbow, though her attention was fixed on Bradamant. 'I assume you're one of Irene's colleagues.'

'Precisely, dear.' Bradamant stepped away from the railings. Her dark hair was cut smooth and short, like black silk against her skin. 'I'm here for that assignment you were given, Irene. There's been a change of plan.'

'What? Within the last ten minutes?'

'Plans change so quickly,' Bradamant said without blinking. 'Be a good girl and hand it over.'

'You don't seriously expect me to believe that.'

'It'd make life easier for both of us, dear.'

'Oh?'

'Yes.' Bradamant smiled. 'It'd mean that the mission was actually completed, for a start.'

'And leaving aside any questions of your competence or my lack of it,' Irene said, calmly, so calmly, 'what could I possibly say to my supervisor?' She was certainly not going to lose control, especially not in front of a student, just on this level of provocation. But she knew from bitter experience just how poisonous Bradamant could be, and there was always politics under the surface.

Bradamant shrugged. Her sheer garments rippled. 'That, my dear, is your problem. Though your record is adequate, I suppose. You'll just be facing a few decades of hard work to get any sort of status back.'

'Wait just a moment,' Kai said. 'Are you seriously suggesting just giving her the assignment?'

'She is,' Irene said. 'I'm not.'

'I'll take the student as well,' Bradamant offered. 'Dear Kai has *such* a good record.'

Irene could hear Kai's suppressed intake of breath. 'That won't be necessary,' she answered. 'I have no reason to hand him over to you. Although you do have *such* a good record of dealing with students.'

Bradamant hissed. 'Slander.'

It was Irene's turn to smile. Bradamant might call it slander as much as she liked, but the facts were on record. The other woman hadn't managed to keep a student for more than a single mission, and whenever there'd been a problem with that mission, the student took the blame. Unfortunate when it occurred once or twice, but a nasty pattern when it recurred. 'No smoke without fire,' said Irene.

'How would you know? Keeping track, are you?' Bradamant seemed disproportionately angry, taking a couple of impatient steps towards them, her heels loud on the bridge.

Irene smiled at Bradamant, making the expression as bland as possible. 'Now why would I want to do something like that?'

The other woman sniffed, composing herself. She studied her fingernails. 'I take it that you are going to be stupid, then.'

'You may take it as you wish,' Irene said. 'But I am not giving you my mission, and I am not giving you my student, and if I were the sort of person who kept pet rats, I would not give you my *rat*. Clear?'

'Very,' Bradamant said coldly. She swept a spare swathe of fabric around her shoulders in a loosely elegant motion. 'Do not expect me to be nice to you when I have to clear up your mess later.'

'Oh,' Irene murmured, 'I'd never expect that.'

Bradamant turned without another word. Her footsteps rang on the iron bridge as she vanished into the dark corridor beyond, then faded into a heavier tapping of high heels on wooden floor, then into silence.

'An explanation would be nice,' Kai said quietly. He didn't try to whisper and his voice echoed in the stillness.

'It would,' Irene agreed. She frowned at the dark corridor. 'I wish I knew whether that was personal or political.'

'You sounded as if you had personal history. Big-time.'

'We don't get on,' Irene said briefly. 'We never have. She gets the job done but she's got a reputation. You wouldn't want to work with her.' She began to walk towards the corridor.

'Irene,' Kai said, and it surprised her in some indefinable way that he'd call her by name like that. 'I get it that you don't like her—'

'I don't like her at all,' Irene cut in, keeping her steps

calm and measured with an effort, not *letting* herself walk away from the conversation. 'I don't want my personal and very strong dislike of her to cause me to slander someone who is an efficient, competent, even *admired* Librarian.'

Kai whistled. 'You really don't like her.'

'We dislike each other enough that she *might* have staged that whole little scene purely as a whim and in order to mess with me,' Irene continued. 'Except that it'd have taken a singularly unlikely set of coincidences for her to have found out that I was on a mission and to be here to intercept me. Which means politics.' She stalked into the dark corridor, still a pace ahead of Kai.

'So who's her supervisor?'

'Kostchei.'

'Oh.' Kai was quiet for a few steps. 'Him. You know, I always kind of thought that was a bit of a dramatic name for him to choose, even for here.'

Irene shrugged, glad of the change of subject. It was true that Russian fairy tale villains weren't the most obvious name choice. But then again her own choice of 'Irene' had hardly been dictated by logic. At least 'the Undying', the epithet usually attached to that name, was fairly accurate for a Librarian who'd made it to his age. 'When we were students, some people spent hours trying to pick what they'd call themselves after they'd been initiated. They'd go round saying, "How about this one?" or "Do you think Mnemosyne sounds all right or is it too obvious?" or "I like Arachne, do you think it suits me?"'

Kai snorted a laugh.

They walked on together, passing room after room of stockpiled books. While there were faster (and non-linear) ways to get around the Library, Irene would have needed authorization from a senior Librarian to use them. In the absence of such shortcuts, all she and Kai could do was walk and watch out for landmarks. Finally the corridor opened out into a small room, whose dominant feature was the iron-barred door on the opposite wall. The walls were covered with full bookshelves, but large posters covered sections of the books. These announced statements such as – CHAOS INFESTATION, ENTRY BY PERMISSION ONLY, KEEP CALM AND STAY OUT and THIS MEANS YOU.

Kai settled his fists on his hips and looked at the posters. 'Tell me,' he said, 'are there some people round here who can't take a hint?'

'You tell me,' Irene said. 'Given some of the people you've probably met here.' She reached into her pocket and pulled out Coppelia's mission briefing.

'Before we go any further,' Kai said, more seriously, 'what about Kostchei and Bradamant? Do you think she's working for him?'

Irene tugged at her earlobe. *We may be overheard.* When Kai didn't seem to take the hint, she tugged at it more obviously.

'Or do you think—'

'I'd rather do my thinking through on the other side,' she snapped. *So much for Kai's potential streetwise criminality and any ability to take hints.* 'Let's get a briefing from the Librarian there first before we come to any conclusions.'

Kai's shoulders slumped. 'Sure,' he said flatly. 'As you say.'

Irene resolved to apologize later – well, to some extent – and turned to slap the mission briefing against the door. The solid metal rang softly, like a distant bell, then re-echoed again, chiming back until the room was full of distant harmonies.

Kai edged closer, apparently willing to drop the sulks for

a moment. 'What would've happened if that had been faked?'

'It wouldn't have sounded half as nice,' Irene replied. She tucked the briefing back into her pocket, then reached down to turn the door handle. It moved easily, swinging open to let her and Kai through into another room full of books, glass cases, and flaring gaslamps.

The room had the indefinable air of all museum collections, somehow simultaneously fascinating yet forlorn. Manuscripts lay beneath glass cases, the gold leaf on their illuminations and illustrations gleaming in the gas-light. A single document was spread out on a desk in the centre of the room, next to a modern-looking notepad and pen. The high arched ceiling had cobwebs in the corners, and dust lurked in the crevices of the panelled walls. Next to the Library entrance was a rattletrap machine, all clockwork and gears and sparking wires, with a primitive-looking printer mechanism and vacuum tubes attached.

Kai looked around the room. 'Do we ring a bell or anything?'

'We probably don't need to,' Irene said. She closed the door behind them, and heard it audibly lock itself. 'I imagine Mr Aubrey has already been alerted. Librarians watching fixed Traverses like this one don't leave them unguarded.'

There was a ping. Several vacuum tubes on the mechanical contraption lit up and the printer juddered into motion, spitting out a long paper tape, letter by letter.

Kai picked it up and looked at it. 'Welcome,' he read out. 'Please make yourselves comfortable and I will be with you—'

The printer came to a halt with a grinding, permanent sort of noise.

'Shortly, I hope,' Irene said.

'This is cool.' Kai began to wander round the manuscripts, peering at them. 'Look, this one says it's an original of Keats's *Lamia*, though I'm not sure what it's doing in Classical Manuscripts in that case—'

'That would be because I'm cross-referencing it with the Plutarch material.' The door at the far end of the room had swung open to reveal a middle-aged, dark-skinned man. 'Good day. I'm Dominic Aubrey. **The action of seeing you is a pleasure,**' he added in the Language.

'**The action of conversing with you is a pleasure,**' Irene replied. 'I'm Irene. This is Kai. We're here about the 1812 Grimm manuscript.' She was conscious of Kai frowning, and remembered from her pre-initiation days how strange the Language could sound. Listeners who weren't trained in it heard it in their native language, but with a certain unplaceable accent. Librarians, of course, heard it for what it was, which made it an ideal tool for cross-checks and passwords and countersigns. Like this.

Dominic Aubrey nodded. 'I'd invite you to take a seat, but there's only one chair. Please lean wherever suits you.' He fiddled nervously with his glasses, pushing them back up on the bridge of his nose, then brushed at his coat. He was in what looked like vaguely Victorian-period garb from the most common timelines. His regalia included the standard white shirt and stiff collar, with a black frock coat, waistcoat and trousers. His straight hair was tied back in a crisp tail, reaching halfway down between his shoulder-blades. 'The situation has, um, developed a bit since I last sent in a report.'

Irene leaned against the edge of the desk, making an effort not to look condemnatory, judgemental, or recriminatory. However much she might feel it. 'I quite understand. This is a chaos-infested world, after all. Perhaps if you'd give us the briefing from the beginning?' She glanced at

Kai, and he nodded in acceptance, waiting for her to take the lead.

'All right.' Dominic sat down in his chair, folded his arms, and leaned forward. 'I originally found out about the Grimm first edition after the death of Edward Bonhomme, when it came into circulation. He was a local property owner and bibliophile. Owned a nice selection of slums and made a very good profit out of them, and put the money into his books. Unfortunately, he was a hoarder of the worst sort. Never invited anyone round, never even let anyone look at his books, just kept them all locked away and gloated over them. You know the sort?'

'I've had to visit a few people like that,' Irene agreed. 'Anything suspicious about his death?'

Dominic shrugged. 'He fell downstairs, broke his neck and was found by the housekeeper in the morning. He was in his eighties, bought the cheapest candles on the market, and the stair carpet was threadbare. A lot of people did quite well out of his death, but none of them seem to have had a significant motive. The police treated it as an accident and it was left as such.'

Irene nodded. 'So, the book?'

'It went up for auction after Bonhomme's death, with some others of his collection. The money was to endow a scholarship in his name at Oxford. Typical post-death snobbery.' He sighed. 'Anyhow. Word got round fast and the bidding went up very quickly. It was bought by Lord Wyndham. He's – he was, rather – more of a general collector of expensive trifles than an actual bibliophile, but the price on the book and the society interest made it something he wanted for his collection. And he got it.'

'He *was*, you say.' Irene had a growing feeling of doom.

'Ah, yes. Precisely. Someone staked him a couple of days ago.'

'Staked.'

'He was a vampire. They used the traditional methods, you know. A stake through the heart, cutting off the head, inserting garlic in the mouth . . . though, to be fair, leaving his head impaled on the railings outside the front door, where all his party guests could see it, could be considered a little extreme.'

'And the book then went missing, right?'

'Yes!' Dominic said brightly. 'How did you guess?'

Kai raised a hand. 'Excuse me. Are vampires considered a normal part of society here?'

'Mm, well.' Dominic held up a finger. '*Being* a vampire or werewolf isn't illegal in itself. Assaulting or murdering someone due to vampiric or werewolf urges is . . . As ever, having lots of money helps ease the rules. Lord Wyndham had a great deal of money.'

Irene nodded. 'So he was murdered – staked, that is – at his party, and someone stole the book?'

'The plot thickens.' Dominic raised his finger again. 'A notorious cat burglar was observed escaping from the mansion that evening. Now while she's never been known to kill anyone before, it seems a bit of a coincidence that she should just happen to be burgling the house on the same night Lord Wyndham was murdered.'

Irene nodded. 'She was seen escaping, you say?'

'Dramatically. She leapt from the roof of the house to catch a ladder dangling from a passing zeppelin.'

'Wait. Zeppelins?'

'It's part of the scientific ethos of this place. Zeppelins, death rays – they haven't quite got those working properly yet, though – and other instruments of destruction. Also they have biomutations, clockwork technology, electrical healthcare spas . . .'

Irene glanced at Kai. He was wearing an expression combining acute interest with admiring attention. 'I told you I dislike chaos infestations?' she asked. 'This is why.'

'But zeppelins are neat,' Kai protested. 'We couldn't have any in my old alternate because of the pollution, but I guess they'd be kind of cool. Up there in the sky, tossed by the winds, driving across the curve of the world with the lands and seas spread out beneath you . . .'

'Falling a very long way down,' Irene added.

He just looked at her.

'I do apologize,' she said hastily to Dominic. 'Please go on. Tell us about this cat burglar.'

'They call her Belphegor,' Dominic said. He seemed more amused than annoyed by their interruptions. 'She's tall. Very tall. Apparently she wears a black leather catsuit and a golden mask.'

'Any details on the mask?'

'I think people are usually too busy looking at the black leather catsuit.'

Irene sighed. 'So we have an incredibly glamorous female cat burglar who slinks around in a black leather catsuit, who kills vampires in her spare time?'

'I'll tackle her,' Kai said enthusiastically.

Irene raised an eyebrow. 'How do you know that I don't want to tackle her?'

'Do you?'

'Involvements with glamorous female cat burglars never end up well.'

'And you've had some?'

'One,' Irene said, and hoped that she wasn't blushing too badly.

'Oh, you're *that* Irene,' Dominic said in tones of surprise. 'I remember Coppelia telling me about it now. Didn't you end up having some sort of showdown in the middle of a reception and—'

Irene held up a hand. 'Could we possibly concentrate on the current problem? Please?'

'It's a pleasure to see that you're taking to this so cheerfully,' Dominic remarked. 'Now some junior Librarians would be running for the Traverse at this point and trying to ditch the job. But not you. No, I can see you're up for the task and all eager to go.' He smiled toothily.

Irene took a deep breath. 'I'm looking on it as a challenge,' she said blandly. *And I'm damned if I'm going to let Bradamant manage this instead of me.*

Kai raised a hand. 'May I ask a question?'

'Please do,' Dominic said.

'Do you have any sort of dossiers about this place that we can read up on?'

Dominic nodded. 'I've a rough set of notes on current affairs, history, geography, all of that. I've also set up some spare identities, both male and female, for when I have Librarians visiting. I'll sign over a couple of these to you, together with funding and so on. Don't worry, I'm not going to hang you out to dry. I just wanted to see how you'd react to the situation.'

'Frankly,' Irene said, 'it sounds like a penny dreadful.'

'Frankly,' Dominic said, 'it is.'

Irene sighed. 'Well. So Lord Wyndham is dead, and not even undead any longer. The book is presumed stolen by the cat burglar Belphegor, and – there is more, I take it?'

'Not much,' Dominic said apologetically. 'All this was only a couple of days ago, you understand. The newspapers are still buzzing about it. In fact, if you want to be researching the story for your cover . . .'

'Good point,' Irene agreed. 'What's the gender situation here?'

'Women are generally accepted in most trades, except as serving soldiers in the army. They often end up in engineering divisions there. Nothing unusual about a female reporter, though they often end up with the high society and scandal pages. So that'll be entirely appropriate.'

'So is there magic?'

'Not per se,' Dominic said slowly, 'though we have vampires, werewolves, and other supernatural creatures and so on. I've got a theory that the weird technology of this place is actually a structural evolution of what would elsewhere have manifested as directed magic, but I can't prove it.'

Irene nodded. 'Do you have any theories about the lack of draconic interference?'

Dominic snorted. 'Typical bureaucratic miscomprehension in summarizing my reports. The dragons don't intervene here because they don't *need* to. There may be a high level of chaos infestation, but there are also a lot of natural spirits inherent to the local order buzzing around the place – metaphorically speaking, that is – and they seem to be acting as a counterweight. In fact,' he said enthusiastically, 'I think we have grounds here for an entire study on how a high level of magic in a world responds to a chaos infestation by working in non-chaotic ways. So, the natural order is reinforced via technology with weird science, and also strengthened supernaturally. The latter happens via a hierarchical structure of guardian spirits and fundamental reinforcement—'

'But you can't get the funding for it?' Irene said sympathetically, before he could get any further.

Dominic slumped. 'Philistines,' he muttered.

Kai raised his hand again. 'So, theoretically, would these local spirits be a useful source of information? I mean, I've been stuck in the Library for the last five years, I know the theory, but not how you go about it in practice . . .'

'Good thinking,' Irene said, but then she saw Dominic frowning. 'Why, is there a problem?'

'They can be dangerous,' Dominic said. He fussed with his glasses again. 'I wouldn't recommend it as a primary option. To be frank, I haven't had much chance to investigate things myself – my cover, you know. There's only so much that I can get away with as Head of Classical Manuscripts. You'll probably be able to find out more at ground level.'

Irene nodded. 'We'll keep it as a fall-back option, then. Do you have any local Language updates that I should be aware of?'

'I've put them in the briefing,' Dominic promised. 'There aren't many, though. The vocab is all fairly generic. A vampire's a vampire as you'd expect, fangs and all etc. Actually, if you want to wait here, I'll go and fetch the documentation, and then the two of you can slip out and get to work.'

Kai looked down at his clothing. 'Like this?' he asked.

'You'll have to claim to be barbarian visitors from Canada,' Dominic said cheerfully. 'I do have some clothing for emergencies, but under the circumstances you can pass for students until you can buy some clothing that fits you better. You'll just need some overcoats until you can get to a shop.' He stood up, brushing his hands together again. 'I'll be back in a moment. Don't fret.'

'Thank you,' Irene said, suppressing a sigh of relief, but he was already out of the door. Perhaps his quick exit was due to embarrassment. Helping visiting Librarians maintain a low profile was supposed to be part of the Librarian-in-Residence's job, after all. It usually involved a *little* more than 'here's an overcoat and there's the nearest shop'. She considered prospective excuses for the shopkeeper. *I'm terribly sorry, but we just had all our luggage stolen while disembarking from the ocean liner . . .*

Kai stretched and looked around restlessly. 'Do you suppose barbarian Canadians wear jeans?'

'I hope female Canadian barbarians wear trousers,' Irene said drily. 'They're easier to run in.'

Kai turned to face her. 'Have you ever seen a really bad chaos infestation?' he asked.

'No,' she said quietly. 'Only mild ones. But I've heard things. I knew someone who went into one, once. I saw some of his reports.'

There's something addictive about it, he'd written. *The world itself seems so much more logical and plausible. There's a feeling that everything makes sense, and I know this is only because the world itself is shaping to fit the gestalt, but you wouldn't believe how comfortable it makes me feel.*

Kai snapped his fingers in front of her face, and she blinked at him. 'Ahem. You could at least share with me, rather than sit there and brood about it and figure that you're protecting me or something.'

'You do rate yourself highly,' Irene said, trying not to feel irritated. 'All right. You remember the stages of infestation? Affective, intuitive, assumptive and conglomerative?'

Kai nodded. 'From what you and Dominic were saying, this world is affective going on intuitive, right? So the theory suggests it's being warped, and it would then reach the stage where things tend to fall into narrative patterns. So instead of natural order prevailing, events start taking on the kind of rhythm or logic you might find in fiction or fairy tales. Which could be terrifying. But it must be hard to spot, surely, as even in order-based worlds fact can prove stranger than fiction . . . It isn't fully there yet, is it?'

'No. And that's interesting. It makes me think that Dominic's got a point with his theory that order is being asserted. I wish I understood more of it.' Irene pushed away from the desk, and began to wander round the room, staring absently at the various glass display cases. 'Now if a world *could* be stalled at this point, so it didn't head further into chaos, it'd be useful to know how it's done. We don't know how many worlds there are, so we don't know how many we lose to chaos. But we lose enough that we do know about. And the dragons aren't interested in talking to us about how *they* do whatever it is that they do.'

Kai coughed. 'Just like we aren't interested in talking to them about how we do what *we* do?'

Irene turned to look at him. Witheringly, she hoped. 'Do you think you're the first person to have made that argument?'

'Course not.' He shrugged. 'Fact remains, though. We don't talk.'

'I met one once,' Irene said.

'What did you talk about?'

'He complimented me on my literary taste.'

Kai blinked. 'Doesn't sound like a life-threatening sort of conversation.'

Irene shrugged. 'Well, he was the one who *got* the scroll we were both after. You see, there was this—' She saw him glance away. 'Oh, never mind.'

There was this room full of fabulous woods and bone, and I'd been escorted there by a couple of servants, and I was honestly afraid that I was going to be killed. I'd trespassed on his private property. I'd negotiated with one of his barons for that scroll without realizing it. I'd been dropped in the deep end and I was sinking fast.

'I don't mean to pry,' Kai said unconvincingly.

He looked almost human. He had scales in the hollows of his cheeks and on the backs of his hands, as fine as feathers or hair. He had claws, manicured to a mother-of-pearl sheen. He had horns. His eyes were like gems in his face. His skin was the colour of fire, and yet it seemed natural; my own skin was blotchy and dull in comparison.

'There isn't much to tell,' Irene said. 'He let me go.'

He discussed the poems in the scroll. He complimented me on my taste. He explained that he did not expect to see me or any other representative of the Library in that area again. I nodded and bowed and thanked him for his kindness.

'Just like that?'

No language that I knew had any words to describe him.

Irene tried to look nonchalant. 'As I said, he approved of my literary taste.'

An hour later, Irene was buttoning herself into a jacket and long skirt while Kai sat outside the dressing room on a rickety chair and read through the dossiers. The cheap clothing shop which Dominic had directed them to was certainly cheap, very definitely cheap, and had little that could be said for it other than the fact that it was cheap. If they were going to infiltrate high society, they'd need better clothing. And costumes that didn't rely on heavy overcoats.

'These lists don't make any sense,' Kai complained. 'They say the same thing on both sides of the page.'

Of course, he was looking at the Language vocabulary pages. Since he wasn't a Librarian, he'd be seeing his native language instead of the Language. 'Yes,' Irene agreed, 'they would, to you. Should I be surprised that you're trying to read them?' She arranged her blouse's neckline so its ruffles sat above her jacket collar, and opened the dressing room door to join him.

'Can't blame me for trying,' Kai said cheerfully. He looked her up and down. 'Are you going to wear the hair-piece? Most of the women we've seen so far wear their hair longer than yours.'

Irene looked unenthusiastically at the tattered partial wig that lay on the table like a mangy dark squirrel. 'Wearing that thing's going to cause more problems than going without,' she decided. 'I'll be counter-fashionable. Let's just be grateful that corsets aren't required wear any longer.'

'Why should *I* be grateful?' Kai asked, raising an eyebrow.

'Because you don't have to deal with me while I'm wearing one,' Irene said flatly. 'Now, give me a summary on what you've just been reading. Think of it as—'

There was a crash from the street, and the sound of screaming. She turned to look at the window. Some sort of huge wind was blowing the smog outside into long grey veils, ripping through the sky like claws.

'As?' Kai asked. He came to his feet in a single neat bound, assuming a smooth attitude of superiority and lack of distraction.

'Imminent disaster takes priority over on-the-job testing,' Irene said. 'Let's see what's going on out there.'

CHAPTER FOUR

Kai made it down the stairs and outside first, and promptly stopped dead, face turned up to gawk at the sky like everyone else in the street. Irene, a step behind, looked up as well.

Five zeppelins hung in the foggy sky, their propellers cutting through the clouds. While all displayed the same dark blue and red livery, one was much larger than the vessels that had taken up positions around it. This particular zeppelin trailed glittering, somewhat tawdry, gold streamers, and flaunted a coat of arms on its side.

Irene strained her eyes, but she couldn't make it out. 'Kai,' she muttered, 'can you see the design painted on that airship?'

Kai raised his hand to shield his eyes, and squinted. 'There's an eagle top left, in black and white on gold. Top right is a green crown on diagonal black and gold stripes. Bottom left is a vertically divided shield in red and white. And bottom right is some sort of harpy, again in black and white on gold. A hunting horn is right at the very bottom, with a horizontally divided shield in red and gold in the middle.'

Irene frowned, trying to remember her heraldry. She'd

been to a few places where it had been important, but surely something that crowded would have stuck in her mind . . . oh, wait, that was it. 'It sounds,' she said slowly, 'like Liechtenstein.'

'I thought that didn't exist,' Kai said blankly.

'Course it does!' a newspaper-seller scolded. He was perched on a battered stool next to his newspapers and a dramatic board that declared – MURDERER STALKS LONDON. 'Best zeppelin-builders in the world, ain't they?'

'I'm terribly sorry,' Irene said. 'My friend's from Canada and he doesn't know much about Europe.'

'Oh. Oh well, then.' The old man nodded as if it made perfect sense. 'Wanna buy a paper, love? Got all the news on the horrible murder of Lord Wyndham.'

'Pay the man, Kai,' Irene directed, and picked up one of the papers. It was thin, coarse paper, with thick black ink that threatened to come off on her gloves.

Kai handed over a few of Dominic's coins. 'Have they made an arrest yet?' he asked.

'Naaah.' The old man leaned forward and tapped the side of his nose, glancing at the zeppelins. 'But you know what they say?'

'That the Liechtensteinians were involved?' Irene guessed, pointing with the rolled-up paper at the zeppelins above.

'Well. I mean. Makes sense, dunnit. What with them turning up like this so soon after that lord died, and all. And they do say that their Ambassador was Lord Wyndham's friend. Very personal friend, if you take my meaning.' The old man winked. 'And they're saying as how he was also his arch-rival and that they were,' he paused to check the front page of his newspaper, 'constantly intriguing against each other in the most diabolical manner.'

'Is the Ambassador a vampire too?' Irene asked. It would be totally inappropriate of her to use Kai as bait, if the Ambassador's tastes ran that way. That was the sort of thing Bradamant would do, she reminded herself.

'Naaah. Where've you been spending your time, love? Nah, he's one of them Fair Folk, see. Always has to have artists draw his picture in the papers, 'cause none of them cameras will work on him, not even the stuff them geniuses make.'

'Fair Folk,' Irene said, a cold feeling gripping the pit of her stomach. This was bad news.

Chaos liked (if liking was quite the word) to manifest into a world where it could take advantage of illogical laws. Vampires and werewolves were particularly vulnerable to chaos. After all, strictly speaking, why should werewolves be allergic to silver, or vampires to garlic, or sticky rice, or a dozen other things. And as for the reasoning behind vampires rising three days after death, or behind most of *Dracula* – anyhow, the point was that chaos used creatures that obeyed illogical laws logically. Fae or fairies or elves or youkai or whatever they were called were among its favourite agents. Some of them were even living pieces of chaos, slipped sideways into various worlds and taking form from human dreams and stories. If there were Fair Folk manifesting in this world, and being accepted by the population, then she needed to know. Dominic had made a note in the briefing about Liechtenstein being a 'potential chaos portal' but hadn't gone into details. She wished that he had. Liechtenstein could be the nexus of all the chaos in this world, if it had perhaps been weakened by too many supernatural or Fae living there, though at this point she could only speculate. However, that would make any agents operating from Liechtenstein particularly suspect.

'Right,' she said briskly, taking a few steps out of the old man's earshot, and gesturing Kai over with a wave of the newspaper. 'We're splitting up. I want you to find out everything you can about the Liechtenstein Ambassador, his Embassy, and his involvement in the current situation. I'll check out Wyndham's place. We'll meet at the hotel in Russell Square – eight o'clock at the latest. Find some way to get a message to me there if you're delayed.'

'Wait,' Kai said slowly. 'You're just sending me off, like that?'

'Of course,' Irene said firmly, and tried to ignore her slight feelings of disquiet. 'You were already competent when the Library recruited you. It won't do either of us any good for me to keep you under my thumb all the time.' *And it'll drive me up the wall and onto the ceiling if I have to constantly operate with someone looking over my shoulder.* 'We need information as fast as possible. I'm relying on you. Do you have any problems with this?'

He looked at her for a moment, then put his right fist to his left shoulder and gave her a formal bow. 'You may rely on me to do my share of the work.'

'Excellent.' She smiled at him. 'Then I'll be seeing you in a few hours.'

He smiled back, his face surprisingly warm for a moment, then turned and headed briskly down the street, shoulders squared for action.

She'd only known him for a few hours, but there was something reliable about him. And she had to admit that the way that he'd said he'd do 'his share' of the work was a well-balanced way of putting it. No attempts to try and do her share as well, no trying to wriggle out of it . . .

Was she actually starting to *like* him? It wouldn't be hard. Kai was likeable. She'd enjoy sharing a mission with someone that she liked. It'd make a nice change.

Irene drew her veil partly across her face to shield her mouth and nose from the smoke and steam in the air. Most of the other women in the street wore veils across the lower parts of their faces too, ranging from filmy drifts of silk for the better-off to thick wads of cotton or linen for the poor. Men wore their scarves drawn up over their mouths. She wondered what they did in summer.

She scanned the newspaper's front page.

LATEST DEVELOPMENTS IN
WYNDHAM MURDER CASE,

it read.

Our correspondent informs us that the police have made great progress and expect an arrest at any moment.

So the odds were that the police were still baffled. Good. It'd be difficult to extract the target document from a police station, if they did manage to catch the cat burglar and lock her up.

Irene rolled the newspaper up, scanning the street. The local type of taxi-cab was black, small, and seemed to be a combination of old-fashioned hansom carriage and electric car. With some determined waving she managed to signal one over, and directed the driver to take her to the Hyde Park Corner Underground Railway station, a couple of streets away from Lord Wyndham's residence.

Lord Wyndham's residence was in an expensive street, with marble frontages and clean-scrubbed gutters, unusual in this grime-stained London. The place stood dark and empty, in contrast to the houses on either side, both already lit up against the afternoon dimness. With practised experience, Irene made her way round to the servants' entrance at the back.

It was locked.

She flicked a quick glance behind her. Although this back alley was far more active than the wide front street, nobody was currently in view – or, more importantly, within earshot – of her. She put her lips next to the lock and commanded in the Language, '**Servants' entry door lock, sealed and closed, now open!**'

The tumblers of the lock shivered and clicked open with gratifying vigour. The door shuddered and the latch came undone, letting the door swing open into a dark passage.

Irene walked through the servants' corridors into the main part of the house. The marks of the police search were obvious: drawers still hung open, there were piles of discarded linen and clothing everywhere and dirty boot-marks on the luxurious crimson carpets. The place hadn't been tidied either, after the 'rude interruption' to the dinner party. Dirty plates and glasses were piled in stacks or left lying on polished tables, and ashtrays were full to overflowing with discarded cigar and cigarette ends.

Despite searching with a certain horrified curiosity, she couldn't find any secret torture chambers or rooms containing strange vampiric devices. She did find that the books displayed prominently in every chamber had been dusted, but the spines were pristine and un-creased. They had the sad, untouched air of literature paraded for display purposes but never actually *used*.

It was profoundly depressing.

Wyndham's study was a large room with far too much pseudo-Degas artwork on the walls; a whole dozen pictures of women in ballet skirts showing off their legs. Thick crimson curtains matched the thick crimson carpet and the dark wood panelling. Her footsteps were silent.

The heavy oak desk was bare of papers, and all the drawers were locked. She could open them later if she had to. A deep score mark marred the desk's surface. Probably from the removal of Wyndham's head. Bloodstains had soaked into the wood, spilling outwards from the line of the cut. She didn't think they'd come out. The big chair behind the desk (ebony with black leather cushions – how vulgar) had been pushed over at some point. It had been repositioned, but had clearly been lying long enough to leave a dent in the plush carpet.

Blood had soaked into the carpet too, but it was barely visible, a slightly darker brown amid the rich thick crimson.

The glass display case in the corner could have held the Grimm book, Irene decided. For one thing, the case was sealed with all manner of complicated locks, catches and alarms. For another thing, it was now empty.

Irene turned thoughtfully, looking around the room. Wyndham was the sort of man who would have needed a safe, and where better to keep it than in his study. She would have bet money on it. Now she just had to try and find it.

Unsurprisingly, the biggest pseudo-Degas hid the safe. She swung the painting back and examined the heavy iron door. Combination lock. Well, she could always talk it open, but . . .

She heard quick approaching footsteps on the main stairs. It must be a man; a woman wouldn't stride like that, not in these skirts. But there wasn't supposed to be anyone in the house! Perhaps another burglar? What marvellous timing.

She quickly concealed the safe, and retreated behind one of the thick curtains. She needn't fear discovery within its thick folds. Merely suffocation.

The door swung open with a heavy creak. Clearly the

intruder wasn't bothering with caution. She waited until she heard the sound of the painting swinging back before she carefully peered round the edge of the curtain.

The man had his back to her. He was of above average height, with well-squared shoulders and a slender waist. His pale hair, a shade somewhere between silver and lavender, was gathered back in a short tail that fell neatly against his perfectly fitted jacket. His trousers were just as well cut, moulded elegantly to his body. It was perfect formal visiting gear. If your host hadn't been murdered. His top hat was tilted insouciantly to one side, and he was wearing pale grey kid gloves.

He reached out a hand to delicately brush the wheel-handle of the safe, then snatched his fingers back with an angry hiss. A thin scent of burning flesh hung in the air, even through his gloves.

Irene let the curtain fall back into place, and considered. Clearly there was more to Lord Wyndham's alliance with the Fair Folk than met the eye, if he'd made sure that his safe was made of cold iron, so proof against Fae. This supported the newspaper's whole 'diabolical intrigue' theory, and it rather fitted what she knew about the Fae. They liked complicated relationships. It didn't matter if they were loved or hated, as long as the other person had strong feelings towards them. Strong enough, for instance, to install a completely Fae-proof safe. And if she'd been able to choose her options a few hours ago, being trapped in a dead vampire's private study with an angry Fae would not have been one of them.

Then, more alarmingly, she heard him sniff. It wasn't the phlegmatic nose-clearing of a cold, it was a hungry sniff, a tasting of the air.

'Ohhhh.' His voice hung on the air like incense. 'Come out, come out, little mouse. Or shall I come looking for you?'

Irene took a deep breath, set her face to an expression of polite unconcern, and moved the curtain back. 'The Liechtenstein Ambassador, I presume?' she guessed.

His face was as pretty as his body had suggested, but his eyes were slitted like a cat's and pure gold. 'Why,' he said, tone smooth as honey, 'you are quite correct. But what sort of little mouse hides behind the curtains? Are you a black-mailer, little mouse? A spy? A detective? A little rat in the arras, just waiting to be stabbed?'

She seized the opportunity to present her cover-story. 'I'm a journalist here to investigate Lord Wyndham's murder, sir. I was hoping to interview you. I hadn't dared hope to catch up with you so soon. If I could ask you for your views on the situation . . .'

He glided a step towards her. 'What paper do you represent?'

'*The Times*,' she said. There was a *Times* in practically every single alternate she'd ever visited.

'And how did you know that I'd come here, pretty little mouse?' There was something very predatory about his face now.

'Well, of course, I had no idea,' she rattled off hastily, reaching into her reticule. 'It was a total surprise to meet you here, sir. But I suppose it's not surprising that on hearing of his death, you naturally hurried to his domicile, with the intention of expressing your condolences to his—'

His hand caught her wrist. 'No guns, little mouse. I don't think we want the police coming. No, this is all going to be very nice and quiet, and you're going to tell me exactly what's going on . . .'

She could lie to him. She could try to resist him. Or she could simply get that cool, elegant, well-gloved, slender hand off her wrist. 'Take your hands off me, sir,' she said, anger sliding into her voice. 'Or you will regret it.'

He paused. 'You're very self-assured,' he said, and for the first time there was a fraction of something other than malice or purring self-satisfaction in his voice. Perhaps an edge of uncertainty. 'I wonder. Are you perhaps a little more than you look?'

'Aren't we all?' Irene answered.

'And is there someone backing you?'

'Someone you don't want to antagonize,' she said. She'd got the measure of his suspicion now. She'd only met lesser Fair Folk before, but they practically defined 'so devious that they'd fall over if they tried to walk in a straight line'. This one was thinking in terms of conspiracies and agents. She could play that game just as well as anyone else. 'But I can't give names. Not even to an Ambassador. But what I can perhaps give is a degree of cooperation.'

He released her wrist and raised a delicate eyebrow. 'You intrigue me.'

She understood that sort of language. She was getting the message that he might find her useful loud and clear – and intrigue had nothing to do with it. Instead, she nodded towards the safe. 'Perhaps we are both looking for the same thing, sir.'

He nodded once, sharply. 'Perhaps we are. Well? Open it.'

'Do you have the combination, sir?'

He rattled off a list of numbers as she worked at the safe's combination mechanism. So it was just the iron that had kept him out. She wondered what he'd have done if she hadn't been here – perhaps enchanted or coerced some passer-by off the street, or brought a human agent here later.

His gloved fingers brushed the back of her neck, and she shivered. *He needs you for the moment, he won't try anything until he's got what he's looking for, the best way to deal with him is to give him something more interesting to pounce on . . .*

'Open it,' he purred from far too close behind her.

Irene swung the safe door open and put some distance between herself and the Fae, physically feeling his focus shift from her to the safe's contents.

Several stacks of papers lay tidily in the large iron cavity. On top of them was a small piece of card, embossed with a golden mask, signed with the name *Belphegor*.

The Fae hissed. His hands clenched, and Irene heard his kid gloves rip. He turned towards her, his face furious.

Saying '*Don't blame me*' or '*It wasn't my fault*' would just have been signalling that she was a victim. As calmly as she could manage, and wishing for a few more feet of distance between them – actually, make that a few yards, or even a few miles – she said, 'This makes no sense. If Belphegor stole the book, and wanted to advertise the fact, why leave her card here inside the safe and not out on the desk?'

He blinked once, and seemed to take a step back mentally. 'Indeed,' he said, pacing the room. 'It's the book that's important here. Keep talking, little mouse. Tell me what you know, what you see here. Tell me what you know about the book. Explain it to me. Make yourself worthwhile to me.'

'There were two factions,' Irene guessed. It was as good a theory as any. It might even be true. She needed more data. The Ambassador seemed to be looking for the book as well, so why not others? Perhaps she could use that. 'And Belphegor wasn't necessarily after the book. She could have been after something Lord Wyndham kept in his safe. So what if the person or people who stole the book and who killed Lord Wyndham were entirely different? If they were waiting here in the study while he was hosting the party downstairs.' She walked over to look at the glass display case where the book had been. 'I can't tell whether they would have taken the book first and then killed him, or vice versa.' Well, of course she couldn't tell, she was deducing all this on the spot, or to be more accurate, guessing wildly. 'But we know they beheaded him on the desk. Then they went out through the house and left his head on the railings outside the front door.'

'Why not out through the window?' he interrupted.

'It wouldn't open.' She'd glanced down at the catch while hiding in the window embrasure. It had been soldered closed. 'It must have been one of Lord Wyndham's precautions. Besides, there was a party going on. It would have been simple enough to walk through the house and out through the front door if they'd concealed the head and if they looked enough like guests or servants.'

'Mm.' He turned and pointed a finger at her. 'And Belphegor?'

'If she escaped by catching a rope from a passing zeppelin, then she must have gone up by the roof.'

He nodded. 'And now a crucial point, little mouse. I'm not asking for the names of any people, but if you don't tell me what group you are working for, I shall be reluctantly forced to . . . Oh, really, why soften things? I won't be reluctant about it at all.' His smile cut like a knife.

Irene was fairly sure that she could invoke the Language against him before he reached her, or simply slam the safe door into him, but fairly sure wasn't enough. She tried to recall Dominic's dossier, as he'd provided a list of the better-known secret societies.

'The Cathedral of Reason. Sir,' she said reluctantly, letting it be drawn out of her. That had been one of the more neutral groups, more concerned with general scientific progress than slaughtering horrific fiends and dangers to humanity. Or being dangers to humanity.

He nodded as if she had confirmed a hypothesis. 'Very good. Now, little mouse, I have a bargain for you. Or rather, for your masters. We both want the manuscript, but we'll get it faster by working together. A copy could be arranged. A deal can be made. Do you agree?'

What Irene truly wanted to say was that she didn't like being called *little mouse*. It wasn't even as if she was that small. She was five foot nine, which was a perfectly good height for a woman in most worlds. Fair Folk or not, this man was an arrogant, insulting, offensive boor, and if she could she would personally make him run a marathon ahead of an oncoming locomotive.

What she said was, 'Yes, sir.' She dropped her eyes sub-missively. Fair Folk were so accustomed to falling into atti-tudes and high drama themselves that they half expected it from humans, and were always gratified to find their expectations borne out. They thought of everything in terms of stories, with themselves as the main character. They played roles – no, they *lived* roles, and they saw the world around them in terms of the mental movie in which they were starring. He wanted her to be a meek little agent. Very well, she'd play the part for him, and use it to get the job done, and try to ignore the burning throb of anger and incipient ulcers.

He smiled at her. This time it was more of a seductive smile than an angry thin-lipped snarl. It was warm enough that she could nearly have smiled back, if she hadn't known how much of a mask it was. It was inviting, somehow sug-gesting darkness and candlelight and closeness, a catch in the breath, a warm hand in hers, a pressure against her body . . .

'Good girl. Wait a moment.' He walked across to the desk, and began throwing drawers open, rifling through them to find paper, pen and ink. 'Where did he keep it – ah, yes.' He dropped a sheet of paper on the dried blood, opened a bottle of purple ink, dipped a quill in it, and scrawled a quick note. 'There. We're having a ball at the Embassy tomorrow. Here's a private invitation for you. Bring a friend. Bring a lover, even. Find me there and tell me what your masters say to my little proposition. And remember . . .'

He let the sentence hang in the air. Obligingly, Irene said, 'Yes, sir?'

'Remember that I would make a better master for you than the Cathedral of Reason.' There was a glow about him, an aura of presence, as if the light that fell on him came from somewhere else, somewhere more beautiful, more *special*. His eyes were pure gold, reassuring, enchanting, all-encompassing. Even the slit cat-pupils now seemed more natural than human eyes ever could. He stepped forward to lay his hands on her shoulders, drawing her close against him. 'I will be everything to you, little one. I will protect and shield you. You will be my adored one, my own special love, my sweet, my pet, my beauty, my heart's delight.'

He smelled of spice and honey. She could feel the coldness of his hands through his torn gloves and the fabric of her clothing.

'Say that you'll be mine,' he murmured, his lips close to hers.

The markings across Irene's back burst into sudden agony, and she pulled away harshly, gasping for breath. He took a step towards her, but she raised her hand, and he paused.

'I belong,' *to the Library*, 'to the Cathedral of Reason,' she spat. 'Seducing me so I'll betray my masters will *not* convince them to form an alliance.'

'Oh well.' He raised his fingers to his lips and blew her a kiss. 'I felt like trying. I'll see you tomorrow, little mouse. Don't forget. Or I'll come and find you.'

He turned on his heel and strode across to the safe,

scooping up the papers and visiting card. She could see the care that he took not to touch the cold metal. 'Merely our private correspondence, my dear,' he tossed over his shoulder. 'About library books. Nothing to concern you.'

Irene bit her tongue hard enough to hurt, trying to keep her face inquisitively bland. He could have used the word 'library' just in passing. He didn't necessarily suspect her. Or he might have been talking in order to keep her attention on him, rather than on anything else . . .

Paranoia gibbered at the back of her mind. Some Fae did know about the Library. The powerful ones. Was this particular Fae that powerful?

The door slammed behind him.

She had nearly given way. He'd been more than she expected, in every sense. If it hadn't been for her bindings to the Library, she might not have been able to resist in time. And what then? The thought literally made her shiver. There had been other cases of Librarians who had been lost to chaos. The stories weren't reassuring. The undocumented cases even more so. And there was the one horror story that every Librarian knew, about the man who'd turned traitor to the Library and sold it out. He had never been caught and was *still out there* –

Her nails dug into her palms as she forced herself into proper posture and composure. She walked across to look at the document on the desk. It was a basic note of admission to the Liechtenstein Embassy, for tomorrow night, for a Grand Ball.

It was signed, *Silver*.

CHAPTER FIVE

'I've found out all about it,' Kai said as he sliced a bread roll into halves. 'Hey, this is real butter. Cool.'

'We're lucky that it isn't flash-frozen with chemical additional supplements,' Irene said. They'd had trouble finding a restaurant that wasn't billing itself as all new and all special, equipped with the latest scientific devices to preserve, enhance and cook the food that was served inside. Post-meal condition of the diners was not mentioned.

'It makes a nice change,' Kai said. He laid the knife down between the two pieces of buttered roll. 'So, do you want to go first, or me?'

Kai was clearly bubbling with enthusiasm to tell her all about his investigation. Irene couldn't help but wonder just how discreet a criminal he'd been in his own alternate, before joining the Library. She made him keep quiet until the waiter had brought their wine and retreated into the curtained shadows of the restaurant, and tried not to be too amused by it all. Five years of enforced study had clearly left him with enough spare energy to run the lights for most of London.

'You first,' Irene said. 'Give me a full breakdown.'

'All right. Now, first of all, Liechtenstein is a major

power in this world. They do the *best* zeppelins. And everyone knows it. That newspaper-seller was right. And they do sell information, but not their big secrets.'

'No industrial espionage?' Irene asked. 'No reverse engineering of technology or attempts to invade other countries?'

'Ah, there's a reason for that.' Kai took a sip of his wine. 'Hey, this isn't bad. For a cheap little hole-in-the-wall place like this.'

Irene nodded. 'So, what's the reason?'

'The Fae keep them out. They keep the entire country well protected to shield their own goings-on, and it keeps out the industrial and national spies as well. Remember the bit about the Ambassador being one of the Fair Folk?' Kai pressed his lips together for a moment, in a gesture of pure disgust. 'It's not just him. There's a lot of them in Liechtenstein. They spawn there, or breed, or something. It's a nexus for their filth. The local populace tolerates them. They've been bought off with trinkets and flashy glamour.'

Irene frowned. It didn't sound as if Kai was going to be thrilled that they were going to the Embassy Ball tomorrow night. 'Ah,' she said neutrally, and sipped her wine. 'So it's quite normal for Fair Folk to be amongst the Liechtenstein Embassy staff?'

Kai nodded. 'They're known for it, even. Newspaper reporters were trying to get interviews at the Embassy gates. One said that other nations dealing with the country carried cold iron talismans now – it was that bad.'

'Good to know that works,' Irene said. 'Assuming it does?'

'Well, they wouldn't carry them unless it did,' Kai said. 'Unless . . .' He paused. 'Unless the Fair Folk are just faking the whole thing in order to lure their victims into a false sense of security.'

'Well, that's possible too,' Irene agreed regretfully. She held up her hand to pause him as the waiter arrived with their soup, and they were quiet until the man had left. 'All right,' she said, picking up her spoon. 'Go on.'

'The current Ambassador has held the post for the last eighty years,' Kai said, picking up his own spoon. 'His name is Silver. Or rather, people call him Silver. It seems nobody knows his real name outside Liechtenstein, if anyone does. Though the fact that it's apparently a reportable fact about him that nobody knows his real name . . .' He sighed. 'Fae. The reporter that I was talking to said that he hadn't changed at all in the last eighty years, except to update his wardrobe. He's got a fairly typical reputation for a Fair Folk. Seductive, arrogant, party-going, patronizes artists.'

Irene thought about that. 'Does he patronize engineers?' she asked.

'The reporter didn't mention that,' Kai said. 'Why?'

Irene shrugged. 'It just seemed relevant, given we're told this alternate favours technology, and if Liechtenstein's economy is based on airships. By the way, you know a lot about the Fair Folk.'

Kai looked as though he was considering spitting on the ground. 'Those *creatures* – we had something like them in the alternate that I came from. Pervasive thieves, wasters, destroyers – they make their way into society and tear it apart. They destabilize reality. They're tools of chaos. They *are* chaos. You can't expect me to approve of things like that.'

'Look, calm down,' Irene said. 'Have some soup. I agree that they're malign. But we're not here on some sort of campaign to root them out. Remember the mission.' She was surprised by his vehemence; it was more than she'd expect from a trainee. But personal experience was probably

74

behind it. She wondered how personal the experience might be. An involvement with one of them? The loss of a friend or lover? 'Our job is to get the text and then we can get the hell out of here.'

Kai stared at her for a moment, then lowered his eyes. 'I apologize for my improper behaviour,' he said, suddenly formal. 'You are the head of this mission, of course. I just wish to convey my feelings on the subject. My extremely strong feelings on the subject.'

Irene tried to think of a way to respond which wouldn't seem dismissive. And he was shifting speech patterns again – from slang to formal and back again. She wondered if he'd noticed it himself. Possibly the influence of the Library, compared to his previous edgy lifestyle?

She set those thoughts aside for later consideration, and did her best to smile. 'It's all right. Really. You aren't the only one who's had problems with chaos. But we can't assess how to handle the situation until we have a full picture of it. Please tell me more about Liechtenstein and the Embassy.'

Kai returned a thin smile, but it was clearly a duty rather than a pleasure. 'Well, as I was going to say, the Fae infestation in Liechtenstein seems to help keep out neighbouring countries. Maybe because they're not sure what the Fae could do, or maybe they're worried about the Fae expanding into their countries. And Liechtenstein's a peach that a lot of people would otherwise want to pluck from the branch and sink their teeth into.'

Irene raised her eyebrows.

'Okay,' Kai said, waving his spoon, 'a dramatic simile, but have you noticed how very balanced and counterbalanced this whole world is? If you take Liechtenstein, there are mad scientists everywhere. The people I questioned implied some kind of mad scientist race. I know I'm just a trainee, but surely the influence of science there could only be to balance the amount of chaos the Fae bring to the table – especially in Liechtenstein itself?'

'Or maybe the Fae are telling stories about science,' Irene hypothesized. 'Or being involved in stories about science. Or maybe Liechtenstein is taking on the role of Belgium in this alternate. My father once did a check on it in as many alternates as he could find. Belgium always seems to get invaded, fall prey to meteorites or get infested by alien fungus or something . . . and don't look now, but someone's just come in and is staring at us.'

'It must be you he's looking at,' Kai said hopefully, tilting his spoon in a vain attempt to catch a reflection of the room behind him. 'Do something odd and see if he reacts.'

'He's coming this way,' Irene said briefly. He appeared every inch the wealthy aristocrat. From the top hat to the silk-lined cape to the silver-headed cane (a sword cane, she suspected). His eyes were fixed on Kai. 'Quickly,' she murmured, 'did you do anything that you should have told me about?'

'Definitely not.' Kai turned to follow Irene's gaze. 'Hm. Wait. I saw him at the Embassy.'

'As I saw you, sir,' the man said, doffing his top hat in a small bow to Kai, then a subsidiary one to Irene. 'May I join you at this table?'

Kai flicked a glance to Irene. She nodded slightly. He turned back to the man. 'Of course,' he said. 'Though I don't think we've been introduced?'

A waiter had come dashing up with an extra chair, and withdrew with the man's hat and cloak.

The man seated himself and leaned forward, steepling his fingers. 'I trust I may speak freely before your associate?' He nodded towards Irene. 'Some of what I have to say may not be fit for the ears of one of the gentler sex.'

Kai looked at Irene for a moment. Irene hesitated, then looked down at her plate in a docile manner. She'd had to play this sort of role before, though admittedly not when coaching a junior at the same time. 'Please let me stay, sir,' she said to Kai. 'I will simply take notes as normal.'

Kai nodded to her in a lordly manner, then turned back to their guest. 'I assure you that Miss – ' he barely faltered – 'Winters here is entirely trustworthy, and is a valued associate of mine. You may speak freely in front of her. Though I would be interested to know what you propose to discuss.'

Part of Irene's mind was surprised at Kai's sudden elegance of speech. He'd shifted again into that extreme formality which she'd noted earlier. And while she could manage such linguistic shifts easily enough from experience in various alternates, she hadn't thought that he'd be so capable. Stranger and stranger from a boy who claimed to be from a cybered-up alternate, where he was a petty criminal. She very much wanted to talk to Coppelia about this. The other part of her mind wondered why he'd dubbed her 'Winters' and what the cultural reference might be.

She watched their guest from under her eyelashes. He had relaxed a little now, and was leaning back in his chair. He was a very aquiline physical type, with a well-defined nose, deep-set shadowy eyes, high cheekbones and long delicate fingers. The perfect example of a lead protagonist in certain types of detective fiction. In fact, she wondered if . . .

'Very well,' the stranger said. 'Permit me to introduce myself. My name is Peregrine Vale, fifteenth Earl of Leeds.'

Kai gave a little nod. 'Kay Strongrock, at your service. Might I ask the nature of your business?'

The waiter cleared away the soup course and brought

the main meal for Irene and Kai. He also brought a spare glass for the visitor, filling it unbidden, before retreating again. The intrusion allowed Irene to bite her lip and refrain from kicking Kai under the table, as she'd just managed to work out where he was getting his pseudonyms from. *Strongrock – Rochefort. Winters – De Winter.* She would have to explain to him why it was a bad idea to pull pseudonyms from literary sources. If the other person had read the book, it gave them far too much information. They'd start looking around for three possible Musketeers or mysterious Richelieu-like manipulators behind the scenes.

Even though she had to admit that being compared to Milady de Winter had its flattering side.

'I observed you this afternoon, Mr Strongrock,' the Earl of Leeds stated. 'You were outside the Liechtenstein Embassy. You arrived while they were unloading their zeppelins. You watched the newspaper reporters and then questioned them afterwards.'

'Your Lordship seems to have paid a great deal of attention to my movements,' Kai said. There was an undertone of threat to his voice.

The Earl of Leeds tilted his hand. 'Call me Vale, please. After all, this is a purely private meeting, in a very unofficial capacity.'

Kai raised an eyebrow, and sliced into his steak. 'Oh?'

'Indeed,' Vale said. He smiled a little.

And it was at that moment that Irene remembered where she'd seen his face before. She'd picked up some newspapers earlier, to get a quick impression of the current political and temporal dynamics. Vale had been on the third page of one; shot half in profile, with him half turned away, clearly unwilling to have the photograph taken. The caption had been NOTED DETECTIVE CONSULTS WITH BRITISH MUSEUM.

Irene continued to eat, thinking furiously. If their companion was indeed a noted detective, investigating the Liechtenstein Embassy and working with the British Museum – they were either unexpectedly lucky, or in very serious trouble.

'So,' Kai said. 'Leaving aside that I saw no sign of your following me . . .'

'That,' Vale said smoothly, 'is what you may expect to see when I am following you.'

Kai choked slightly on his wine. 'Pardon me. But then, sir, why were you following me? What was so interesting about my activities?'

Vale's smile narrowed even further. 'Why, Mr Strongrock, the fact that they mirrored my own. I suspect that we are investigating the same matter. To be frank, sir, if we are both chasing the same hare, I would rather that you did not start it and cause us both to lose it.'

Kai darted Irene a glance. Clear as daylight, she read a desperate plea for help in his eyes. 'Mm,' he said meditatively.

Irene gasped. It was probably a little theatrical, but, she hoped, not too much so. 'Mr Strongrock! Our investigation is strictly private! Even if His Lord— that is, even if Mr Vale is a famous private detective, we could be looking into entirely different matters!'

She hoped that conveyed the message of *we need more information* thoroughly enough.

Kai patted her on the hand soothingly. 'My associate has a point, Mr Vale,' he said. 'We are operating under conditions of strict confidentiality.'

'As am I, sir,' Vale said with equanimity, not seeming at all put off. 'Whatever minor assumptions I might make about you are simply the result of anything you may have revealed to me yourselves, rather than from any investigations on my part.'

Kai raised his eyebrows. 'But we have revealed nothing to you,' he said, a moment before Irene could kick his ankle.

'Forgive me when I say that it is obvious that you are strangers to London,' Vale said. He turned his glass in his hand, regarding it with a dry smugness. 'I am not speaking merely of Mr Strongrock's need to check the street signs when leaving the Liechtenstein Embassy. Neither of you have the accent of native Londoners, and to be truthful, I cannot place either of you within the British Isles.' He frowned a little. 'Which is unusual. Miss Winters might perhaps have a trace of Germanic brutality to her verbs – possibly the result of a governess or boarding school at an impressionable age? Mr Strongrock, on the other hand, has the accent and the bearing characteristic of certain noble families of Shanghai. While neither of these in themselves is that unusual in London, both of you are dressed in a manner that suggests a hasty choice of clothing from a second-rate supplier. Miss Winters's gloves, for instance.'

Irene glanced down at her gloves, which lay next to her table setting, unable to resist the impulse. She knew that they clashed with her dress, but there hadn't been much of a choice in the shop.

'Precisely,' Vale said. 'A woman as carefully turned out as Miss Winters would not commit such an elementary error in dress. Similarly, Mr Strongrock's shoes – ' Kai shuffled his feet further under his chair – 'were clearly worn before him by a man with the habit of kicking the right side of his forefoot against his chair, but Mr Strongrock himself does not do so. And if the two of you had been in London for a while now, and making enquiries about Lord Wyndham and the Liechtenstein Embassy, then I assure you that I would have known about it.'

Kai opened his mouth, and Irene realized that he was about to say something like *how did you know I asked about Lord Wyndham?* Apparently he had never been taught the first defence in the science of provocative questioning: Keep Your Mouth Shut. This time she did manage to kick him under the table. He shut his mouth again.

'Mm,' Vale said, apparently satisfied. 'A sharing of information could be quite useful. But on the other hand, as Miss Winters has said, we could be looking into entirely different matters. I believe we have come to the point where we decide whether or not to trust one another.'

'So it seems,' Kai said, making a recovery. 'Some more wine?'

'Thank you,' Vale said, extending his glass to be filled.

There was silence for a few minutes. Irene turned over various strategies in her mind. Unfortunately, most of them involved Vale briefly leaving the table so that she could talk urgently with Kai, and this seemed unlikely to happen. She was simultaneously impressed by the man's skills of observation, and significantly worried by them. This sort of intellect was splendid in fictional characters, but in practice it risked making their task a great deal more awkward.

Fortunately, the situation was interrupted by screams and loud grinding noises from the street. Diners dropped their knives and forks to turn towards the doorway. A couple of men leaped to their feet, wineglasses still in their hands.

Kai managed an infinitesimal blink at Irene, then turned to Vale. 'Do you think we should investigate, sir?'

'Of course!' Vale exclaimed, rising. He picked up his swordstick, balancing it casually in his left hand. 'Madam, kindly stay here. Mr Strongrock, if you would accompany me – ' He strode towards the door.

'What do I do?' Kai hissed at Irene.

'Stay with him,' Irene whispered. 'I'll hold back. Find out what's going on. Be careful, he's a detective.'

'I'd worked that bit out,' Kai muttered. But he displayed a wild enthusiasm as he raced after Vale, an eagerness for action.

Irene glanced around as the two men raced off. Nobody creeping out of the shadows to try to abduct her while their attention was elsewhere. Good. She picked up her bag and walked after them.

The restaurant's reception area had large glass windows which provided a convenient view of the street outside. The place was in total chaos. A giant mechanical centipede – well, some sort of segmented insect with multiple legs, Irene was hardly going to stand there and count them all – was wreaking havoc in the narrow alleyway outside. She spotted a badly damaged cart and several broken windows. There was barely room for it to navigate, let alone turn around, and it was dancing a few steps forward and then a few steps back as its front feelers seemed to quest for something or someone. Oil oozed from its crevices, while steam puffed from its head-segment and mingled with the ambient fog. She noticed that a couple of people had already been hurt and bystanders were screaming and running in all directions. Then of course pausing, at a theoretically safe distance, to watch what it did next.

Kai and Vale were standing in the doorway, assessing it. At least, Vale looked as if he was assessing it. Kai just looked stunned.

'How the hell did that thing get through the streets?' Kai asked.

Vale sniffed. 'It probably came up from the sewers. The recent renovation programme has been a godsend to criminals across London.'

'*Vale!*' The creature's echoing voice boomed down the street. '*Prepare to face your doom!*'

'Ah,' Vale said cheerfully, 'it's for me.'

Kai looked hurt. 'It might have got us confused,' he said. 'Perhaps it's for me.'

'No, no, I assure you it's for me,' Vale said. 'But would you mind watching the rear end while I distract the front? Sometimes they have high-emission scintillotherms located there.'

'Of course,' Kai said. 'Not a problem.'

Irene leaned against the wall and tried not to sigh. Perhaps Vale was an ethical person, if his enemy was happy to risk innocent lives to hunt him down. Assuming that he hadn't staged the entire thing of course – but it was also just one more distraction. How on earth was she supposed to manage an investigation with these constant interruptions?

The two men ran out into the street: Vale to the right, towards the creature's head, and Kai to the left, towards its rear. Irene debated which one to follow. Kai was under her protection, but following Vale could be far more informative.

The question was settled for her as the centipede threw itself into rapid reverse, metal claws scraping on the pavement as it danced backwards. Its head came into view: a monstrous steel model of mandibles and huge faceted glass eyes, large enough for a man to sit in, with steam jetting out in thick squealing bursts on either side. Vale stood before it, his sword unsheathed from its cane and blazing with electricity. Each time that the centipede lowered its head to try to bite at him, he parried, and sparks flew to sizzle against pavement and walls.

With a dazzling burst of speed, he darted forward between the gnashing mandibles, and leapt up onto the main part of the centipede's head, balancing there for a moment. He raised his blade, and brought it down into one of the creature's eyes.

Electricity blazed up in a great sparking column. The centipede gave a hissing scream, and thrashed all along its length, one segment jolting into the next, with steam gushing out from all the apertures. A hatch dropped open beneath the creature, and a man in a greasy black boiler suit came rolling out of it, coughing and spitting.

Vale leapt down from the head, landing in a billow of coat-tails. He pointed his sword at the man. 'Talk, sir, or—'

At that point Irene's attention was distracted by someone attempting to tug her bag out from under her arm. She turned to see one of the waiters – no, it *wasn't* one of the waiters. It was a man in evening dress, with a napkin hastily thrown over one arm, posing as a waiter. His watch was far too expensive to be a waiter's, his grey moustache too well groomed. And his right hand, she noted in the clarity of the moment, had thin electrical burnlines running from knuckles to wrist.

He tugged again. Irene released the bag, keeping hold of the strap, letting him tug at it. She dropped into a semi-squat, balancing on her left heel, then brought her right leg out in a straight wide pivot. It caught him off-balance and he fell to the ground with a curse.

She straightened again smoothly, pulling her bag back against her body, and picked up one of the flimsy restaurant chairs. It was of dubious quality and, as her antagonist tried to get up, it broke very thoroughly when it slammed into his body.

He staggered back. She picked up another chair.

Outside there were more explosions. Inside, people were gasping and pointing at her and the pseudo-waiter.

Irene tried to decide whether it was more important to maintain her cover as a helplessly feminine secretary, or to beat the bag-snatcher over the head with the chair and take him prisoner. After all, he wasn't definitely involved with any larger conspiracies, and might simply be a petty thief . . .

. . . the hell with it. She brought the chair down on his head, and he went backwards like a sack of potatoes.

She dropped the remnants of the chair, and put her free hand to her chest, hyperventilating. 'I – ' she gasped. 'I come here on holiday, and this man, this *thief* tries to snatch my bag, and nobody tries to help me. Not a single person comes to a helpless woman's defence . . .'

'My dear Miss Winters, I am so sorry.' Vale had stepped back into the restaurant, sheathing his sword. 'I do regret that you should have suffered assault at the hands of some hooligan—'

He looked at the face of the prostrate man, and blinked. 'Do I understand that this man assaulted you?'

'He attempted to snatch my bag,' Irene said, sniffling a little. 'I – I simply reacted on instinct – '

'You.' Vale snapped his fingers, and two of the waiters responded. 'Have this man taken to the nearest prison at once.'

It's good to be an Earl and a noted detective, Irene reminded herself, a little wistfully.

Kai walked into the restaurant, brushing ashes and powder off his jacket. 'Well, that seems to be— Irene! That is, Miss Winters! What happened?' He glanced warily from Irene to Vale, and back to Irene again, clearly wondering if the whole thing had been some sort of diversion.

Irene pointed a finger at the man being dragged off by the waiters. 'That person attempted to grab my bag. I resisted.'

'I suggest we return to our table at once,' Vale said, lowering his voice. 'This merely confirms my suspicions.'

Five minutes later, they were round the table again. The steak had gone cold, but the wine was still drinkable. The general buzz of conversation had resumed its former level. Irene was surprised at how quickly people seemed to have forgotten the centipede attack. It implied that such things were common, which wasn't a comforting thought.

'Forgive me my earlier discretion,' Vale said. 'And thank you for your assistance, Mr Strongrock. But this attack on Miss Winters only proves what I suspected.'

'And what is that?' Kai demanded, turning towards Vale. Irene had the impression that he was slightly miffed that she hadn't asked about his valiant conduct vis-à-vis the centipede's tail. She made a note to get the full details at some point – when a valuable contact wasn't engaged in sharing useful information.

'That your investigations into the Fair Folk have been noted.' Vale leaned forward. 'I observed your questions at the Embassy, Mr Strongrock. And now, a man whom I know to be a Fae agent tries to steal Miss Winters's handbag. Am I wrong to suspect a link?'

Kai threw Irene a frantic glance. She gave him a slight nod.

'You are not wrong, sir,' Kai said firmly. 'There is a link.'

'I thought as much!' Vale glanced between them. 'In that case, we are investigating the same matter – though possibly from different directions. I too am concerned with the Fair Folk, Mr Strongrock. With the recent thefts of occult material. And with Belphegor.'

'Belphegor?' Irene gasped. 'The mysterious cat burglar?'

'Indeed.' Vale's brows drew together. 'I have suspicions as to her identity. And what is more, I believe that all these things are connected. Even though you are both visitors to our city . . .' He let the sentence trail away, as though expecting to be challenged on his deductions, then continued. 'Even though you haven't been here long, the news-papers have been blatant about the thefts. You can hardly open a paper without seeing a new headline. Let me be frank: is this what you are investigating?'

Irene caught Kai's eye, and gave him a very slight nod. She suspected that Vale would pick up on this, but she hoped that he'd interpret it as a suggestion rather than the order that it was.

'You are correct,' Kai said.

'Then I suggest we combine forces. My card.' He flipped out a silver card-case, selected a card from it, and slid it across the table to Kai. 'Please call on me tomorrow morning, when we can talk more privately. Your associate is also welcome, of course.' He gave Irene a dry nod, which made her wonder just how much he *had* guessed. 'Thank you for your time and assistance.'

Vale rose. Kai and Irene rose too. There was a quick confusion of bows and curtseys, followed by Vale striding off, the waiter hurrying after him with hat and cloak.

Kai and Irene sat back down.

'I'm sorry,' Kai said. 'I didn't see him following me earlier at all.'

'Don't worry,' Irene said. 'I suspect he's rarely spotted. But I think he could be a very useful contact.'

Kai perked up. 'So we got lucky?'

'It happens,' Irene said. 'From time to time. Now finish your wine and tell me about the centipede.'

She was already working out a list of things that she needed to ask Kai later, in private. But for the moment, the centipede would do.

CHAPTER SIX

'Right,' Irene said as they finished their coffee. 'We have to assume that our cover's blown.'

'Because of Vale?' Kai asked.

'No.' Irene tilted the cup, staring at the dregs. 'The man who tried to snatch my purse. If he's working for the Fae, I can only think he saw me at Lord Wyndham's house. And if that's the case, then he knows my face, he probably knows my hotel, and now he knows you as well. We need to break our trail.'

'But all our things are in the hotel room!' Kai said. 'All the clothes we bought—'

'How many did you buy?'

Kai tried to meet her gaze, but his eyes wandered down to his coffee cup. 'I was just setting up several possible identities, in case we needed to move among different circles of society,' he said, unconvincingly.

Irene patted his hand. 'Don't worry. In that case, they'll be sure we'll return, and you'll have tied up some of their resources.'

Kai sighed.

'So,' Irene said briskly. 'Standard measures.' These were taught in the Library alongside languages and research, but were rather harder to practise inside the Library's boundaries. But Kai's personal experience should mean he was good at this sort of thing. 'We'll leave here separately; I'll go first, and draw off anyone obvious. They may only have a single watcher. You go to the hotel room, pick up our papers and our cash supply, then leave via the back of the hotel. Do your best to lose any followers. Meet me in front of . . .' she considered, then checked her new clockwork watch. There was no point wearing something electronic when she might have to take it into the Library. 'Holborn Tube station at eleven o'clock. That should be busy enough to throw off any watchers. Damn. I'm never sure whether I prefer worlds that have invented mobile phone equivalents or not.'

'It'd make communication easier,' Kai said.

'But it would make it easier to track us, too,' Irene said. 'And would empower anyone who's trying to catch up with us. All right, are you okay with those instructions?'

Kai nodded. 'What do I do if you don't turn up at Holborn?'

'Contact Dominic,' Irene said. 'He'll put you in touch with Coppelia, and she'll work out what to do next. But I don't expect that to be necessary.'

Kai nodded. He picked up his coffee cup, and tilted it sadly, looking at the dregs in the bottom. 'We're not doing very well so far, are we?'

Irene blinked. 'What? Where do you get that idea?'

'Well, the book's been stolen, enemies are tracking us, we're having to abandon our base—'

'Get that out of your head right this minute,' Irene said. 'Did you expect us to just be able to waltz in and pick it up?'

Kai shrugged. 'I had sort of got the idea that it would be appropriate for an assignment involving a novice like me.'

Irene leaned forward in her chair. 'Point one: the Library never has enough people to be able to give novices "easy" assignments. Never expect an assignment to be "easy". Point two: yes, the manuscript has been stolen, but we already have several leads to follow, including an appointment to meet a famous detective.' The thought made her smile. Perhaps sometimes wishes did come true. 'Point three: it's not a base, it's a hotel room. Point four: the fact that we are being tracked is a lead in itself, and means we can use *them* to work backwards to find the book. And point five: we've an invitation to attend a ball at the Liechtenstein Embassy, which ought to be very interesting.'

Kai stiffened. 'We've got *what*?'

'See you at Holborn,' Irene said, rising and collecting her bag.

There was indeed someone waiting outside the restaurant. She spotted him while checking her reflection in a shop window. The glare of the actinic streetlamps made them better mirrors than the flyspecked piece of glass in the hotel room. *Small loss.* The tail was an average-looking type, with a cheap bowler hat and a frock coat frayed at lapels and elbows. He also wasn't very good at being inconspicuous. Maybe that was usually the job of the colleague who'd tried to snatch her bag.

At the next street corner, she managed a surreptitious glance back while waiting to cross the road, and saw him murmuring into cupped hands. He opened them, and something buzzed out, circling his head before zooming upwards in a clockwork clatter of wings.

Two streets later, he'd rather obviously acquired re-inforcements. She stopped to check her hat in another shop window, and caught another glimpse of him, clearly gesturing to three newcomers and pointing in her direction.

Irene jabbed a hatpin back into place viciously, and considered how best to lose them. This London was laid out like most Londons, and she was on the edge of Soho. It'd be easy enough to lose followers there, but a woman on her own would attract the wrong sort of attention, and it might take too long for her to extract herself inconspicuously. A department store might work, but if they had any sense they'd put watchers at front and back before searching for her inside. Also now there were at least four of them, and there could be others that she hadn't spotted. The Tube itself was a possibility, but she hadn't investigated it yet. And while the crowds might let her hide herself from her pursuers, they'd also be ideal cover for an 'accident' or kidnapping. She was halfway to Piccadilly by now, too, so she needed to start turning back if she was to meet Kai comfortably by Holborn at eleven.

Hm. Wait. Covent Garden usually had a market of some sort in most alternate Londons, whether it was selling flowers or curios or simply a tourist trap. Even if there weren't many stalls open at this time of night, it should still be busy enough for her to lose her pursuers. That should do the trick.

Irene should have expected it: Covent Garden market was a technology extravaganza. Stalls teetered on collapsible legs and sprayed rays of light from dangling ether-lamps. The path between them was a constantly shifting maze as each stall manoeuvred for yet more space on its automated feet, bouncing and jarring against the ones next to it. Much like Covent Gardens she'd seen elsewhere, there were several open yards, and a central area with a high glass roof and several banks of permanent shops. Pavement cafes added their own influxes of shoppers to the area, and regular jets of steam came shooting out of the sewer gratings and manholes.

She put on a burst of speed as she entered the crowd, before the men following her could get any closer. She then allowed herself to be drawn into a whirlpool of spectators orbiting a display of mechanical exsanguinators. (She decided that the little jabbing steel needles weren't specifically unpleasant in themselves, but the oiliness from the self-slathering antiseptics somehow made the whole thing inexpressibly gruesome. It was something about the way that it glistened under the electric flares.)

There were as many women here as men, but the real difference was between those she suspected were genuine artisans and engineers and everyone else. The former had neat equipment cases tucked under their arms or chained to their wrists. The latter included wanderers on the lookout for an interesting bargain, slumming upper classes or fascinated onlookers. The women all wore scarves or veils against the sooty fog, just as Irene did, concealing anything from just their mouth to their entire face. Many of the men had wound mufflers around the lower part of their faces in a similar way. It gave the whole place a very seedy feeling, akin to a market for Victorian bank-robbers, a shady shoppery for shady people.

Nearby, bustling market stalls touted portable notebooks with self-adhesive toolsets, and she spotted pocket watches with built-in lasers (she nearly bought one for Kai). Then there were Constructa-Kit automata, followed by freshly fried doughnuts and self-tattooing kits (just add ink!), then shawls with attached portable heating units, then—

It hit her like a whiplash across her back, throwing her to her knees on the dirty pavement. She could feel every inch of her Library tattoo burning, feel it mapped out across her back as clearly as if she could see it. The world shivered around her. She tasted bile in her mouth, and struggled not to throw up.

The words were everywhere. She could see them on the newspaper stands, swimming up through the whiteness to crawl across the paper. She could see them on the back of the paperback novel which the man in front of her had tucked into his pocket, on the crudely printed advertisements fluttering from every stall and on the receipts which the woman to her left was checking. They printed themselves on everything legible in a spreading circle around her.

BEWARE ALBERICH

People were calling out and swearing in surprise and alarm, blaming the engineers and stallholders for some sort of experimental side-effect (and what that said about this place, Irene reflected in some distracted corner of her mind, didn't bear thinking about). In some cases shoppers were shaking the affected items in the hopes that the words would fall off. Some hope. Irene had never before been the victim of an urgent message from the Library, but she knew the words would be permanently burned in. It was a shocking thing to do to printed media, which was why it was only saved for the most desperate purposes. Members of the public could read them, but at least no one would know what the words meant.

If Alberich was involved in this, then the warning was definitely desperate and necessary.

She pulled herself together with an effort that set her teeth on edge, and glanced over her shoulder to check on the men who'd been following her. Damn. They were closing fast. They must have decided to pick her up now rather than risk losing her.

Irene allowed herself a vicious smile. Pester an agent of the Library, would they? Hassle her when she'd just received an urgent message? Get in her *way*? Oh, they were going to regret that.

She waited for a breathless half-minute until the shifting patterns of moving stalls closed up behind her, blocking her pursuers. They'd open again in a moment, of course . . .

She spat out in the Language, loud enough for it to carry, **'Clockwork legs on moving stalls, seize up and halt, hold and be still!'**

'I beg your pardon?' the man next to her said. 'Were you speaking to me—' He cut off as, in a widening circle within range of Irene's voice, the moving stalls all came stuttering to a halt, jointed legs going abruptly rigid and stopping where they were. The general swirl of people and stalls was thrown into sudden and shocking confusion, far more dramatic than the earlier printing incident. People who'd been preparing to zig suddenly found themselves forced to zag. Piles of goods teetered on the edges of stalls and were barely saved from sliding off – or not saved, in quite a few cases, adding to the general uproar.

Before anyone could come to awkward conclusions about the centre of the circle, Irene darted forward and elbowed her way past several complaining clots of shoppers. She could hear the grinding whir of gears and levers struggling with disobedient mechanical legs. The flow of people carried her forward out of her cul-de-sac, leaving her pursuers trapped behind the barricade of frozen stalls (and, she hoped, being trampled underfoot by angry shoppers). Irene headed for the nearest opening in the maze of tables, then from there to an alleyway. After a bit of rearrangement to veil and jacket, it was out onto the main street again – heading back and round towards Holborn. With nobody following her this time.

With each step the reality of the message from the

Library sank more deeply into her guts. *Beware Alberich. Beware Alberich. Beware Alberich.*

She didn't need this. She really didn't need this. She was already in the middle of a complicated mission, with a trainee to handle on top of it all. She'd given Kai an optimistic summary to keep his spirits up, but that didn't mean that anything was going to be *easy*.

And now this.

Alberich was a figure out of nightmare. He was the one Librarian who'd betrayed the Library, got away with it and was still somewhere out there. His true name was long since lost, and only his chosen name as a Librarian was remembered. He'd sold out to chaos. He'd betrayed the other Librarians who'd been working with him. And he was still alive. Somehow, in spite of age and time and the course of years that would afflict any Librarian who lived outside the Library, he was still alive.

Irene found herself shivering. She pulled her shawl more tightly around her shoulders, and tried to rein her thoughts back from a train of needlessly baroque images. Stupid thoughts. After all, it wasn't as if Alberich was on her trail at this very moment . . .

. . . was it?

The message from the Library couldn't have been faked. It must have been sent by one of the senior Librarians, probably Coppelia. It wouldn't have been sent unless things were urgent, which meant that she had to assume that Alberich was in the area. Worst-case scenario.

She glanced back into a shop window. Nobody seemed to be following her.

She needed to talk to Dominic, urgently, but the British Library would be shut at this time of night. He'd be at home – the address being somewhere in the papers Kai was safeguarding. Tomorrow morning would be easier. For the moment, she and Kai had to find a new hotel and go undercover.

Irene wanted to go very deeply undercover. She wanted to go so deeply undercover that it'd take an automated steam-shovel to excavate her out of it. She also had to decide how much to tell Kai. It was too dangerous to leave him in the dark, not to mention simply unfair, but at the same time she didn't want to panic him. After all, look how panicked she was herself. One panicked person was quite enough. Two would be overkill.

Possibly he'd be ignorant enough not to realize just how bad the situation might be. Possibly he wouldn't have heard the horror stories that had been traded round in quiet alcoves about some of the things that Alberich had done.

And possibly, Irene decided, as she came into sight of Holborn Tube station and saw Kai loitering under a streetlamp, pigs would fly – which would at least mean bacon for breakfast. Oh well. Hotel first. Dramatic explanations later.

CHAPTER SEVEN

'I don't want to complain or anything,' Kai said, 'but we're currently holed up in a cheap hotel.'

'We are,' Irene agreed. She sat down and began to work her buttoned boots off, with a sigh of relief.

'This place isn't just cheap, it's filthy!' Kai gestured round at the tatty yellow wallpaper, the dirt-streaked window, the threadbare counterpane on the double bed, the sallow mirror on the rickety dresser. 'You can't seriously expect us to—'

'Kai,' Irene said firmly. 'You're spoilt. What happened to the shady but useful background? What happened to being a cool street runner who could handle that sort of thing? Have five years in the Library really softened you up that much?'

Kai looked around, and his nose wrinkled. 'Yes,' he finally said. 'They have.' He sat down on the very edge of the bed. 'Is this much deep cover really necessary? Couldn't we, you know, go and hide out at the most expensive hotel in town and claim we're Canadians?'

'No,' Irene said. She removed one boot and started to work on the other. 'Deep cover. For the moment, I want us untraceable. We'll clean up tomorrow and find a nicer place.'

'Is something the matter?'

Irene pulled off the second boot. 'Oof.' She had to tell him; it wouldn't be safe to keep him ignorant. 'There is a potential problem,' she admitted slowly. 'I don't know that it's an immediate issue.'

Kai just looked at her.

'I had an urgent message from the Library.' The next few words were difficult to say, and even more difficult to keep calm and reasonable. 'It warned me to beware Alberich. You can pour me some of that brandy now.'

Kai's hand halted halfway to the brandy bottle, on Irene's list of essential supplies. 'Wait,' he said slowly. 'When you say Alberich, do you mean the one who's supposed to be . . .' He trailed off, leaving it hanging. And, Irene noted to her displeasure, not pouring her brandy either.

'No,' Irene said. 'I don't mean the one who's supposed to be. I mean the one who is. Not that I've ever met him, and with any luck we won't have to, and this is just a precaution.' She hoped. 'Now can I have that brandy?'

'He's real?' Kai said. Still no brandy.

'He's recorded in the Library. How could he not be real?'

Kai looked blank. 'He could be fictional?'

Irene gritted her teeth. 'No. He was formally marked for the Library, given the initiation and everything. That's why he can't go back there. It'd know he was there. But it proves that he is real, that he's not some sort of urban legend like the thing about the pipes and the tentacle monster.' That had been one of the popular ones when she was a trainee. The logic was that if rooms of the Library could be connected by the plumbing, then there was some sort of dark central cistern with a huge tentacle monster living in it which ate old Librarians. And of course it was all covered up by order from on high . . . She and other trainees had spent several hopeful hours rapping on pipes and trying to pass messages or find tentacles. 'Brandy?' she finished.

Kai finally remembered to get up and open the bottle. He splashed a bare quarter-inch into a battered china cup, and offered it to her.

'Thank you,' Irene said, and knocked it back in one gulp, then offered the cup for a refill. 'A bit more this time, please.'

Kai stared at her. 'Are you *sure* you're all right?'

'It's been a busy evening,' Irene said. 'And I'm going to be sitting up for the next few hours studying the local Language listings that Dominic gave us. You can get some sleep.'

'But we ought to tell Dominic at once! After all, if Alberich's here, it proves how important the book is! And we should warn Dominic—'

'How?' Irene enquired. She'd decided a while back that Socratic questioning was a good idea, because (a) it got students thinking for themselves, (b) sometimes they came up with ideas she hadn't thought of, and (c) it gave her more time to think while they were trying to find answers.

'We can go to the British Library – oh, wait. It won't be open at this time of night.'

'It won't,' Irene agreed, 'which is going to be annoying if we need to sneak back in there at some point to get back to the Library. And he didn't give us a home address.' It should have been in those papers he'd given them. It wasn't. Which, a niggling voice at the back of her mind pointed out, had been careless of Dominic. Almost to the point of outright dereliction of duty in such a dangerous location. She might have needed his help urgently.

'We can use the Language to contact him,' Kai said triumphantly.

Irene considered that. 'I can make a construct and send it to warn him, but it will need to travel and find him.'

'Magic,' Kai said.

'Not my field,' Irene replied. 'Are you any good at it?'

'I can command some spirits,' Kai said modestly. 'But I haven't had time to introduce myself to any local ones. I wouldn't want to try that unless we have no other choice.'

Irene nodded. 'And Dominic did say they could be dangerous. So we'll go to the British Library in the morning and talk to Dominic in person, then. The Library will have updated him in any case, just as they did me. It's not as if we're leaving him in danger. This isn't a bad horror film.' She smiled, hopefully reassuringly.

'Oh,' Kai said. He glanced at the small case by the door with the documents in it. 'So,' he said, with a little too much casualness, 'can you show me some of the Language words in there?'

'I could, but it wouldn't do you any good.' Irene put down the cup. 'It won't be any different from how it is inside the Library. It still won't look like anything other than normal speech to you.'

'Did it hurt?'

Irene blinked at the change of subject. 'Did what hurt?'

'Getting the Library mark.' Kai threw himself back down on the bed. It creaked under him. 'If that's the only way to understand the Language.'

'Yes, and yes.' Since Kai evidently wasn't going to bring it over to her, Irene got up and walked across to fetch the case. 'Look, you should get some sleep. There's no point us both staying up all night.'

Kai rolled onto his front, resting his chin on his hands, and looked up at her. 'Irene,' he said, and there was something low and stroking in his voice. 'When you say sleep, do you really mean just sleep?'

Irene looked at him, the case in her hands, and raised her eyebrows pointedly. 'Yes. I do really mean just sleep.'

'But you, me – we're sharing rather a small space, don't you think?' He stretched, and she noticed his trousers clung appealingly tightly. 'You're not feeling some kind of *loco parentis* responsibility towards a novice, are you? Is that what it is?'

'No,' Irene said briefly. 'But it's irrelevant in any case.'

'But . . .'

'Look,' she cut him off, before he got any ideas about standing up and taking her in his arms or anything like that. 'Kai, I like you, you're extremely handsome, and I hope we'll stay good friends, but you are not my type.'

'Oh,' he said.

She walked back, sat down, and opened the case, starting to thumb through the papers inside.

'What is your type?' Kai asked hopefully.

Irene looked up to see that he'd removed his cravat, unbuttoned his shirt, and was showing a triangle of muscular, smooth, pale chest. She could imagine what he would feel like under her fingers.

She swallowed. 'Do we really have to do this?'

'I'm not just trying to flatter you,' Kai said. There was a thread of annoyance in his voice now. 'But I like you, I think you're clever and witty and charming and I have a lot of respect for you. And believe me when I say I am *marvellous* in bed.'

'I do believe you,' Irene said, looking for a way out of this. 'I'm sure that we would spend a very nice evening. But I wouldn't get any study done then.'

'After the study,' Kai said hopefully.

Irene rubbed her forehead with the back of one hand. She was getting a headache. 'Look, I appreciate you being polite about this, I appreciate you being absolutely charming, and I wish I could be more polite about turning you down. But it's been a long day, and I still have work to do, and you're not really my type. And before this goes any further, my type is darkly dangerous and fascinating, of dubious morality. And yes, this caused the whole problem in the cat burglar scandal that was mentioned earlier. Which was deeply embarrassing at the time. And still is. Also, let me make myself perfectly clear that if you repeat this I will *skin you alive*. Right?'

Kai looked at her with big disappointed eyes. 'I would have enjoyed partnering you,' he said. 'Really. You would, too.'

'Allow me to inform you that I am an *exquisite* bed partner,' Irene said, a little sniffily. 'I have travelled through hundreds of alternates and sampled partners from many different cultures. If I took you to bed, you certainly wouldn't be complaining.'

Kai gave her another deep stare from those drowning-dark eyes of his.

She sighed. 'But right now, we have a book to find, I have to study, and you need to sleep. Please?'

Eventually he did, and she could work in peace, with only the occasional side-thought about tempting offers and beautifully contoured muscles.

A couple of hours later, with Kai soundly asleep, Irene put down her papers and rubbed her sore temples. She'd just memorized a dozen different adverbs for the way that an airship moved, and fifteen adjectives for types of smog. She was due a break.

Unfortunately, thought came along with it.

Alberich was known to be allied with some of the Fae; he'd gone to them when he first went renegade. Now he allegedly played on their various factions with the energy of a lunatic musician with a pipe organ. The few fragmented reports that the Library had on him – at least those that were accessible to juniors like herself – suggested that he was after immortality.

She stared at the papers without really seeing them. Immortality. The Library gave an effective sort of immortality, or at least a continued life until the person involved grew tired of it. As long as a Library initiate bearing its mark was *inside* the Library, they didn't age. Out in the multiple worlds, one grew old, but inside the Library ageing just stopped. She'd spent years in the Library herself while she was training. She'd had years of experience that didn't show anywhere obvious. Except perhaps her eyes sometimes, but she tried not to think about that.

That was why the Library hierarchy functioned as it did. Junior Librarians operated out in the divergent worlds while they still had the years to spare. Once they grew old, they retreated to work in the Library for as long as they chose, with only the occasional trip outside if necessary. These were people like Coppelia and Kostchei, spending their days in the endless rooms, finally able to get their research done properly. Some Librarians just lived on and on, until they decided that they'd had enough, or went out into the alternate worlds to finish their days somewhere that they liked. The Library paid for it, however expensive or exotic, on the grounds that 'nothing is too good for those who've spent their lives in service to the Library'. Of course, it was similarly aged Librarians who voted for the funding on that sort of thing . . .

Irene wasn't going to start thinking about that sort of thing yet. She had years in the field ahead of her yet. Decades. Things to do. People to see.

But then there was Alberich. He'd left the Library *five hundred years ago*. There was no way that he could still be alive by the Library's normal methods. He must have made some sort of bargain with the Fae, creatures defined by their impossibility. Common horror or fantasy literature supplied half a dozen unpleasant ideas on how Alberich could still exist, though some of them might not count as living.

And what did he want to do with that continued existence? The Library could use unique books to connect and bind itself to particular alternate worlds. But what could someone else – someone from outside the Library – do with those linking books? It wasn't an area within which junior Librarians had been encouraged to speculate. The best answer she could come up with at the moment was *something bad*.

After all, what might it imply if Alberich could *influence whole worlds simply by owning certain key texts . . .* ?

Irene seriously considered another brandy. This was all growing overly complicated. Bradamant wanting to take over the mission, the Fae involvement, Alberich . . . and then there was Kai.

She looked across at his sleeping form. He didn't snore. Kai breathed gently and regularly, like an advertisement for particularly comfortable pillows. And he'd managed to fall asleep in just the sort of position that might require her to smooth his brow or wake him with a kiss. As for that earlier shift of persona from street punk to semi-aristocrat – he'd handled that detective like a gentleman born. And his current interest in wardrobe, seduction and general adventure really didn't fit the young man who'd introduced himself to her as Coppelia's latest student. There was something off. Coppelia *had* to have noticed it herself.

Irene realized that she was tapping her finger against the papers. She deliberately stopped herself. Habits were dangerous; they could get you killed.

Had Bradamant's interest in Kai been suspicious?

Irene had her own history with Bradamant, which she

certainly wasn't going to discuss in front of Kai, or behind Kai, or in any place where Kai might end up hearing about it. The woman was a poisonous snake. No, that was unfair to snakes. Irene had been Bradamant's student once, and she knew exactly what it meant. Get used as a live decoy, somehow miss any of the credit but catch all the blame. Then spend years putting your research credentials back together again, after the blot on your record caused by rejecting an older Librarian's offer to take you out on another mission.

With an effort, she stopped herself tapping on the papers again.

It was just three in the morning; she could hear distant church bells and clock chimes, drifting through the fog outside. Another hour of study, then she'd sleep and Kai could keep watch. She was paranoid enough to want someone keeping watch, however unlikely it was that Alberich or anyone else could find them here.

Paranoia was one of the few habits that was worth keeping.

At eight o'clock the next morning, the doors of the combined British Museum and British Library opened. Irene and Kai joined the crowd of people heading in. Luckily nobody was in the mood for talking at that hour of the morning. People kept their gazes fixed on their boots, stared blankly ahead, or buried themselves ferociously in notebooks.

The Department of Classical Manuscripts was open, but Dominic Aubrey's office was closed. The door was locked, bolted, and possibly even barred on the inside, for all that Irene could tell. She didn't remember noticing a bar when she'd been inside, but she might have missed it.

'Shall I pick the lock?' Kai asked as they (not for the first time) straightened from peering at it and did their best to imitate hopeful students, just in time to smile at passing staff.

'I'll do it,' Irene said. 'He may have put some sort of wards up against physical or sorcerous lockpicking, but he can't ward against the Language.' She paused. 'Stand back.'

'Oh?' Kai said, doing as she'd told him.

'Well, wards are one thing, but traps and alarms are something else.' She ignored Kai's expression of sudden dismay (really, he should be grateful, he was getting an excellent education) and quickly went down on one knee. There she informed the door in the Language that all seals and bars on it were undone, all locks and bolts opened, and all wards gone.

It swung open quietly when she set her hand on the handle. She beckoned Kai in quickly after her, and closed the door behind him.

The room was just as it had been yesterday. Early morning sunlight came in dimly through the windows, muffled by the fog beyond, and gleamed on the gold leaf and glass cases. The Library door itself was secured by means of a chain and padlock, the chain running through both the door handle and a metal link set into the wall. It would be useless to prevent anyone coming from the other side, as the power of the Library would prevail, but it was efficient enough to stop people trying it from this side.

'Irene,' Kai said uneasily.

'Yes?'

'If the door out was bolted from this side, and if the door to the Library was padlocked from this side too, how did anyone leave the room?'

'A good point,' Irene said. *Encourage useful habits of thought.* 'There must be a secret door here somewhere. Or he left through sorcery.'

'So can you use the Language to find the secret door?'

Irene sat down on the chair behind the desk. It was clearly Dominic Aubrey's personal chair. It yielded with the ease of long use with a single graceful creak, and smelled of snuff and coffee. 'Not exactly. Field exam; tell me why.'

'Oh, that's not fair . . .' Kai started, then looked at her expression and shut his mouth to think. 'Okay,' he said a moment later. 'Sorry. I think I've got it. Everything within range of the Language reacts to it unless the command or sentence specifies otherwise, right. So if you just tell everything within range to unlock . . .'

Irene nodded. 'Then I'll end up opening the cases, the drawers, the cabinets along the wall there, the padlock on the Library door, and quite possibly my handbag and your wallet and the windows while we're at it. It's a reasonable suggestion, but it won't do unless we have absolutely no other choice. Now tell me why I'm not going to use sorcery.'

Kai thought, then shrugged. 'Because Dominic may have put wards on any secret door which will blow up when you use sorcery to detect them?'

'Actually, no.' Irene leaned her elbows on the desk. 'It's because I'm bad at sorcery.'

'What? But anyone can do sorcery!'

She lifted her eyebrows.

'Seriously,' Kai said. 'You must be joking. Sorcery's one of the simplest skills around. Even my – my youngest brother could command the simpler spirits and invoke the elements. You're not telling me that . . .' He ran out of words mid-sentence, with the uneasy look of someone who'd spotted that he'd said the wrong thing.

Irene had noticed it too. 'Your youngest brother,' she repeated softly.

'Irene, I—'

'*If I'd had a family*, you told me before.' She remembered

the conversation in the Library, as forgetting was the last thing a fully-trained Librarian should do. Memories were as important as books, and almost as important as proper indexing. 'Kai, you've been lying to me about some things, and hiding others. I know it, and you know it.' She wished that she could run her hands through her hair in the way that he was doing now, but she was the older Librarian, and he was her apprentice, and she couldn't afford to show weakness. She had to be in control. She liked him, and she didn't actually like many people, and she didn't want to accuse him. She didn't want to . . . drive him away. 'Do you want to talk about it?'

He drew himself up and stood in front of her, suddenly appearing very tall and yet somehow fragile. 'I can't,' he said.

'You can,' Irene corrected him. 'But it seems you won't.'

'Irene.' He swallowed. 'I swear to you that it has nothing to do with the current situation. By my name and my honour and my descent, I swear it.'

Saying *as far as you know* was the obvious response, but it would have made light of his obvious struggle and sincerity. And he was sincere, Irene was certain of that.

Of course, that didn't necessarily mean that he was right, or that he wasn't an idiot.

She sighed. 'I accept your word, and won't ask for more unless the current situation dictates otherwise. But I will have to tell Coppelia about this, Kai. I can't keep it secret.'

'I'd expect that,' Kai said. He raised his eyes to look nobly at the opposite wall. 'I would have known that you would report it, seeing as—'

'Assuming she doesn't already know,' Irene said thoughtfully.

Kai twitched. 'She can't,' he said, in a tone that was more desperate hope than genuine conviction.

'If I can spot something being odd in two days, then she

can probably notice it in five years.' Irene stood up and patted Kai on the shoulder. 'Relax. Now let's find this secret door. I'll check the cabinets on this wall, you check the shelves on that wall.'

She could hear Kai muttering behind her as she walked across to check the ranks of cabinets. They were full of carefully pinned-down pages, shards of pottery, pens, quills, typewriters, and other bits and pieces that obviously hadn't been dusted for at least a couple of years. The locks on the cabinets were good, but the wood was dry and fragile. Any serious thief (such as herself, on more than one occasion) would simply have broken the frame or cut out the glass rather than trying to pick the lock.

Kai sneezed.

'Found anything?' she called across, not bothering to turn and look.

'Only dust,' he said, and sneezed again.

Irene went down on her hands and knees to check the bottom edge of the cabinets, looking for traces that they'd been moved. If this didn't get her anywhere, then she'd forget about confidentiality and go through the drawers of Dominic's desk. She didn't seriously expect him to keep anything incriminating or important there, but it might at least give them his home address. Failing that, she and Kai could check with the British Library administration. Failing that—

Kai sneezed again.

'If there's that much dust,' she called across, 'then any secret doors should be fairly obvious.'

'It's not just dust,' Kai said. He took a step. Paused. Took another step. 'There's something in this room which smells odd.'

Irene gave up on the cabinets, and pulled herself to her feet, brushing off her skirt. 'What is it?'

Kai sniffed. 'I'm not sure. Spicy. Salty. Somewhere round here . . .' He wandered along the bookcases, sniffing again.

She followed him, fascinated by this new approach to finding secret doors.

'Got it!' Kai leaned in and pointed at the small cabinet at the end of the shelves. Half a dozen volumes of *The Perfumed Garden Summarized for the Young* were piled on top of it, but the actual door of the cabinet was accessible, if locked.

'Let me see.' Irene went down on her knees again to check it. 'Hm. Looks like a normal cabinet. Anything odd about the lock?'

'Not that I can see,' Kai replied, joining her at ground level. 'Do you want to open it or shall I?'

'Oh, allow me.' Irene leaned in, and ordered the lock open in the Language.

The cabinet door didn't open.

'That's interesting,' she said.

'How can it *not* open?' Kai asked.

'The easiest explanation is that it's sealed by some other method, on top of the lock,' Irene explained. 'Something that's not obvious, so I wouldn't know it's there to tell it to open. Or then again . . . you were saying you could smell something. On which side of the cabinet is the smell strongest?'

Kai gave her a look suggesting that he wasn't here to sniff on her behalf, but complied after a moment. 'This side,' he said, tapping the right-hand panel of the cabinet.

'Right.' Irene shuffled round to get a better look at it, then prodded carefully at the corners and the inlaid design. 'Hm. Yes. Thought so. When is a door not a door?'

Kai just looked at her.

'When,' Irene said triumphantly, 'it's a fake. Here.' She pressed the upper corners simultaneously, and the whole side of the cabinet swung open on a hidden hinge. 'There. Now . . .' She would have said more, but a powerful stink of vinegar hit her, and she rocked back on her knees, fanning the air in front of her nose.

'That's rather raw,' Kai said. 'Is it a Library way of preserving documents?'

'Not one that I've ever heard of.' Irene regained her self-control, and drew out the contents of the cabinet. It was a single Canopic jar in the ancient Egyptian style. 'So let's see what's in here.'

'Should we?' Kai asked.

'Kai,' Irene said gently. 'If Dominic really wanted to keep this secret from us, he wouldn't have hidden it and then been late for work, knowing we'd snoop around.'

'Just purely for information,' Kai said, 'are all Librarians like this over private stuff?'

Irene didn't dignify his question with an answer. Besides, he'd learn better. A Librarian's mission to seek out books for the Library developed, after a few years, into an urge to find out everything that was going on around one. It wasn't even a personal curiosity. It was a simple, impersonal, uncontrollable need to know. One came to terms with it. She lifted off the Canopic jar's stylized jackal-head lid. 'There's something in here,' she reported.

Kai forgot moral scruples and leaned in closer. 'What is it?'

'Some sort of leather.' Irene rolled back her sleeves and pulled it out. It was larger than it looked, thin delicate stuff with long trailing attachments. She shook it out to get an idea of its full length and shape, then froze, horrified. Behind her she could sense Kai's stillness and shock.

It was a complete human skin, all in one piece, with a single slit down the front from chin to groin.

It was Dominic Aubrey's skin.

CHAPTER EIGHT

Kai drew back with an indrawn hiss, raising his hands in front of him like claws. The skin lay there on the floor, limp and wet, staining the polished boards with vinegar.

Irene swallowed, holding on to the smell of the vinegar to keep her own nausea at bay. Dominic Aubrey's features looked so different like this. The flattened face was recognizable, but lacking shape, spirit and the congenial warmth that had animated it just the day before.

'Is it some sort of fake?' Kai demanded.

Irene flipped it over. The Library mark ran across its back in a complex tracery of flourishes. It was unmistakeable; the Language couldn't be faked, even if someone tried to copy it. She felt the mark across her own shoulders twitch in a kind of sympathy. 'No,' she said, numbly. 'It's real. But it's not *possible* for someone to shed their skin like this . . . I mean, it may just be possible to remove your skin, if you consider some wilder fictional texts, but you couldn't remove the Library's mark and survive.'

'Alberich,' Kai said.

Irene didn't need to ask him what he meant. 'Certainly possible,' she agreed. 'Even likely. But there's the Fae to consider as well, and there may be other factions at work. Right. We have to report this.'

Kai sighed deeply in relief. 'I was afraid you were going to say that we had to investigate it ourselves.'

'Don't be ridiculous,' Irene said briskly. 'We may collect fiction, but we are not required to imitate the stupider parts of it.' *And let's hope we don't just get told to investigate this mess without backup anyway.* 'First things first. We'll hide this thing again, then I'll open the door to the Library.'

The handle of the outer door began to turn.

Irene barely had time to think *But I know I locked it!* She hastily shoved skin and jar behind one of the display tables and rose to shield it further with her skirts.

Kai managed two paces towards the door before it swung fully open.

A tall young woman stood there, clutching some books to her chest. She looked at the two of them.

'I'm terribly sorry,' Irene said quickly. 'Mr Aubrey isn't here yet. Can we help you?'

The woman stared at the two of them. 'I beg your pardon?' she said slowly. 'Who are you?' Her brown hair was looped untidily on the back of her head and smeared with dust, and there were traces of dust and ash on her grey skirt and jacket.

'Vermin preventative defence,' Irene invented quickly. 'We're working through all the rooms, looking for signs of infestation. Tell me, Miss – ' She paused invitingly.

'Todd,' the woman said. 'Rebecca Todd. He told me to come in this morning about the *Lamia* manuscript.' She shifted her grip on her books.

'He should be in soon,' Irene said. 'I'm terribly sorry, but I can't ask you to wait inside because we need to deploy some hazardous chemicals while we're testing for silverfish. Would you mind waiting outside in the corridor? We'll be out in a minute.'

'Of course,' Miss Todd said readily. 'If Mr Aubrey does arrive while you're still testing, I'll let him know.'

'Thank you,' Irene said with a smile. She waited until Miss Todd was safely out of the room before breathing a sigh of relief.

'Silverfish?' Kai muttered.

'Hush,' Irene said. 'We'll be out of here before she knows it.' She knelt down again, avoiding the growing puddle of vinegar, and hastily stuffed the skin back into the jar. 'Ugh. I need to wash my hands. Actually, I'll take this with us. Perhaps Coppelia or one of the others will know what it means.' She passed the jar to Kai. 'You hold this.'

'Must I?' he said, taking it distastefully.

'I need to open the door.' Irene walked across to the Library door. She remembered seeing the chain last time, but she rather thought it wasn't in use then, perhaps freed by their own journey through the door. It was clearly for show rather than substance, presumably to discourage outsiders from using it. And, of course, anyone like Irene could just use the Language.

'**Chain, open,**' she said, laying her hand on the padlock.

It didn't explode. It burst open. It unfurled like a chrysanthemum and then fastened onto her palm, spreading across her skin in a slick of white-hot metal. But there was more to it than heat. Through the acute pain, Irene sensed active malice and deliberate will. Behind it all, as she almost lost consciousness, she caught a dazzle of brightness that ultimately faded to darkness.

'Irene,' Kai was saying, but she had fallen to her knees, and didn't have the space in her head to register his words or his expression. Or anything except the blazing pain crackling from her hand to shoot up her arm. 'Irene!'

The mark across her back flared to life, automatically resisting the invasive chaotic forces linked to the padlock. Order and chaos now battled for authority over her body. And it was too late to recognize this as a trap laid for someone who'd use the Language, even though it was so clearly that in hindsight.

She could smell something burning. That would be her dress. Fabric was so flammable.

'Get me loose,' she gasped. If only she could break the physical link that held her to the padlock, or the forces powering it, that might be enough to let her regain control and finish cleansing herself.

Kai closed a hand round her wrist and pulled. He didn't try touching the padlock.

The padlock was stuck to her hand. She couldn't even shift the grip that she had on it; her fingers were locked round what was left of it in a spasm that she couldn't break. Through the agony, she recognized this as a chaos-fuelled trap. A normal human being, one not sealed to the Library, would already have been warped to something on the verge of possible. Or they would have been accelerated all the way into something that couldn't exist in this alternate, and outright destroyed. Though a normal human being wouldn't have triggered the trap . . .

She felt her grip slipping.

For the moment her Library seal was saving her, but it couldn't last. The two competing forces would burn her out like an understrength fuse if she couldn't break the connection somehow.

'Irene!' Kai yelled in her ear, as if volume would make a difference. 'Can I get you into the Library? Will that help?'

She jerked her head in a shake. 'No,' she gasped. She couldn't enter the Library in this state. 'I'm polluted – can't –' She tried to think of any teachings covering this, but could only remember it was called the 'Babelfish Principle', which was no use. And it was hurting, it was *hurting* . . .

Then a solution came to her. But if the Library door wasn't the trap's power-source, she was so screwed. 'Break my link to the door . . . break the chain!'

'Right,' Kai said as he pulled the chain taut, trying to wrench out the flimsy-looking loop holding it to the wall by brute force. It shifted, but not nearly enough, and he slipped a knife from his sleeve, trying to prise open the links. One parted with a sudden snap, weakened by the forces flowing to the lock. Then the chain whipped free, and he yanked it through what remained of the original padlock.

With the chain gone, the power circuit broke – and the padlock clicked open to fall from Irene's hand to the floor. Irene knelt there, breathing in deep sobbing gasps, unable to quite look at her hand yet and see what damage had been done.

'Irene?' Kai said. 'What the hell was that? Are you all right? How did you get it loose?'

She looked up at him. Her vision was a little blurry. Maybe that was why he was swaying. 'It was a trap,' she tried to explain. 'Set to react to the Language and bind to the user, using the Library door as an energy source. That was why it stopped functioning when you broke the chain. It was very energy-efficient.' There was a buzzing in her ears. 'Kai? Can you hear something? Is it the silverfish?'

'Irene,' Kai said. He went down on one knee beside her. 'Are you all right?'

Irene looked at her hand. It was red all over the fingers and down the palm. 'Oh,' she said, in deep comprehension. 'Kai. I think I'm . . .' The buzzing was getting louder. 'I think I have to lie down for a bit.'

'Irene!'

The world slipped sideways. She felt him catching her as it all went dark.

When the lights came on again, they did so slowly and blearily, through a haze of smoke and a drift of odd smells. She was propped at a strange angle, her skirts carefully draped to hide her ankles. The back of a sofa dug into her shoulders and her head was tilted to one side, hat still pinned to her hair. Someone had pushed a cushion under her cheek. It was horsehair. It prickled.

From under her eyelashes, she could make out a room that had been forced into ruthless order by someone who believed in making large piles of things. Books. Documents. Clothing. Glassware. A dream-catcher in Lissajous lines of wire and ebony spun in the window, turning slowly in a drift of breeze and fog. The walls were also crammed with books, and someone had hung paintings and sketches in front of them, and piled small objects on top of the shelves. The place was crammed with . . . with stuff. She was surprised there was room for her on the sofa.

Her hand ached less now. Someone had slathered it in something wet and wrapped it in bandages, and it lay like a foreign object in her lap. She twitched a finger, stifling a scream, and was pleased to see that it functioned.

'Irene!' Kai said from behind her, far too loudly. 'Are you awake?'

'Yes,' she murmured, 'but please don't shout.' She pulled herself upright and managed to knock the horsehair cushion to the ground. 'Sorry. Where are we?'

'In my rooms.' Peregrine Vale stepped forward. 'Mr Strongrock brought you here an hour ago. Miss Winters, you have been the victim of an appalling assault. Do you feel well enough to speak?'

Irene put her undamaged hand to her head. 'I'm so sorry. I have a dreadful headache,' she said, not entirely untruthfully, 'and I don't know what's going on. The last thing I remember is touching this door handle which was booby-trapped . . .'

'It was some sort of electric shock,' Kai said helpfully. He went down on one knee next to her, looking up into her face. 'I didn't know what to do. I wanted to try to get somewhere safe while we worked out what to do next, Irene. The only person who I was sure we could trust was the Earl of Leeds here—'

'Please,' Vale interrupted, 'call me Vale. The title is unimportant. What *is* important now is locating and arresting the fiends who set this lethal trap.'

'Well, I . . .' Irene tried to think what to say next. 'I . . .'

Vale held up a commanding hand. 'Say no more. I am aware that Mr Strongrock here is your subordinate.'

'Oh,' Irene said.

'It was blatantly obvious,' Vale went on. 'Your signals to him in the restaurant, your ability to handle yourself in combat, and his unwillingness to speak while you were unconscious – these all made it quite clear that you were in command of the mission. Miss Winters, I realize that you have your own agenda, but I ask you – I appeal to you – to trust me. I believe that our aims are congruent. I think we can help each other.'

'Then Kai's told you . . .' Irene let the sentence trail off meaningfully. This wasn't what she'd wanted. The man was a near-total stranger to her. However impressive his skills were, and while he fitted the character type of nobleman, so he should understand the principles of noblesse oblige well enough, there was still risk. There was always a risk. She was supposed to be manipulator, not manipulated.

Her hand hurt. It was distracting her.

'He has told me nothing,' Vale said, and Kai nodded in agreement. 'He turned up in a cab on my doorstep with you unconscious in his arms, and he asked for shelter until you were awake again.'

Irene pushed straggling tendrils of hair back from her forehead. She didn't have to feign pain or confusion. 'I don't think that we're the only ones keeping secrets here, Mr Vale. The attack on you last night was too deliberately timed to be coincidence.' It was a guess on her part, but it hit a mark; his eyelids twitched very slightly. She looked up at him. 'I think there's more to all this – the murder, the theft of the book, Belphegor – than just a simple crime of greed. When we met last night, you referred to "thefts of occult material". This isn't the only book that's gone missing, is it?'

Vale threw himself down into another armchair. 'You're correct, Miss Winters. Oh, sit down, sit down, Strongrock. To be frank, I need people that I can trust. The Fair Folk have contacts at every level of society. My enemies have even more. You two are strangers in London, and though you have no apparent links to the Fae, you have nobody to vouch for you or speak in your favour. I may have reasons to believe that you are reliable . . .' He frowned. 'No. Leave that for the moment. I will explain my part in this affair, and then perhaps you will explain yours.'

Irene looked down at her hand. She wished she could rip off the bandages and see just how bad it was – surely not a permanent injury? It was that infernal urge that came with any injury, wanting to see how it 'looked' every minute of the day, as if she'd actually be able to see it getting better or worse. And if it did get worse, if she'd damaged herself for life? She couldn't stand the thought of being crippled . . . but investigating would have broken the flow of Vale's confidences, and she needed his information. 'Please,' she said softly, looking up from her hand and trying to stop herself fiddling with the bandages. 'Please, do go on.'

Vale interlaced his fingers. 'When I introduced myself as the Earl of Leeds, it was accurate enough, but it is not a title that I care to use often. The dark associations of the city of Leeds and its Earls go back to King Edward's reign in the fourteenth century. I broke from my family under – under somewhat unpleasant conditions, and have no wish for further connection with them. My father is dead, and I cannot be disinherited, but equally I have no interest in the family lands, properties and secrets.'

'Is that why you live in London?' Kai asked. Irene stole a glance at him. He was leaning forward with an expression of keen interest, but there were lines of clear disapproval in his face. His mouth was pursed in what was very nearly a censorious frown.

Vale nodded. 'My family have no interest in seeing me, nor I them. They hope that I will not marry, and that the title will pass to my brother Aquila. However, a week ago I received a letter from my – ' he hesitated a moment – 'my mother.' The words came with difficulty. 'She wished to advise me of a theft which had taken place, and to ask me, as detective if not as son . . .' He fell silent for a moment, staring at his fingers as if they were somehow stained. 'To ask me if I would investigate the matter for her.'

'And the subject of the theft?' Irene enquired delicately.

'A book,' Vale said. 'It was a family journal – that is, not a printed work, but a collection of handwritten notes and studies, herbal references and fairy tales.'

'Fairy tales,' Kai said slowly.

Vale nodded. 'You will see why I am intrigued by Lord Wyndham's murder and the disappearance of his book. Taken in conjunction with certain other thefts which have taken place, it suggests a culmination of events. None of the other thefts have involved murder. And as for the explosion last night beneath the Opera—'

'What?' Irene said, coming upright.

'Ah, you wouldn't have read the morning paper yet,' Vale said. 'The incident bears the hallmarks of secret society activity. A number of cellars were collapsed, but the foundations seem to be undamaged. The police have not requested my assistance – ' Irene could almost hear the unspoken *yet* – 'so I can only make do with the public reports.'

'But what makes you think this is connected with the thefts?' Kai asked.

'Two things,' Vale said. 'Firstly, the timing. It took place the very night after the airships arrived in convoy from Liechtenstein. I do not think that I need to remind you about that.' He looked up from his contemplation of his fingers. 'And secondly ...' He hesitated again before continuing. 'My family was involved with a certain society, and they believe it was connected with the loss of their book. The same group met beneath the Opera.'

'You're being very careful not to name that society, Mr Vale,' Irene commented.

'Indeed I am,' Vale said.

'Are they connected to the Fair Folk?' she probed.

Vale laughed, a surprised bark of a laugh. 'My dear Miss Winters! Show me a society that *isn't* connected to the Fair Folk. I suppose you could say no more than most of them.'

'And its connection to Liechtenstein?' she continued.

'Ah. Now here we come to the nub of the problem.' Vale frowned. 'I should probably have offered you tea. I do apologize. I always forget that sort of thing. But in any case, from what I've heard, the Liechtenstein Fair Folk are very definitely not affiliated with – well, let us call

121

them the Society. So the Ambassador's arrival, just before the Society was targeted in this way, is notable for its timing.'

'You think *he* caused the explosion?' Kai asked. 'Or the Society? Or were they the targets of the explosion?'

'Possible.' Vale waved a hand. 'Possible. Certainly it is worthy of further investigation. And now, Miss Winters, Mr Strongrock, since I have done my part and told you why I am involved in all of this, I ask you to do the same.' He leaned forward in his chair, his eyes hooded, and Irene wondered how much of what he'd said had been a carefully constructed bluff. *Trust me. I've told you everything. Really I have. Now it's your turn.* 'If we are to progress, then there must be some trust on both sides.'

Irene held up her good hand before Kai could speak. 'Before that, Mr Vale, I'd like the answer to one more question.'

'Within reason, I am at your disposal,' Vale said.

'Why do you feel that you can trust us?' she asked. Certainly she'd like to cooperate with him. It would make matters much easier; it might even make success in this mission possible, as opposed to out of the question. But it might also be a trap.

He might even be Alberich. How could she tell? The very thought made her swallow, and made her bandaged hand throb and twinge again.

'That is a fair question,' Vale allowed. 'I will be honest with you. I do have a few gifts from my family heritage. One of them is – well, not exactly prognostication, but an ability to tell when something is going to be important in my future. I have used it to advantage in a number of my cases, though I do not discuss it with the public. When I met Mr Strongrock the other day, I *knew*, in a way which I fear I cannot describe to you, that he was going to be closely involved with me in the near future. I had the same sensation upon meeting you, Miss Winters. On assessment of your characters, I choose to assume that you will be my allies rather than my enemies. I hope that you will not disappoint me.'

Irene glanced at Kai for a moment. He shrugged neutrally. But it wasn't as if it was his decision, in any case; this wasn't a democracy and he wasn't an equal partner. The decision, the risks and the potential for disaster were all hers.

Vale's story hung together and made sense, which was more than one could usually expect of events. More than that, Irene had the feeling that she could trust him. She *wanted* to trust him. (Should that in itself make her suspicious?) And there was nothing that said they had to tell him everything. And this was only a single mission, after all. They could leave this entire alternate behind them, and he'd have no way to follow them. There wouldn't be any repercussions afterwards. And, well – if he *had* been Alberich, then they'd already be dead. Just like Dominic Aubrey.

She made her decision, and leaned forward to offer her good hand. 'Mr Vale, I am grateful for what you have said. I believe we can cooperate.'

Vale smiled briefly, and clasped her hand. 'Thank you. Then perhaps you can tell me about yourselves?'

Irene glanced at Kai. 'You have already made it clear that you believe we're not English.'

'Indeed not,' Vale said crisply. 'Nor are you Canadians.'

'Ah,' Irene said, and quickly rephrased her next statement. 'We are representatives of – a Society. You will understand if we don't name it, I hope.'

Vale's smile was a little bitter. 'If you can vouch for its good intentions, that will be sufficient.'

'I can vouch for its non-interference,' Irene said scrupulously. 'We're after one thing: the book that was stolen from Lord Wyndham's house. We arrived here with the intention of purchasing it,' *well, that would have been one option*, 'only to find the man, ah, vampire, murdered, and the book stolen. Now we want to recover it. If together we can discover the truth behind the book thefts, the murder, and the explosion, well, that would surely be the best of all possible ends.' *And*, she thought privately, *the Library might be interested in those other books as well. Except for the one from Vale's family. That one they could afford to give back, and he'd appreciate it.*

'And your enemy?' Vale gestured at Irene's bandaged hand.

'We only have his name,' Irene said. It was probably safe enough to give that. 'Alberich.'

Vale shook his head. 'I know no player in London by that name. But for the moment, yes: I think we can work together.'

'Excuse me,' Kai said. Irene turned to look up at him. He was clearly holding himself in check with a great effort. 'May I speak to Miss Winters alone for a moment?'

'Certainly,' Vale said. He rose from his chair. 'I will have some tea fetched. That is – your Society does drink tea?'

'Always,' Irene said.

CHAPTER NINE

'This is a bad idea,' Kai said as soon as the door had closed behind Vale.

'I am listening,' Irene said as she began to pick at her bandage, 'and I am paying attention, and if I do scream, it's because my hand is in worse condition than I thought. Go on.'

'Why do you trust him?' Kai demanded.

'I don't.' Irene didn't look up from the tightly wrapped bandages. 'Not totally. But I think he's telling the truth about his family and about his gift. I'm not sure he trusts *us*, either.'

'And that's another thing,' Kai said. 'How can we possibly trust someone who'd betray their family?'

Irene let the bandages be and looked across at him. He had clenched his fists in his lap so tightly that she could see all the bones of the hand, and the blue veins up the inside of his wrist, clear beneath his pale, pale skin. 'We don't know the whole of that,' she said. 'We don't know what they may have done to drive him away. If—'

'But he left them!' Kai was nearly shouting. He controlled himself with an effort, rising to stand in front of Irene. 'He admitted as much. If he really disagreed with them, then he should have stayed with them and tried to change them from the inside. To just leave them, to walk out on them, to disobey his own parents – how can that possibly be justified?'

Irene looked down at her hand again, partly to think, partly so that Kai shouldn't see her own expression. Didn't he realize how much he was giving away about himself? Or did he just not care? That sort of openness was, in its way . . . intoxicating. 'I hardly ever see my own parents,' she said, and wondered at the quietness of her own voice.

'But you haven't defied them or deserted them.' Kai dropped to his knees, looking up into her face. 'You've followed their tradition. They were Librarians and so are you. I'm not saying that he should *love* his family, not if they really were malicious, but he shouldn't have left them. You can't trust a man who'd do that.'

'I'm not saying we should trust him,' Irene said. 'I'm saying that we need to work with him.' She felt very cold, and she wasn't sure if it was because of her hand, or the earlier shock, or her own words. 'To serve the Library, I would work with murderers, or thieves, or revolutionaries, or traitors, or anyone who will give me what I need. Do you understand me, Kai? This is important.' She reached out with her unwounded hand to touch the side of his face. 'I am sealed to the Library. I can make my own choices to some extent – but at the end of the day, bringing back the book the Library wants is my duty and my honour, and that is all there is to it.'

'Have you ever been forced to choose between the Library and your honour?' Kai demanded.

'Kai,' Irene said, 'the Library *is* my honour. And if you seal yourself to it, then it'll be yours too.' She could feel herself smiling grimly. 'But you've already told me that you don't have any living family, haven't you? So it's not a choice you'll ever have to make.'

Kai didn't even flinch at that, he simply glared at her. 'You're confusing the issue. There ought to be a way of finding our book that doesn't involve allying ourselves with an honourless, family-betraying creature like this. Irene, please. Walk out now and tell him no. We don't need this kind of help.'

Irene tried to think of a way to make him understand. Perhaps she was being too abstract in an attempt to make him comprehend this specific case – but, damn it all, he was going to have to face tough moral choices himself some day. If he really wanted to be a Librarian. If he survived.

'Leaving aside the question of his personal honour,' she said, 'we're not in a good situation. Dominic Aubrey's dead. There's an enemy in the city, quite possibly Alberich, and maybe others too. We're cut off from a direct retreat, and though I may be able to open a way back—'

'May?' Kai broke in. 'What do you mean, may?'

Irene raised her bandaged hand. 'I mean that I may be chaos-contaminated. I need to find out. It should get better in a few days, but at the moment I may not be able to open a way to the Library. It would keep me out in the same way that it'd keep out anything chaos-tainted. So we don't have a convenient escape route.'

'Oh,' Kai said. He bit his lip.

She was actually far less certain than she was willing to admit about how long it might take for her to access the Library again. It wasn't something that had happened to her before. She knew the theory, but this was her first case of actual contamination. Thinking about it made her feel ill. She wanted peace and quiet and a chance to actually look at her hand, plus a small library where she could run some tests.

Unfortunately, what she had here and now was a nervous and highly principled subordinate to reassure. It wasn't a leader's place to cast oneself trembling on a junior's shoulder and confess uncertainty. It wasn't even a leader's place to suggest that they might be in an indefensible position and should be grateful for any allies that they could get. It was a leader's job to project a calm mastery of the situation, while also encouraging subordinates to develop decision-making skills. Assuming that they made the right decisions.

A leader's job was a crock of shit.

This was becoming one of Irene's least favourite missions ever. And that included the one with the evil dwarves under Belgium (what was it about Belgium?), and the one requiring a cartload of carved amber plaques to be shipped across Russia. Or even the one with the cat burglar.

'Would it help if we could find out more about his family?' she offered. 'If we find out that they're not as bad as he's painting, we can re-evaluate how much we trust him.'

Kai shook his head decisively. 'That makes no difference. We should reject his offer of help.'

'That,' Irene said quietly, 'is not an option.'

They looked at each other for a moment. Kai's lips were drawn together, his eyes darkly furious as he stood there, glaring down at her. In that moment, there was something almost inhuman about him, something fiercer – more elemental, perhaps. For the first time, she thought he might actually disobey her.

In the end, he was the first to drop his eyes. 'As you command,' he said. *But I don't approve of it* was unspoken and unnecessary.

Irene had met other Librarians who tried to manage their subordinates using shallow gender tactics. Bradamant, for one. She hadn't liked it. She wasn't going to try to sugar-coat this for Kai by softening now or by fluttering her eyelashes at him. 'Did you bring our stuff along when you got me out of the British Library?' she asked.

'I did,' Kai answered stiffly. 'Both your document case and the jar with the . . . the skin.'

'I'm impressed,' Irene said. 'It must have been difficult to handle both them and me.'

Kai shrugged, but she had the feeling that he was pleased. 'I found a larger suitcase in the room, and I managed to get the jar and your document case in it. Do we tell Vale about *those*?'

'No,' Irene said quickly. 'That he doesn't need to know. Did anything else happen while you were getting me out of there? People following us, attacks, whatever?'

'Nothing worth mentioning,' Kai said smugly. 'I wrapped your face in your veil and propped you against my shoulder and got my arm round your waist, and sort of steered you, and I kept on telling you how you shouldn't have had so much gin last night. Nobody looked at us twice.'

'Very prompt thinking,' Irene said drily. 'Well done. Good job. And good selection of a place to hole up.'

'If I'd known then what I know now . . .' Kai muttered, but not quite as sullenly as before.

'You did the best you could on the information you had,' Irene said. She started peeling off the bandage again.

'Are you sure it's safe to do that?' Kai asked. 'You don't want it to get infected.'

'I just want to see how bad it is . . .' A chunk of bandage fell back to reveal a layer of ointment-soaked dressing. Bits of raw skin showed at the edges, red and oozing. A twinge of pain ran through her hand, and Irene suppressed a wince. 'All right,' she said through gritted teeth. 'Who saw to this?'

'I did,' Kai said. 'That trap took the skin off your hand as neatly as if – well, as if it was a glove being peeled off.' He went down on one knee and took her hand in his, winding the bandage round it again. 'Vale gave me some antiseptics and bandages, and I set some healing spells on it, but try not to use it too much.' His touch was careful and precise, his fingers dry and hot when they brushed her wrist. 'Normally I'd say that you can take the bandages off in a couple of days, but I don't know about chaos contamination.'

'I can check that easily enough,' Irene said confidently. 'This room has enough books in it for me to try asserting basic resonance.'

Kai glanced around at the heavily shelved walls. 'You don't need to be in a real library for that?'

Irene shrugged, then grimaced in pain as the movement twisted her hand in Kai's hold. 'Sorry,' she said, as he gave her a disapproving look. 'Not exactly. I'd need to be in a real library to open a passage, but a single room of books is enough for me to reaffirm my links. Of course, it has to be a lot of books . . .' She smiled for a moment, remembering the smell of old celluloid and dustless air. 'Actually, any significant store of knowledge or fiction can be made to function. I did it in a film storage section once, an archive of old television programmes. Not a single book in sight, all film reels and computer data, but the similarity in purpose and function was enough.'

'Go on.' Kai leaned forward eagerly. 'Do it.'

'All right.' Irene was nervous, now that it actually came down to it. She'd spoken glibly enough about contamination, and while she knew the theory on the subject – it'll wear off, just be sensible and avoid further exposure and stay away from the Library until you're clear – she'd never actually experienced it herself. 'You may want to stand away from the walls.'

'I'm nowhere near the walls,' Kai pointed out.

'Oh. Right.' Irene swallowed. 'Okay.'

She took a deep breath, wetted her dry lips, and invoked the Library by her name and by her rank as Librarian, speaking the words in the Language which described it. Unlike nouns or other parts of speech, words that described the Library or the Language themselves were among the few parts of the Language that never changed.

The bandages covering her hand burst into flame. The shelves on the walls shuddered and groaned, wrenching from side to side and creaking like living trees in a winter storm, and books tumbled to crash on the floor. Tossed-aside newspapers and piles of notes rustled and moved, crawling along the floor in fractions of an inch, writhing away from her like crushed moths. The fountain pen on the desk jolted and rolled across the open notebook where it had been balanced, trailing ink behind it in a dark wet line.

'What the devil!' Vale burst in, carrying an enamelled tea-tray. 'What do you think you're doing—'

'Excuse me,' Kai snapped, grabbing the blue and white milk jug off the tray. He caught Irene's wrist in his other hand, and shoved her blazing bandaged hand into the jug, flames and all.

There was a hiss and a gout of steam, and her hand went out.

'Thank you,' Irene said, trying to get her breathing stable again. Her hand ached as if it had been stung by wasps all over and then left to get sunburned. 'I'm so sorry about the milk, but I take my tea black anyway . . .' She was conscious that she was babbling, but she had to say something to try to explain things, and besides, her hand *hurt*.

'My books!' Vale exclaimed in horror, looking around the room. 'My notes! My – my – ' He stood there, tea-tray shaking in his hands, glaring down at her in fury. 'Miss Winters, *kindly explain yourself*!'

Irene considered a number of things. She considered fainting. She considered claiming that it was a magical attack. She considered just giving up on Vale and walking out of the door. She also, with a pang of regret, considered how she'd feel if it had been *her* books all over the floor. Finally, she said, 'I'm sorry, Mr Vale. I was trying something and it went wrong.'

Vale set down his tray on the nearest bit of uncluttered table with an audible thump and tinkle. 'Something. Went. Wrong,' he said coldly.

'Yes,' Irene said. She pulled her hand out of the jug. It dripped milk. 'I'm terribly sorry.'

Vale tapped his fingers against the surface of the tray. 'May I ask if something is going to go "wrong" again in the near future?'

'I think it very unlikely,' Irene said hopefully. 'I'm terribly sorry. Could I have some clean bandages, please?'

Vale stared at her.

'I've never seen her do it before,' Kai put in. 'It was an accident.'

'Simply an accident,' Irene agreed. 'I truly am extremely sorry.'

'I'm sure you are,' Vale spat out. 'Very well. Bandages.'

He slammed the door behind him as he left the room.

'What does that mean?' Kai demanded. 'The books! The papers!'

'It means I'm contaminated after all,' Irene said quickly and quietly. 'We can't get into the Library until I'm clear. And I can't use the Language reliably.'

Kai stared at her. 'You're being awfully calm about this.'

'Having your hand catch fire puts things into perspective . . .' Irene said. Any words would do, anything that kept her from panicking. She couldn't afford to panic. She was contaminated with chaos, *sick* with the stuff, and she could only hope that she was right, that it would go away in time. But now, she had to hold together and be in charge. '. . . I find that it distracts me.'

Kai just looked at her for a few seconds longer, then turned to glare at the door. 'I don't believe Vale swallowed that.'

'I'd say it's fairly conclusive proof that he needs our help badly,' Irene said.

Vale stalked back in with a basin of water and some bandages. 'Far be it from me to criticize,' he said, 'but setting the afflicted body part on fire is not a usual form of treatment for an injured hand. Though I hear that milk is high in calcium.'

Kai gave Vale one of his affronted looks. 'Are you challenging Miss Winters's actions, sir?'

'Oh, no, no,' Vale said. 'I will go so far as to spend the next half-hour or so picking up the books which are for some reason all over my floor, and let you tend to her hand. Unless the lady herself has something to contribute.'

'Actually,' Irene said, 'I do. But I can do it while Kai's seeing to my hand, if you don't mind.' Fortunately, staring at her hand gave her an excuse not to look at Vale. She knew that she must be blushing. Of all the stupid, ridiculous things to happen. This was not calculated to impress him at all.

Kai snorted, then sat down next to her and began to remove the soaked bandages. 'Please do go ahead,' he said. 'What do you have in mind?' *Besides your inability to contact the Library* came through the words quite clearly.

'I think we are all agreed that the Liechtenstein Embassy is involved in – *ow, careful* – this,' Irene said, clenching her free hand.

'Sorry,' Kai said, more as a pro forma than in genuine apology. 'Hold still.'

'I would agree,' Vale said. He picked a couple of the books off the floor, and dusted their covers tenderly. 'Especially given that Lord Silver placed a very high bid by proxy for that book when it was being auctioned. Quite interesting, don't you think?'

Irene nodded. That was extremely interesting. 'Then I suggest we attend the Embassy Ball tonight,' she said firmly.

'What?' Kai said in horror. 'Mingle with the . . . that is, are you serious? Do you realize the danger we'd be putting ourselves in?'

'Mr Strongrock overstates the situation,' Vale observed, 'but it isn't possible in any case. I agree that it is worth investigating, but unfortunately we won't be able to get in. The affair is strictly invitation only, and even if I can enter the place disguised, I am not sure that either of you would be able to do so.'

'I agree that the Fae are probably behind it,' Kai put in, 'but there has to be a better way of investigating them. As this one isn't going to work.'

'No.' Irene said. 'It will work. Because I have an invitation.'

'Excellent!' Vale exclaimed.

'And,' she added, 'I'll need a new dress.'

'And a new hand?' Kai asked through gritted teeth.

Irene managed to catch his eye. 'Trust me,' she said.

'Oh, I do,' Kai said. 'I just happen to think that this is one of the most reckless, hare-brained, soul-endangering plans I have heard of since—' He broke off. 'Never mind. I'm under your orders. But that invitation had better be for three people.'

'It'll do,' Irene said serenely, and tried to stay calm, and composed, and everything that she didn't feel.

CHAPTER TEN

Irene stood back and watched Kai at the buffet. There was something fascinating about the pure, focused dedication that he gave the caviar: it seemed to somehow elevate the little black grains into something holy, even divine. The curve of his wrist as he scooped it onto a triangle of toast was the last word in elegant efficiency. Of course, there were other reasons to watch. Thanks to Vale's tailoring recommendations, Irene was decorously gowned in a nice dark green, but Kai . . . well.

Kai managed to wear evening dress with a personal style that made Irene work very hard on repressing jealousy – and on stifling a half-formed wish that she'd accepted his offer last night. It was not *her* business that Kai had such an air of inherent power, or the elegance of a nobleman combined with a somehow touching air of raffishness . . .

That made her think. When she'd first seen him he'd been in leather jacket and jeans, with a young ruffian attitude to match. But once they'd established themselves here, he'd shifted his style and his language as effectively as any spy (and that wasn't a comforting thought), easing into a more cheerful politeness that had certainly mollified her. At the ball, he'd adjusted himself again without a moment's hesitation. She took a sip from her glass of wine, held in her left hand. Dry white, appropriate to the largely fish buffet.

She still trusted him. That enthusiasm – that vigorous, cheerful offering of himself that night – and even his unwillingness to accept what he thought was a dangerous course of action, both rang true to her. Whoever he was, *whatever* he was, he was sincere and he was on her side.

He couldn't be a fully-fledged Librarian. He wouldn't have been so willing to share a bed with her if he'd needed to hide the requisite Library brand. That was one thing which make-up wouldn't cover, as Irene knew from personal experience. And she didn't think he was a creature of chaos. His distrust of all things Fae seemed very real. A nature-spirit, perhaps? But from what she'd read, non-human spirits didn't actually *like* taking human form that much. And then again, there was one significant alternative. She stared at the back of Kai's head and thought about everything that she knew about dragons, and wished she knew more.

There were dragons, after all, who looked like – well – dragons. And then dragons could take a partly human form. She'd met one of those and sensed a pride so sublimely unaware of itself that it was somehow graceful. There had been the sense of a being apart, and definitely not human. She didn't get that from Kai, except he did have the dignity. And Kai looked human. Impossibly handsome, but entirely human. Yet she'd been told that dragons could take that shape as well, if they wanted. Irene felt a rising sense of outrage at the thought that Coppelia must have known – if this was true. So why hadn't she said – and why had Bradamant wanted him?

'My little mouse, I believe,' a voice said from behind her. 'How good of you to come.'

Irene had enough of a grip on herself not to spill her

wine. Just about. And she hadn't been so engrossed in her student that she'd forgotten to watch the crowd. She just hadn't seen him coming. She turned and dropped into a curtsey, flicking a brief glance up at his face before lowering her eyes. 'Lord Silver.' She had no idea whether or not he deserved the title, but it'd probably please him. He was as formally dressed as Kai, with some unspecified military order on his chest, and his pale hair was draped loosely over his shoulders. 'Thank you for your kind invitation.'

'You do pick the most interesting people to accompany you,' he said. His tone was amused rather than dangerous. 'But I appreciate it. I'd have invited Leeds myself if I'd thought of it.'

'I didn't realize you were on those sorts of terms with him, sir,' Irene said.

'I'm not.' His lips curved in a private smile. 'Very definitely not.'

Irene straightened out of her curtsey. 'The ball seems very successful,' she said neutrally.

Silver glanced across the room with a smile of casual ownership. He scooped up a plate from the buffet, casually loaded it with a handful of crab pâté puffs, and offered it to her. 'I should hope so,' he said. 'I've invited all the best people. Lords, ladies, authors, ambassadors, debauchers, grave-robbers, perverts, sorcerers, courtesans, deranged scientists, and doll-makers. And a few innocent socialites, of course, but generally I receive polite notes of refusal from their parents – or invitations to be horsewhipped.'

'Invitations?' Irene said.

'Notes offering to horsewhip me in front of my club if I even approach their daughters . . . '

Irene swallowed nervously. Was it a joke? Should she so much as touch the crab pâté puffs? 'Some people might call that a threat, sir.'

'A threat?' He looked at her, genuine puzzlement in his eyes. 'Why on earth would you think that?'

She couldn't quite bring herself to look him in the eyes while replying. If that was an example of Fae tastes, then she wasn't going to push it any further. 'They must be people of very limited scope, sir. Clearly.'

He patted her shoulder fondly. His gloves were white kid, soft against her skin, and she could feel the heat of his flesh through them. It was more of a casual flash of power, as a shark might show its fin, than a deliberate attempt to englamour and seduce her, but she could feel it all the same.

Kai was still over by the caviar, but watching her with narrowed eyes, as sharp as a snake. She shook her head minutely, warning him to *keep away*. Vale looked bored, and was talking on the other side of the room to a hunched man with a brass-rimmed monocle screwed into his right eye.

The room itself was large enough to hold about a hundred and fifty people comfortably, with buffet tables around the edges and waiters circulating silently. Improbable swords and lances hung along the walls in glittering decoration, with Liechtenstein banners positioned above. A string quartet in the corner picked through something light and unobtrusive. The whole room had an unwholesome feel to it, a hothouse sort of closeness and oppression, even though the temperature was perfectly normal. Irene wondered whether everyone present was hiding secrets, something that affected their every word and action.

Even me, she thought with more than a touch of irony.

Silver squeezed her shoulder again. 'I'll be back,' he said smoothly. 'Don't go away.'

Between one blink and the next, he was gone.

Irene put her glass down before she was tempted to

drink even more wine. There had to be some way to lure out Belphegor, or whoever had killed the vampire and taken the book. And if this ball was as packed with key society suspects as she expected, here would be the perfect place to gather information.

Several conversations and about fifteen minutes later, she'd reached the Yoruban Ambassador – a kindly-looking man a full head taller than her. He was sporting some sort of ceremonial outfit with gold bracelets that weighed more than her entire gown. She wondered how Silver had got him to visit. 'So, you see,' she lied with the utmost sincerity, 'I'm writing an article on important figures in the literary world. I was going to interview Lord Wyndham, but his tragic death . . .' She let her voice trail away artistically.

'I never knew that Lord Wyndham was a literary figure?' the Ambassador queried.

'Well, not as such. But he does seem to have been very *au fait* with up-and-coming novelists. I'd heard that he acted as patron to some.'

'Ah,' the Ambassador said comprehendingly. 'I only knew about his collection.'

Since Irene had entirely invented the bit about his patronage of new writers, she wasn't surprised. 'It was a fine one,' she agreed. 'And he was always so good about making books available to other experts in the field. Not like some bibliophiles who hoard everything and then just gloat about it privately.'

The Ambassador looked slightly furtive, then loomed forward. 'One hesitates to speak ill of the dead,' he said in lowered tones, 'but I think that is giving the gentleman a little too much credit. He was inclined to boast. His nature, you know. Vampires. They just can't resist it. I've known some very pleasant ones, of course,' he added hastily.

'Oh, of course,' Irene agreed quickly and meaninglessly.

'But I do think that you're right, Your Excellency. They are so very proud of their advantages.'

'Exactly,' the Ambassador said approvingly. 'I am glad that our host hasn't brought any here tonight. They always demand to be catered for in such an obtrusive manner – the blood, the open veins, all that manner of thing. It does get in the way of a simple conversation.'

Irene nodded, suppressing annoyance that Silver hadn't invited any. She'd have liked the chance to question a few. In fact, why hadn't Silver invited them, if he enjoyed their company? Or even if he was feuding with them? From what Silver had said about the guest list, inviting half a dozen antagonistic vampires seemed like just the sort of thing that he'd do. 'It does make matters simpler for everyone else,' she agreed.

'And we're spared the anti-blood-sports protestors.' The Ambassador collected a fresh glass of wine from a passing waiter. 'But if you're a reporter, you've probably interviewed a few of them already!' He rumbled a deep laugh.

'I like to think there's something to be said on both sides,' Irene temporized. 'But about Lord Wyndham's boasts . . . oh, I beg your pardon.' Vale was walking towards them, a slight urgency to his movement. 'If you will excuse me a moment, Your Excellency . . .'

'Of course,' the Ambassador said. 'About that interview later—'

'I will contact your Embassy staff, sir,' Irene said, and retreated with another polite curtsey.

Vale shepherded her back over to the buffet table (was she ever going to get away from it?) and made an obvious show of getting her some canapés. 'Miss Winters, we need to be careful,' he muttered. 'One of my contacts tells me that there's going to be a strike here, at the Liechtenstein Embassy, this evening.'

Irene suppressed a groan. How many factions were involved in this thing? How was she supposed to conduct a rational investigation with this sort of interference? 'Who's doing the striking?' she demanded in a murmur. 'And can we use it as a diversion to search the Embassy?'

Vale regarded her from under lowered eyebrows. 'Miss Winters, that's a very felonious suggestion.'

'But it's a very practical one,' she said, reminding herself that he *was* a private detective. Though he didn't seem to be particularly disapproving. Perhaps it was the fact that she'd suggested it, rather than him, which had forced him to condemn it.

'Hmph.' He shovelled more salmon onto her plate. At this rate she'd have indigestion. 'In answer to your first question, the protestors are the Iron Brotherhood. They are notoriously anti-Fae, so it wouldn't be out of character for them.'

'Do you think it would be worth notifying the Embassy staff?' she asked.

Vale shook his head. 'They'll already be expecting something like this. I checked earlier, and they have all the usual precautions – anti-zeppelin guns, glamours, whatever. But do be careful, Miss Winters. Now if you'll excuse me, I need to speak to that lady who just came in.'

The lady in question was currently invisible behind a squadron of male admirers, so Irene watched Vale edge across the ballroom, and tried to hide her overstuffed plate behind a bowl of soup.

'There's something going on,' Kai said from behind her shoulder.

Irene very nearly spilled the soup. 'Really,' she said through gritted teeth.

'Absolutely,' Kai said. 'Let me get you some of those blinis.' He picked up a new plate and started depositing more food on it. 'You need to eat more: it'll help the healing process.'

'I also need to be able to walk without falling over,' Irene said, watching with growing unease as he ladled on something involving crabmeat. 'Or dance.'

Kai edged a little closer. 'Have you found out anything yet?' he muttered.

Irene considered the facts she'd picked up so far. 'I think Silver's waiting for something. Or someone. He seemed on edge. But he's being distracted by the glitterati.' She could see him at the other side of the ballroom, talking to a voluptuous pair of women in black who hung on each other's shoulders, clearly already half-drunk. 'I've been talking to a couple of other people. Apparently it's odd that Silver hasn't invited any other vampires tonight. I'm wondering if Wyndham's attack might have been anti-vampire rather than anti-Fae, and I'd like to ask Vale a few more questions about his family and if they have any links to vampires. Oh, and Vale thinks there's going to be an attack on the Liechtenstein Embassy by an anti-Fae society called the Iron Brotherhood, and – oh, Kai, *please* not the sour cream.'

'You need it for a proper contrast with the blinis,' Kai said firmly.

'Have you found out anything?' Irene asked.

'Nothing definite,' Kai said slowly. 'And – well, I haven't actually been *trying* to talk to any of the other Fae here. I don't think they'd tell us anything useful.'

'Uh-huh,' Irene agreed neutrally. 'But have you found out anything from anyone else?'

'That lady in the corner.' Kai flicked a glance to their left. The woman in question was elderly, rouged, half buried under a vast white wig, and dressed in a construction of black and white striped satin that was viciously corseted and heavily underwired. 'She's very well informed. And she actually *is* part of the literary world, not just a poseur like Wyndham was.'

'What's her name?' Irene asked.

'Miss Olga Retrograde,' Kai said. 'The elder Miss Olga Retrograde. She said so several times.'

Irene wondered what the younger Miss Retrograde looked like, as she moved towards her. 'You'd better introduce us. What is she?'

'A retired lady of pleasure,' Kai said, rather flatly.

'Well, at least she won't assume I'm looking for a job,' Irene said cheerfully. 'Oh, Kai, don't look at me like that – '

The crowd drifted apart, and Irene could finally see who had just entered the room.

It was Bradamant.

She was as perfect as a black and white photograph, her slender neck rising out of the deep grey silk folds of her bodice like a swan, the train of her dress undulating in smooth liquid elegance.

Kai frowned as Irene broke off mid-sentence, then followed her gaze. 'What?' he hissed. 'Her? Here? How?'

'Four very good questions,' Irene said through gritted teeth. 'My god, she's wearing a Worth gown. That has to be a Worth gown.'

Kai turned to stare at Irene. 'What's the gown got to do with it?' he asked. 'Is it particularly effective in concealing weapons or something?'

'No,' Irene spat. 'It's just one of the best dresses from one of the best dressmakers of the period, or whatever the equivalent is in this alternate. Dear heavens, not only does she come in here to try to steal my mission from under me, she has the *nerve* to do it while wearing something which screams *here-I-am-everyone-look-at-me*. I mean, do I go round collecting outfits from alternates just so I can be the best-dressed person at a party?'

'Irene,' Kai said, 'you're holding my arm a bit tightly.'

Irene had to stop herself grinding her teeth. 'A Librarian is supposed to be about subtlety,' she muttered. 'Getting the job done. Not being noticed—oh, sorry.' She removed her hand from Kai's forearm and watched Kai affrontedly smooth out the wrinkles on his jacket sleeve. 'Um.' She could feel herself flushing. 'I apologize.' What she wanted to do was scream *How dare she!* until the chandeliers tinkled. But she couldn't.

'Perhaps she has important information and wanted to talk to you,' Kai said.

'But how would she know we were here? Or – wait.' Irene frowned. 'Dominic Aubrey could have told her – did she enter this alternate before he died?'

'Or did she have something to do with it?' Kai said slowly, completing Irene's own thought.

Irene was silent for a long moment, turning possibilities over in her head. 'Unthinkable,' she finally said. 'I won't believe that of her.'

At that moment the crowd shifted again, and Bradamant turned her head. She looked across the ballroom, and for a moment their eyes met. And in that moment, Irene saw something in Bradamant's face which she hadn't expected to see. Shock.

'She didn't expect us to be here,' she murmured.

Bradamant recovered almost instantaneously, and turned away with a contemptuous little twitch of her shoulder to bestow her attention on the man next to her, a skinny white-haired man in his eighties with his chest so encrusted with military medals and orders that it was a wonder he didn't fall over.

'Why don't you introduce me to Miss Olga Retrograde,' Irene said to Kai, composing her face into what should with any luck be a pleasant smile. She'd work out what was going on. And this time she wasn't going to be Bradamant's stalking horse, decoy or tool.

Not this time. Not again.

'Very well,' Kai said, glancing at Bradamant over Irene's shoulder. 'But what *is* she doing here? I know she said she wanted the mission . . .' His face lightened as a thought obviously occurred to him. 'If she's your senior, then maybe she has clearance now for you to cooperate on the mission. That would make things simpler, with the chaos contamination.'

'Such a thing is possible,' Irene said slowly, to give herself time to think and to find an answer why this could not, *would* not be the case. She wasn't sure that she would be able to physically obey if it were. Her loathing of the other woman was too bone-deep for that. 'But if it were the case,' how careful, how conditional, 'then she would have some sort of token from the Library, and she'd show it to me. She hasn't even tried to find me yet. So I'm dubious.'

'I trust you,' Kai said. He touched her hand briefly, reassuringly. 'I do trust you, Irene. I wish that you could tell me why you don't trust her.'

She could have said, *It's private*, but something in her felt that he deserved better than that from her. Instead she said, 'It's personal, and if you really do want to know, I'll tell you later. It doesn't make her any the worse as a Librarian. Just as a person, to me. But later. All right?'

Kai nodded, and then they were there. 'Miss Retrograde?' he said. 'May I introduce my friend, Miss Winters?'

Irene gave a small curtsey. 'Miss Retrograde. It's a pleasure to meet you.'

'And you, my dear,' the elderly woman said. Close up, her face was all rouge, white paint and beauty patches. She deserved an award for thoroughness in concealing wrinkles, if not for artistry in doing so. Her dress might be heavily corseted and old-fashioned, but the fabric was high-quality, and the diamonds on her fingers looked genuine. 'I understand that you're not from these parts.'

Kai must have given her the Canadian cover story. 'Oh no,' Irene agreed. 'But I'm working as a freelance reporter at the moment—'

'Oh no you're not,' Miss Retrograde cut in.

Irene shut her mouth before it could gape open too wide. 'I beg your pardon?' she hastily said.

'My dear,' Miss Retrograde said, 'I make it my business to know all the members of the fourth estate in London. I wouldn't have missed an intelligent-looking girl like yourself.'

Irene would have given Kai a venomous look, along the lines of *what have you got me into and why didn't you tell me more about this*, but it would have been too obvious a betrayal. 'I'm very new on the scene,' she said quickly.

'I've been watching Silver,' Miss Retrograde said. She leaned forward with a creak of whalebone. Her beady eyes focused in their heavily shadowed sockets. 'He spoke to you. I'd like to know why.'

Irene suspected that playing the innocent wasn't going to work here. She could feel Kai's arm tense under her hand, waiting (hopefully) for her to tell him which way to jump. 'I'm afraid that would depend on why you want to know,' she finally said, letting the humour drain out of her face.

'I could make it worth your while,' Miss Retrograde said, rubbing the ball of her thumb against one of her diamond rings suggestively.

Irene tilted an eyebrow. There was some sort of noise in the corridor outside, thumping and crashes, but she didn't take her eyes off the older woman. If the Iron Brotherhood, or whoever, was attacking, then hopefully someone else would deal with it.

'Oh, very well,' the woman said pettishly. 'That was crass, I admit it. Let's get down to business. Take a seat, young woman. Have your bodyguard – I'm not stupid, young man – have your bodyguard fetch us both some more wine. Then we can discuss matters—'

And at that moment the alligators burst into the room.

CHAPTER ELEVEN

Irene had only ever seen alligators at the zoo before. She remembered them as being lazy, log-like objects, draped over cement 'rock formations' or dozing in muddy pools.

The creatures invading the room moved with disturbing speed. If they were logs, then they were logs on a river in full flood. Some of them were fifteen feet or so long. Their mouths opened and closed as they scuttled forwards. One of them clamped its jaws on the leg of a waiter and rolled sideways; the man screamed and went down. His leg came off in the alligator's jaws, wrenched off like a chicken wing, spraying blood across the polished floor. Through the melee, Irene spotted metal contraptions bolted onto their skulls, and metal screwed onto their claws, before the press of the crowd became too great.

Guests and waiters were screaming and running for the other doors, as alligators continued to spill through the main entrance. A few of the guests were firing previously concealed weapons, a mixture of pistols and ray-guns, but most were simply trying to escape. The smell of blood was sharp and coppery on the air, rising above the blend of perfume and food.

'Have no fear!' Silver shouted, leaping onto a convenient

table, bestriding a centrepiece of oysters. 'The powers of my kind shall scourge these creatures back to the slime from which they crawled –'

Amazing grammar in a crisis, Irene couldn't help noticing.

– 'Behold!' Silver raised his hand. Fire flared round his fingers dramatically, then leapt to strike the alligators in burning orange whips.

It fizzled. There was no other word for it. The flames drooped and went out as if they'd been doused with cold water, leaving the alligators to rumble forward undeterred.

'Damnation!' Silver swore. 'They have been armoured in cold iron! Johnson! My elephant gun!'

Much as Irene would have enjoyed watching whatever happened next, fleeing the room before she was trampled by the crowd or eaten by alligators seemed a better idea. 'Quick!' she snapped at Kai. 'Help Miss Retrograde—'

'The elder Miss Retrograde, if you please, young lady,' the older woman said, rising to her feet. 'I knew I should have brought my pistol with me.' They were jostled and bumped, but there was still just enough space to move freely as long as they kept next to the walls.

'Does this happen often at these balls?' Kai asked. He seemed half fascinated by the chaos, half appalled by it. There were enough screaming, fleeing waiters and party-goers that the alligators weren't going to reach them for at least a few minutes. Hopefully Bradamant could take care of herself.

The elder Miss Retrograde clicked her tongue. 'People should know what to expect at a party thrown by Lord Silver,' she said. 'Now – what *is* going on over there?'

The headlong escape was curdling in its tracks, as people came running back into the room. Over the hubbub, Irene could hear yelling about the outer doors being locked.

'This smells planned,' Kai remarked.

'It is,' Irene said. 'The Iron Brotherhood?'

'It has their stink,' the elder Miss Retrograde sniffed. 'Did you notice the cold iron on the alligators' claws? The easiest way to deflect Fae sorcery. I'm afraid we can't expect anything from Lord Silver tonight.'

'Won't his subordinates be trying to rescue him?' Kai asked. He cast a thoughtful glance at the weapons hanging on the wall.

The elder Miss Retrograde twitched a ruffled shoulder. 'A couple of them may, but I can almost guarantee that the rest will be thinking about promotion, so will take care not to rescue anyone until it's too late. Are either of you two young people skilled with alligators? Do they teach alligator training in Canada?'

'Let me try something,' Irene said, stepping forward.

An alligator turned its head and upper body. One rolling eye focused on her.

Irene swallowed. This was not a time to give in to the roiling fear which churned in her stomach. This was not a time to consider that all she knew about alligators came from reading Rudyard Kipling. (Or had those been crocodiles?) This was the time to remember she was a Librarian, and that she had a responsibility to protect Kai.

She suppressed the urge to cross her fingers, raised her hand and pointed it at the nearest alligator, and commanded it in the Language to lock its legs and stay still.

It nearly worked.

The words were clear in her mouth, but something in the air, or still lingering in her body, twisted them and wrenched them out of focus. She felt the marks on her hand reopen under the bandages, and saw traces of scarlet start to seep up through her glove.

The alligator's legs locked: that much worked. It squinted at her with a reptilian look of cold hatred as it skidded on the polished floor, and came sliding right at her, gliding like a doom-laden missile with huge (and getting huger by the minute) jaws.

There was something hypnotic about those jaws. She should have been fleeing, but the sight held her until she thought that she could count every one of the approaching teeth.

'Hell,' Kai said, and caught her by the waist, tossing her up onto the nearby table. Irene managed to catch herself with her good hand, pulling her skirts away from a steaming tureen of soup as the alligator went sliding by under the table. The white tablecloth rippled as the alligator went under one side and came out on the other, continuing its skid along the highly polished floor until it crashed nose-first into the wall. It lay there, opening and closing its mouth and rolling from side to side, tail thrashing, apparently unable to flex its legs.

'I'm afraid it's not working properly,' Irene informed Kai.

'Well, that much is obvious!' Kai offered the elder Miss Retrograde his arm. 'Madam, if you'd kindly get up on the table—'

'And what are you going to do, young man?' the woman demanded.

Irene could tell what Kai *wanted* to do. It was evident in the set of his shoulders, the tension of his face. *One of the most important aspects of command is not giving orders that won't be obeyed*, she reminded herself. 'Get a sword down from the wall, Kai,' she said. 'Find Vale, help him if he needs it. Do what you can to sort this out. I'll take care of myself.'

Kai raised his head, and there was a dangerous gladness in his eyes. 'Do you really mean that?' he asked.

'I am perfectly capable of staying out of the way of a few

alligators,' Irene said coolly. Especially if she stayed up on the table, but it would spoil the statement to add that. 'I don't think they can climb.'

'I hope not.' The elder Miss Retrograde rapped Kai on the shoulder. 'I'll take that assistance, young man. You two can tell me why you're pretending to be Canadian later.'

Kai put one hand under the elder Miss Retrograde's elbow, bent to put the other under her shoe, and boosted her up on the table with barely a sign of effort. 'Later,' he promised, and ran. He was heading for a low-hanging banner, which dangled temptingly near a pair of ornate sabres hanging eight feet up.

Elsewhere around the room, Irene could see other men and women climbing on the tables, some of which had given way in the process. It was sheer luck that there had only been a few people left in their corner of the room, and so the tables were comparatively unoccupied. This was apparently not one of those alternate worlds where the British Empire mandated a tradition of women and children first. It was a case of survival of the fittest, and alligators take the hindmost.

From her vantage point she looked around, finally sighting Bradamant. She was athletically swinging herself onto a free table and tossing a platter of mussels into the jaws of the pursuing alligator in one smooth motion. The alligator paused, grunting and shaking its head, as Bradamant smoothed her skirts and looked around.

Irene's and Bradamant's eyes met. For a moment they looked at each other across the room, then Bradamant turned away, with a jerk of her head and a little smile. She scanned the crowd, clearly looking for someone else. Irene swallowed bile. Was she still so preoccupied by Bradamant that she had to look for where she was first, and be sure that she was safe? Interest in a fellow Librarian's welfare only went so far.

And where was Vale? With a pang of guilt she scanned the crowd for him too, finally managing to catch sight of him. He'd been backed into a corner by two alligators, and was defending himself with a silver tray as best he could. Of course, he would have had to leave his swordstick at the door. It didn't look good.

'Kai!' Irene turned to find him. He'd managed to climb up the banner, almost high enough to reach the sabres. 'Help Vale! Over there!'

Judging by his frown, Kai could see Vale struggling even better than she could. He clamped the banner between his legs, reached up with both hands, and grabbed the hilts of both sabres: then he simply let go. The sabres came free from their brackets with a shriek of metal, and Kai fell the eight feet to the ground, twisting smoothly in mid-air to land on both feet.

'Vale!' he shouted, loud enough to be heard over the screaming mob. 'Here!' People backed away from him at his shout, and he tossed one of the blades in a high arc through the air; it spun above the crowd in a shimmer of steel. Vale snatched it out of the air, the throw perfectly weighted to slap the hilt into his hand. Then he sheared the metal contraption off a lunging alligator's skull with one vicious slice.

Irene let out a breath, unaware that she'd stopped breathing. Apparently both Kai and Vale possessed previously unappreciated keen fighting reflexes. Taking down a giant robot centipede seemed comparatively simple in retrospect.

Kai shouted something in a Chinese dialect that Irene didn't recognize, perhaps a battle cry or a curse, and leapt into the fight. He impaled one alligator, closing its jaws with a single sabre thrust just before the creature could bite into a waiter.

Irene sidled further along the table, and tried to think of a plan. The alligators weren't showing any interest in the piles of spilled food that littered the floor. And while she wasn't an expert on reptilian psychology, animals would normally go for an abundance of convenient meals rather than armed dinner guests. Whether in the grip of a feeding frenzy or not. So maybe the buzzing metal things bolted onto their heads were controlling their behaviour – a theory that seemed borne out from observation of Vale's former aggressor.

The alligator which had been de-metal-objected by Vale had retreated, and was currently wandering around in a dazed way. That was promising. If they could de-weaponize all the alligators, then they'd have ... well, they'd have a mob of normal alligators. Which wasn't much, but it would be something. Especially as neither Fae magic nor the Language use was working. Bradamant, however ...

Irene sprinted along her table, skirts in hand. Bradamant was a table and an alligator-infested stretch of floor away. The table wasn't a problem. The chunk of floor was – and there were people dying out there.

She just didn't have time to think about that. It was clear to her left. Clear to her right.

'Stay up here!' an elderly gentleman sputtered behind her. 'Dash it, girl, don't go committing suicide! Wait just a minute and the police will be here – '

No. She couldn't wait. She tried to rationalize why, as really all the screaming, shooting and sounds of ripping flesh were irrelevant to her mission to get the book – to her duty as a Librarian. She could just stay put. But as she tried to shut out all the unimportant noises, she found herself already acting. She swung away from the man and dropped onto the floor, running for the other table.

A man was lying under it, tumbled across a fold of fallen white cloth. He was bleeding freely, which meant that he was still alive.

Irene pulled herself up onto the table, vaguely conscious that her skirt was fouled with blood and salmon. 'Bradamant!' she called, pitching her voice to carry above the noise.

'Yes?' Bradamant came stalking down the table, brushing aside other men and women by sheer force of personality. Her hair was still perfect, and her gown was only stained at the very edges. 'I hope you have something useful to say.'

Irene forced down her hostility. 'I do. I have an idea, but I'm having problems with the Language. I need your help.'

For a moment she wondered if Bradamant was going to put conditions on that help, but the other woman barely hesitated. 'What do you have in mind?'

Irene pointed up at the chandelier – the elegant, huge, electric-lit chandelier. 'The things on the alligators' heads are specific and discrete. Use the Language to call electricity down into them. Even if it doesn't kill them, it'll wreck their control systems.'

Bradamant turned her head to follow Irene's gesture. 'It might also kill some of the guests if they're in contact,' she said neutrally.

Irene hadn't thought of that. It only took a moment to imagine Vale or Kai with their blades in an alligator. 'So be precise in your language!' she snapped. 'Or do you want me to find the vocabulary for you?'

Bradamant sniffed. 'I don't think that I will need your help for *that* endeavour.' Her tone suggested Irene's total incompetence would render any assistance worthless.

Irene should have let her get on with it, but a sudden thought struck her. 'When did you come through from the Library?'

'We have no time for this discussion,' Bradamant declared. 'Stand back and let me work.'

Irene stepped back and scanned the crowd as Bradamant prepared. Silver was easiest to spot. He'd found an ornate pike and was busy impaling an alligator with it, gullet to tail. Vale and Kai were back to back, surrounded by half a dozen alligators. No one else was being targeted so heavily. She couldn't recall anything from Dominic Aubrey's notes about the Iron Brotherhood. They were fairly obviously anti-Fae, what with shoeing their alligators with cold iron and staging the attack here and now. But she wouldn't have thought that made them anti-Vale. Quite the opposite, really: Vale clearly had no particular liking for the Fae, and his attendance here was adversarial rather than friendly towards Silver. Were the alligators being somehow specifically directed? Or were they simply attacking those people who offered the most resistance?

Irene turned back to Bradamant as the other Librarian called out a crisp string of orders in the Language. Fortunately the people around her were too preoccupied by the alligators to pay much attention.

The chandelier trembled where it hung, then shattered, prisms chiming and blowing apart in puffs of crystal dust. Electricity forked down in visible arcs of lightning, targeting the alligators' electronic attachments. The reptiles spasmed and thrashed, tails sweeping in wide curves as their jaws opened and closed on empty air.

Irene watched in relief as Vale and Kai dodged the alligators that had been surrounding them. 'Nicely done,' she said to Bradamant.

Bradamant sniffed, somehow managing to suggest that

the words *Of course* were simply beneath her. 'I can't see why you didn't do it yourself,' she said.

'Chaos contamination,' Irene replied reluctantly. The alligators were slowing their thrashing now, their wild spasms becoming mere squirming wriggles. 'The door to the Library was sabotaged on this side. We think it must have been Alberich—'

'Wait.' Bradamant grabbed her shoulder. Some of the high colour drained from her face. 'Alberich is *here*?'

'Yes,' Irene said bluntly. 'Didn't you get notified?'

The expression on Bradamant's face spoke for itself. Belatedly, Irene put two and two together. 'You're here without authorization, aren't you? You came here even though this is a quarantined world and it was my mission—'

'And I just saved you and your student from getting eaten by alligators,' Bradamant snapped. 'You owe me. I want the precise details about Alberich being here. Now.'

'So why did you come here anyhow?' Irene asked, ignoring the demand, as she checked there was still enough chaos to cover their conversation. She and Bradamant weren't the only people to be staying up on the tables. A lot of other people were waiting to be absolutely sure that the alligators were dead before they came down to ground level again. 'To this party, that is. Not just to this alternate.'

Bradamant was silent for a moment. There might even have been a trace of shame in her eyes, but Irene wasn't sure if it was shame at having stolen another Librarian's mission, or just embarrassment at being caught. Finally she said, 'I needed to investigate the Iron Brotherhood.'

'Congratulations,' Irene said, and jerked her head in the direction of the alligators. 'You found them. Were they supposed to meet you here, or was it just a happy coincidence?'

'You're very insolent tonight,' Bradamant said softly, dangerously.

'Oh, don't you think that I have reason?' Irene had enough control to keep her voice down, but not enough to keep back her words. 'If you have anything, *anything* to do with this piece of bloody lunacy—'

'I'd have thought that Alberich was more important than collateral civilian casualties,' Bradamant said. Her eyes glittered. 'Shouldn't you be briefing me on that rather than wasting time on those people?'

'Did you have anything to do with this?' Irene repeated.

'No,' Bradamant said. 'If that helps you answer my question.'

Irene glanced at the dying alligators again. She didn't trust Bradamant, but she couldn't refuse to warn her. 'Yesterday I was told to beware of Alberich, a direct communication from the Library. This morning Kai and I went to talk with Dominic Aubrey, at our Library entrance point. We didn't find him there, but we found his skin rolled up in a jar of vinegar, and a chaos trap on the door to the Library itself.'

Bradamant blinked slowly. 'Dominic Aubrey is dead? Actually dead?'

'Yes,' Irene said. 'Well, probably. Given the alternatives. When did you get here? Did you see him when you came through? If we can pin down when Alberich killed him and trapped the door—'

'Irene!' Kai and Vale had converged on them unexpectedly. Vale had several cuts, but Kai was elegantly unruffled. He offered his hands to Irene. 'If you'd like a hand down – and Bradamant, of course . . .'

'Of course,' Bradamant said in suddenly sweetened tones. She stepped past Irene, hips swinging, and placed her hands in Kai's, letting him assist her down.

Kai threw a martyred glance over Bradamant's shoulder at Irene. It said, more clearly than words, *I couldn't possibly leave her to fall into the remains of the herring, could I?*

Irene sighed. She set her chin, sat down on the edge of the table and swung off it to stand on the floor. Her gown was already ruined, anyhow. 'I'm glad to see that both you gentlemen are safe and well,' she said flatly. She could feel Vale's measuring stare on her, Kai and Bradamant, and tried to ignore it. There was no reason *whatever* for her to have any feelings on the subject at all.

The doors slammed open. A squad of men in vaguely military uniforms came barrelling through, rifles shouldered. They were led by a dark-skinned man with turban and moustache, his uniform differentiated by a wide green sash. They pointed their guns at the alligators, and began to riddle them with bullets, ignoring the fact that the poor reptiles were now barely moving.

'Ah,' Silver said from behind Irene's shoulder, 'the police at last. Inspector Singh is as vigorous as ever.' He took Irene's hand between his. 'My dearest girl, you are wounded.'

Irene was conscious of both Kai and Vale staring at Silver in a distinctly freezing way. She wished that she could just have had even five minutes to get some answers out of them and Bradamant before Silver had turned up. 'A scratch,' she said quickly, gingerly trying to slide her hand out of his grasp. 'Sir, no doubt Inspector Singh will want to speak to you . . .'

'And you must introduce me to your beautiful friend,' Silver said, his eyes on Bradamant, his grip on Irene's hand painfully firm.

Irene glanced at Bradamant. Bradamant gave a small nod of agreement, her lips curling in a sweet smile.

'Lord Silver,' Irene said formally, 'this is my friend

Bradamant; I had no idea that she would be at this party, but of course I am delighted to see her.' *And I hope she falls over and plants her face in a dish of salmon roe.* 'Bradamant, this is Lord Silver, one of the Liechtenstein Fae, who is visiting England—'

' – and who would have come much sooner,' Silver cut in smoothly, dropping Irene's hand and stepping forward to take Bradamant's elegant fingers in his, 'had I known that such beauty was to be found. How could I have missed a gem like you? Sweet lady, do me the favour to say that I may have the honour of your closer acquaintance?'

Irene could recognize an opportunity when it sat up and begged in front of her. She began to quietly edge away, as Silver raised Bradamant's hand to his lips.

Silver's nostrils flared. He sniffed at Bradamant's hand, eyes brightening to an utterly inhuman shade of yellow. 'I know that smell!' he spat. 'Belphegor! I have you at last!'

CHAPTER TWELVE

'What?' Bradamant said, but her attitude was wrong. It was one of denial, not blank incomprehension.

'What?' Vale said, in a very different tone of voice, taking a step forward.

'Impossible!' Irene said, without too much hope of being believed.

'I'd be accusing you too, little mouse,' Silver said, 'but you were there when we opened the safe, and I know you were as surprised as I was. You should be glad that I've identified one of our enemies. This woman is Belphegor. She is responsible for stealing a highly valuable book from Lord Wyndham, and maybe for his death. I recognized her scent from the card she left in his safe. Johnson! My horsewhip!'

A thin, pale-faced man in grey stepped up, and offered a coiled horsewhip to Silver.

'This is all a terrible mistake,' Bradamant said firmly. 'I demand that you release me.'

Silver looked at her with dangerous sharpness, lips curling to show unnaturally white teeth. 'Belphegor, you have no idea what you have blundered into. Give me your word to restore the book to me, and I will consider letting you go. For the moment, at least.'

'Hst!' Irene said loudly. 'The police are approaching. We don't want them to hear about this –'

Everyone twitched and turned to see the inspector in the green sash marching towards them. His demeanour fairly shouted determination, and there was something worryingly satisfied about his smile.

'Inspector Singh,' Vale murmured in Irene's ear. 'Over from the Indian Empire for the last two months, on a formal officer exchange between police forces. He didn't like the Fae there and he doesn't like them here. He'll take any opportunity to pry.'

'Do we object to that?' Irene murmured back, just as quietly. Bradamant was trying to wrench her wrist loose from Silver, clearly not quite willing to use the Language in front of him, but he was effortlessly maintaining his grip.

'That might depend on what we have to offer him,' Vale said. His eyes were on Bradamant.

While Irene could think of several ways for her, Kai and Bradamant to get out of the current situation, very few of them involved keeping Vale as a reliable contact, much less Silver. Having the law hunt them as criminals would only make things more complicated. And she needed to know what Silver knew about the book, and why he wanted it. 'If Singh doesn't like Fae,' she pointed out, 'then he won't accept Lord Silver's identification of her as Belphegor. We may be able to get more information out of her later if we help her now.'

'She is your friend, you said,' Vale murmured. His gaze was cold.

'She wasn't supposed to be here!' Irene nearly spat in frustration. 'And I knew nothing about her being this criminal.'

The inspector stopped, and inclined his head slightly to Silver. It wasn't a bow. It was very definitely not a bow. It was barely a nod. 'Good evening, sir.' He had a perceptible accent, but an Oxford one rather than Punjabi or any of the other Indian accents that Irene recognized. 'I understand that you've had some sort of minor problem this evening.'

'A minor problem?' Silver hissed. He whirled to point at the dead alligators and the human corpses, still grasping Bradamant's wrist in his other hand. 'You call that a minor problem?'

'To you, sir,' Inspector Singh said coldly. 'I am sure that it was far more serious to the unfortunate people caught up in this, and my men are handling the casualties. I would be grateful if you could inform me exactly what took place.'

As Silver filled him in, in melodramatic but fundamentally accurate detail, Irene took a silent breath of relief. He hadn't seen who controlled the electricity that took out the alligator threat. She noticed Bradamant relaxing a fraction as well.

'. . . That is all,' Silver concluded. 'You may inform me when you have any further details.' He turned his back on the inspector.

'Actually, sir,' Inspector Singh said, 'we are aware of the identity of your aggressors.'

Everyone stared at him.

'The Iron Brotherhood.' He turned another page in his notebook, and deliberately made a note before proceeding. 'Of course, sir, we are most interested in why they should try to attack your party in such a way.'

'Oh,' Bradamant said, 'I think I can answer that.'

Everyone looked at her.

She lowered her head demurely, batted her eyelashes, and took a cute little gasp of breath that made her bosom heave in a way that was neither cute nor little. 'They were after a book which they thought was being kept here. In fact, I believe that this attack was a distraction—'

Silver's eyes went wide. He flung Bradamant into Inspector Singh's arms with a muffled curse (she bounced), and ran for the door, Johnson two paces behind him.

'Well,' Inspector Singh said, setting Bradamant back on her feet. 'I'm afraid I must ask you to come down to the station with me, madam. We have a few questions.'

Bradamant rubbed the hand which Silver had mangled, the imprints of his fingers scarlet against her pale skin. 'May I just have a word aside with my friend Irene, Inspector? If you would be so kind?'

'Of course, madam,' Inspector Singh said, without taking so much as one step back.

Bradamant clasped Irene's non-bandaged hand between her own before Irene could react. Very rapidly, in the Language, but pitched low, she said, '**I bind myself by my name, by my oath, and by my word that if I find the book I will bring it to you before returning to the Library, and that I will consult with you tomorrow morning, if I am free to do so, about what to do next.**' She dropped back to English, but kept her voice low. 'But for the moment I need you to do something about that Fae.'

Inspector Singh stiffened, staring at the two of them from under heavy dark brows. Well, of course: to him it must have sounded as if Bradamant was talking in his native language and dialect. Irene tried to suppress an urge to feel smug about Bradamant having to explain that, along with everything else.

'Of course,' she said in English. 'I will see you then. Please be careful.'

However, Bradamant had bound herself in the Language. She couldn't break that. She might be able to evade the precise spirit of the oath. Indeed, Irene could think of several ways to get around it, the first one being that 'bring you the book' was not the same as 'give you the book'. But even so, that still brought the book a lot closer than it was right now. And, to be completely frank, she was almost too exhausted to care. The oath would do for the moment.

Bradamant nodded, and turned back to Inspector Singh. 'I am at your disposal, sir,' she said.

'Perhaps we might also consider leaving,' Vale suggested. 'Unless you want to discuss matters further with Lord Silver, Miss Winters?'

Irene thought about having to explain things to Silver. Having to explain anything to Silver. 'What an excellent idea,' she agreed enthusiastically. 'Kai, unless you can think of anything that we've left undone, this might be a good moment to leave.'

Kai wiped his sword with an unstained bit of tablecloth, and put it down on the table. 'I am entirely at your disposal,' he said. 'Where are we going?'

Then Irene remembered that they didn't have hotel rooms. Wonderful. One more thing to sort out.

Her dismay must have shown on her face, and Vale stepped in, almost smiling. 'Allow me to offer you the hospitality of my rooms for the night, Miss Winters. I have a couple of spare bedrooms – and what's more, it will allow your friend and Inspector Singh to find you in the morning.'

Inspector Singh nodded, and Irene revised her opinion of his relationship with Vale by a few notches. Clearly the two men were used to working together. She'd have to bear that in mind.

She tried to remember exactly where India stood in the history of this alternate. It had become an independent trade partner of Great Britain rather than a colony (not due to any particular lack of imperialism on Britain's part, sadly) and the two Empires still maintained close ties. That'd explain Singh's accent.

Kai stepped forward and offered Irene his arm. She took it, suddenly conscious of her weariness, and of the confusion around her. The air was heavy with the smell of blood. Human bodies littered the floor together with alligator corpses – mauled limbs, bloody torsos, screaming faces. Some men and women were still sobbing in corners. Others were filing out of the room, talking to the policemen, or simply drinking. Only a few of the tables were still upright; others had been battered down or had collapsed under the weight of people crowding onto them. The lovely floor was scarred by claws and gunshots, and soaked with blood.

There was so much blood.

'Are you all right?' Kai said softly.

There might have been a time when Irene would have said, *No, I'm not*, and shut her eyes for just a few minutes. But it was not now, and definitely not in front of Bradamant. She swallowed, and tried not to breathe the air more than she could help. 'I will manage,' she said curtly. 'Thank you.'

'Your cloak, Miss Winters,' Vale said, draping it over her shoulders. She must have been dangerously distracted, as he'd retrieved it without her noticing. She made a note to be more careful, and filed it along with all the other notes to be more precise, more attentive, less squeamish, and less inclined to curl up and cry on someone's shoulder.

Inspector Singh clicked his heels together, half-bowed, and turned away with Bradamant, staying a very precise half-foot away from her. Bradamant didn't look back as she followed him.

Outside, on the steps of the Liechtenstein Embassy, there was a mob of photographers, reporters and interested parties. Street vendors were even selling roasted chestnuts, doughnuts and candied peanuts. Their fragrance blended with the taint of Irene's bloodstained dress, and she had to struggle not to be sick.

'Did you see the elder Miss Retrograde leave?' Kai asked.

Irene shook her head. 'I saw her alive at the end, but didn't see her go. I suppose she may be useful. If she knows something.'

Vale came to a sharp halt, looking down at her. 'The elder Miss Retrograde? Miss *Olga* Retrograde?'

'That was the lady in question,' Irene said. 'Is there something that we should know about her, sir?'

'Only that she's the biggest society blackmailer in London,' Vale said. 'The lady is extremely well known for knowing things. The unfortunate thing is that what she knows is rarely advantageous to anyone except herself. As to your acquaintance with her . . .'

'It was the first time we'd met,' Irene said hastily. The curl of Vale's lip made his opinion of the lady extremely clear. 'She realized that we weren't Canadians.'

Vale snorted, and turned away to signal a cab.

'Do you think we'll have a problem?' Kai murmured.

'We're probably the least likely people in that room to have a problem with her,' Irene answered, equally quietly. 'After all, what can she blackmail us with?'

Kai laughed. 'True.'

'Over here!' Vale called. One of the swarming cabs had answered his uplifted hand. They had to elbow their way to it through the edges of the crowd, avoiding reporters with notebooks and cameras. Vale drew the shade across the window as they set off.

'Do you expect us to be watched?' Irene asked.

'It seems likely, Miss Winters,' Vale answered. 'In my own defence, I will say that I am not unknown to the criminal section of London – nor them to me. But since I have not attempted to hide *my* identity, we may as well return to my lodgings directly.'

Irene nodded, settling back into her seat. The passenger

compartment of the cab had two wide leather-covered benches facing each other. Its basic structure was similar to that of a classical hansom carriage, but it was electric-powered rather than horse-drawn, and built of metal rather than wood. She'd been in hansoms before now, and it was strange to be in something so close to one without hearing the sound of hoofbeats.

'About your *friend*,' Vale said, leaning forward, bracing his elbows on his knees. The cab jolted as it turned a corner. 'Do you think Silver's accusations regarding her identity are correct?'

Irene would have liked to meet his eyes and unflinchingly deny it, but she honestly didn't think it would work. She wondered how much Vale might have deduced about Bradamant, simply from their brief meeting. It was the sort of thing that she would expect him to do. 'I wish that I knew myself,' she finally said. 'I hadn't thought that she'd been in London,' *or in this alternate*, 'long enough to have done such a thing. And I can't think *why* she'd do it!'

'It is a common enough technique,' Vale said austerely, 'to establish a pattern of thefts in order to conceal a single one. If she was planning to steal that book, then she could also have been the perpetrator of those early thefts to camouflage its significance.'

Irene considered that idea. It sounded uncomfortably plausible. 'But why would Bradamant have needed to hide the theft?' she said out loud. After all, Bradamant herself could have just left the alternate immediately after stealing the book. But did she want the book for herself, or was she seeking it for the Library? She *was* here without authorization . . . Irene's blood went cold. Could Bradamant have turned traitor to the Library?

Kai was only a step behind her. 'But if she was trying to hide her theft from *us* as well as the authorities—' he began.

Vale frowned. He raised a hand to interrupt Kai. 'A moment, please, Mr Strongrock. Driver!' He hammered with the head of his cane on the roof of the carriage. 'Driver! Why are we going this way?'

Irene pulled back the window shade. She couldn't recognize the buildings going past outside, but they were clearly on a main street. 'I think we're going faster,' she began, then yelped in shock as chaotic power flared across the window. She managed to snatch her fingers back just in time before it could touch them. Across the carriage, Kai flinched back from the window on his side, bumping into Vale.

'Driver!' Vale shouted. 'What is going on?'

The cab jolted as it speeded up again. 'The name is Alberich,' a voice called from above, audible over the rattling of the wheels and the creaking of the carriage. 'I suggest you ask your friends what that means, Mr Vale.'

Irene was conscious that she'd probably gone pale, but she was too busy trying not to shake with sheer terror to spend much time bothering about it. She couldn't handle this – she couldn't – her hand was still infected – this was Alberich, *the* Alberich, the one who had been cast out of the Library, there was no way she could handle this . . .

'Brace, Miss Winters,' Vale instructed Kai, then kicked out at the door with a coiled strength that should have burst it open.

It didn't. The door stayed firmly in position, and the walls of the cab flexed with it as if it was a continuous part of the cab's structure. Vale recoiled into his seat, thrown back by his own force, and bit back a muffled oath.

'I'm afraid you Librarians have become an inconvenience,' the voice called down. Male, Irene noted with the part of her brain that was capable of doing something other than shudder and try to hide. No discernible accent. Precise. Something about the rhythm of it was vaguely familiar, as though she'd heard someone else speak in the same way. 'I require that book for my own collection. A pity to lose you as well, Mr Vale, but I draw the line at stopping the cab to let you out.'

Someone in the street ahead of them screamed as they dived out of the way of the speeding cab.

'I think not,' Vale said coldly. He spun his cane in his hands, and smashed the silver head against the window.

The glass took the blow without breaking or even splintering.

'He's sealed the cab.' Irene forced the words out, nearly shouting against the banging and clattering of the wheels on cobblestones. 'Chaos magic – he's somehow bound it into a coherent whole, so nothing can get in or out – you'd have to break the whole thing to break part of it.'

'Quite accurate,' the voice said. 'Though it's not airtight – or watertight. A logical paradox which I'm afraid you won't have the time to appreciate.'

'The river,' Kai said, barely audibly, and the same knowledge was in Vale's eyes.

Irene's thoughts ran round inside her head. *There must be something I can do – even if the Language isn't working reliably for me, could I use it enough to save us? But the cab itself is chaos-contaminated and Alberich too, so maybe it would cancel out any Library powers anyway . . .*

'Adieu,' Alberich said. The cab rocked again, and speeded up in one last rush towards the river.

'Together!' Vale shouted. 'Enough weight and we can force it over – ' He threw himself against the side of the cab, and a moment later Irene and Kai joined him, struggling together in the confined space. The cab tilted, regained balance, tilted again –

'Yes!' Kai exulted.

– and the cab went over into the river.

CHAPTER THIRTEEN

The carriage did not sink elegantly into the water like a dying swan: it hit the surface of the river with a rattling crash that threw Irene into Kai, and Kai into Vale, and Vale into the wall of the carriage.

Force equals mass times acceleration, Irene thought dizzily. She should be thinking of a way out of this, but her thoughts cowered like frightened rabbits. She didn't *want* to think.

The carriage tumbled as it began to sink, rolling over as the river tugged at it. The three of them automatically grabbed handles and benches, wedging themselves into corners until the vehicle came to a jolting stop on its side. Black Thames water covered the windows, not entirely cutting off all light, but making it only barely possible for the three of them to see each other.

'The usual protocol in these cases is to wait until we are fully submerged, then open a window to equalize the water pressure, and swim up to the surface,' Vale stated. Irene could hear the sheer control in his voice, over the creaking of the carriage and the slow trickling sound of water. 'But if that person has sealed the carriage, given that I could not break the window earlier, this tactic would be ineffective.'

Right. She had to explain to Vale about Alberich. She owed him an explanation about a great many things now. But what was the point, if they were just going to die – well, it did remove the need for justifications. Yet there were other ways of dodging that sort of thing, and she was avoiding the subject again. And the water was pressing down, and they were all going to die . . .

He doesn't just want us dead. He wants us dying in fear, in the dark, and slowly. This isn't just wanting to get us out of the way, so he can work undisturbed. It's malice, pure and simple.

She had been afraid. She had been so very afraid that she'd been cringing in the corner, unwilling to speak, let alone act. But now something else woke in her.

I will not tolerate this.

'Then we're just going to have to find a way to break it,' Irene said. She forced herself to lean forward. 'What one man can do another can undo.' Saying the words made them possible, gave her strength.

'But you can't touch his magic!' Kai said. 'When it infected you before it nearly killed you!'

She wished that she had time to think this through calmly, to plan, to consider. 'Wait,' she said, pulling the glove off her damaged hand and pointing her fingers at the window. 'I've got an idea.'

'Would you care to explain?' Vale invited tensely.

'I was attacked by the same forces he used earlier,' Irene said. She could feel the cold water soaking into her slippers and stockings, curling up around her ankles. 'If I can identify them and expel them, it should break the binding, and we can swim out of here.'

'Very good.' Vale eased himself further back in his seat. Perhaps it was only the dim light that made Irene think that he was trying to position himself as far away from her as possible. She'd sort things out later. She'd explain things later. Right now she just had to make sure there would *be* a later.

Irene held her fingers a fraction of an inch away from the window and focused – away from the water, the darkness, the two men in the carriage with her, and into a world where language structured reality.

It was a fact that Alberich controlled and used chaotic forces. The chaotic forces must therefore be discrete and identifiable. But she had no words in the Language for these forces, and she could only control what she could name or describe.

However, she could name and describe *herself*.

It wasn't a thing that the Librarians did very often. Oh, certainly if you had a broken left arm you could try saying, **'My left tibia is in fact not fractured but perfectly whole.'** But while your tibia might obey, your muscles would still be torn and any wound would still be open. Unless you could name every single thing that required naming, you would probably end up with a partly healed wound that would be more trouble than letting it heal in the normal way. While some Librarians went in for that level of detail, and were very sought-after, Irene was not one of them.

But a person, especially a Librarian, could be named and described holistically as a single entity. She bore the Library's mark on her flesh, and her name was in the Language. If she could enforce that strongly enough, deliberately enough, there would be no space for the chaos forces inside her. Without that to contend with, she could finally access her full powers as a Librarian.

This was not something she'd ever tried. Then again, she'd never been infested to this degree before. Only imminent death would force her to play with dangerous, untested, theoretical techniques, otherwise maybe she'd have thought of this earlier.

Her life was far too full of learning experiences.

Before she could lose her nerve, she shaped the words with her lips, barely audible, speaking in the Language. '**I am Irene: I am a Librarian: I am a servant of the Library.**'

Her brand burned across her back as she enforced her will. But she felt curiously distanced from the pain, as though she could shrug it away and wish it gone. In a flash of insight, she realized that would be disastrous. What she felt in her was the conflict between self-definition and the contamination. She couldn't afford to ignore it. She had to embrace it.

But it *hurt*. She heard her breath catch, the sound strange in her ears.

'Irene?' Kai said, his voice concerned. It was too dark to see him now.

With a racking surge, like vomit after eating spoiled food, the chaos power came jolting out of her. She tried not to think of the buffet earlier that evening (salmon, mussels, crab, soup, little prawns in sauce) and failed. It spilled from her hand, boiling off her fingers in waves of shadow that rippled in the air – and like any living thing, it looked for shelter, for something like itself.

It jumped for the window, arcing through the narrow span of air, and crackled into the glass. Irene had just enough time to wonder if she should jump away from the window, when it broke.

Not just the window.

The whole carriage came apart. First the window, splintering into shards of glass, then sections of the carriage were toppling away from each other like a badly glued model. She barely had time to feel the splinters of glass in her arm before the water came in like a hammerblow. And, surprisingly clearly in the near-darkness, she saw Kai's face looking strangely decisive. His mouth was moving, he was saying something –

She had several seconds of thrashing panic before she realized that she could breathe.

The three of them were drifting along together at the bottom of the river, enclosed in a long continuous coil of dark water. It was a flexing shifting *visible* current in the river, separate from the rest of the water. It even felt cleaner. The shattered remnants of the carriage were already invisible in the shifting mud of the bottom, some distance behind them. Above, through the surface of the water, streetlamps glimmered in hazy balls of white and orange. Kai floated a few paces ahead of herself and Vale, moving at the same pace as them. He was saying something, but the river water filled her ears and she couldn't hear him.

Vale grasped at her sleeve. He mouthed something that was probably *What is going on, Miss Winters?*

On the positive side, Irene reassured herself, he must be feeling more composed if he was back to calling her Miss Winters. She shrugged as obviously as she could, gesturing soothingly. *It is all under control,* she mouthed back.

Vale didn't look as if he believed her, which was a shame, because she was now sure that things actually were back under control. To the extent that the three of them weren't about to drown, at least.

No, the real problem was something else entirely. Now she was sure what Kai really was. A river-spirit might have changed himself to water to save them, and a nature-spirit of some other type might have cajoled or persuaded the river to help them, but only one sort of being would give orders to a river.

Kai was a dragon. What the hell was she supposed to do about that?

And he'd chosen to reveal himself in order to save them.

Not himself: he would presumably have managed quite comfortably on his own. But them. Her and Vale. It was a commitment on Kai's part that made her worry whether she would be able to answer it. She didn't like commitments to other people. They could get . . . messy.

The tumbling rush of the current veered towards the far bank, and then lifted the three of them out of the water itself, rising in an arc of dark water. They were placed on the dockside, deposited as lightly as driftwood. A couple of beggars who'd been nursing their hands over a small fire just sat there, looking at the three of them numbly as the water sloshed over the pavement and ebbed back to the river again.

A curl of the river still held itself aloft, curving towards where Kai stood. It wasn't quite like a serpent: the head had features something like a human and something like a dragon (yes, that again). There was also something of the lion, mane wet and draggled with weeds and dirt. Its eyes gleamed yellow as fog lamps, burning under heavy brows. This spirit was as polluted as the water itself, its body entwined with fragments of garbage and long streaks of filth. A heavy smell of oil and weed clung to it, wafting thickly along the dock.

Kai faced it and gave a small, precise inclination of his head. 'Your service is acknowledged,' he said firmly. 'Return with my thanks and the thanks of my family.'

The river-spirit bowed its head in a long fluctuation that rippled along its body, then reared up and crashed back into the river in a spray of black water. The eyes were the last thing to vanish beneath the surface of the river, disappearing slowly rather than simply closing, visible for a long moment under the dark water.

Vale took a step forward. 'What was that?' he demanded,

shocked. 'What did you *do*? What is it that you have brought into my London, sir?'

Kai turned with a snarl, his eyes an inhuman shade of blue, as fierce and dangerous as gas flames. 'What it was, sir, was—'

'Was under my orders,' Irene said, stepping between them. She couldn't allow this to degenerate into a shouting match. And more than that, she could sense something archaic and furious within Kai, the dragon under the human skin now very close to the surface. She had to divert it now, give him familiar channels to work in, and give Vale a target – herself – who he simply couldn't shout down without shattering his own rules of custom and propriety. She regarded Vale firmly, refusing to show him an inch of fear or terror or even, she hoped, nervousness. 'I have promised you more information, sir, and you shall have it, but I suggest we return to your lodgings first. Mr Strongrock acted on my instructions to *protect* and *save* us all.' It was a fairly small lie, really only a half-lie as lies went, because Kai had certainly known she would want him to protect all of them. 'And this is no time for us to be arguing, when we are all fighting a greater enemy.'

Vale regarded her for a moment, then granted her a small nod, nearly the mirror-image of Kai's own salutation to the river-spirit. 'Very well, Miss Winters. We shall return to my lodgings. I can only have faith in you, I suppose, as I have done before.'

That stung. As no doubt it was meant to. She smiled as sweetly as she could, then turned to Kai. 'We can talk later,' she said softly, 'or we can talk now, but either way, I know what you are, and it doesn't matter.'

'You think very highly of yourself,' Kai answered, equally quietly, but far more deadly, 'if you believe that it doesn't matter.'

This was very different to handling Vale. There she had needed to hide her fear to convince him to wait for information. Here, with Kai, she needed to show her control and dispassion or, she could feel it in her bones, she would lose him to his true nature.

She couldn't afford that. She had a responsibility to the Library. And she had a responsibility to him.

'Are you still my student?' she asked him directly. 'Am I still your mentor?' Nothing more than that. The bond of loyalty, and the bond of trust. Anything else was something that they would have to work out later.

He looked at her, and something inhuman seethed behind his eyes. 'Do you think you can command me?'

'**Yes**,' she said, and she spoke in the Language.

The word hung in the air between them. Then Kai closed his eyes, and reopened them, and now they were a human blue, sharp but no longer alien. 'Then I believe I am still under your orders,' he said, and he managed a very small smile.

'Miss Winters, Mr Strongrock, over here!' Vale called. He had walked to where the dock ended and the houses began, and had somehow managed to conjure up a carriage. As Irene followed Kai across to the carriage, struggling with her soaked skirts and cloak, she couldn't help but notice that Kai was perfectly dry. It didn't seem fair. But it was a comforting, small thing on which to concentrate. She could be aggravated by something simple, rather than floundering in terror at what she had just faced down.

CHAPTER FOURTEEN

'I would appreciate that explanation, Miss Winters,' Vale said as he refilled their teacups.

There had been hot baths and bandaging of injuries. Even Kai, untouched by the dirty water of the Thames, needed to clean himself after the exertions of the reception and its accompanying alligator blood. As for Vale and Irene, they were soaked and filthy. The driver had been muttering audibly about getting his carriage cleaned, even after a very generous tip from Vale.

Irene would gladly have soaked for a few more hours, but she hadn't felt it safe to leave Vale and Kai alone to talk for too long. Kai's temper was still touchy, and Vale might ask a question that was more dangerous than he realized. With a virtuous feeling of self-sacrifice, she'd dragged herself out of the hip-bath that she'd been allotted, wrapped herself up in the heavy flannel dressing-gown Vale had lent her, turbaned her hair in a towel, and gone out to join the others in Vale's study for tea and interrogation.

(She hadn't asked why Vale had a spare woman's dressing-gown in his wardrobe. Presumably specifically for female victims of crime who'd had a drenching. However, she didn't think it belonged to any close female associate of

179

Vale's. For one thing, it clearly hadn't been used for months, and for another, any female trying to be flirtatious would not choose a dressing-gown made of heavy flannel. For a third thing, Vale hadn't offered her any *other* female clothing. And Vale hadn't given her the sort of attention that even the politest of men might give a soaked wet woman in dripping clothing. He'd bustled her off towards the hot tub as briskly as the matron from her old boarding school. Not that she wanted him to give her that sort of attention, anyhow . . .)

Irene sipped her tea. Milk. Two lumps of sugar – suitable for people suffering from shock. 'I should warn you that it is a little, ah, far-fetched,' she said, trying to think how best to explain it, or failing all else, lie about it.

Vale shrugged. *His* dressing-gown was red and black silk. His hair was still damp, combed into position and gleaming darkly in the light from the lamps. 'I can hardly object until I have heard it.' Somewhere amidst the confusion he had found time to rearrange his books, after the disorder which Irene had inflicted on them, and neat piles of half-sorted literature sat around his chair like patient children.

Kai sipped his own tea (no milk, no sugar, black and brooding) and watched the two of them. There was still that feeling of distance about him. He was wearing what was obviously Vale's second-best dressing-gown – the same colours and design, but more worn on the elbows, and with small burn holes marring the embroidery of the cuffs. His mouth was pinched in stubborn lines.

'Mr Strongrock and I are agents of a library,' Irene started. 'It is often known as the Invisible Library among those who have heard of it, as it's hidden from most.'

'A reasonable enough name,' Vale granted. 'Where is it based? I would hardly think that it could be London.' *Since I have never heard of it*, he didn't bother to add.

'Ah. Now this would be the implausible bit,' Irene said. 'Are you familiar with the concept of alternate worlds?'

Vale put down his cup, his regard assessing rather than outright disbelieving. 'The theory has been mooted by some of the more metaphysically inclined philosophers and scientists. While I do not necessarily *believe* in it, I must admit that it has a certain quality of inherent satisfaction. That is, to coin a phrase – it "makes sense" that possible fulcrum points in history have created alternate worlds where things might have been different.'

Irene nodded. That way of looking at it would do for the moment. 'I and Mr Strongrock are agents of a library which exists between the alternate worlds. Our task is to collect books for the Library from all those worlds, to preserve them.' She glanced meaningfully at his crowded bookshelves. 'You must admit that to a keen reader – like yourself, or like me – that also would "make sense".'

'Mm. Your argument would appeal to any bibliophile, Miss Winters. Should I take it that you are here in pursuit of a particular book?'

Irene nodded again. 'The copy of Grimm that Lord Wyndham had before his death. But it seems that we aren't the only people after it.'

Vale hesitated for a long moment. 'Very well. I can postulate an interdimensional library hunting down rare books. I can accept the agents of that library having unusual powers.' He glanced at Kai. 'Once one accepts the basic concept as possible, today's events become – well, not entirely inexplicable. I have a great many questions, but one query in particular intrigues me, and I trust that you can give me a solid answer to it. Why should you be looking for Grimm's Fairy Tales? Why not the latest scientific advances?'

Irene smiled. This part had always warmed her some-where deep inside. She leaned forward in turn, putting her cup down. 'Mr Vale, while all the alternate worlds exist, and while they may have different *metaphysical* laws, their *physical* laws are the same. Iron is iron, radium is radium, gunpowder is gunpowder, and if you drop an object, it will fall according to the law of gravity. Scientific discoveries are the same across the alternates, and while they are no doubt important, we don't value them as we do creative work. There may be a hundred brothers Jakob and Wilhelm Grimm in a hundred different worlds, and each time they may have written a different set of fairy tales. That's where our interest lies.'

Vale blinked. 'But in that case, you could import the dis-coveries from other worlds! You could bring more than simply fiction – new technologies, new wonders of science. Have you no concept of the good you could do for these – ' he remembered himself – 'hypothetical alternate worlds.'

'Wouldn't work,' Kai said, staring at his tea.

'What my colleague is trying to say,' Irene said patiently, 'is that, while it has been tried, firstly, the Library does not care to make itself public. Secondly, we cannot introduce material for which there is no support infrastructure. This is what would happen if we tried to bring in discoveries that your current science didn't support, and as a result the dis-covery wouldn't take root. It would probably be written off as a fake in short order. Also, please consider. What would be the dangers facing a person attempting to introduce entirely new scientific knowledge to this world? To this country?'

Vale nodded slowly, his expression bitter. 'I take your point,' he said. He didn't sound convinced, though.

'And lastly,' Irene said, a little embarrassed that she had to point it out, 'all of us who are sealed to the Library are people who have chosen this way of life because we loved books. None of us wanted to save worlds. I mean, not that we object to saving worlds . . .' She shrugged, picking up her teacup again. 'We want books. We love books. We live with books. Someone who joined the Library just so that they could try to use the Library to benefit their own world . . . well, I suppose it would be ethical, but it isn't the purpose of the Library.'

'Then what is the purpose of the Library?' Vale asked.

'To save books,' Irene said firmly. The words were so automatic that she didn't even need to think about them. She'd spent all her life with the idea. But they had never sounded hollow to her before. She made herself focus on the familiar justification. 'To save created works. In time, if their original alternate loses them, we can give them back copies, so that they aren't lost. And in the meantime, the Library exists and endures.'

'So why did Alberich leave?' Vale asked.

Irene swallowed. She hadn't expected him to get to that point quite that fast. The little that she knew about Alberich was bad enough that she had been *happy* to write him off as a myth. She didn't really want to think of him as a real person with potentially terrifying motivations. Then she blinked. 'Wait. How did you know that?'

Vale waved a hand dismissively. 'Simple enough. The fellow is clearly a deserter from your own organization. Given what I know about it from you, his possible motives are either personal advantage, or he has overarching principles that conflict with your own stated mission – which is to save books and not interfere in the workings of other worlds. But if it were a question of personal advantage, why bother to hunt down and assassinate other Librarians? If he wanted money, fame or adventure, presumably other Librarians wouldn't get in his way, as long as he didn't obstruct your searches for specific books. And what specific book would be that important to him, if he were pursuing personal gain? So perhaps he has a larger plan, one that requires your non-interference. This would require him to be motivated by personal power or have some goal which he believes is more important than your Library's search for books. Your own response confirms this – why else would Library agents feel such a sense of dread towards a mere rogue agent?'

Irene reminded herself bitterly not to underestimate Vale again. She also ignored Kai, who was twiddling his fingers in his lap with an air of smug unconcern. *Fine. I suppose I should be glad his mood's improving.* 'Alberich left the Library a while ago,' she said reluctantly. 'I lack the clearance for full information on why.' *Or any information beyond the bare minimum.*

'So – this Alberich is a continual threat. Has he crossed your path before?'

Irene shook her head. 'No. Thank heavens. I had heard about him, of course, everyone hears about him—'

'Even I'd heard about him,' Kai put in, not very helpfully.

'Kai is my junior,' Irene said before Vale could ask for clarification of that statement. 'And I know that the idea of an evil rogue Librarian must sound like some kind of rumour. The sort of rumour which gets passed down through the years to frighten the novices. But there were stories about things happening to people one actually knew.'

'Things?' Vale asked.

'People dying,' Irene said bluntly. 'With pieces of them being sent back.'

Kai started. 'Was that why Dominic—' he began, then stopped a fraction too late.

'I don't know,' Irene said. She turned to Vale again. 'What Kai is trying to say is that the Librarian who was supposed to be stationed locally, in this alternate world, has apparently been killed and mutilated. We found out just before I triggered the trap I mentioned – a trap set using chaos forces. These – forces – are something that Alberich uses.' She couldn't keep the distaste out of her voice.

Vale nodded. 'So *chaos* . . . Is that what we would term "magic"?'

Irene tried to think how to explain it. She'd been planning to sidestep this part as much as possible, given Vale's apparent dislike of magic. 'Not exactly. According to our cosmological model – ' there, that was tactful and avoided saying, *this is how things really work* – 'there are lawful and chaotic forces active in all worlds. Sometimes they take on a physical form, appearing as entities – or personifications of law or disorder if you like. The lawful forces support reason and natural laws. The chaotic forces support impossibility, and things that are blatantly irrational or disorderly. For example, dragons are lawful forces and the Fae support chaos. Fact versus fiction, if you like.'

Vale stiffened like a hound catching the scent. 'So Lord Silver is a supporter of chaos itself?'

Irene nodded. 'This alternate is strongly affected by chaos. Silver is certainly at least one of the lesser Fae, who are usually confined inside a single alternate. I don't know if he is one of the greater ones, but I sincerely hope not. Such creatures even have the power to move between worlds. But they have nothing to do with the Library.' She wanted to make this extremely clear. 'We do not associate with them.'

'Except when obtaining party invitations,' Vale said drily.

'I want that book,' Irene said flatly. 'So does he, it seems.

And so does Alberich. I need to know who has it. If Silver or Alberich already had it, they wouldn't be looking for it. Once I have it, Mr Strongrock and I will be out of this alternate and won't need to bother you again.'

Vale nodded. 'Very well.' Again there was the feeling of a confrontation being postponed until he had sufficient ammunition. Perhaps he wanted to bring her to justice as well. Or perhaps he simply wanted to visit the Library. 'So, tell me,' he went on, 'when was the Librarian stationed here murdered, where, and how?'

Irene glanced at Kai. 'Well, it must have been somewhere between yesterday afternoon and this morning, because we first met him yesterday afternoon when we came through from the Library proper. The entrance is in the British Library,' she added, a little reluctantly.

'Really,' Vale said thoughtfully.

'And when we came back this morning to speak with him . . .' Irene trailed off, wishing she didn't have to go into the next bit. 'Ah, we have reason to assume that he was dead by that point, possibly for several hours.'

'Why?' Vale demanded. 'You found his body?'

'We found his skin,' Irene said. 'In a jar of vinegar.'

Kai reached across and touched her wrist. She knew that it was inappropriate for her to show weakness, but she found it comforting.

Vale sat back in his chair. 'I see,' he said. 'That must have been a great shock for you, Miss Winters.'

Irene remembered the pungent smell. Her stomach twisted. 'Yes,' she said. 'It was. I am sorry, I'm afraid I find it difficult to be as detached as I should be.' He'd been friendly, helpful, kind, just simply *nice* . . .

'And you are quite sure that it was your contact?' Vale prompted.

Irene nodded reluctantly. She hadn't wanted to admit

this bit if she could have avoided it. 'All Librarians have a mark on their body,' she said. 'It looks like a tattoo done in black ink. It cannot be removed.'

Vale was quite clearly considering asking whether he could see hers, but after a moment's hesitation he nodded. Possibly the fact that she hadn't offered to show it was hint enough. 'And – if I may be frank – would the trap that had been set possibly have killed you?'

Irene had been trying to avoid thinking about it. She had plenty of productive ways to occupy her mind besides yet one more way in which she had almost died in the last couple of days. 'Yes,' she said. 'If Mr Strongrock had not broken my link to it, it might well have done. It would certainly have incapacitated me and left me helpless. And . . .' She frowned, her mind sensing something important. 'Let me think. Alberich would have known I would touch the door, not Mr Strongrock, because only I can access the Library. Even if I survived, he'd know the chaos contamination would prevent me accessing the Library. He'd also be aware that the contamination would only last for a few days.'

Vale nodded. A spark kindled in his eyes. 'That seems logical,' he said with more warmth than he had shown at any point previously. 'Let us theorize that your Alberich—'

'Hardly *my* Alberich,' Irene snapped.

Vale snorted. 'Alberich, then. Let us theorize that he expected to have completed his plans in a few days, at which point it would no longer matter if you contacted the Library. As he was still around earlier today, with our murder in mind, those plans can't be completed yet. Especially as he was still trying to get us, or rather you, out of the way.'

'That seems plausible,' Kai said, emerging from his moody self-absorption. 'But, if he doesn't have the book,

187

and *we* don't have the book, and Bradamant doesn't have the book, and Silver doesn't have the book – and if the Iron Brotherhood is responsible for the alligators, so still on the offensive, then they don't have the book . . .' He shrugged. 'Who *does* have the book?'

'I dislike dismissing possible culprits without firm evidence,' Vale murmured. 'But I see little reason why the Iron Brotherhood would be interested in a book of fairy tales. They tend more towards technological paradigms. Now had it been one of the lost notebooks of Leonardo da Vinci, that would be entirely different. Come to think of it . . .' He levelled a stare at Irene. 'Why would your Alberich want to steal a book of fairy tales? Out of spite?'

'Maybe there's something unusual about this particular copy of the book,' Kai offered. 'Possibly there's something hidden in the binding, or a coded message . . .'

Irene shook her head. 'I don't think so. The reason I think the Library wants it is because it might contain something which other versions of Grimm's Fairy Tales in other alternates don't. That is, a new story, or several new stories. There would be no point in collecting it if it were just the same as the ones in other worlds. But if Alberich wants it? I don't even know what Alberich wants.' She became aware that she was starting to whine, and made herself concentrate. 'It can't be because there's a significant connection between the book and this alternate. It's not individual enough for that. There are too many other versions of Grimm out there. That sort of connection requires a very specific book with relevance to that alternate.' Her hand twinged, and she rubbed it nervously, then tried to stop herself before she could make it any worse. Bradamant certainly wouldn't approve of what she was about to say. And her mentor Coppelia would undoubtedly have forbidden her to voice her suspicions.

But Coppelia couldn't have foreseen any of this. Could she?

'Sometimes information about the Library gets out,' she said slowly. 'Not just in conversations like this. Librarians are observed, or they talk too much, or maybe the Fae are involved. It's not exactly something that I've been tutored in.' She paused to translate her thoughts into a theory that would also make sense to Vale. 'And often when this does happen, this information ends up being recorded in works of – well, fiction.'

Kai blinked, eyelids flickering, without moving. 'I've heard as much.'

And that confirmed his nature for her. Trainees did not get told about this. Ever. Only Librarians fully sealed to the Library got even the most basic of briefings about it. Irene herself was a full Librarian, albeit a junior one, and even she had only had a few hints about it. If Kai had 'heard as much', then it had been from other dragons, not from Librarians.

'Indeed,' she said, keeping her voice even. 'And if there is some secret pertaining to the Library in this book, then that might explain why Alberich is so eager to get his hands on it. Silver, too. Some Fae know about the Library, and have an interest in it. If Silver believes that the book holds some secret – if only because other people are trying to get their hands on it – that would make it irresistible to someone like him.'

Kai frowned. 'But if it's such a big secret, why send – um, forgive me for this, Irene – but why send someone who's just a journeyman Librarian after it? Why not send in an expert? Several experts?'

'That could actually be construed as support for Miss Winters's theory,' Vale said thoughtfully. 'In order not to attract Alberich's attention, your superiors could have chosen to send someone who had no idea of the book's importance. Someone who would not be seen as an obvious choice for important missions.'

Irene decided that this was not the time to have a hissy fit or make pointed comments about her status in the Library. Especially as Vale was right. 'But unfortunately Alberich found out about it anyhow,' Irene continued the hypothesis. 'And, come to think of it, that would explain Bradamant. One of the senior Librarians might have thought I wouldn't be up to the task, and decided to send her in.' With an effort, she added, 'She does have more experience than I do, after all.'

And then there was Kai. Apparently just an apprentice, but in fact a dragon. Well, probably a dragon. She needed to have a private talk with him. They simply hadn't had a chance since the river incident. If Coppelia had *known* that, then assigning him to the mission was far more significant backup than it had originally seemed.

Vale nodded. 'So if your associate Bradamant – another code name, I take it?'

Irene nodded. 'We all have them.' It was simpler than trying to explain the whole Librarianly choice of names to him.

'Very well. Your associate Bradamant arrived here before you did, and created an identity as the thief Belphegor. An intelligent piece of work. She must have planned to conceal her theft of this specific book among the thefts of other books. A needle in a haystack, as the saying goes. Do you suppose she would be prepared to return the other ones?'

Irene thought about it. Vale's theory made a great deal of sense, and was a step ahead of where she'd managed to get to. (She'd always wondered, or even daydreamed, what it was like to actually work with great detectives, rather than just read about them. It was more annoying than she'd expected.) The odds were that Bradamant had kept the books – after all, if her private mission had been successful, then she could have donated them to the Library as well. 'I can ask her,' she offered. 'The current mission is definitely more important than these other books.'

'But it's *our* mission!' Kai put in.

Irene sighed. It was well past midnight. It had been a very full day. She was tired to the bone. 'Look, Kai. At the moment, the most important thing is keeping that book out of Alberich's hands. If he wants it, then it's paramount that he doesn't get it. And the second most important thing is getting it to the Library. I admit it's not going to look good on my record if I fail. But when it comes down to it, I don't care if I bring it in, or you bring it in, or if Bradamant brings it in and takes the credit and ends up spending the next ten years rubbing my nose in it. And if that means promising her the book in exchange for handing back the other books to Vale, then I will do it.'

'That's very noble,' Kai said dubiously, 'but it doesn't solve our original problem. Where is the book?'

'I believe that is something we can discover when Madame Bradamant is here to be questioned,' Vale said briskly. 'She agreed to come and see you tomorrow, I think? And if Singh does not release her, then we can go and question her in prison.'

Irene nodded. She was about to continue, when Vale held up his hand. 'One thing more. When you made that reference to "significant connections" and "books specific to an alternate" – would you mind expanding on that?'

Damn him. Irene had been hoping to skate past that without going into further detail. Belatedly, she decided that she should never have mentioned that bit in the first place. *Stupid* of her. 'Some books have a significant connection to the alternate that they come from,' she said reluctantly. 'They help anchor the Library to that alternate. It's not a bad thing in itself. The Library's a stabilizing force, so it even helps ward off chaos influences like Fae.'

That was half of it. The other half of it – the possibility that books with a significant connection to the alternate world could affect that world itself, could somehow even change it – was only a theory at her level in the Library. It was a theory that she was increasingly wanting to research in more detail, but there wasn't time for that at the moment. It was also something that she definitely wasn't going to tell Vale. Call her a cynic, but Irene suspected that if she were to tell him that, then there would be no way in hell that he'd cooperate in getting the book for her. He'd be far too concerned at what it might mean for his own world. After all, he'd made it clear that he didn't necessarily trust the Library's intentions.

'And my world?' Vale pounced on her words. 'Which books are "significant" here?'

'I don't know, sir.' She saw Vale was about to object, and she shook her head. 'No, please. Believe me, Mr Vale. We don't get told. They don't tell us. It's dangerous knowledge.'

He leaned back in his chair, his expression hungry and unsatisfied. 'And aren't you ever curious, Miss Winters? Don't you want to know?'

'You're suggesting that I have some sort of academic curiosity about the fact,' Irene said curtly. Out of the corner of her eye she could see Kai leaning forward. 'I've already told you that our interest is in books. Not . . .' She looked for words that would convey her meaning with sufficient strength. 'Not in overarching world-changing forces.'

'Yes, Miss Winters,' Vale said drily. 'That is indeed *what you have told me*.'

The unspoken accusation of lying, or at the very least prevarication, hit her like a slap across the face. It didn't help matters that it was in some respects true. She lowered her eyes and couldn't answer him. Worst of all, for the first time in years, *we're just doing this to save the books* sounded petty, and choosing not to know more seemed childish.

'And yet there might be good reasons for not knowing,' Vale went on, talking over her bowed head. 'Perhaps for fear this Alberich fellow might find out. Perhaps simply the senior members of this library would refuse to tell you, if they knew themselves. And perhaps you would simply refuse to tell me, for your own safety, or for mine.' His voice was dispassionately kind. She didn't deserve it. 'It must be very frustrating, Miss Winters. Wondering.'

She still couldn't bring herself to look up. 'If it was important,' she said, 'then they'd tell me.'

'Or possibly it is too important to tell you,' Vale answered. 'Just as with the suggestion that the book contains classified information, which we discussed earlier. We lack sufficient information to know for certain which is true. But one thing is sure. We cannot allow this book to fall into Alberich's hands.'

'You'll accept that?' Kai demanded, his face brightening.

'I may be suspicious,' Vale said, 'but I hope that I am not stupid. He has already made his position towards me extremely clear, after all.'

Irene took a deep breath. 'If you have no objection, there is one more thing I would like to do before we sleep.'

'What is that?'

Irene smiled a little. It was good to know that this was within her power again, now that the chaos contamination was out of her system, and that Vale trusted her enough to consider it. It helped her feel less ashamed of herself. 'It's possible to link a suitably similar space to the Library.' She surveyed Vale's office again. 'In practice, that means there has to be a reasonable number of books present, or some other sort of storage media. It won't enable passage, but it will ... well, it can make that area a sort of annex of the Library, and that would prohibit creatures of chaos from entering. Or, more specifically, it will prevent Alberich from being able to get in. If he does realize that we survived ...'

'Ah. A good thought. Will this involve any sort of "magic"?'

'Only the innate force of the Library itself,' Irene said, she hoped reassuringly. She didn't want to go into the whole question of the Language. She'd already said more than enough for one night, to an outsider. 'You probably won't notice anything at all.'

'Why did your colleague who was murdered not do this?' Vale asked. 'Or did he?'

'It wouldn't have lasted,' Irene answered. She'd been through this in basic training. 'The problem with declaring an area in sympathy with the Library is that it only works as long as nobody takes any books away from it. Your lodgings will be safe because nobody will be removing any books from here this evening. Mr Aubrey couldn't have done the same to the British Library. The protection would have come down the moment someone took a book out of it.'

'Ah.' Vale sat back in his chair. 'Very well. You may proceed, Miss Winters.'

It didn't take long. She simply invoked the Library, in the Language, in the shortest possible way that it could conveniently be done without damage to the speaker or the surroundings. The more *precise* the definition, the more harm it might do to everything around it by linguistically shaking its surroundings into conformity. Declaring the Library's unabbreviated name, a single word, would remove everything that was not Library.

Irene therefore used half a dozen sentences. She felt the

snap of coherence as the synchronization took place, and with it a greater sense of comfort. She felt in control again.

'Odd,' Vale said. He rubbed at the bridge of his nose, frowning. 'I thought that I would feel something more than that.'

'What did you feel?' Irene asked curiously.

'Something of a headache, like the high pressure before a storm.' Vale shrugged. 'I have no talent for such sorceries. Another reason for my differences with my family.'

Irene was about to say, *It's hardly sorcery*, but decided that it wasn't worth the argument. She was also wildly curious about Vale's break with his family, but this was hardly the moment to pry. 'It should keep Alberich out, which is the important thing,' she reiterated.

'Excellent.' Vale brushed his hands together and rose to his feet, all business once more. 'Then, for the moment, I suggest we all get some sleep. Madame Bradamant's information is necessary for any further hypotheses. Unless it is possible for you to reach her via some arcane method?' he added hopefully.

'I'm sorry,' Irene said. 'I have no specific link that I can use to reach her.'

'Your connection to the Library?' Vale suggested. 'Would that work on its own, or could it be used as the focal point for some other spell?'

'That wouldn't work,' Kai said. 'The Library link is to the Library rather than other Librarians, and it surpasses lesser sorceries. Irene and Bradamant are safe from Fae glamours and minor spells because they're directly connected to a greater power. Such glamours would be as insignificant as starlight in sunlight.'

Vale raised his brows. 'But not yourself?' he asked, giving Kai more friendly attention than he had done since the river-spirit incident.

'I'm still a trainee,' Kai said, smiling as he stood in turn, then offering Irene a hand to help her rise. 'For the moment I don't have that sort of connection. What powers I have are my own and my family's.'

'Your . . . family?' Vale enquired, in a tone that was an invitation to expand on the subject.

'There is a temporary disagreement on the subject of my future,' Kai said. 'I hope to win them round.'

Irene suspected there was more to it than that. The dragons – very well, the single dragon whom she had met – seemed to tolerate the Library as some sort of human eccentricity. It seemed notable only for its admirable taste in fiction, and certainly not a prospective life for one of their children. (Spawn? Eggs? Younglings? She didn't have vocabulary for this.) It was now quite obvious why Kai had claimed that his family was dead; she could understand why he'd told the lie, in view of the greater secret. What she didn't know was how he was going to resolve the situation. Or how the Library would resolve it for him.

But then again, if Coppelia knew about Kai's true nature, perhaps there were other dragons at large in the Library. Maybe there was a Secret Alliance. (That sort of thing would demand capital letters.) Perhaps the lower depths of the Library sheltered great slithering coils of ancient dragons and . . .

. . . and she was going to drive herself into paranoia at this rate. 'I agree that sleep would be a good idea,' she said, causing both Vale and Kai to give her aggrieved looks. They could have a bonding session some other time, or after she had gone to sleep. Dragons might be stand-offish in general, but this particular dragon seemed inclined to be friendly, or even outright demonstrative, and possibly even a thorough Romantic. She was much more detached. Semi-detached. Her brain was tired enough that her thoughts were making stupid connections. 'I hate to impose on you for a bed, Mr Vale, but . . .'

'Of course,' Vale said, giving in gracefully. 'The bed in the spare room has already been made up for you. I'm afraid that Mr Strongrock will have to make do with the couch in here. My housekeeper has put out some blankets. I'll just fetch them.'

The moment he was out of the room, Kai turned to Irene. 'Well?'

'Well, what?'

He folded his arms defensively, drawing himself to his full height. 'I expected you'd want to talk about . . . well, you know. You've probably guessed.'

She'd thought about how to handle this. She'd run through several different scenarios in her head, and none of them that started out 'so explain why you're a dragon' had ended well. He was proud. She was familiar with the emotion. 'No,' she said. 'I'm not going to ask you any questions.'

Kai stood there like a beautiful statue (in a second-hand dressing-gown with frayed cuffs), blinking at her. The rain was audible on the window for several seconds before he could bring himself to speak again. 'You're not?'

'My trust in you hasn't changed.' She put her unbandaged hand on his wrist. 'I believe that if it mattered, if it was truly important, then you would tell me. You wouldn't jeopardize the mission for the sake of your own pride. But when it comes to your private matters – yours and your family's – I don't intend to pry.'

'Irene.' He swallowed. 'That's very generous of you.'

'Think nothing of it,' she said, turning away.

'And it makes me feel like hell,' he said to her back.

Ah, guilt. Which Irene was very definitely feeling herself at the moment, for what she'd said and also what she *hadn't* said to Vale, and for the way that she'd manipulated Kai. She could tell herself that she'd only acted as was necessary in a dangerous situation, but she knew perfectly well that he'd confessed his nature to save her life, and she'd just . . . well, given him orders and enforced their relationship as superior and trainee. All her feelings of natural justice encouraged her to confess something to him in return, but she wasn't sure what she could say.

And now he was offering her another chance to manipulate him. Under some conditions, Irene would happily have encouraged his guilt in the hopes of getting him to spill the full details, but in the middle of a mission wasn't one of them. *I am not a nice person,* she thought, *to be thinking only of the mission, sparing nothing for my responsibilities to him.*

'What do you want me to say?' she asked, turning round to look at him. 'I'm grateful that you saved our lives. Thank you.'

'You're taking this far too calmly.' He ran one hand through his hair. 'You should be demanding answers, being furious—'

'I thought you said you knew me.' She pointed a finger at him. 'Look. So far – so far just *today* – I have coped with discovering the skin of a senior Librarian, with running into a trap of chaos energies, with an attack by alligators, with an encounter with Alberich himself, and with an attempt to drown us in the Thames. And you have the nerve, the insolence, the *undiluted gall,*' she could hear her voice rising, and at this point she didn't much care, 'to expect me to throw my hands in the air and run round in little circles just because you happen to be a dragon?'

Kai made desperate calm-down gestures with his hands. 'I thought you were going to interrogate me! I was trying to think what to tell you!'

'Well, I'm not going to interrogate you.' Irene lowered

her voice. 'So calm down. Will it make you feel better if I promise that later on we'll have some coffee and I'll ask you a lot of personal questions?' Yes, she could look forward to that. She *would* look forward to that.

It surprised her that she was indeed looking forward to that.

He sighed. 'At least I'll have that to dread, I suppose.'

'Kai.' Irene gave him a very deliberate stare. 'Were you actually looking forward to telling me everything?'

Kai tried to meet her eyes in a decisive way. He settled for looking over her shoulder. 'It isn't as if I've done this before,' he muttered.

'Later,' she said meaningfully. 'I promise.'

She turned to see Vale at the door with an armful of blankets. 'Am I interrupting?' he asked politely.

'Not at all,' Irene said firmly, and swept past him with as much dignity as she could manage. He and Kai could stay up talking as long as they wanted.

Hopefully Bradamant wouldn't turn up with any emergencies until *after* breakfast.

CHAPTER FIFTEEN

Kai and Vale were both up before Irene, and she walked in to find them sharing breakfast. Yesterday's awkwardness seemed to have vanished, and they were talking amiably enough now. They seemed to be enjoying discussing politics (a hindrance to all right-minded men), previous investigations that Vale had undertaken (though generally without books being involved), zeppelins, and the proper method for eliminating giant centipedes.

Irene made the proper noises of *good morning* and *yes, I slept very well, thank you for asking* and *please pass the marmalade* as she took a seat. She then inhaled coffee by the cupful until she felt more human, letting the men resume their conversation. Her hand was feeling much better, even if it was still in bandages. Last night's rain had passed, and outside the window the sky was – well, as clear as could be expected, given the constant smog. Rays of sunlight were filtering down. No doubt birds were singing in the countryside. Things weren't too bad.

She wondered if she could actually get to quite like this alternate.

The door banged downstairs, and two sets of feet came hastening up the stairs.

'Ah!' Vale said, dusting toast crumbs off his fingers with a napkin, and pushing aside the spoon and egg which he'd been using to demonstrate the finer points of zeppelin control. 'That would be Singh. I know his step. And no doubt Madame Bradamant with him.'

Irene hastily refilled her coffee cup and tried to ignore feelings of imminent doom. It had been such a nice morning, too. 'They're up early,' she commented.

'Oh, Singh is always welcome here for breakfast,' Vale said cheerfully. 'Especially when I'm working on a case that involves him.'

Perhaps that was why Singh had allowed Bradamant to meet them here, rather than keeping her at the station. Irene wondered a bit nervously if there had been any communication between Vale and Singh last night after she'd gone to bed. She stiffened her spine and was smiling pleasantly when Bradamant and Singh came in. Bradamant had somehow managed proper morning dress, neat and pristine in dove grey with violet cuffs and jabot, and had an umbrella tucked under one arm. Singh, behind her, was still in the same uniform as last night, but his moustache and beard had a spruce, freshly combed look to them. He carried a well-stuffed black briefcase that looked as though it had seen an investigation or two.

'Ah!' Singh said, his eyes fixing on the breakfast table.

'My dear Singh,' Vale said, springing to his feet and seizing the coffee pot, 'we must speak a moment. Ladies, Mr Strongrock, please excuse us. Miss Winters, please do invite your friend to some breakfast. We will be back in a moment.' With one bound he had swept Singh out of the room, taking the coffee with him, and abandoning Bradamant in the process.

'Would you like some toast?' Kai said helpfully, rising to his feet.

'By all means.' Bradamant furled her skirts and seated herself on the sofa next to Irene. 'Is our host usually prone to such dramatic moments?'

'I think he wanted to explain something to Inspector Singh,' Irene replied. Her feeling of imminent doom was getting worse. She passed the toast and butter. 'They're old friends, and no doubt they wanted to discuss things without us listening. Quite reasonable.'

'Oh, absolutely.' Bradamant drew off her gloves, picked up a knife, and swiped butter across the toast. 'So what do we all have to say to each other while they're out of the room?'

Irene ran through her mental list of languages and their applicability to this alternate. She wouldn't put it past Vale to be listening to the conversation. Imperial Russia had conquered China and Japan a while back in this alternate, so the odds were against Vale knowing Japanese. However, Bradamant did know it, and all things considered, she rather thought Kai would as well. '*Last night I told Vale the basics of the Library,*' she said bluntly in Japanese.

The toast cracked and splintered in Bradamant's hand. '*You what?*'

Irene returned the other woman's glare. '*We were attacked by Alberich on our way back here.*' She decided to leave Kai's contribution out of it. '*He trapped us in a carriage in the river and left us to drown. We escaped, but after that I had to give Vale some sort of explanation.*'

Now she recognized the churning in her guts, the uncertainty in her mind. It was the nervous reaction she always used to get when reporting to Bradamant, decades back, when she had been a student and Bradamant had been mentoring her in the field. It was, apparently, something she still had to get over, if she could figure out how.

Bradamant hadn't been the type to insist on formality

while Irene reported back. No, they'd always sat together or facing each other, as comfortable as one could *possibly* ask. And every time Irene had tried to explain something, she had been wrong. Always.

Bradamant considered the reply, clearly looking for holes. '*You could have given him a story about a secret society,*' she said. '*That's what I told Inspector Singh.*'

Irene was going to answer in the negative again, say something like *I didn't think that it would work* or *I couldn't think of a way to make it convincing,* when she felt Kai's eyes on her. He clearly understood what they were saying. He was looking at her with something that took her a moment to identify as trust, as expectation that she could handle things. She had to deserve that trust.

She composed herself, took a firm grip on her cup of coffee, and turned to meet Bradamant's eyes. '*I took a field decision that Vale would be more useful and cooperative if he knew the truth – well, some of the truth,*' she said. '*In this place and time, I am not a courtier to present an opinion to a king, but a general in the field, expected to handle things as they arise for the good of the Library. Vale is a highly intelligent man, well informed on the current situation and trained in noticing discrepancies. Alberich had already made reference to the Library, and I was forced to use my own abilities to break free from his trap.*' Out of the corner of her eye, she saw Kai relax a fraction, leaning back into his chair. '*An incomplete story would only have roused Vale's distrust. We have enough enemies in this place and time as it is . . . Belphegor.*'

Bradamant snorted. '*My actions were a valid response to the situation.*'

'*Do you still have the books?*'

Bradamant hesitated a moment. Possibly she could guess what Irene was about to suggest. '*I do. Some of them are rarities, you know. They would be appreciated by other Librarians.*'

'*I have no doubt,*' Irene said wryly. '*You have always had excellent taste. But it may be necessary to return those stolen books to their owners in order to secure cooperation.*'

Bradamant put down her toast very deliberately, and stared at Irene. '*You have no authority to order me to do such a thing. Or are you planning to turn me over to your new friends instead?*'

'*Don't be ridiculous,*' Irene said, and tried to ignore the mental voice that pointed out that yes, it would certainly convince Vale and Singh that she was on their side. And Bradamant could easily escape from any prison cell anyway. '*I am assuming that you were sent by one of our superiors. Why?*'

'*To find the Grimm book,*' Bradamant answered. '*And yes, let me reassure you: I do have orders from one of our superiors to that effect.*'

Irene tried not to show her relief. Bradamant was still loyal to the Library. A number of unpleasant possibilities had just been ruled out. Even if there was some sort of internal dispute going on inside the Library about who was supposed to be fetching the damned book, at least she didn't have to worry about Bradamant being in league with Alberich. '*It's possible that our target is one of those books that's linked to the whole alternate,*' she said. '*The fact that Alberich's after it shows just how important it is. And you could only know of my mission from someone highly placed. Surely these factors make it an absolute priority for us to work together to find the book and bring it to the Library? Or do you have some other goal?*'

Bradamant brushed crumbs off her fingers. The toast lay on her plate, slowly cooling. '*Certainly my highest priority is to bring the book back,*' she replied. '*But I cannot see why Alberich should want to kill you. It isn't as if you have the book.*'

'*And you do?*' Kai put in, his tone highly formal. But it

wasn't the formality of junior-to-senior: it was the formality of someone with authority in his own right, to a peer in another discipline.

From the look on his face, he realized that a second too late.

Bradamant didn't seem to mind. She graced him with a delicate smile, and Irene wondered if anyone who didn't know her would have recognized the calculation in her eyes. '*If I did,*' she said, '*I wouldn't be here now.*'

'*I think we would profit from a council of war,*' Irene said. '*Or we will all assuredly hang separately.*'

Bradamant thought about it, dusting her fingers again and again until not even the smallest crumb could have remained on them. Finally she said, '*I will agree to that much. For the moment.*'

Irene nodded. She turned towards the door. 'You can come in now, gentlemen,' she called. *She*'d have been listening if it had been the other way round, after all.

Vale opened the door, and held it for Singh to enter. Both men looked a little irritated, Singh more than Vale – but then, Irene reminded herself, who knew what Bradamant had been telling him last night? There were few things worse than thinking you knew everything about secret goings-on, and then finding out you'd been fed a nice plausible mess of lies.

Vale occupied his armchair again. Singh looked at Kai in a way which suggested that *he* usually got the comfortable chair Kai was sitting in, then pulled over the high-backed chair from by the desk. He cleared off a stack of newspapers, and settled down with a snort, flipping out notebook and pen.

'I have been discussing the situation with Inspector Singh here,' Vale said. He steepled his fingers. 'It has become quite clear that we are all in pursuit of the same thing. Several members of the Iron Brotherhood were questioned last night – with Madame Bradamant's cooperation – ' he nodded to Bradamant – 'which has established some interesting facts.'

'May I ask what you've found?' Irene said, glancing at Kai, who looked impatient for news.

Inspector Singh regarded her with the same wary distrust that he was displaying towards Bradamant. What fun. 'You may recall the explosion a couple of nights ago, under the Opera House?'

'I'm afraid I only know the very basic details about that,' Irene said. 'Was it related to the Iron Brotherhood?'

Inspector Singh nodded. 'It was indeed, madam. They happened to meet there, and unfortunately the blast took out a number of their more senior members.'

'Unfortunately?' Kai said. 'Surely, if these people are criminals . . .'

Inspector Singh shook his head. 'Your reaction is understandable, sir, but you must understand that we have infiltrated some of these societies to a degree. We know who runs them, Mr Strongrock, and we know who's in charge. We have some idea of which way they're going to jump in a crisis, even if we can't bring any charges against them. For the moment,' he added ominously. 'The unfortunate result of this little affair was that a woman of whom we know little is now leading the society. The Grand Hammer, I believe they call her. And this woman is, shall we say, an unknown quantity. I don't like unknown quantities, Mr Strongrock. They don't fill my notebook and they don't go to prison as they should.'

Irene leaned forward. 'Are you saying, Inspector, that this "unknown quantity" is linked to last night's events at the Liechtenstein Embassy?'

'You would be quite correct, Miss Winters,' Inspector

Singh said. He rearranged his lips in a thin distrustful smile. 'Now from what Mr Vale here has told me, I'm inclined to wonder if this woman is linked to the person you know as "Alberich". Given that one of the aims of last night's little exposition, alligators and all, was to search Lord Silver's rooms while he was otherwise occupied.'

'For a book,' Vale interjected.

'Indeed,' Inspector Singh agreed. 'That's what our questioning confirmed. For a very specific book. The same book that was stolen from Lord Wyndham recently by a certain thief. Or should I say, believed to have been stolen?' He shot a glance at Bradamant. His face was inexpressive enough, but his eyes were very dark and very angry.

Bradamant seemed to crumple in on herself. If she had had a handkerchief, no doubt she would have held it to her eyes and sniffled bravely. As it was, her lower lip quavered and her eyes were wide and limpid. 'If Irene has told you about the Library,' she said, 'then there's nothing more that I can say. I admit that I took,' Irene admired her careful avoidance of the word stolen, 'some books in order to make the Grimm's disappearance look unimportant. But I certainly didn't kill Lord Wyndham. Why would I have wanted to? I didn't even know the man.'

Irene raised her hand to get Vale and Singh's attention. 'Would you mind if I ask Bradamant a couple of questions, gentlemen? To fill in a part of the story on my side.'

'Certainly, Miss Winters,' Vale said. Singh gave her a brief nod.

Irene turned back to Bradamant. 'I saw a card in Wyndham's safe. It was embossed with a gold mask and signed with the name Belphegor. Was that you?'

Bradamant sighed. 'Yes. It was. I had the plans of the house from a local contact—'

'This Dominic Aubrey person?' Vale cut in.

Bradamant glanced to Irene, with an *I see you've been giving away all our local secrets* look, then nodded. 'He and Wyndham had been acquaintances for a while. I think Aubrey may have actually been rather indiscreet in what he told Wyndham, but that's a different problem.' *Just as you've been with Vale,* was the unspoken message. 'Anyhow, I came in by the roof while Wyndham was at his party downstairs. It was comparatively easy to deactivate the alarms on the display case where he kept the book – '

'Oh, was it now,' Singh muttered.

– 'and after I'd taken the book, I left the card in the case before leaving, by the roof again. I don't know why it should have been in the safe.' She shrugged.

'What time was this?' Singh asked.

'About half past eleven,' Bradamant answered. 'The party was in full swing downstairs. I didn't expect anyone to come up to Wyndham's study at that point.'

Singh nodded. He turned to Irene. 'According to our forensic specialists, Lord Wyndham was slaughtered somewhere between midnight and one o'clock. It is difficult to tell with vampires, but the fact that his head was found on the palings outside at one o'clock gives us some idea of the time frame.'

Irene wasn't sure whether or not that was supposed to be a joke. 'I see,' she said neutrally. 'So in that case, who put the card in the safe? Lord Wyndham himself?'

'It seems the most likely hypothesis,' Vale agreed. 'The man – I apologize, the vampire – was beheaded in his study, at his desk. Some of the other guests at the party said that he went upstairs at midnight, saying that he was going to arrange a surprise.'

Kai nodded. 'So when he walked in to find the book gone, he determined to preserve Belphegor's card for future investigation. Though it seems overly careful to put it in the safe rather than simply leave it in a drawer of his desk. But then he was attacked?'

'That is so,' Singh said. 'By members of the Iron Brotherhood. I have information from some of our agents. We believe they must have been masquerading as guests. They simply lopped his head off, walked out normally, and impaled it upon the palings as they left.'

Irene frowned. 'But then Wyndham's murder was before the Opera explosion and change in command in the Brotherhood. Is there a connection?'

Singh and Bradamant traded glances. 'That is a very interesting question, Miss Winters,' Singh said. 'But at the moment, I am more interested in knowing the whereabouts of the book which Madame Bradamant stole.'

Bradamant regarded him stonily. 'It was a fake.'

For a moment everyone was talking, mostly along the lines of *What?* and *Are you certain?*

'And I know it was a fake,' Bradamant said, cutting through the noise, 'because when I took it back to my superior, he looked at it and then explained to me that he was not interested in facsimiles. Especially those which were missing certain relevant parts.'

'Which relevant parts?' Irene demanded. She was fairly sure who the superior in question must have been. Bradamant answered directly to Kostchei, just as Irene answered directly to Coppelia. The possibility of someone else having been involved, and giving Bradamant orders . . . well, it wasn't impossible, but it was too unlikely. At the moment the principles of Occam's Razor, starting with the most obvious answer, seemed the best plan. 'Did he tell you?'

'No,' Bradamant said bitterly. For a moment her face betrayed genuine emotion: anger, bitterness, and sheer thwarted curiosity. 'I was given the strong impression that it was better for me not to know.'

Irene worked out times and dates in her head. 'Then, when you met myself and,' she almost said *Kai*, but caught herself in time, 'Mr Strongrock, on our way to our assignment, this was after you'd discovered the book was a fake?'

'It was,' Bradamant agreed. *See how honest and forthcoming I'm being*, her vague smile said, her expression under control again. 'I thought that if I could intercept you on the way, then I could try to find the real book without your interference. Pardon my phrasing.'

'Of course,' Irene said blandly. She was conscious of the three men listening. 'So after that, you decided to come through anyhow?'

'I had the advantage of already knowing this place,' Bradamant said. 'I didn't expect you to work as fast as you did.'

Irene glanced round at the three men. Somehow they shared a similar demeanour, whatever their reaction to this new information. Perhaps it was a kind of aristocratic poise, an inbuilt certainty that the world was going to co-operate with their needs.

She wished she shared it.

'Wyndham is the obvious candidate to have created the fake, since records show he had the original book,' Vale said briskly. 'Inspector Singh, if you would – '

'Of course,' Singh said. He pulled a sheaf of papers from his briefcase. 'The clerks and difference engines at the Yard have tabulated records of Lord Wyndham's last few weeks. He only obtained the book two and a half weeks ago, at an auction of the late Mr Bonhomme's effects. And it was certified as genuine by the auction house at the time, which resulted in a quite remarkable price being set on it.'

Vale nodded. 'I managed to trace one of the proxy bids to Lord Silver, through the solicitor that he employed. We can be sure of his interest.'

'There were some threats after the auction, too,' Singh went on. 'This all resulted in the book being under tight guard. So if he had the fake made, then it was within that time period.'

'Could it have been done that quickly?' Irene asked, startled.

Vale leaned back in his chair. 'There are precisely three forgers in London at the present moment who could have done it,' he said. 'And even they would have taken at least two weeks to do so.'

'So there are,' Singh agreed. 'And a delivery came from one of them—'

Vale held up a hand. 'Matthias?'

'No, Levandis,' Singh said smugly.

'I thought Matthias was the one he'd dealt with before,' Vale said.

'Possibly why he chose not to deal with him this time,' Singh said. 'In any case, one of our people was watching Levandis at the time – the Severn matter, you know – and she confirms that he was making daily trips to Wyndham's house. The servants agree that he called, but they had him down as a workman doing some alterations on the panelling in Wyndham's study. They can confirm that was where he was spending his time daily. He sent a final delivery to Wyndham three days before Wyndham's murder, and didn't visit again after that.'

Vale nodded. 'Convenient.'

'Sometimes we get lucky,' Singh agreed. 'She wasn't able to determine what was going on at the time, but given this other business . . .'

'Wait,' Kai said, frowning. 'Assuming that Wyndham

211

had a forgery made for some reason and then displayed it, what did he do with the original?'

'He hadn't given it to Lord Silver,' Irene said thoughtfully, remembering the encounter in Wyndham's study. She saw Singh's lips twitch in an expression of distaste. 'Silver was searching Wyndham's study and his safe, and I think it was the book that he was looking for. Maybe Wyndham had intended to give it to Silver, or promised it to him.'

'If Silver's involved, there could be all sorts of reasons Wyndham might have had a fake made,' Bradamant agreed. 'If the book was hugely valuable, Wyndham might have wanted to safeguard it by only displaying the fake. Or perhaps he meant it as bait for Silver to attempt to steal it; we know that the Fae love things they can't have. Also they had a very close, if antagonistic relationship at times – the papers have made a great deal of that. Maybe Wyndham wanted to show off by loaning Silver the real thing, or had even promised him it to repay a favour. Or maybe he meant to fob him off with the fake. It's impossible to know without questioning Silver.'

Or maybe the copy was meant for Alberich, Irene thought. Was that where Alberich fitted in all this? But if that was the case, then why didn't Alberich already have the book?

'Lord Silver was certainly Wyndham's best-known ally and contact,' Vale was saying. 'As well as one of his best-known enemies. Fae relationships.' His lips pursed in disapproval. 'But in that case, the book may still be in Wyndham's house.'

Singh was shaking his head. 'If it is, sir, then it's very well hidden.' Irene suspected the *sir* was due to the presence of outsiders. 'We, ah, searched the place thoroughly after Lord Wyndham's murder. We did find a number of interesting items and documents, which have been enlightening with respect to other cases, but the Grimm book was not there.'

'It could perhaps be *very* well hidden,' Kai said hopefully.

'We had our best searchers on the job, Mr Strongrock,' Singh said, in a tone which closed the subject.

'So the real book is not in Wyndham's house,' Irene re-iterated, thinking aloud, 'and the forgery Bradamant stole couldn't have been started until Wyndham actually had the book. This would have taken at least two weeks to create. So was it moved during that period or copied before it arrived?' She turned to Singh. 'Can we confirm that the book entered Wyndham's house directly after the auction, and remained in a public place there until it was stolen?'

Singh nodded. 'We can. And after it arrived, testimony from the servants confirms that the book – or a very good copy of it – was in Lord Wyndham's study all day every day, madam. The maid who dusted it was quite definite on the subject. Lord Wyndham wanted it kept in perfect condition.'

'Very good. So ... either the real thing or an excellent copy was on display throughout, but Bradamant definitely picked up the fake. And the real book cannot have been removed until the forgery was ready. If the forgery was only ready a few days before Wyndham's murder – given that the auction was a little over two weeks before the murder, and the forgery would have taken two weeks – then the real book must have been taken from the house in those last few days. That is, if it isn't there now.'

'An interesting train of thought,' Vale murmured, and Irene had to work to suppress a blush of pride. *It's nice to have just one little daydream come true. And it's even better when it's actually deserved.* 'But why not keep it in the house?'

'There is a risk of theft – from someone other than Belphegor, that is,' Singh suggested. 'His safe might be impregnable to the Fae, given that it was cold iron, but human thieves could have opened it.' He gave Bradamant a meaningful look. 'If the real book wasn't hidden very thoroughly, and it came to light, it would show Wyndham's display copy was a fake – whatever the reason for all this cloak-and-dagger subterfuge. I wonder what he was up to . . .' Finally he nodded to Irene. 'I agree with your theory, madam. Although it does mean we'd have to assume Lord Wyndham handled the book himself, rather than passing it to some agent or third party to deal with.'

'Let us commence with that as a working hypothesis,' Vale said briskly. 'In those three days, where *did* he go? And when could he have been carrying a book with him? How large is the book, in any case?'

'A large hardback,' Bradamant said, sketching the shape in the air with her hands. 'Leather-bound and illustrated. Perhaps six inches by eight. Impossible to conceal under a fashionable coat. It could be carried in a briefcase easily enough.'

'Excellent,' Vale said. 'That limits the possibilities. Lord Wyndham did not favour overcoats. What can you give us based on that, Inspector?'

'Just a moment, please, sir,' Singh said, flicking through the papers. 'I have some statements here from Lord Wyndham's valet, concerning his comings and goings over the last few days before his murder. We managed to assemble quite a timetable of the gentleman's movements while we were establishing who might have wanted to kill him. He didn't make that many outings during that period, so I believe we should be able to rule out a number of possibilities.'

Tension hung in the room. The seconds went by painfully slowly. Irene considered suggesting that they all help by taking a paper each and checking them separately. Then she decided it was a stupid idea. Then she considered it again. Then she watched Singh's moustache and beard twitching as he muttered under his breath and turned pages.

With an effort, she glanced towards the window rather than watching Singh read. The weather outside still seemed to be good – for this alternate, anyhow – with high-flying clouds and sunshine. The dream-catcher that she'd noticed earlier was dark against the pale sky.

She wondered what sort of dreams Vale had, that he, sceptic and logician, should hang a dream-catcher in the window.

'Ah,' Singh finally said. 'I think we may have something here.'

CHAPTER SIXTEEN

'The day before his murder, Lord Wyndham visited his bank,' Singh said. 'It wasn't a scheduled visit. Apparently he couldn't be seen immediately, and he made a few complaints, which caused some of the tellers to recall his visit when we were questioning them. While none of the statements there confirm that he was carrying a briefcase, they don't say that he wasn't either. It'd be quite the normal sort of thing for a gentleman consulting his banker to be carrying.'

'Who did he bank with?' Bradamant asked.

'Lloyds,' Singh said. He frowned. 'I'll need to get a search warrant if we're to look inside his safe deposit box, sir. That'll take a few hours at least. And it'd be easier with a bit of evidence that we could take before the judge.'

There was a glum silence throughout the room.

'Not impossible, of course,' Singh added. 'But it might get us a warrant a trifle faster.'

'If the Iron Brotherhood were behind last night's attack on the Embassy, and they're looking for this book too, then they might try and steal the deposit box from Lloyds,' Irene offered hopefully.

Singh looked disappointed in her. 'I said evidence, madam. Not conjecture.'

'Well!' Vale brought his hands together in a brisk clap. 'Inspector, I suggest you set that in motion – and if there's anywhere else that the gentleman might have concealed the book, we can review the possibilities while we're waiting. Is there anywhere else that's reasonably plausible, or even possible?'

'There is one other thing,' Singh said. He turned back to one of the earlier pages in his bundle of papers. 'Apparently Lord Wyndham did regularly donate books to various museums around London. They were usually ones which he had collected earlier, but which were no longer of interest to him or his associates.'

Irene twitched at the very notion. Give books *away*? 'How very frivolous,' she finally said.

'More altruistic than keeping them to himself,' Vale corrected her. 'Please go on, Inspector.'

Singh rustled his papers, just enough to emphasize that he was in charge of the situation. 'Two days before Lord Wyndham's murder, he sent a small box of such books to the Natural History Museum. Herbariums, bestiaries, that sort of thing. My men looked into it as a matter of course while in the process of investigating the goings-on before his murder. The clerk to whom they spoke said that nobody had got round to looking at it yet. Please don't stare at me like that, madam. It's quite regular for persons of quality to make donations to the museums. It might be months before anyone gets round to checking it, unless they'd been specifically notified that there was something of importance in it.'

Kai frowned. 'Are you suggesting that he hid the genuine book in the crate of donations? Wasn't that, well, extremely risky? If even one person had found it there, he would have lost it. His bank deposit box seems much more likely.'

'No, I can see the logic of it,' Bradamant contradicted

him. 'If there is a backlog of such donations, it could have been as much as a year before anyone opened it, and he could have asked for it back if he needed it to present to Silver – or to anyone else,' she added thoughtfully.

'Well, the gentleman was a vampire,' Vale agreed, 'so it would fit certain scheming aspects of his character – even though one should probably not speak ill of the *undead*.' He paused, but nobody laughed. 'Oh, very well. Are there any other possible ways by which the book could have been smuggled out of the house, Inspector?'

'Possible, certainly, sir,' Singh said cautiously, 'but none plausible. I had my men check the cellars very thoroughly. There are no connections to the local sewers, or to the Underground. Of course, if he trusted it to one of his servants, then we have a whole new set of possibilities. If that's the case, then we might do better watching the black market for such things to see if it shows up. Or we could see how the Iron Brotherhood go about finding it – if they're after the damn thing too.'

Irene and Bradamant glanced at each other, and Irene could guess what the other woman was thinking. If they did have to resort to scouring the black market, or liaising with secret society members, then it might be better for Bradamant to break away from the group. She could then use any contacts that she'd made as 'Belphegor', rather than be known to be working with Singh and Vale. Of course, Bradamant could then find the book, and be the one who took it back to the Library. So which was more important for Irene? Finding the book herself, or making sure that it was found? She knew what the answer *should* be, but that didn't mean that she liked it.

Vale and Singh were also looking thoughtfully at each other. Then Vale leapt to his feet. 'Well, then! I believe this calls for a visit to the Natural History Museum. Ladies, Mr

Strongrock, I trust I can prevail upon you to accompany us. Inspector, do you have a cab downstairs? You can give us a lift there before going on to get your search warrant.'

Singh looked at Bradamant, Irene and Kai with less than total enthusiasm, but controlled his expression. 'I have one, sir, but I believe that we may require a second one if we are not to subject the ladies to unduly close quarters.'

'I'd rather not delay,' Irene broke in. A growing sense of urgency was pricking at her. Maybe the bank deposit box was the more likely possibility, but what if they were wrong? 'Inspector, do you think you were followed here?'

Singh frowned. 'I can't deny that it is possible, madam. Not that anyone would find it strange. A great many people from the Yard come to visit Mr Vale here, and very frequently at that.'

Vale stepped across to the window, and stood to one side of it, peering down at the street below. 'I can't say whether they followed you, Inspector, or whether they're watching me,' he reported, 'but Hairy Jimmy of the Whitechapel Roaring Boys is watching my front door.'

'That'll be Lord Silver, I believe,' Singh said, slipping his papers back into his case. 'The Iron Brotherhood wouldn't have anything to do with werewolves.'

Vale considered for a moment. 'Well, with London traffic the way it is at this hour of the morning, even if they are going to the museum, we should still make it there before they do.' He snatched a coat from the overloaded hatstand, flung it on, and caught up his hat and sword cane. 'Let us be off.'

Kai had also sprung to his feet in wild enthusiasm, and was busy finding his own hat and coat, which allowed Irene to tug Bradamant into the passage for a word in private.

'What is it?' Bradamant asked quietly.

'What are the identifying marks for the book?' She saw Bradamant begin to say something, and held up a hand to stop her. 'Look. You said that you've already been fooled once with a fake. If it was your superior who sent you back – if you're actually here with *permission* . . .' She saw Bradamant's eyes narrow in anger at that. 'Then he wouldn't have sent you back again without giving you some sort of way to identify the genuine article. Are you really going to risk losing the book because you're not prepared to share that with me? A book which may be that important to this world?'

Bradamant's glare was pure poison. 'Don't rush me,' she said. 'I'm thinking.'

'Think fast,' Irene said. 'Vale will be coming to find us in a moment.'

'Tale eighty-seven,' Bradamant said. 'The Story of the Stone from the Tower of Babel. If it's there, then it's genuine.'

'Thank you,' Irene said. She picked up her hat and veil, and skewered them in place with a hatpin.

Bradamant seemed about to say something but, with a visible struggle, managed to contain herself. She adjusted her own hat, then swept out, calling sweetly, 'We're coming!'

A few seconds later they were jumbled together into a hansom cab and heading to the Natural History Museum. From what Irene could remember of London's geography, it was at least half an hour away – more, if the traffic was bad. Singh had muttered the instructions to the driver rather than shouting them loud enough to be heard across the street, and was now brooding in the corner of the cab. Kai, Vale and Singh were all sandwiched onto one seat, while Irene and Bradamant shared the seat opposite and tried not to look too comfortable.

'Do you know who we need to speak to when we get there, Inspector?' Vale asked Singh.

Singh nodded. 'I have the name from last time – Professor Betony, and even if you can't find her, then you can find her office in the Department of Cryptidology downstairs. With any luck, you can be in and out of there before anyone who might be following you catches up. We can then establish if the book's here or not. And I'll be getting that search warrant in the meantime.' He gave Bradamant one of his flat looks. 'And then this young lady can return the other books that she made off with.'

Bradamant flushed, lowered her eyes, played with the strap of her handbag. She looked in every way like an innocent young woman who had been led into crime by bad company and wanted nothing more than to make amends. Irene had to admire the performance, especially given Bradamant's probable feelings of rage towards her.

'Do you often get sent on missions like this for this Library of yours, Miss Winter?' Vale asked Irene. He tried to make it sound like casual conversation, but she could feel the deeper curiosity beneath his words.

'This one is a bit more . . . ah, dramatic, than most of them,' Irene said, a little relieved that Vale was asking her rather than Bradamant. And that was perfectly true. She'd had dozens of missions where she'd simply wandered in, quietly bought a copy of the book in question, and left without anyone so much as noticing her. And at least ten assignments where there had been some minor illegality involved, but none had featured chases through the streets, dangerously flamboyant personalities or cyborg alligators. 'There was a time before this when I was in France.' Well, a France. There were a lot of Frances. 'I was trying to secure a copy of a book about alchemy by someone called Michael Maier, a few hundred years old. It was called . . .' She frowned. 'Something about nine triads, and it contained intellectual songs about the resurrection of the phoenix, or something along those lines. I ended up getting involved with a group of Templars and having to leave in something of a hurry.' About five minutes before they'd broken the door down, to be precise, but no need to tell Vale *that* bit.

'And then there was the cat burglar affair,' Bradamant said sweetly.

Irene felt her hands tighten in her gloves. She forced herself to stay calm. 'Yes,' she agreed. 'There was that.'

Kai leaned forward. 'What *was* this cat burglar affair?' he asked.

Bradamant smiled in a sympathetic, understanding, non-judgemental sort of way. 'Oh, it was when I was mentoring Irene, when she was first working in the field. We were trying to locate a book which had been stolen by a notorious thief. Everyone knew who she was. The best police officers in the city were watching her every move and still they couldn't catch her. And when Irene and I were trying to investigate her, well . . .' She smiled again, tolerantly. 'The lady in question *was* very charming. And it isn't as if I was in any significant danger while Irene was so, shall we say, "preoccupied" with her. And I managed to find the book, so all's well that ends well.'

Irene looked down at her knees and bit her tongue. It hadn't been like that at all, it hadn't, but that was all the story that anyone would know now. Bradamant had cheerfully spread it all over the Library in murmured detail, and anything that Irene had said then, or could say now, would simply make her sound as if she was making excuses. The alternate had been one with a very specific set of social standards. Theft was a comparatively petty transgression there, even if it was illegal; immoral behaviour was the sort of thing which could entirely destroy a woman's reputation. Bradamant had set the whole thing up, arranging an identity for Irene as a freelance thief herself, suggesting that perhaps the woman could be persuaded to hand the book over, and even fixing up an assignation. And then she'd simply burgled the woman's house while Irene had been sincerely trying to talk her round. And Irene had been left floundering and making excuses, and trying to explain what had happened to the other woman's house, and her possessions, and her reputation . . .

She had come out of it with a bitter, lasting fury against Bradamant, and a resolution that she would never do the same thing to someone who actually trusted her. Never. *Never.*

And if she tried to object now, it'd be just the same as before. She'd look as if she was trying to make excuses for something which must have been her fault if she was making excuses for it. She'd look guilty. She'd look petty . . .

She'd look like a child.

'Yes,' she agreed, with a smile as pleasant as Bradamant's own. 'All's well that ends well.'

Kai glanced from Irene to Bradamant, then back again. 'Of course, this is the first time I've worked with Miss Winters,' he said, a fraction too quickly. 'I was rather hoping we might be sent to fetch some poetry at some point. I have a high regard for poetry. My father and uncles always felt that it was very important for anyone who had any claim to culture.'

'Hm!' Singh leaned forward, looking genuinely interested. 'The epic poem, or shorter forms?'

The conversation shifted, much to Irene's relief, into a debate on poetry that lasted for most of the journey. She herself was mostly silent, being more used to acquiring it than reading it. Bradamant put in a word or two in favour of the Elizabethan styles, and fortunately there had been an Elizabeth on this alternate. Vale had a fondness for Persian poets, though his pronunciation of their names was bad enough that Singh twitched. Singh himself refused to consider anything shorter than an epic poem as worthy of serious study. And Kai, not too surprisingly, favoured classical Chinese modes, with a passing nod to constructions like the sestina and villanelle.

It took a moment for her to realize that she was actually enjoying herself. Even if she wasn't contributing much to the conversation, she was taking part in it. She was speaking her mind, she was having an honest exchange of opinion, she was . . .

Among equals, the back of her mind supplied, with the unwillingness that came with the recognition of an unwanted truth. *You are discussing a common interest without worrying about betrayal or about losing them, and you are enjoying it. How long is it since you did that?*

She looked around at her party's various interested expressions and felt as if she had known them for years. It was ridiculous, and yet . . . it wasn't unwelcome.

The traffic outside had descended from merely bad to abominable, and their cab's progress had slowed to a walking pace, with occasional jolts at the traffic lights.

'There isn't any risk of us being overtaken, is there?' Irene asked nervously.

'Very unlikely, madam,' Singh answered. 'For that, they would need to know where we're going, and there are far too many places where we could be going for them to be certain.'

'There is one thing that I've been wondering about,' Kai said. 'While I know that you have difference engines and calculating mechanisms, I have yet to see any sort of long-distance communication device. Now I – ' He became conscious of Irene's glare. 'That is, hasn't that sort of thing been investigated?'

Vale sighed. 'Another of your alternate-world advanced pieces of technology, Mr Strongrock? There has indeed been some research into the subject, but it proved simply too prone to demonic possession. While there have been a few successes with various forms of theologically based shieldings, on the whole the area cannot be said to reward investigation. Certainly it would be unsafe to put such things in the hands of the masses.'

'But how do zeppelin pilots communicate with the ground?' Irene asked.

Vale sniffed, and Singh looked disgusted. 'Fae magic,' Vale said. 'Another reason why Liechtenstein has so heavy an influence on the zeppelin industry. I believe they also make some machinery for submersibles, but of course the large quantity of iron reduces the magic's efficiency.'

Irene nodded, and wished that some of this had been in the information pack which Dominic Aubrey had provided. He'd completely neglected the subject: there had been plenty of material on the current non-Fae situation, but hardly any on the Fae themselves, their political implications, and their ongoing plans for world domination – since Fae always had plans for world domination. (It was more dramatic that way, after all.) Possibly he'd thought that she would be able to avoid Fae interference – though, given Wyndham's involvement with Silver, that would scarcely have been possible. Could someone have managed to remove part of the information pack? And if so, how and when?

She also wished that she was sitting on Kai's side of the cab so that she could kick his ankle without it being obvious. Discussions along the lines of 'so why haven't you introduced this bit of technology in your alternate world' rarely went well. Often there were perfectly good reasons why it hadn't been introduced, and you opened a whole can of worms by just asking. And on the few occasions when it simply hadn't been invented and you had indeed introduced the alternate to a whole new concept, you could end up with problems like cold fusion. (Not that she'd been involved in *that* one, but stories had got around.)

The cab jolted to a stop, and the driver leaned down to the opening. 'I'm sorry, sir, but I'm afraid as how traffic's very bad today, it'll be another ten minutes before I could reach the steps of the museum – though you can see its wall there. If it won't be inconveniencing you, sir, yourself and your friends might be finding it easier to walk from here.'

'Certainly,' Vale exclaimed, flinging the cab door open. He glanced up to the driver. 'Wait here. We shouldn't be long. Here.' He tossed a coin up to the driver. There was a keen energy driving his movements as they neared possible action. 'For your time.'

Kai assisted Irene out of the cab, giving a little extra squeeze to her wrist as he helped her down the step. 'Almost there,' he murmured.

Bradamant coughed meaningfully. With an apologetic look, Kai let go of Irene and turned to help Bradamant down as well.

The streets were full of traffic, moving slowly with a lot of shouting, and the air was full of smog. Irene folded her veil up across her face, and stepped over to the museum wall to let people hurry past. The others joined her, waiting for Singh, who was talking to the driver. The wall was stained a deep filthy brown from decades of ingrained smoke and smog. The surrounding buildings were old brick and marble, similarly smog-stained. Many of the people bustling by were carrying books or briefcases. From what she remembered of the geography of some Londons, there was a university near here, sited conveniently near the museum.

A passing zeppelin high above caught the corner of her eye, and she glanced upwards. Several small zeppelins were moored to the roof of the museum, with pennants hanging from them emblazoned with the museum's name. As she looked further down the street, she could see more of them moored to the roof of other large buildings.

'Ah,' Vale said, following her line of sight. 'Splendid contraptions, aren't they? And so much faster than a cab, but sadly not as controllable. One of those little skimmers can make it across the Channel and back without needing to refuel.'

'Across the Channel?' Irene asked. 'Does the museum use them for such trips, then?'

Vale nodded. 'They can transfer important small items and particular rarities. I understand that most large museums keep a few these days. And of course, much less risk of theft.' His narrow gaze shifted to Bradamant for a moment, and brooded on her oblivious back. It seemed that he hadn't forgiven or forgotten any little details about cat burglars.

'If you are from an alternate world yourself,' Vale said, turning back to her, 'what is it like?'

Irene noticed that Kai had edged close enough to listen. The problem was that she didn't have a good answer. 'It was . . . well, it was just another world. The technology was a little more controlled than it is here. There weren't so many zeppelins, and there weren't any vampires or werewolves. My parents used to take me to the Library as often as they could, but I spent a lot of time in boarding school. It was in Switzerland, and very good for languages.' She wasn't going to mention some of the other things that they'd taught. The school had prided itself on sending out pupils who were ready for anything, and some parts of that world had been very dangerous.

'I did visit other alternates with my parents too,' Irene added. 'Sometimes when they were on a mission, and they didn't think that it was too dangerous. Sometimes I was even helpful.' She found herself smiling. 'And there were years in the Library, though there weren't many other children there. But I had to grow up mainly outside the Library.'

'Why is that?' Vale asked. 'Surely it would have been better for you to stay there and be tutored in safety, rather than taken into danger?'

Irene knew she was on dangerous ground here. There were some things that she shouldn't tell him. For his own safety. 'Time passes differently in the Library,' she eventually said. 'My parents wanted me to grow up naturally. Well, moderately naturally. And if I was to be a useful Librarian, I had to know how to function outside the place.'

'Is that why they usually recruit from outside the Library, rather than the children of Librarians?' Kai asked.

Irene nodded. 'That, and . . . well, to be honest, I don't think Librarians tend to have children very often, and even then there's no guarantee they'd want to become Librarians in turn. I think I'm the only one in a generation or so.'

She caught a movement out of the corner of her eye. Bradamant was turning away, but not quite fast enough to hide the expression on her face. There had been a corrosive jealousy in her eyes. Irene didn't think that she'd seen it in the other woman before . . . or had she? She'd tried to forget so many other things about Bradamant, and failed so badly.

Singh walked up to Vale, having finished his low-voiced conversation with the cab-driver. 'I'll send the cab back here for you, sir, once he's dropped me off at the Old Bailey.

It shouldn't take you long to check whether the book's here.'

Irene controlled her impatience. It was a great relief to think that in half an hour she could even be heading back to the Library, book in hand, Kai in tow, Bradamant in ... well, she didn't *consciously* want to think about Bradamant in disgrace. After all, everyone had a failure now and again. Things like glamorous cat burglars. Whatever.

Maybe an hour. She didn't want to be too optimistic.

Inside the museum, the building widened out into a glorious cathedral-like hall, with a high curving ceiling inset with windows, and a mosaic-inlaid floor. A diplodocus skeleton leered down bonily from high above the heads of the onlookers, and some harassed-sounding mother implored her little darling not to try and climb on its foot. A white marble statue at the head of the room's main stairway overlooked the whole thing with an air of dignified approval. It was about the only piece of non-smog-stained marble that Irene had seen in this alternate London.

She supposed that it was interesting enough. But it was sadly lacking in books.

Vale clearly knew his way around and led them up one of the staircases, through several minor rooms of exhibits, then past a wide range of stuffed animals, stuffed plants, and possibly stuffed mineral deposits (she didn't have time to check). Next they hurried down another staircase and into an even more cluttered and confused set of corridors, which was clearly where work actually got done. Crates were stacked against the walls, many with notes attached saying OPEN THIS TODAY. The only things that weren't dirty or dusty were the office doors' brass nameplates. These gleamed with a rather desperate shine, as if trying to compensate for their surroundings.

'Here we are,' Vale said, pausing before one which

apparently belonged to Professor Amelia Betony, MSc, PhD, and Doctor of Divinity. 'This was the person to whom the crate was addressed. Let's see if we can eliminate this possibility.' He shoved the door open without bothering to knock.

Inside, the low-ceilinged office was larger than expected. The small desk in the corner was piled high with unopened envelopes and packages, and the large table in the middle of the room was strewn with bones, gluepots and measuring devices. The air smelt of dust and drying solvent. Then a young man entered from a side-door, a steaming mug of tea in his hand. He stood there, blinking at the four of them.

'Mr Ramsbottom, I presume?' Vale said, stepping forward briskly. 'Professor Betony's secretary?'

The young man nodded and peered at Vale, and his eyes widened in recognition. 'Ah, I'm so terribly sorry, but the Professor is away on the Egypt expedition, if you were wanting to consult her over a case – '

'Fortunately, I believe that you will suffice, Mr Ramsbottom,' Vale said. 'We are here to look into the matter of a parcel that may have gone astray.'

Ramsbottom glanced guiltily at the stacks of incoming mail on the corner desk.

'We are looking for a crate from Lord Wyndham,' Vale said. To his side, Irene could see Kai tense with excitement, watching Ramsbottom with a glare of anticipation that was probably unnerving the nervous-looking fellow. 'It would have been delivered about five days ago.'

Was it really that short a time since Wyndham's death, since Irene and Kai had arrived here? It felt so much longer, Irene thought.

'Ah,' Ramsbottom said, sidling towards the desk. He abandoned his mug and selected a ledger. 'Actually, I think I do remember that one.'

'You do?' Vale asked.

Ramsbottom nodded. 'There were particular instructions enclosed with it. Please, um, gentlemen, ladies, Professor Betony will no doubt answer everything with full dispatch as soon as she returns.' He glanced guiltily at the pile of post again. 'But she does have a very specific dislike of anyone else reading her post, and when she left, she told me that unless a letter or package specifically said that it should be opened . . .'

'The crate, man!' Vale snapped, striding forward. 'What happened to it?'

'Ah, ahem.' Ramsbottom twitched at his collar. 'The accompanying note stipulated that if Professor Betony did not return to open it within three days of its receipt, then her assigned subordinate, which is myself, was to open it and take all necessary actions with the contents.'

Irene swallowed. To one side, she could see Bradamant going white. To her other side, she could hear the hoarseness in Kai's breathing. This must have been some sort of last gambit by Wyndham, in case he wasn't able to collect his prized book . . . In *expectation* of his murder?! As just one more step in whatever relationship he'd had with Silver? As a deliberate ploy against Silver getting his hands on the book, or to hide it from someone else?

'The package contained an *Archaeopteryx* skeleton,' Ramsbottom went on, more nervous by the second, 'and another parcel, to be forwarded elsewhere – ' He stuttered to an anxious stop.

'And where would that be?' Vale prompted.

Ramsbottom hesitated. 'This is a matter of confidentiality, Mr Vale, and while I do know your connections with the police, I, ah, that is . . .' He trailed off, apparently unable to utter the words *I'm not going to tell you*.

'Mr Ramsbottom.' Vale stepped forward. 'Naturally I

will not press the matter. But I would be grateful if you could reassure me that there will be no difficulty in tracing the package, should such a thing prove necessary.'

'Of course!' Ramsbottom exclaimed, looking deeply relieved. He tapped a small blue ledger. 'I have full details here of where the package went.'

Then the door in the opposite side of the room slammed open, and Silver strode through, followed by his bland-looking manservant and half a dozen hairy men in cheap suits and bad hats. 'At last!' he declaimed, pointing dramatically. 'I have you now, my dear enemy!'

He was pointing at Bradamant.

CHAPTER SEVENTEEN

'What?' Bradamant said, then quickly converted it to, 'But, ah, how did you find us so quickly?'

Silver laughed merrily. His hair, loose over his shoulders, tossed in a wind which somehow blew around him and ruffled his clothing, but failed to stir a single hair on the louche, bearded thugs who crowded in behind him and leered at the room in general. Their clothing was as dirty and unkempt as Silver's was elegant and stylish, and they all had eyebrows which met in the middle.

'Hah!' Silver preened. He pointed his cane at the unfortunate Ramsbottom, who was trying to retreat into a corner. Any corner. 'You! Hand over the book at once, and your rewards will be beyond your imagination!'

'Careful, Silver,' Vale said. His grip on his swordstick was no longer quite as casual as it had been a few seconds ago. 'You wouldn't want to have any witnesses to illegal actions on your part, would you?'

'Illegal actions?' Silver turned to his manservant. 'Johnson! Have I committed any illegal actions?'

Johnson checked his watch. 'Not within the last three minutes, sir.'

Silver turned back to Vale. 'There you have it. Rest

assured that I am not at the moment committing any illegal actions. I am merely promising this hireling here that if he hands over the book I am looking for, then he will receive rewards beyond his wildest imaginings.'

'Well, if there's nothing *illegal* in it . . .' Ramsbottom said vaguely. His eyes followed Silver dreamily, watching his every gesture, his every breath. Irene remembered the glamour that Silver had tried to lay on her, back in Wyndham's study.

'My dear sir,' Bradamant said, with a nerve that Irene wasn't quite sure she'd have managed to muster, 'you still have not explained how you managed to track us here.' She stepped to her left, forcing Silver to take his attention off Ramsbottom if he wanted to keep his eyes on her.

Silver waved a hand vaguely. 'The simplest of matters. I subcontracted. Knowing that I could not track an agent of the Library – ah, you fooled me once, but not again! – I approached the elder Miss Olga Retrograde.'

Irene and Bradamant exchanged quick shocked looks. It was one thing to think that Silver might be aware of the Library – many Fae and dragons were, after all, just as the Library was aware of them – but to have him say it so baldly and in front of witnesses was rather worrying, in that it suggested there would shortly *be* no witnesses. And how had Silver known, in any case? What had he seen? How *much* did he know about the Library?

Vale, meanwhile, looked outraged. 'You dealt with *her*?'

'Merely a matter of convenience,' Silver said airily. 'Normally she is far too sordid for me to do more than invite her to my parties. I don't suppose you would care to comment on that, would you, my dear private detective? From a, shall we say, *family* perspective?'

Vale looked even more furious, if that were possible. 'I have nothing that I would wish to say about her,' he spat.

'Then allow me to clarify,' Silver said with great satisfaction. 'Her scrying attempts proved useless until you left your lodgings this morning. She caught the directions given to the cab-driver. From then it was simply a matter of reaching this museum first, and having my minions here locate your destination.' He smiled at the hirsute thugs.

'We know Mr Vale's smell,' one of them growled, his tongue coming unsettlingly far out of his mouth as he panted. 'We all know Mr Vale's smell. There's a lot of us want to have a nice quiet little chat with Mr Vale down some dark alley sometime.'

'There, there,' Silver said. 'I'm sure you'll get your chance some day very soon now – if Mr Vale doesn't advise his Library associate to comply with my requests.' He smiled at Bradamant dazzlingly. Irene felt a little of the overspill of it, the burning surge of slavish desire and passionate adoration, and felt the brand across her back burn like raw ice in reaction. She also felt a quick burst of relief that apparently Silver hadn't recognized *her* as a Library agent. She was still incognito for the moment.

Ramsbottom's hands fell to his sides, and he gave up all attempts to be helpful to stare at Silver in mute fascination. Vale didn't seem to be affected. Irene was tempted to look behind her to see what Kai was doing, but as a dragon, he should surely be immune to anything that Silver could throw at him. At least, she hoped so.

Silver thought that the book was still here. There had to be some way that they could use that. At least Bradamant was playing along and keeping Silver occupied.

'But how did you know I was from the Library?' Bradamant asked, edging still further to the left.

One of the thugs twitched forward as if to make a grab for her, but Silver shook his head. 'No, my adversary deserves to know at least that much. How well you fooled me, my dear! I was quite distracted by your mousy little minion over there in her drab dress,' he gestured at Irene, 'and by your cunning thefts. How could I have realized that you were the mastermind behind it all? It was only after I put it all together that I saw you in your true light.'

Irene was torn between relief that he wasn't focusing on *her*, and a certain amount of irritation that she was apparently a mousy little minion unworthy of his attention. Was she so utterly unnoticeable? Why wasn't he pointing a finger at Irene and declaiming about *her* being an impressive mastermind? In fact, why was Silver claiming that there was a mastermind at all?

Part of her was aware that this was an incredibly stupid attitude to take, a reaction to his Fae charm or something. The same thing that was making her want to pout and preen at him. Maybe bare a shoulder or breathe deeply or somehow get him to notice her. To have him touch her with those beautiful long hands, his body pressing. . .

Right.

A thought at the back of her head was trying to get her attention. *This is the problem with interacting with the Fae.* An instructor's voice from back at the Library, talking to half a dozen trainees while they made notes (or surreptitiously tried to plot out best-selling novels), droning away while rain spattered against the window that looked out onto a deserted grey stone square full of empty market stalls. *They see everything in terms of their own personal drama. If you are not careful, they will drag you into it. This is in fact a problem and a risk with all chaos-infected alternates . . .*

'I see.' Bradamant did a good job of drooping in response to Silver's accusations. 'Then you know everything.'

'Everything!' Silver declared. 'I am not surprised that Aubrey should have called for reinforcements from the Library with such a prize at stake, but now he will have to admit that he has failed. Our long rivalry is at an end!'

Irene blinked in shock. No. No. That couldn't be right. If Silver had known Dominic Aubrey, and had learnt that he was a Library agent, then Dominic should have known about Silver being a threat. But Dominic hadn't said a single word about Silver being an enemy of his, or warned them about him, or even told them that Silver existed . . .

. . . and why was Bradamant nodding? What did she know? 'Aubrey warned me about you,' she said, 'but I believe he did not prepare me enough.'

No, surely this was *impossible*. There was no conceivable reason for Dominic to warn Bradamant, but not her or Kai. They could well have come into contact, as the only door to the Library was in Aubrey's office. But there had been no sign that they had exchanged this sort of intelligence. Of course Dominic might have had his own patrons in the Library, who wanted Bradamant to find the book first. That was entirely plausible, and wasn't even an offence as such. But deliberately hiding the threat of Silver from her and Kai wasn't just a casual slip, it was a *betrayal*. If she'd got back and told her superiors, then Dominic might well have been removed from his post.

Could Bradamant be lying? Her thoughts rattled in her head like computer keys. And the tension in the room escalated as Silver considered his next dramatic reply, as Vale and Kai shifted their positions behind her, and as the werewolves panted and waited to lunge.

No. It didn't fit. Oh, all right, maybe Bradamant and Silver might be secret allies staging an argument to convince her. But that was taking paranoia too far. So if Dominic knew about Silver and considered him significant enough to warn Bradamant – but didn't even bother mentioning him to Irene on the next day, when he knew Irene was on a confirmed mission – then what did that imply? What had changed?

She thought back to her brief contact with Dominic Aubrey. His use of the Language was strangely old-fashioned. And then there was Dominic Aubrey's disappearance and skinning, which left his library tattoo intact but no sign of his body at all. And how did Alberich operate in this alternate world? Alberich, who had lived for long enough to be a legend even among the Librarians . . . but nobody knew how, and nobody even knew what he looked like.

An idea was forming, an idea that she mentally flinched from, but one that answered a lot of questions. Stealing someone's skin and identity was covered in obscure folklore treatises, but it wasn't something that she ever expected to be real. She didn't *want* it to be real.

Silver had advanced on Vale and was flourishing his cane menacingly. 'Wyndham only wanted the book because of information *I* gave him. Then he thought he could bargain for it. With me! Why, if the Iron Brotherhood hadn't disposed of him, I might have been forced to do so myself . . . But all is not lost, my dear.'

So it was the Iron Brotherhood that had killed Wyndham. Assuming Silver was correct about it, that tied off one loose end. *Good*, Irene thought, *at least that's one less unidentified group of assassins running around the place.*

Silver took a step forward, smiling brilliantly. Irene felt the air tingle with suppressed longing again. 'Hand over the book and I will be glad to agree to any terms that you might desire.'

Over by the desk, Ramsbottom seemed poised to tell all. His hand wavered towards the small blue ledger.

Kai was the one who moved. He sprang forward like a leopard, and threw himself into a running dive across the desk, snatching the incriminating ledger out of

Ramsbottom's hands. He tossed the ledger across the room to Irene and it spun through the air in a flutter of pages.

'*Get that!*' Silver shrieked.

Irene caught it.

'Back, ladies,' Vale snapped, as a swift twist of his hand revealed the sword inside his walking cane. The length of steel glittered in the burning glow of the lamps, and with a sudden crack sparks cascaded down it, flaring up harshly between them. 'Lord Silver, restrain your dogs!'

Kai was pushing Ramsbottom back against the wall, getting between him and Silver's snarling minions. Good for Kai, keeping the civilians out of it. Silver's minions were getting hairier by the second. Irene could see the spreading patches of iron-grey and black matted fur on their hands, their lengthening nails, their bulging jaws with sprouting teeth . . .

'Come on!' Bradamant grabbed Irene's shoulder, pulling her towards the door.

Pure animal terror at the thought of being torn apart by half a dozen large wolves voted in favour of escape. Explanations could wait.

She stumbled out into the corridor behind Bradamant. If they ran to the right, they'd be leading the chase back towards regular museum visitors. And that would not only be morally invidious, but would probably put them off museums for life.

Irene tucked the ledger under one arm, picked up her skirts, and sprinted leftwards. She heard a muffled curse as Bradamant followed.

Two junctions later, she paused at a spot where two corridors crossed. The place was a rabbit-warren. The air to the right smelled fresher, which argued a way out to the ground floor, or at least a fire escape of some sort, but the passage to the left was better lit. The passage directly in front had nothing to recommend it.

'Keep going,' Bradamant ordered, pausing to catch her breath. 'The werewolves are right behind us – '

But the floor was shuddering violently underneath them. It felt like a passing underground train, but more worryingly close to the surface. Then the floorboards directly ahead buckled upwards in slow motion, and something clawed and dark tore its way up and through. It dragged itself up into the passageway in a vast clashing of gears and clinking of metal. It was all oil-smeared steel except for the head, which was glass-panelled on either side to make two huge flat translucent eyes. It was clearly from the same root design as the metal creature that Kai and Vale had fought two nights ago, but smaller and faster.

'What's this?' Bradamant asked calmly, her words oddly distinct against the sound of splintering wood, grinding metal and distant howling.

'I think it must be the Iron Brotherhood,' Irene answered. 'They probably followed Silver.'

'Oh, this is simply getting ridiculous,' Bradamant sniffed. 'Which way next?'

The insectoid robot head swivelled to focus on Irene and Bradamant. It took a jointed pace down the corridor towards them, the claws attached to each segment of the body dragging it along and leaving horrible gashes in the wood. Its top scraped the ceiling, bringing down cobwebs that had probably been centuries in the making, leaving a long swathe of scoured white plaster in its wake.

'Go right,' Irene shouted to Bradamant on no particular evidence, and ran in that direction. She was already calling vocabulary to her mind – words for gears, joints, pedals, steel, glass, struts and nuts and bolts. But there was always the chance that the construct would decide to chase Silver and the werewolves rather than them, and it seemed a shame to wreck it if so.

'It won't work, you know,' Bradamant said, catching up and outpacing her. 'Do you seriously think that thing won't chase us?'

'It's worth a try,' Irene gasped. She turned and looked back over her shoulder.

The iron automaton came jolting forward in a screeching rattle of steps, then halted as it reached the junction. With a whirr the head turned to edge itself into the passage that Bradamant and Irene were running down. Its shoulders began to creak after it, manoeuvring so it could bear down the passage after them like an oncoming train.

Irene and Bradamant looked at each other.

'I'll do the gears if you do the joints,' Irene said.

'Right,' Bradamant said. 'Give it a moment so that it can block the junction.'

The robot managed to half-negotiate the turn. Its claws dug into the floor as inner springs rewound themselves. The huge lenses set into the head reflected the two women, mirror-like. If they were in fact windows, it was impossible to see who might be lurking behind them.

'**Gears, lock up!**' Irene shouted, pitching her voice to carry as far as possible. '**In head, in claws, in body, and in every part which can hear me – gears, seize solid and stand firm!**'

The robot came to a standstill in a horrific mechanical screaming of blocked joints and gears. Even the distant howling of the werewolves was drowned out. Wires and cables tensed and broke. One claw rotated backwards, caught itself in the floor at an angle, and snapped. And a fragment of steel went flying, pinging off the wall with a high-toned ring of metal, audible even over the noise of the machine destroying itself.

Both women turned, and ran down the corridor away from the thing, past closed offices and storerooms. The air was full of fresh dust, the smell of oil and burnt metal. A part of Irene's mind wondered if it'd make tomorrow's front pages. Probably. She didn't like making headlines. A good Librarian was supposed to read headlines, not *make* them.

'There!' Bradamant pointed unnecessarily to a stairway ahead of them. They plunged down it at a run, Bradamant swinging wide on the banister at the curve and almost hip-checking Irene. The door at its base opened on to the ground floor, revealing a room full of shells and corals. Several family groups turned to look at them disapprovingly.

Irene smiled her iciest smile, brushed some of the dust off her skirts, and took a firmer grip on the precious ledger. Behind her, Bradamant whispered something to the door lock. Irene couldn't quite make it out, but it had the cadence of the Language.

Hopefully they had a couple of minutes before any were-wolves, Fae, Iron Brotherhood, or other book-hunters caught up with them. Irene spotted a small office on the other side of the room and caught Bradamant's eye. 'Over there,' she suggested, jerking her chin towards it.

'Absolutely,' Bradamant agreed.

The two of them walked decorously across the room, skirting glass cases full of dried sea anemones, brittle polyps, and other brightly coloured objects that were probably happier when they'd been underwater. With a polite nod to an elderly man shuffling along behind a walking frame, Irene quietly tried the handle of the office door.

'Is it shut, dear?' Bradamant enquired quietly.

'Oh no,' Irene said, keeping her voice down. 'In fact, **this door is open**.' The Language rolled in her mouth, and the handle loosened under her hand, turning obediently to let the pair of them in.

'Not bad,' Bradamant said, closing the door behind them. She looked around for a key, saw none, and muttered, '**Door lock, shut.**' The lock clicked to again.

Irene glanced round the room. It was clearly someone important's office: the desk and chairs were newer than the ones downstairs, the pieces of artwork and diagrams hanging on the walls had frames, and there wasn't any dust. 'We'd better not take too long,' she said, walking over to the desk. She sat down and flipped the ledger open. 'Someone might come in at any moment.'

'My dear Irene,' Bradamant said, raising her hands to adjust her hat and her hair, 'I may not be able to handle a set of werewolves and an angry Fae, but I can certainly handle one museum official. Especially as he is overweight.'

'Overweight?'

Bradamant's smirk was obvious in her voice. 'I don't need to be a great detective like your Vale to look at the chair you're sitting in and see that it's usually sat in by an extremely fat man.'

'Oh,' Irene said, a little stung. Just because she had her own particular tastes in fiction didn't mean that she liked to be sneered at about them. She flipped through the pages, looking for entries dating two days ago. *It arrived five days ago, then three days after that he would have sent it on . . .* 'Ah!' she said, finding the date. 'Mm. He's had a lot of packages going through. Professor Betony must get a lot of mail.' She ran her finger down the page, looking for a mention of Wyndham's name. 'Got it. Package from Lord Wyndham, redispatched to—'

'To *Dominic Aubrey, British Library!*' Bradamant said in shock, reading over her shoulder.

'Of course!' Irene slapped her hand against the desk.

'You said it yourself, Dominic was indiscreet in what he told Wyndham! And Wyndham was afraid of Silver striking at him or trying to steal the book.' Well, technically a cold iron safe would keep a book safe from any thieves, not just Fae ones, but Silver had known to look there for the book. 'If Wyndham wanted to hide the book from Silver, and if he knew more or less about Dominic, or at least if he knew for certain that Dominic was an enemy of Fae in general, and Silver in particular . . . Wyndham must have sent this package before his death, once he had the copy of the book made, the one that you stole.' She was aware that she was getting incoherent, and she took a deep breath. 'He must have expected to get the book back from Dominic later.' Suddenly her earlier fears about Dominic returned to her. 'But that means—'

A bright pain knifed into the side of her neck, as sharp and vivid as a wasp's sting. She would have exclaimed in shock, but the words were somehow fuzzy in her mouth and her lips were numb. She was sagging back into the wide seat, thoughts clear but body numb and loose, unable to form a single deliberate word.

'But that means,' Bradamant said, wiping the end of her hatpin on the shoulder of Irene's coat before sliding it back into her own hat, 'that I don't need you any more.'

CHAPTER EIGHTEEN

'What'reyoudoin'?' Irene slurred. She could barely form the words in English, let alone in the Language.

'Making sure that this mission will be a success,' Bradamant answered. 'I haven't broken my word. I promised you that if I found the book, I'd bring it to you before returning to the Library. I will still do so once I've collected it from Dominic Aubrey's office. But that will be at my own convenience and in a way that I choose. In the meantime, I don't want you interfering any longer.'

'Stpd,' Irene mumbled. *Stupid.* She needed to tell Bradamant what she suspected about Alberich, but Bradamant's attack on her had just made that impossible.

'Don't worry,' Bradamant said. She stroked a fragment of strayed hair back under her hat. 'It's a curare derivative. You should be back on your feet in half an hour or so. It probably won't affect your breathing or your heart.' She smiled maliciously. 'Or perhaps it will. It's not as if I've tested it *that* often, after all. Cheer up, Irene dear! Soon you'll be free of all these annoying worries about the Library and your actual job, and you can concentrate on your friends here instead. Perhaps you'll get another mission more commensurate with your talents. Gathering toilet paper, for example.'

Irene glared up at her, struggling to form words. *You stupid idiot, don't you realize that I was about to tell you something important?*

This would have been the perfect time to develop telepathy, except that as far as she knew, it was purely fictional.

Bradamant leaned across to retrieve the ledger. 'I'm not blind, you know,' she said. 'I have been aware of you watching me. Your little sneers at the fact that I enjoy nice clothing. I've seen you turn up your little nose at my interest in completing the mission, and my willingness to lie to get the job done. Your general . . . dislike of me? Yes, dislike is a good word. We wouldn't call it quite scorn now, but you don't like me at all.'

I suspect Dominic Aubrey isn't really Dominic Aubrey, Irene tried to convey with her eyes. *I think Alberich replaced him days ago. I think that the kind man who Kai and I met was actually something old and vicious wearing Dominic Aubrey's skin. And I think the only reason he hasn't found the book yet is that he didn't know about Dominic Aubrey's contacts. And, crucially, he hasn't bothered to check Dominic Aubrey's mail.*

'Get over it.' Bradamant smiled down at Irene. 'Some of us aren't the spoiled offspring of lucky parents, who then spend the rest of their lives being treated like little angels. Some of us are grateful to be out of places worse than *you* can imagine.' A shadow flickered behind her eyes. 'We appreciate what we've been given. And we would do anything, anything at *all*, to do our job properly. You can play around with your great detective as much as you like, Irene – oh, don't think I never worked that one out. I know who you want to be. But I know who I *am*. I'll sacrifice whoever and whatever I must sacrifice to complete the mission. If you really understood, if you were really a *proper* Librarian, then you'd do the same. Perhaps some day you will understand that.'

You're about to walk right into his arms. Irene could feel tears burning at the corners of her eyes. *You're going to walk in there and you have no idea.*

'I'll lock the door behind me,' Bradamant said helpfully. 'You shouldn't have any werewolves bursting in on you while you're helpless.'

I hope they bite your bloody nose off, Irene thought vengefully.

'Don't think of me as malicious,' Bradamant said, then paused. 'Actually, do think of me as malicious. Think of me as a malicious bitch who's going to take your mission, your credit, and possibly your apprentice if you haven't spoiled him too much. Think what you like. But – ' She leaned forward and patted Irene's cheek gently.

Irene couldn't even feel the touch of Bradamant's hand against her skin.

'Think of me as a bitch who gets the job done,' Bradamant said. She walked across to the door. 'Don't call me. I'll call you.'

The door clicked shut behind her.

Irene stared at the bare desk in front of her, sprawled like a doll in the chair. She couldn't turn her head, and she didn't have the muscular focus to scream. She tasted bitterness and despair.

Perhaps she had been wrong to bind Bradamant by an oath in the Language, she thought through the confusion. Perhaps this betrayal ultimately came down to her own insult to Bradamant's integrity.

Or then again, perhaps Bradamant was a *back-stabbing bitch*.

A nagging twitch of guilt lurked at the back of her mind. Yes, she had to admit it, she had enjoyed working with

Vale. It wasn't just a case of her Great Detective fixation. (She'd always loved the Holmes stories. And the Watson stories. And even the Moriarty stories.) But there was more to Vale than just being a Great Detective. There was the prickly man who'd confessed to his split with his family, but who was still ready to help them when they asked. There was his surprising generosity and courtesy. There was even the humanizing touch that he'd lent Kai his dressing-gown, and she'd found them sitting over breakfast discussing airships.

She wasn't a child looking for a role. She was a Librarian with a job to do, and sharing information with Vale and Singh had resulted in things getting done.

Letting herself be immobilized by guilt would be as poisonous as Bradamant's curare, and as harmful.

There was something deeper to this, though. As she struggled to stay alert, as her mind fought not to follow her body into lassitude, she tried to think it through. She had nothing better to do, after all. Librarians *didn't* betray other Librarians like this. Bradamant had been playing the part thoroughly but, just once or twice, she'd seen that Bradamant had been afraid. She'd taken up someone else's mission – something which was, if not actively forbidden, at least a serious breach of convention. She'd already tried and failed once to get the book. Now she'd assaulted Irene and left her in danger in order to reach the book first. Who could have pushed her that far?

Irene felt chilled. Some of the older Librarians had . . . unsavoury reputations. A lifetime among books didn't cultivate depravity or debauchery, as much as a love of mind games and politics. And those games could turn dark. Even Coppelia could have her own objectives. Look at Kai, for instance. He'd been planted on Irene in the middle of a mission involving Alberich. What precisely was going on there? How many people had guessed the truth about him?

Her mind felt as if it was stuffed with marshmallows, clogged at the edges and fuzzy in the middle. It must be the drug. But she had to *think*: she had to work this out. She had the facts. She just needed to apply them.

Compared with Coppelia, there were people like Kostchei, Bradamant's patron. He was reclusive and exacting. Nobody dared argue with his messengers when he 'requested' a specific book. Rumour had it that he had a great deal of influence among the older Librarians, when he cared to use it. The fact that he'd chosen Bradamant as a protégée was interesting in itself. The fact that she would assault other Librarians and steal their work in order to avoid disappointing him . . . was even more so.

Irene was abruptly filled with a burning desire to read the damned elusive book, if it was so very important. (She was aware that this sort of logic had landed people in trouble before. Screw logic. She was furious.)

Was that her finger twitching? Please let it be her finger twitching.

She tried to cough. Something resembling coherent noise came out.

She was *so* going to have Bradamant's ass for this. Metaphorically speaking.

The door handle rattled. She could hear the murmur of voices outside, but nothing distinct. She struggled to call out intelligibly, but only a ragged gurgle emerged. In desperation she jerked her leg, kicking out at the desk. There was a thud as her shoe banged into the hollow side.

Another brief exchange of conversation. A pause.

The door swung open with a bang. Out of the corner of her eye she could see Vale and Kai standing there, Vale refolding something about the size of a wallet and sliding it into his pocket. Both of them looked mildly battered and unkempt, but not lethally so.

'Irene!' Kai exclaimed, rushing into the room. 'Are you all right?'

No, I'm currently suffering from curare poisoning, she attempted to communicate. A gargle came out of her mouth.

Kai's eyes went to the scratch on her neck. 'Heaven and earth!' he exclaimed. 'She's poisoned! Silver must have got here before us! I'm going to kill him—'

'Excuse me,' Vale said, and picked up Irene's hand where it lay limply on the arm of the chair. He slid back her cuff and checked her pulse. 'The lady is conscious, as you can see, and seems in good enough health otherwise, so one must assume a paralytic . . .'

'Irene, say something!' Kai leaned forward and cupped her face in his hands, staring into her eyes. She could just barely feel the touch of his skin against her face. 'Can you hear us?'

'Hear . . .' she managed to force out. 'Cur . . . curare . . .'

'She's been poisoned with curare!' Kai swung round to Vale. 'Quick! Where can we find a doctor?'

Irene wondered sourly if dragons were particularly prone to stating the obvious at moments of crisis, or if it was just him.

'Aha.' Vale brightened, his eyes flashing with enthusiasm. 'I believe we can deal with this here and now. I have a small amount of a strychnine derivative with me, which I use as a stimulant in moments of emergency – '

Much is now explained, Irene thought, even more sourly.

– 'and while there may be some minor side-effects, with any luck it should restore her enough to speak. Mr Strongrock, if you would be good enough to hold her shoulders steady?'

'Of course,' Kai said, stepping round behind her chair to grasp her shoulders. She could actually feel his fingers biting into her through the folds of clothing. Either the curare was wearing off, or that was a very firm grasp indeed.

Vale removed a small glass tube from an inner pocket of his coat. Leaning forward and turning his head away, he flipped the lid off and briefly passed it under Irene's nose.

Irene inhaled. Her whole body jolted in an undignified convulsion, legs kicking wildly and tangling in her long skirt, the muscles in her arms clenching and contracting. Her head snapped back and without Kai's grip on her shoulders, she would have sprawled out of the chair to thrash on the floor.

'Miss Winter?' Vale said, closing the glass tube and putting it back in his pocket. 'Can you understand me?'

Irene coughed and focused on breathing for a moment, as the twitching in her limbs slowly eased. It just felt like cramps now. Really bad cramps. The sort of cramps that would ideally warrant a long, extremely slow rubdown in a hot bathhouse . . .

That must be the strychnine. She wouldn't normally let her mind wander like that.

'Mm, okay,' she managed to mumble. 'Thank – thank you. Got to – it was Bradamant, the book's with Aubrey, not really Aubrey – '

Vale exchanged a meaningful glance with Kai. She could guess what they were thinking: *She's still delirious.*

She had to make herself understood.

Irene closed her eyes for a moment, focused, thought vicious curses down upon Bradamant's head, and opened her eyes again. 'Three things,' she said distinctly. 'First. The book was posted to Dominic Aubrey. I believe Wyndham must have wanted him to keep it safe from Silver. Second.

Bradamant poisoned me. She wants to get the book first. Third. I think Alberich killed Dominic Aubrey before we arrived. Think he was posing as him when we arrived. The only reason he doesn't have the book yet is because he hasn't checked Aubrey's post.'

Her leg spasmed. She leaned over awkwardly and banged it with her fist. 'Ow,' she said.

Vale and Kai exchanged glances again. She had the feeling that more was being communicated than she could see. Perhaps it was a manly thing. Perhaps it was a dragon thing on one side and a Great Detective thing on the other.

'Could Bradamant be working with Alberich?' Kai asked. 'If she poisoned you?'

Irene shook her head and regretted it. She put her hands on the arms of her chair and struggled to push herself up to a standing position, glaring at Kai when he tried to help her. 'Bradamant has no *clue*,' she snapped. 'Bradamant is an idiot. Bradamant ran off to get the book . . . I didn't get to tell her about Alberich and Dominic. I'm not sure she even believed me that Alberich is here. And if he's still around the British Library when she arrives . . .' The thought made her throat go dry. She wanted to take some sort of painful and pointed revenge on Bradamant, but she didn't hate her *that* much. 'We have to get there first,' she said firmly.

She took a step, and almost fell over.

Vale caught her elbow and supported her. 'Miss Winters, you are in no condition to accompany us. You should rest here while Mr Strongrock and I go in search of your errant comrade.'

'While I would normally agree with you,' Kai said, 'there are those werewolves.'

'Didn't you even deal with the werewolves?' Irene snapped. She was aware that she was being just a *little* unfair here, but at least presumed allies hadn't stabbed them in the back while they were trying to do their job. Or their neck. Whatever.

'True,' Vale said. 'The werewolves may be a problem. We only inconvenienced them, rather than finishing them off. I have sent for the police, but they will need to reach here first. Perhaps if we—'

'Perhaps if yer what?' a snarling voice enquired. A ragged figure stood in the open doorway, hair sprouting from his clothes at neck and cuffs, with snarling teeth gaping in his mouth. 'This time it's too late for Mr bleedin' Vale—'

Kai snatched up the inkwell from the desk, and threw it straight at the werewolf's face. Ink splattered everywhere, on the varnished floor and the papered walls, but mostly on the werewolf. He had time for a single black-drooling look of surprise before Kai's kick caught him in the chest and sent him stumbling back into the central hall. Kai followed it up with an elbow blow to the werewolf's chin, another kick to the back of his knee, and a two-handed smash to the back of his neck.

The werewolf lay flat in a splatter of drool and ink. Vale half supported, half dragged Irene out of the office and into the main hall. 'It seems you will have to come with us after all, Miss Winters,' he said.

'Quick,' Kai exclaimed, ignoring the general mob of bystanders either shrieking or staring. 'We need to catch a cab.'

'A cab? My dear fellow, a cab would be far too slow,' Vale said. 'We need to get to the roof.'

'The roof?' Irene said. She was possibly being a bit slow here, but she wasn't sure that Kai turning into a dragon and flying them there would be much use, unless . . . 'Oh. Of course. *The airships.*'

'Precisely,' Vale said, hurrying her to the stairs. 'Of

course, there may be some problems with mooring subsequently, but it's our best option.'

Kai caught up with them, and grabbed Irene's other elbow to assist in the dragging-her-along-like-a-giant-doll process. 'I hear more of them coming . . . Which way, Vale?'

'Left at the top,' Vale instructed. They dashed past two astonished tour groups and turned left, entering a wide gallery full of large glass cases. Here, stuffed hyenas menaced stuffed deer, a giant stuffed polar bear towered over some bored-looking stuffed seals, and a rainbow of stuffed birds sat mournfully among dried flowers.

'Catch them!' she heard Silver's voice calling from behind them.

An utterly blood-chilling howling rose up ahead of them. Panicked visitors fled the room, forcing Irene and the two men to one side as they stampeded out of the far doors.

'Get me a megaphone,' Irene said quietly to Kai. Her legs were still cramping, and she had to hold on to Vale to stay upright. But she had an idea and this time, just this time, she had the feeling it was going to work. 'The tour guides have them . . . '

Kai grabbed a tour guide as he rushed past, and swiftly relieved him of his megaphone. 'Will this do?'

The first werewolf came howling into sight, rounding one of the glass cases. Its head and hands were totally wolf-like now, and its clothing was splitting down the seams as it changed shape.

Irene tried the megaphone. 'IS THIS THING ON?' Feedback fuzz echoed in the room.

The werewolf seemed to laugh. Another one joined it. They were approaching slowly. Clearly they were just as interested in fear as they were in bloodshed.

'Miss Winters,' Vale began, 'if you have anything in mind – '

Irene held up her hand in apology. Very precisely, she directed the Language through the megaphone, '**Stuffed creatures, come to life and attack werewolves**.'

The words shook in the air and drew energy from her to make themselves real in the world. It was simple enough to tell a lock to open, or a door to shut. These actions came naturally to those objects, and the universe was glad to oblige. But stuffed animals weren't in the habit of reanimating to attack things.

Except now, as Vale looked at her in growing comprehension and Kai smiled a sharp-edged smile, it was coming true.

The polar bear burst from its case with a silent roar, mouth open to display all those carefully preserved teeth. The glass panes crashed in a waterfall of shards onto the tiled floor, shattering in all directions. The seals came crawling after it, flopping in spasmodic jerks across the floor. Elsewhere in the room, more glass cracked as a flood of creatures fought their way out. A wolf pack staggered forward on stiff legs, and a carefully wired boa constrictor came writhing out of its own case, uncaring of the glass daggers stuck into its sawdust-stuffed body, and even the birds threw themselves at the walls of their cases, struggling on the ends of their wires.

'Dear heavens,' Vale said. 'Miss Winters. What have you *done*?'

'They'll only attack the werewolves,' Irene said, tossing the megaphone to one side. It crunched and tinkled as it hit the floor. 'We need to run while they're distracted, before Silver gets here.'

Vale had a good instinct for knowing when to act now and ask questions later. It must be part of being a Great Detective, Irene decided giddily, wondering if the strychnine/curare cocktail was making her delirious. One of the werewolves tried to break away from the attacking mob of otters and crocodiles to get at them, but a persistent baby alligator (*Observe the Young of the Species, Only Two Feet Long*) chomped on its ankle and dragged it back into the melee.

Vale navigated confidently though more stairs and corridors, and then they were on the roof. The air outside was smoggy and cold. It hit Irene's throat and made her cough. Two small airships bobbed on the end of moorings in a darkly ominous sky, hovering perhaps twenty feet above the roof of the museum.

A guard came hurrying towards them. 'Mr Vale!' he said, moustache quivering. 'Now excuse me, sir, I'm sure that you have very urgent business up here, but this is off limits.'

'There is no time for that, man!' Vale declared. 'Barricade the doors. There are werewolves at large in the museum. Inspector Singh is bringing a force from Scotland Yard to sweep the place. In the meantime, I require one of your zeppelins to stop the perpetrator before he can escape.'

The guard's eyes widened. He stroked his moustache nervously. 'Is it that urgent, sir?'

'It's a matter of life and death,' Vale snapped. 'Inspector Singh will explain everything when he gets here. Are you with me, man?'

'Yes, sir,' the guard declared, nearly snapping his heels together in his enthusiasm. Werewolves and assisting great detectives must be somewhat unusual. He turned to look up at the floating airships, waving an arm. 'Jenkins! Throw down a ladder, girl, you've a run to do!'

With a certain amount of pushing from below and pulling from above, Irene was assisted up the swaying rope ladder. She decided to be grateful that firstly, she hadn't just been left behind, and secondly, that she was wearing traditional underpants rather than anything scantier. The rest of her mind was preoccupied with clutching the rope ladder with sweating hands, trying not to fall off and die.

The pilot was a woman, in canvas and leather clothing – the first that Irene had seen in trousers so far in this alternate. Her goggles were shoved back over a coiled heavy braid of hair and she looked more suspicious than the guard had been. 'I don't know what's going on,' she said, 'but I'll have to see some authorization.'

'My name is Vale,' Vale announced. 'I require your assistance to reach the British Library as fast as possible.'

'That and a shilling'll buy you a pound of onions,' the woman said. Unimpressed, she leaned back in her seat, a hammock-like sling of leather straps and creaking rubber. 'Go find some other poor sod to risk their job if you want to chase criminals.'

Irene considered the possible mental damage of what she was about to do. Librarians were generally supposed to avoid it, because of the risks of imposing on people's minds, not to mention the universe occasionally backlashing in interesting ways. But they were running out of time. 'Miss Jenkins—'

'That's Mrs Jenkins to you,' the woman snapped. 'I'm a respectable married woman, I am.'

'**Mrs Jenkins**,' Irene continued, switching fluidly into the Language, '**you perceive that the detective here is showing you reliable and acceptable authorization.**'

Mrs Jenkins frowned, staring at Vale. '. . . well, I can't say as I like it,' she finally said, 'but that seems to all be in order. British Library, you said?'

'At once,' Vale said, with only a quick frown at Irene. 'There is no time to lose.'

'Very good, sir,' the woman said. 'Kindly have you and your friends hang on to the straps further back in the

257

cabin. This is going to be a bumpy ride. The wind's against us.'

Irene heard shouting in the background and looked down. Silver was standing on the roof, his cape billowing behind him as he pointed at the zeppelin.

Kai saw him too and took rapid action, casting off the mooring cable. The whole zeppelin rocked, and Irene had to grab for the straps, but they were moving, jerking away from the museum at the sudden loss of their tether.

'Damn dilettante amateurs,' Mrs Jenkins muttered, and ran her hands over the controls, flipping two switches and spinning a dial before hauling on a joystick. The zeppelin tilted and jolted into forward motion. 'Passengers, we are now in the open air and heading for the British Library. Please talk among yourselves while I pilot this damn thing because I don't like being distracted.'

'Yes,' Vale said, turning to Irene. 'We need to talk, Miss Winters.'

CHAPTER NINETEEN

Irene could think of so many things that Vale might want to discuss that it wasn't even funny. But she was going to sit down first.

She decided, as she perched on a ledge which might be a seat, that this sort of transport must be reserved for very small antiques. The compartment was cramped, with hardly enough room for the three of them, let alone the storage of large items. The engine was also incredibly noisy, which was good – Irene didn't really want Mrs Jenkins listening in on this.

Vale himself remained standing, holding on to an overhead strap, using the advantage of his height to tower over Irene. Possibly in response, Kai also stayed on his feet, moving over to loom behind Irene's shoulder supportively.

Irene wished that they'd both been poisoned too: perhaps then they'd be a bit more understanding about wanting to sit down.

'Miss Winters,' Vale said, retreating into formality, 'am I to understand that you have the Fae-like power to glamour and delude the minds of others?'

Oh. So that was what had disturbed him. 'No,' she said,

then qualified it with, 'not precisely. And you're probably wondering why I didn't do such a thing before.'

'Or why you suddenly revealed it now, after using it on me without my realizing it,' Vale suggested, brows drawn together suspiciously.

Damn. It was a logical suspicion which she'd been hoping that he wouldn't have. Why did he have to use those qualities that she admired against her? 'I'm hardly that stupid,' she said.

'But you might have been that desperate,' Vale answered. 'An explanation, if you please.'

Irene sighed. She'd been hoping to avoid this. 'All right. You know that I can use the Language to, in blunt terms, make things do things. I can't change a door from a locked door to an open door, but I can make the lock on a door open itself. There are some subtleties to this, but I hope you'll understand that I can't explain *everything* in full detail and with footnotes. I can get away with telling my superiors that I explained some things to you, but there are limits.'

'You show a sudden high regard for your superiors' opinion,' Vale commented.

She was suddenly furious, his words reviving Bradamant's taunts on not involving others and doing the job – no matter what. 'I'm not supposed to be sharing anything with you at all!' She could feel her control slipping, which just made it worse. She should be handling this dispassionately like a capable Librarian, as Bradamant would have done. She shouldn't feel this sudden lurch at the thought of ruining any sort of friendship with Vale. She was not supposed to be involved with him at all. With anyone. 'Standard procedure is getting in and out, leaving no traces. Standard procedure does not involve investigating local murders, going to local receptions, getting involved with local secret societies—'

'Or visiting local detectives,' Kai put in.

Or forming friendships, Irene heard behind his words. She wished that she had a spare hatpin to jab into Vale. Or possibly Kai, who wasn't helping. 'Standard procedure tends to advise against high-speed chases in borrowed zeppelins, too,' she said flatly. 'Bradamant would have told you all this. Perhaps she's the one you should have been working with from the beginning.' Yes. Bradamant would never have got so . . . involved. 'I still don't understand why your, ah, *foretelling urges* pointed you at us rather than at her. If you'd been working together, you'd probably have managed to track things down a great deal faster.'

Vale simply stared down at her. 'None of this explains your ability to control the minds of others.'

'Well . . .' Irene tried to think how to explain it. 'When I use the Language to tell something to do something which is against its nature, the universe resists. This is why those stuffed animals are going to return to that state, probably quite soon. I hope Inspector Singh is there to sort that one out. It's easy to tell a lock to unlock – these things are in a lock's nature. It's much harder to order something to behave in an unnatural manner.'

'Such as having stuffed animals come to life,' Vale agreed.

'Well, that's only mostly unnatural,' Irene said. 'After all, they were once living animals. I couldn't require a building to jump up and fall on someone, but I could tell a roof tile to come loose. Do you understand me so far?'

'I can see your logic,' Vale said, clearly interested but also clearly lacking patience. 'But again, how is this relevant to controlling minds?'

'I can tell someone that they're perceiving something

other than what they're actually seeing,' Irene said, wishing that English was better adapted for this sort of discussion. 'The problem is that the universe resists, as with objects asked to do unnatural things. Specifically, the person's mind resists, and continually resists until – ' She paused. 'Well, some individuals manage better than others, but generally the results aren't pretty. That's what I was told in classes. But that's not the same as what I just did, and it won't last like a glamour does either.' She was fairly sure that Mrs Jenkins couldn't hear this. She certainly hoped so. 'At the moment, Mrs Jenkins's mind is telling her that no, she did *not* see full authorization. When that overcomes my temporary adjustment, probably within the hour, then she will remember everything. But would you rather I'd just *let* Silver catch us?'

Vale gave Irene a cold look and glanced out of the window at London beneath them, not deigning to answer.

Irene propped her elbows on her knees. 'If the Library told us not to meddle with minds because it was unethical, that might be virtuous. But the fact is, it's very unreliable. And once the subject regains their memory, it can make a mission so much more dangerous.' Irene tried not to dwell on her own lack of ethics. Surely she was more than just a book thief? Or was the only real difference between her and Bradamant, that Bradamant looked good in black leather? It was easier to think of herself as a valiant preserver of books when there wasn't someone looking her in the eyes and questioning that. 'All I've done is applied a very temporary patch.' She looked up at Vale. 'Because I couldn't see any other alternative, and we were in a desperate hurry. As you saw.'

'Were we?' Vale turned away.

Irene raised her eyebrows, even if he wasn't looking at her. 'I realize that you don't see Alberich as a personal

262

threat,' she said, 'or even as a threat to public law and order.'

'I admit the fellow did try to kill me,' Vale said generously.

'He will continue to be a threat to you all as long as the book is here,' Irene went on. She felt Kai squeeze her shoulder encouragingly. 'Once it's gone, he and Silver won't be competing for it any longer.'

'Silver is hardly your concern, Miss Winters,' Vale said. 'And I fail to understand your distress over one world, when you doubtless have so many to occupy your time. Why should you care about us, except as a source of books?'

Irene swallowed, and felt her cheeks flush with mingled anger and embarrassment. There was an uncomfortable grain of truth to what he was saying. This was just one alternate world, and one book. 'So far, I have been assaulted, attacked by cyborg alligators, almost drowned in the Thames, had most of the skin stripped off my hand, poisoned with curare, revived with strychnine, and chased by both werewolves and giant robots. Are you accusing me of not taking this seriously, sir?'

'On the contrary, madam. I consider that you are taking this extremely seriously. Such devotion is worthy of a good cause. But consider this.' Vale leaned back, bracing his shoulders against the cabin walls. 'I see a woman – and her assistant – who are prepared to go to extremes to secure a single book. I have watched you hijack a zeppelin in order to achieve your aims. I ask myself, Miss Winters, just how far are you prepared to go?'

Wonderful. First Bradamant sneered at her for not going far enough, and now Vale was eyeing her as though she were a prize specimen of the criminal underworld. 'I just want to do my job,' she said. 'I have a duty to the Library.'

'Has the Library laws?' Vale cut in. 'Has it signed treaties with all the worlds allowing it to steal books? Has it any authority save that which it claims for itself? I would like to know if there is any reason in the world why I should respect it or its servants.'

Irene set her jaw mulishly. 'Have I personally broken any laws?'

'Not yet,' Vale said. 'At least, none of which I am aware.' The tone of his voice made it clear that he suspected she wouldn't hesitate.

And would she? Well, it would depend on the law. Her body was humming like a high-tension wire, probably the effects of the mingled drugs. 'I don't want to harm your world,' she said quietly, bowing her head. 'I just want a single book.'

She could feel the weight of Vale's accusing stare. 'And so we have to hurry across London, deceiving the pilot and endangering her as well as ourselves, because you must have this book.'

'Watch what you say,' Kai said softly.

Vale shrugged. 'I ask Miss Winters questions to which she should have answers – if such answers exist. If she has none, then perhaps you should consider your own allegiances. What is the point of this Library, if it demands such sacrifices?'

Irene pushed herself to her feet. 'Thank you, Kai, but you don't need to defend me. In answer to your questions, Mr Vale, I am going to get this book. Not just because the Library wants it, but also because Alberich wants it, and he is *far* more dangerous than you seem to think I am.' She gave him a withering look. 'Has it occurred to you that besides trying to kill us, he *has* killed other people? Librarians, people that I know about, even if you don't – and we have no idea what he may have done in this world?

That if I don't get this book out of here, he will probably kill others? And if I don't get to the British Library first, then –' Her brain caught up with what she was saying. '– then he is going to kill Bradamant,' she finished.

Vale snorted. 'The woman is clearly capable of taking care of herself.'

'Maybe she is,' Irene said. 'But that's not the point. I am not going to let her just walk in there and . . .' She thought of Dominic Aubrey, and wondered with a shudder how his skin had ended up in that jar. She would not, *could* not, let that happen to someone else she knew when there was a chance of stopping it. 'You may think of me as you wish. I intend to save Bradamant. I refuse to feel guilty for what I've just done.'

'Ah.' Vale stepped away from the side of the zeppelin, and offered her his hand. 'Then I believe we can work together, Miss Winters.'

Irene nearly said *Huh?* – which would have been inappropriate in so many ways. She just stood there limply. 'But, you were saying . . .'

'Tch,' Vale said. 'Really, madam. I can accept that you are an effective agent, much like your colleague Bradamant. I wanted to be sure that there was more to you than that. If the Library employs persons like yourself, then I suppose there must be something to be said for it after all.'

'Excuse *me*,' Kai began.

'You were doing your duty in following orders, and no man could ask for more,' Vale said. 'But Miss Winters is your commanding officer. The truth needed to come from her.'

Having won the point, Irene felt a curious mix of emotions – including rage. How dare he consider her ethics from such a lofty height? How dare he *judge* her? She took a deep breath, forcing down the anger with whatever justifications she could bring to mind. He had to make his own decisions. He needed to understand her to do so.

Still, it stung.

She reached out and clasped his hand briefly. 'Thank you,' she said. 'I appreciate that.'

Kai stepped up and laid his hand across their joined hands. 'Together we shall put Alberich down and rescue Bradamant. Though personally, as she'd so disloyally betrayed—' He caught Irene's glare. 'Still, I am under your orders,' he said heroically.

Irene disengaged her hand as tactfully as was possible. Heroic fiction had plenty of manly handclasps in it, and she'd read enough of them. But it had never gone into how you retrieved your hand afterwards, and whether there were any relevant squeezes or other manoeuvres. 'I've been trying to think how to deal with Alberich,' she said, though didn't add *in my copious spare time* as she was tempted to, 'and I'd be interested to know if you have anything to suggest.'

'Shoot the bounder,' Vale suggested. 'That works on vampires or werewolves, and even on Fae under some circumstances.'

Kai flexed his long-fingered hands. He seemed, for once, to be hesitating.

'Kai?' Irene prompted.

'There are certain ways that we – that is, um, my family – ' which was probably the closest he was going to come to saying the d-word for the moment – 'can reinforce an area against chaos. Alberich uses chaos, so he must be contaminated by it, so it should work against him too.'

'How large an area?' Vale said. 'And can you make it permanent?' Clearly he had grand visions of driving the Fae out of his entire world, or at least the British Empire part of it.

Kai shook his head. 'If we could, then we wouldn't have this ongoing problem. We could just push them out and keep them out. The best I can do is mark out an area and ward it. And it has to be an area that I can travel around in a set period of time.' He brightened up. 'Greater powers like my father or my uncles could guard an entire ocean within a single turning of the sun!'

Irene bit the inside of her cheek hard before she could make any comments about *putting a girdle round the world in forty minutes*. It probably wasn't an appropriate moment for Shakespeare, and she didn't think Kai would find the analogy funny. 'And yourself?' she asked.

Kai's shoulders slumped, showing a hint of sulking adolescent. 'I'm more bound by physical constraints,' he mumbled. 'And I can't actually force one of those creatures out if it's already inside my wards. I can only set up a boundary so that it can't get in or out.'

'Yes, but how large an area?' Vale pressed. 'The whole of London?'

'Maybe,' Kai said. 'If you gave me all night. And I'd have to, ah, it would attract attention.'

'From whom?' Irene asked. 'The Fae?'

'My relatives,' Kai said. He looked as if he'd like to shrink into a corner at the thought. He seemed to be displaying the heroic nobility of a teenager doing the right thing, combined with the hangdog despair of anticipating the removal of privileges for the next *decade*. She wondered how old – or how young – he was in terms of dragon ageing. He was so mature in some ways, and so young in others.

Irene frowned. 'Well, I can ward an area against chaos by attuning it to the Library. That might force Alberich out of an area if he's already in it – but I can only cover a relatively small area that way. And there are issues of power . . .' Yes, that was one way of putting it. Warding Vale's rooms the previous night had been fairly simple. Trying to block a larger area of reality, as it were, would take much more of her energy. She would also need a very thorough description of the area that she was trying to ward. But there had to be some way that she could use this . . .

The zeppelin rocked, throwing Irene off her feet. Something whirred and chittered like locusts in the air outside. Kai grabbed her round the waist, catching hold of a hanging strap with his free hand. Vale managed to balance himself against the far wall. 'What's going on?' he shouted in Mrs Jenkins's direction.

'We're under attack,' Mrs Jenkins snapped back. She didn't look away from the controls. Her right hand was locked into the middle of a brass and pewter orrery, and her left hand was pulling at a range of levers. She tugged at something that looked like an organ stop, and frowned when it wouldn't respond. 'Trouble to starboard!'

Irene and the others crowded to the window.

'I can't see anything,' Irene said. The only things in sight were rooftops and smog.

'There!' Vale declared, pointing a finger. 'See that vapour trail?'

'Something small,' Kai said, leaning over Irene's shoulder. 'But I can't sense any Fae interference.'

'You forget the Iron Brotherhood,' Vale interrupted. 'They have their agents after us too.'

'Hang on!' Mrs Jenkins called from the cockpit. The zeppelin lurched again, dragging sideways in a painful, ungainly movement that shook the cabin like a dice cup. Irene and the two men clung to handholds. Lengths of rope that hadn't been strapped to the walls swung out and flailed in the air, and an unsecured teacup bounced from wall to wall, leaving a trail of cold tea droplets.

'There he is!' Vale exclaimed. A man had flown into view. He was strapped into some sort of mobile helicopter unit that whirred its tarnished blades dangerously close to his head, and was wearing an oil-smeared leather helmet and overalls. In one hand he held a heavy pistol, with a cable running from it to something strapped to his lower back. He bobbed in the air, steadying the pistol with his free hand as he tried to line up a shot.

'Is there some way we can shoot back?' Kai asked, reverting to smooth competence.

'Over here.' Vale leapt into the cockpit and wrenched at a panel above Mrs Jenkins's head. She ignored him, concentrating on steering the zeppelin. 'The weapons are kept here on museum vehicles – ah, here they are.'

He pulled out a brace of pistols, tossing one to Kai and another to Irene, who wasn't too confident about popping off shots at a flying target. 'Isn't there anything larger on board?' she asked. 'A flare pistol or something?'

Vale spared his attention from smashing a window to give her a sharp look. 'Really, Miss Winters! A flare pistol on a zeppelin? I thought you were more sensible than that.'

'It's not something I've ever studied,' Irene muttered, and decided to keep any other bright ideas to herself for the moment. Kai and Vale were both shooting out of the window and could certainly do so without her assistance. She staggered forward to the cockpit. 'How much further to the library, Mrs Jenkins?'

'Almost at it,' Mrs Jenkins said bluntly, 'but it's not going to be a rat's ass of use, because we can't land with that maniac out there firing at us. I don't know what sort of stories you've heard about what zeppelins can and can't do, miss, but I need to hover while someone throws us a line and makes us secure. And that's what we call, in aviator parlance, a 'sitting target'. So I hope your friends are good shots, or I'm going to be making altitude and heading north until we lose him. Can't risk crashing with the streets this busy.'

Vale shouldered over to grab Irene's arm. Apparently their shots had all gone wide. 'Miss Winters, can your abilities be of use here?'

Irene shook her head. 'I can't affect him or his gear. They can't hear me.'

Vale stared at her. '*Hear* you?'

'The Language only works on the universe if the universe can hear it,' Irene snapped. She was sure that she'd explained this to him earlier. Perhaps she hadn't. 'I can affect this zeppelin, but I don't see what good that would be—'

Vale suddenly snapped his fingers. 'I do! Mrs Jenkins, bring us in to above the British Library, right now, if you please. And be ready for an abrupt descent.'

'What are we trying?' Kai asked, looking round from the window.

'I wouldn't mind knowing that myself,' Mrs Jenkins said. The zeppelin wheeled to the left, throwing them all off balance again. 'We're three hundred yards off, coming in at forty-five miles an hour, and the landing roof's only fifty yards long.'

'On my word, Miss Winters,' Vale instructed, 'tell all the structural components of the zeppelin to increase their weight by fifty per cent. Mrs Jenkins, you are to deploy landing flaps.' He checked his watch.

Another burst of chittering sounded outside. 'Damn,' Mrs Jenkins commented. 'I hate those things.'

'Which things?' Irene asked, frantically trying to remember vocabulary for zeppelin parts.

'Seed ammunition,' Mrs Jenkins said, adjusting the

organ-stop controls. 'They chew right through an airbag. Stand by for rapid braking.'

'Now!' Vale declared.

'**All zeppelin structure parts, increase your weight by a half again!**' Irene shouted, projecting her voice to ensure it would carry through both cabin and cockpit. She didn't want half the struts deciding to stay their original weight, making the whole thing break up in mid-air. Imagination could supply too many images, and none of them good.

Mrs Jenkins slammed down half a dozen of the organ stops simultaneously, using her left hand and forearm, and threw herself back in her seat.

The zeppelin shuddered, leather straining and metal creaking, and the whirling motors outside howled in near-human agony. Kai had dropped his gun and was hanging on to the straps with one hand and Irene with the other, and Irene couldn't complain. Vale had tucked his elbow through a strap and was watching the view through the shattered window with keen curiosity.

They were sinking in the air, dragged down as if someone was hauling the craft's mooring rope from below, but they were still moving forward. The braking flaps were working, but, Irene thought, maybe not fast enough.

'Should I make it heavier?' she shouted at Vale, her voice barely carrying above the howling of the air and the tortured noise of the metal struts.

Vale shook his head in clear negation.

It was at times like this that Irene really wished she believed in prayer. Sudden death was easy to cope with, seeing as you had no time to ponder. But their impending crash and burn over the British Museum was leaving too much time for dread, with an inevitable fiery doom at the end. Every second seemed to stretch out into an eternal moment of panic.

Then the zeppelin settled on solid ground with a thump that threw Irene entirely onto Kai, knocked Mrs Jenkins back in her seat, and made Vale drop his watch. Irene could vaguely hear screams and shouts outside. Hopefully anyone who was standing on the roof had had the sense to run away.

With a muffled curse, Mrs Jenkins started throwing switches. The hum of the motors began to slow, as they shut down one by one. Suddenly the zeppelin was absurdly quiet after all the earlier noise, with only the cabin's creaks and groans as an eerie backdrop.

'Thank you,' Vale said. 'Excellent piloting. I will be mentioning your conduct to your superior.'

Mrs Jenkins looked at him for a long moment, then picked up a rag and wiped her goggles with it. 'You'll find the exit to your right,' she said flatly.

Kai released Irene, and went to open the zeppelin door.

Irene saw it coming, but it was too fast for the Language to stop it. The man in his mini-copter was hovering there, levelling his gun to shoot directly through the open door at the people in the cabin. At Kai standing there with his back half turned.

She didn't have time to speak, but she did have time to move. She threw herself at Kai, and the two of them went sprawling on the floor together, Kai's mouth open in shock, as a whirring mass of silver flecks sliced through the air where he had been standing. The metal pieces sliced into the leather and wooden parts of the structure, chewing long gashes into them, and ricocheted off the metal struts, leaving long silver scars against the dark oiled surfaces. A couple of them sliced along Irene's left arm, cutting through the cloth of her sleeve and drawing blood.

Vale went down on one knee, snatched up Kai's pistol from where it had fallen, and fired.

There was a long, dwindling scream, and a distant crash.

Irene looked down at Kai's face for a moment. He was looking up at her with that lost, puppy-like look again, as if she had somehow perfectly filled a hole in his personal universe. It was no doubt immensely flattering, but she didn't have time for that. She didn't have time to tell him that she trusted him, or that he could trust her. She didn't have time for the immense feeling of gratitude that he was safe – or for anything except finding the book, stopping Alberich, and saving Bradamant. She had to finish the job, or all their efforts and the danger she'd put people in would be wasted.

And she couldn't waste time indulging herself with personal feelings. Even if she wanted to.

'All right?' she said briskly, pulling herself to her knees. 'Good. Come on.'

Vale offered his hand, and pulled her to her feet. 'Good reflexes, Miss Winters.'

'Good shooting, Mr Vale,' she replied. 'Thank you. Now let's find that book.'

CHAPTER TWENTY

There were several guards on the roof who would have liked to discuss their crash-landing and the ensuing gun-fire. But Vale simply strode past, and Irene and Kai marched along in his wake. Their commanding poise was spoiled a little by Kai's sidelong glances whenever he thought her back was turned. What did he *expect* from her?

'Through here,' Vale said, pointing at a door in one of the smaller battlements circling the landing area. Beyond that bulged the wide glass curved roof of what must be the Reading Room. Irene hadn't had time to admire it in this alternate, but she'd seen versions of it in other Londons, and she shuddered to think how close they came to landing on it. Though surely in a world of airships and personal helicopters, the curators must have taken some sort of pre-cautions against things or people crashing through it from above?

She really hoped so. She'd seen too many glass pyramids and domed roofs and huge chandeliers that were just acci-dents waiting to happen.

Vale had a few quick words with the guard, who flung the door open and practically saluted them through. And then they were inside, and out of the wind, and surrounded by comforting walls and walls of books. The rich, delightful smell of old paper, leather and ink permeated the place, washing away the pettier odours of blood and oil and smog.

Irene felt a desperate surge of nostalgia for her Library. Her life was more than just airship chases, cyborg alligator attacks, and hanging out with this alternate universe's nearest analogue to Sherlock Holmes. She was a Librarian, and the deepest, most fundamental part of her life involved a love of books. Right now, she wanted nothing more than to shut the rest of the world out, and have nothing to worry about, except the next page of whatever she was reading.

'Which way is Aubrey's office?' Vale demanded.

Irene frowned, trying to remember the route. 'Third floor,' she said, 'along from the south stairs, two rooms east, then one south, then east again, I think that most of the stuff along there was European history.'

'This way,' Vale said, leading the way down a gallery of drawings and prints. 'Do you have a strategy?'

A couple of men looked up disapprovingly from their sketchbooks at the noise. Their faces were full of *we are far too polite to say so, but really you shouldn't be making any noise at all.*

Irene ignored them. 'Get the book,' she said to Vale. 'Secure this building against Alberich. My invoking the Library won't keep Bradamant out, so she'll be safe once she gets here. I'll contact my central authority for direct assistance.'

Vale raised an eyebrow. 'Aren't you going to tackle the fellow directly?'

Irene couldn't meet his gaze. 'I'd lose,' she said.

'This language of yours—' Vale started.

'I'd find it very hard to believe that other Librarians haven't tried that against him already,' Irene snapped before she could help herself. 'And confrontations with Alberich generally end with him sending parts of their internal organs back to the Library. In neatly wrapped parcels. Someone said that they can tell it's a parcel from Alberich because he always folds the paper in the same way.'

'Miss Winters, just because this fellow has reached the status of an urban legend . . .'

'He's more than that,' Kai said urgently. Their footsteps were loud in the stairwell. 'You were there last night, Vale. He sealed us in the carriage and put a block on it which even I couldn't undo.' There was an unconscious arrogance to his voice. 'And Aubrey, the Librarian stationed here previously. He would have been more experienced than Irene – no insult, Irene, but—'

'Oh, don't worry,' Irene said with a shrug, surreptitiously flexing her hands and trying to decide how fully recovered she was. For the moment she was functional, if damaged. 'You're quite right. He wouldn't have been stationed in an alternate like this unless he was competent, and he was older and more experienced than I am.'

'It's this floor,' Vale said. They came out of the stairwell into a room blazingly full of painted hieroglyphics, icons and crosses with pointy end bits – Coptic, Irene decided. The light was artificial, presumably to spare the papyri from natural sunlight, but the colours leapt at them in a riot of gold, red and turquoise. 'Straight ahead, then left. And may I suggest that Mr Aubrey had no warning that Alberich was coming. Presumably if he had done, then he could have secured himself and called for help from the Library, just as you intend to do?'

She didn't want to hear this.

Casual strollers saw them coming and stepped out of the way. A couple of elderly ladies muttered something condemnatory about young people these days, as Irene strained to listen.

Irene knew that this was displacement behaviour, as the last thing she wanted to do was listen to Vale talking about tackling Alberich. Playing chess matches against masters who were certain to defeat you was one thing: you learnt about chess, and you didn't die in the process. Getting into a fight with someone who would kill you (messily) failed to teach you anything useful, unless reincarnation was genuine, and you did die in the process. It was hard enough to have to consider how important the book might be to this world. She could only think in small steps. If Alberich wanted the book, that meant it was important, possibly even vital, to this world, and he mustn't have it . . .

She was also trying to ignore Kai's sympathetic glances from behind Vale's back. Maybe there was a whole genre of literature written by dragons for dragons about how they sensibly stayed out of fights that they couldn't hope to win, and flew away to do something very important somewhere else. Or maybe it was a bad idea to be distracting herself quite so thoroughly when they were almost at Aubrey's office.

'We can't possibly know how Aubrey tried to handle Alberich,' she finally said. 'I believe the Aubrey I met was simply Alberich disguised. I never even met the real man. All I know is that I am not going to get into a fight which I can't win, when there are alternatives.'

Vale nodded towards the exit. 'Through that way, then straight on for the next seven rooms, then turn left. Very well. I accept your judgement. Can you fetch help rapidly?'

Irene was glad she could agree. 'From what I've heard, the main problem is that my superiors rarely know where Alberich is. If they can actually pinpoint him to this world, then they can take steps—'

Vale cut in, and Irene realized it was a sign of his urgency that he'd actually interrupt. 'Miss Winters! A little logic, if you please. They already know he is in this world, as they warned you about him.'

Something in Irene's stomach went cold. 'Oh,' she said. She hadn't thought that through. 'Maybe – maybe they just suspected he was here, but had no actual proof . . .'

Vale didn't say anything, but then again, he didn't need to, as Irene could feel the shallowness of her reasoning. Oh, it was fashionable among Librarians of her age to impute dubious motives to their seniors. She'd heard the gossip – *they'd use us as bait if they thought it was necessary, they edit the information they give us, they'd sacrifice us to get their hands on a text.* But that didn't mean they *believed* it. At the bottom of her heart, Irene had faith in her superiors.

Genuine doubt was worse than fashionable adolescent doubt had ever been.

'And possibly I've been misinformed,' she said, forcing firmness into her voice. 'Can we at least assess the situation before we start assuming the worst?'

'As you wish,' Vale said, in tones stating *I know perfectly well you aren't going to stop thinking about it now.* 'But why wouldn't he be in his office, though we might wish him elsewhere?'

'The automaton attack at the museum,' Kai suggested. 'If that was him, and if he expected to find the book there, wouldn't he be on the spot to collect it?'

Vale rubbed his chin thoughtfully. 'That assumes that he *was* responsible for the automaton attack. And it would be rather overly controlling, wouldn't you say, to be there in person if he could command underlings . . .'

'He did try to drown us in person,' Kai answered. 'Isn't that the sort of thing that people usually have their subordinates do?'

'True, true.' Vale's frown lightened. 'If that should be so, let us by all means take advantage of it. And if not, well, I believe we may have the advantage in that he will not be expecting us. In either case, surprise and speed are our best option.' He looked around at the vast quantity of rather dull Romano-Celtic objects in the room, noting, 'And I do believe we are almost there.'

'We should clear the area,' Kai said firmly.

'We can't without raising the alarm,' Irene pointed out. If Alberich were in the immediate area, he'd react to something like fire alarms going off, security guards clearing the area, or any sort of disturbance involving people running round shrieking. And people always ended up running round shrieking. It was a law of nature or something. She wondered if she could use the Language to pre-warn them as to whether or not Alberich was in his office. Nothing came to mind. 'I think we'll just have to knock on the door and play innocent.'

'Hm. I believe it might work,' Vale agreed. 'He has no reason to believe you have penetrated his imposture. I will hold back and be ready with my gun.'

Irene tried to think of how this plan might go wrong. Alberich couldn't have laid any sort of kill-everyone-who-touches-the-door spell on his office door (assuming that such a spell existed, something about which she had no clue whatsoever). That would be too likely to slaughter innocent British Library staff and visiting children. So that was positive. What he might have done – what she would have done if she knew how – would be to set a ward against Language use. Again, she had no idea whether or not it was possible, but she would assume for the moment that it was. So she should avoid the Language for the moment.

This bit of paranoid planning had helped her stroll

through a number of Dark Ages exhibits without looking as panicked as she felt. Now, at last, their goal was through some last cases, then directly on the left.

Irene took a deep breath. She gathered her determination, smiled blandly at Kai and Vale, then strolled forward. She tried to ignore the grandfather with a complaining brat to her right and the students over by the archway ahead. Possible witnesses also included the woman squinting near-sightedly at a display card, who did look vaguely familiar – maybe she'd seen her before when she came here last time – oh dear, she was procrastinating again, wasn't she?

Why couldn't this be the sort of story where she kicked the door down and burst in with a loaded gun? Probably because it was a heavy door, she was in long skirts, and she didn't have a loaded gun.

Plastering her best look of sincere concern and gullibility on her face, she knocked on the door.

No answer.

She knocked again. A couple of the bystanders glanced across, then turned back to whatever they'd been doing.

Still no answer.

'Cover me,' Kai said in a low voice. He stepped forward, fishing a thin metal probe out of an inner pocket. He tapped it against the doorknob as Irene shielded him from view. She glanced around but nobody was paying them any attention – except for Vale, who was hanging back and ostensibly ignoring them.

The tapping having drawn no visible reaction, Kai tried the handle. It didn't move, so he bent over and began picking the lock. Clearly his time as a juvenile criminal hadn't been a total fiction.

Irene spread out her skirts, and turned to watch the room, a smile pinned to her face. *No, nothing going on here, absolutely normal, my friend here likes to stare into locks and wiggle bits of metal round in them, he does it every day and twice on Sundays . . .*

A moment later Kai was tapping her on the shoulder, with a cool look of superiority.

Irene gave him a nod and tried the door. It didn't explode.

This is good. I'm already ahead of the game.

She turned the handle and walked into the room. A quick glance around showed that it looked just as they had left it the last time. No sign of anyone. Nobody hiding under tables. Nobody hiding behind the door. No Alberich.

She breathed out a sigh of relief which she hadn't realized that she'd been holding, and stepped aside so that Kai could come in. Vale followed a few seconds later, closing the door behind him.

Irene cast around, looking for anything that resembled an in-tray. Score! There was a blatantly obvious one on Aubrey's desk. She remembered it having been tidy when they first arrived, but it was now crowded with papers and oddments. She quickly sorted through it, and the packet with the Natural History Museum's address on the back (return to sender) was the seventh item. It was an unobtrusive package in plain brown paper.

'Paper knife,' she said, extending one hand.

Vale slapped a knife handle into her palm. It was elegant, made in ivory or whalebone, and had no doubt contributed to the extinction of at least one endangered species. It was also nice and sharp.

Irene sliced through the twine and unfolded the wrappings. Inside was a book and an envelope. The book's title was *Kinder und Hausmärchen. Children's and Household Tales*, she translated automatically, and breathed a sigh of relief. She flipped the book open to check the publication date:

1812. Better and better. Now what was the definite proof that Bradamant had mentioned?

She turned to the index. There were eighty-eight stories listed. The eighty-seventh was titled, in German, *The Story of the Stone from the Tower of Babel.*

She breathed a sigh of relief. 'It's the one,' she said.

'Yes!' Kai said exultantly, and slammed his palm down on the desk. 'We've got it!'

'What does the letter say?' Vale asked.

Irene put the book down again for the moment and opened the envelope. Thoughts of letter bombs came a few seconds too late. With a sigh, she shook the letter gently onto the desk. No bombs. Good.

Kai leaned across to read over her shoulder, then paused, tilting his head.

A fraction of a second later, Irene heard it as well. Screams. Screams, and a horrid sort of rustling with a nightmarish familiarity to it.

She thrust the letter into her jacket. There would be time to read it later.

The door slammed open with a heavy boom, and a woman ran in, looking round desperately. She had been amongst the browsers outside, but now looked panicked and in a state of disarray. 'Where's the way out?' she gasped.

Behind her, through the open door, Irene could see more people running in all directions, but ultimately all in the direction of *away*. There was a spreading tide of something silver oozing across the floor in a horrible stop-motion way. It would reach a row of cases, and then it was suddenly crawling round the foundations of the next row. The noise it was making, a fierce hungry rustling and skritching, echoed in the large room, underpinning the shouting. Further back, the silver flood was oozing over ominously shaped lumps on the floor, covering them so densely that she couldn't see the colour of clothing, hair or skin.

'Silverfish!' the woman screamed at them. 'Get out of here now!'

The oncoming menace had nearly reached the chamber door.

Irene was an intelligent, self-possessed, practical woman. (Or at least, that was how she would describe herself on a performance review to any senior Librarian.) She yelped in panic and scrambled on top of the desk, pulling her skirts up and crouching there in horror. She desperately tried to remember if the Language had vocabulary for *silverfish* or *instantly lethal insecticide* and, if so, what it was.

Kai swept across the room in a motion almost as smooth as the approaching silverfish. He picked up the screaming woman, and tossed her up onto the table beside Irene before joining them. Vale leapt onto a chair.

'You said you were here to do something about the silverfish!' the woman screamed at Kai. 'Why didn't you get rid of them?'

Irene remembered her now. She'd been here when they were looking for Aubrey and found his skin instead. They'd fobbed her off with a story about insect infestation. Marvellous. She hated dramatic irony. 'Can they eat wood?' she asked.

'You're the exterminators, you tell me,' the woman snapped.

'Silverfish eat anything starch-based,' Vale informed them from his chair. 'Glue, book bindings, papers, carpet, clothing, tapestries . . . I imagine theoretically they could eat wood.'

'If they don't crawl up here first,' Kai said, leaning over the edge of the table to look down at the floor. The silverfish weren't actually trying to crawl vertically up the table legs yet, but Irene wasn't going to wait for empirical evidence. More and more of them were now flooding into the room, crawling over each other on the floor in a thick seething mass of unhealthy silver.

Something at the back of Irene's mind was trying to get her attention. It wasn't the silverfish. It wasn't the woman next to her. It was the way that she could see a newspaper on top of a display case, and it was *moving*. Without the aid of silverfish, it was actually shifting itself, millimetre by millimetre, across the top of the glass, in a light rustling drift . . .

'Vale!' she gasped. 'Could this be triggered by subsonic frequencies? Do you have knowledge of such things?' She gestured at the swarming creatures covering the floor.

Vale caught her meaning. 'Possible,' he said. He frowned at the silverfish as though they weren't starting to crawl up the legs of his chair. 'Though any frequency that could provoke those creatures would surely also have some sort of effect on humans. Causing panic, perhaps—'

'Oh, I'm definitely panicking,' the woman said, with a little half-hysterical catch in her voice. 'And they're still coming in here, they keep on coming – '

'Right,' Irene said, trying to keep her voice calm, deliberately not thinking about the insects crawling up inside her skirts and on her and . . . She swallowed. 'Right. They keep on coming *in here*. If there's a subsonic generator somewhere then it must be either driving them or luring them in here.'

'Heaven and earth,' Kai swore with violent emphasis. 'It must have been keyed to our opening the door – look at the timing of it!'

'But if it was linked to the door, how did it—' Irene started to say, and at the same moment Vale pointed at the door's hinges. 'There!' he snapped. 'That wire. It follows the skirting and leads to the cupboard in that corner. And they're swarming more thickly around it . . .'

Irene could barely see any traces of a wire, but she was prepared to trust Vale's eyes. The dark-wood cupboard was set back into the corner of the room and the silverfish were writhing around its base. They'd swarmed up to a foot off the floor, and now that she was paying attention, they were perceptibly more heavily concentrated there.

'That'll do,' she muttered. Luckily, there was enough detailing on that particular piece of furniture for her to be precise. She'd meant to avoid Language usage in case of booby-traps, but she was prepared to be flexible. Any booby-traps would just have to look after themselves. She raised her voice. **'Oak-leaf-handle cupboard doors. Unlock and open.'**

The cupboard doors sprang open, swinging wide and ripping out bolts at both top and bottom. Inside the cupboard was an intricate tangle of machinery and wires, barely visible under the silverfish which were pouring over it like scaly water. Lights on it glinted and something was humming.

'That's it!' Vale said.

'Kai—' Irene began.

'Already there,' Kai said. He leapt from the table towards the cupboard. The silverfish crunched under his shoes as he hit the floor. Then he was already spinning, body turning gracefully as he launched into a high flying kick. His leading foot crashed into the twisted machinery with a resounding thud and tinkle.

The humming stopped.

Silverfish all over the room paused, then began to pour *away*. Some trickled down through imperceptible cracks in the flooring and skirting-boards. Others flowed out through the door again, scattering in all directions as soon as they could. A few still lurked around the machine, all trying to squirm underneath it and only about half of them succeeding. Kai hopped on one foot, trying to extract his other foot from the mangled device. He was swearing in what Irene assumed were words well-brought-up dragons used when they didn't want to shock lesser creatures.

'I was about to say, please hit it with a chair,' Irene said as the hissing of moving silverfish died away to leave them in relative quiet. 'But thank you. Thank you very much. Nice work.' The book lay safely in Dominic Aubrey's in-tray, untouched, unharmed. It hadn't been eaten. So much for Alberich's final gambit.

'Is that normally how you perform exterminations?' the woman asked. She wasn't showing any sign of getting down from the table yet. To be fair, neither was Irene.

'I think they're in my shoes,' Kai said in tones of deep disgust.

Vale cautiously stepped down from his chair. The few remaining silverfish took no interest in him. He walked gingerly over to Irene's table, and offered her a hand down. 'Nicely done, Miss Winters.'

'Thank you for noticing the wire,' Irene replied. She took his hand and eased her way off the table, trying not to show too much leg in the process. She was going to enjoy being back in an alternate world where trousers were regular wear for women. 'Do you think that means – ' She was about to continue, *that Alberich is elsewhere, and he left this trap*, when she noticed the meaningful glance Vale was giving over her shoulder. Oh. Of course. The woman. The sooner they could get her out of here, the better. – 'Ah, thank you,' she concluded.

'A trap for us?' Kai said softly as she joined him.

'Plausible,' Irene agreed, also keeping her voice down. Vale and the woman were murmuring to each other, so they

286

shouldn't be overheard. 'A bit careless, though. It'd be bound to draw attention here, to this room. Unless it was a delaying action.'

'It was a delaying action,' the woman said.

Kai and Irene turned to look.

Both she and Vale were now wedged against the table, and Vale had an odd rigidity to his posture. His eyes were furious, but his body was entirely still, hands raised as if he'd just been helping the woman down and hadn't got round to lowering them. The woman had a knife to his throat. It didn't look elegant, but it did look brutally efficient. And maybe sharp enough to remove someone's skin.

'**Door, close**,' the woman said. The room and cupboard doors both slammed shut. 'There. Now we should have a few minutes uninterrupted.'

Irene could feel her heart thudding painfully in her chest. 'You're Alberich?' she said tentatively.

'Yes,' the woman said. 'Our fourth meeting. And I hope that you are paying attention this time. Because if you do not do *exactly* as I tell you, then your friend will die.' She paused. 'That is, he will die *first*, and with you watching.'

CHAPTER TWENTY-ONE

'We're listening,' Irene said. She kept her hands still, avoiding anything that could be taken as provocation to slit Vale's throat. 'Please go on.'

She hadn't realized that a change of skin could be quite so all-encompassing. She (no, *he*) spoke with a woman's voice, and it was quite different from the voice she'd heard from inside their ill-fated cab. It was also different again from Aubrey's voice. Was he transplanting the vocal cords too? No, probably just a consequence of the entire magic transferral of skin, however that worked. It would be so helpful if she could see anything unusual in his (or her) appearance. But there was nothing at all.

'I'm willing to make concessions,' Alberich said. 'You aren't all necessarily going to die. Be sensible about this, and we can all walk away.'

Irene did her best to smile in response. *Somehow I don't believe you.* 'I'm interested in staying alive,' she said. 'So's Kai. Aren't you, Kai?'

'Let Vale go and we can talk,' Kai snarled. There was something in his voice which Irene hadn't heard before. For want of a better word, it sounded like possessiveness. *A draconic emotion?*

288

'Silence, boy,' Alberich said. He very deliberately moved the knife in a fraction of an inch, and a trickle of blood ran down Vale's neck to mark his white collar. 'Stay where you are, don't try to jump me, and let your superior do the talking. Well. Do you have the book, Irene?'

Surely he'd noticed the book in the in-tray? If he hadn't, then she wasn't going to draw his attention to it. 'I can get hold of it,' she offered. 'Is that the price?'

'I want more than that.' There was a glitter behind his eyes, and *that* she would recognize if she ever saw it again. A rapacious hunger, an endless emptiness that would never be filled, with all the madness that went with it. 'I have a number of questions. You can even sit down, if you like.'

'We'd really rather stand,' Irene said quickly.

'Suit yourself.' His lips curved in a smile that was somehow more a man's than a woman's. 'Shall I go through the usual literary conventions? First I tell you that you've been told slanders about me, and you nod understandingly while not believing a word of it. Then I promise that you can go free if you hand over the book and you lie and give me a forged copy. Then I kill you.' He shrugged. The knife stayed in place. 'Or shall we break from the usual tropes and actually do something different? Something that might mean you survive this?'

Irene thought about how many other Librarians must have been in this position. There was a reason why he was an urban legend.

Though if they all get killed, who comes back to tell the stories, an irritating part of her mind pointed out. She ignored it.

'I don't see how you can use both the Language and Fae magic,' she blurted out, her mouth running on automatic while she tried to think. It wasn't hard to sound vaguely admiring, even if he'd see right through it.

'I'll give you that one for free,' Alberich said generously, and Irene mentally lowered the odds on him letting them live even further. 'Once a person can use the Language, that can't be taken away. I've learned to use chaos since then. It involves a certain amount of personal redefinition. Difficult, but not impossible. One doesn't *have* to die. Something to take into account in your future career, perhaps? There are far more opportunities open to you than you might think.'

Opportunities . . . What opportunities did she have right now? Kai might be able to use amazing dragon powers to stop Alberich entering an area, but that wasn't much use when he was already inside it. And she might be able to force Alberich out of an area using Language, but again that wasn't much help if he could simply wait outside its boundaries . . .

Boundaries. A half-plausible thought moved through the back of her mind. She wished she'd had more time to ask Kai about his capabilities. When he warded an area, did the warding simply follow the track that he left? Or was it a more metaphysical sort of thing, with the boundaries of his warding being linked to whatever he *intended* to ward?

'Let's reduce the potential hostages,' she said briskly, ignoring Kai's intake of breath from behind her. If this was going to work, she needed him outside and free to act. 'I'm the one you want. As you said, I'm Kai's superior. Having him stand here and maybe lose his temper won't help either of us.' She tried to look gullible. Impressionable. As if she believed Alberich when he said she might survive this. 'You've already got one hostage, and you know I'm concerned about his well-being. If I wasn't, we'd already be attacking or running away. Let's clear the ground. Let Kai here go as a start to the negotiations.'

Alberich surveyed her thoughtfully, and again there was that flash of hunger in his eyes. 'It's true that my questions concern you, not him,' he said slowly. 'And he's no initiate.

I needn't fear him trying to open a door to the Library behind my back. Very well. I'll be reasonable. In return for a similar concession from you.'

Irene remembered to breathe. 'Such as?' she said.

'Your birth name,' Alberich said quickly, and she realized this had been his plan all along.

Magic had never been Irene's field of expertise. It still wasn't. But she didn't need to be an expert to know that Alberich's Fae magic, with knowledge of her true name, could be very bad news for her.

'Hah!' Kai said. She suspected he was sneering.

Irene nodded to Alberich, then turned to Kai. As she had thought, he was sneering. 'Kai,' she said. 'I want you to do something very straightforward for me. I want you to go outside and stay outside. I don't want you setting one foot inside this library.' How to convey to him *I want you to set up that warding you talked about and do it as fast as possible*? 'I'll handle this.'

Kai blinked at her, totally blindsided. 'But—' he started.

'But me no buts,' Irene snapped. 'It's as Alberich said. You're not a Librarian and there's *nothing* you can do in this situation. You don't have the Language and you can't fight him. I'm not going to endanger yet another person. Now are you going to obey my orders and get *out*,' she could hear her voice rising, 'or am I going to have to worry about you as well as Vale here?'

Kai gave her a long stare. It felt like a reproach. It was a reproach. She didn't want to do this to him, but Alberich wasn't stupid. The slightest hint of collusion would get Vale killed, and she could only hope that Kai understood that. 'You know perfectly well there's nothing I can do if I'm outside these walls,' he said. Could he have grasped what she wanted? 'I'm supposed to be your colleague, not your brain-damaged dependent! At least let me stay nearby.'

'It's all one to me,' Alberich said blandly.

Irene jerked her thumb at the door. 'These are your orders, Kai. Out, and stay outside, and I don't want to see your face until we're done.' She glanced up at the window for a moment. 'And don't get any ideas about flying around on the zeppelins.'

Kai's eyes narrowed fractionally, and she could only hope that he'd grasped the idea. 'Don't think I'm happy about this,' he said, shoulders slumping to the very angle of their first meeting. It had looked better in a leather jacket.

Irene nodded and turned back to Alberich. 'The door, please.'

'Your name, please,' he said, with the same intonation that she had just used.

'I give you my word that I will give you my birth name the moment Kai stands safely outside that closed door,' Irene said in the Language.

'Neat,' Alberich commented. 'You think quickly. **Room door, open.'**

The door swung open, squashing silverfish in its wake, and thudded against the wall. There was nobody in the room beyond – at least, there was nobody alive. Just the huddled mounds of the few unfortunate bodies caught in the silverfish attack. Irene hoped queasily that they were just unconscious, overcome by ultrasonic waves or something like that. She couldn't handle more deaths.

'If you hurt her,' Kai said softly, 'I swear by my father and his brothers, and by the bones of my grandfathers, that you shall pay for this.'

Alberich regarded him thoughtfully. 'What a curious way of putting it. I'm sure I've heard that somewhere before . . . oh, never mind, I daresay I can dissect you later if it's absolutely necessary. Out of here now, before I change my mind.'

Irene didn't say anything, in case Alberich did change his mind. She gestured Kai towards the door, and wondered how long it would take him to set up a barrier. And also how long she had before Alberich was finished with her.

Kai hunched his shoulders angrily and stalked out of the office.

'**Close, room door**,' Alberich said, and it slammed shut with another squelch of splattered silverfish, leaving the three of them alone together.

Irene felt the compulsion of her own oath like a noose around her neck. 'My parents gave me the name of Ray,' she said, quickly choosing her words, before it could force out even more detail. The phrasing was more convoluted than it might have been, but it was true enough. 'I don't know their birth names, so I can't give you a family name.'

'Ray.' Alberich looked as if he was about to laugh. 'And did they call you their little ray of sunshine?'

Actually, yes, they had. Irene raised her brows. 'Is that relevant?'

'Not particularly, but I have always been a curious man.' His hand didn't move, and the knife at Vale's throat stayed steady. 'Why don't you know their birth names?'

There was no way she was telling him they were Librarians too. And now she'd answered, she wasn't bound and could lie as much as she wanted. 'They always kept secrets from me,' she invented. 'I'm answering your question as best I can.'

Alberich narrowed his eyes, and she suspected with a chill that he didn't believe her. 'Relevant questions, then. What precisely has been going on?'

She hadn't expected that one. 'Er, in what sort of detail?'

'There have been far too many people interfering in what

might otherwise have been a perfectly straightforward extraction. Believe me, Ray – '

She knew he saw her twitch when he used her name. She couldn't help it. She hadn't heard anyone use it to her for *years*. It was a childhood name and she wasn't a child any longer.

– 'I didn't ask for any of this,' he went on smoothly. 'I would much rather have simply taken the book and left. No mess. No fuss. So I'm asking you, in a perfectly reasonable way, to stand up straight, stop stammering, and give me a full report. Imagine I'm one of your superiors.'

He could have been one of her superiors too. It was easy to imagine. They were diverse enough – such as Coppelia with her clockwork limbs or Kostchei with his thousand-yard gaze. But all had the same air of authority that Alberich was displaying. Other than that and the rumours, she knew *nothing* about him. She didn't even know what he looked like. And he terrified her.

'Under the circumstances—' Vale put in.

'Remember that I can and will freeze your vocal cords too,' Alberich said. 'And your lungs. Unless you want to explain events yourself? In which case, Ray here becomes worthless . . .'

'I believe Miss Winters can handle this,' Vale said. 'I will only interrupt if I have something important to add.'

He was probably used to coping while people held knives at his throat, Irene reflected savagely. 'Allow me,' she put in. 'I believe that the main factor here was that Wyndham knew too much.'

'Quite a claim, given how much Vale seems to know of Library business,' Alberich said pleasantly.

Irene decided to ignore that as she wondered how long Kai would take. And would she know when he'd finished? She needed to spin this out as long as possible, weave all her guesswork into a convincing narrative, and pray that Alberich would accept it. 'Wyndham had connections with the Fae,' she started confidently, 'but he also knew that Dominic Aubrey was a Librarian and, as such, opposed to the Fae. Wyndham knew the book was significant to Silver and thought that he could use it as a bargaining chip to gain something in return. Or he might have been taking some sort of complicated revenge. It was one of those Fae relationships. He decided to make sure that the book was somewhere safe while he negotiated. So he sent it under cover of another parcel to the Natural History Museum.' Could she persuade Alberich to go there to look for it? 'And then he was murdered.'

'Oh yes,' Alberich said. 'I arranged his killing. My agents didn't find the book while they were there, but that would be because Belphegor got there first. The Iron Brotherhood were extremely useful. Vampire-killing assassins, automata to send after you, and other things too. It seemed the easiest way for me to get hold of the book. I didn't feel like dealing with Silver or the other local Fae. Some of my allies have issues with certain factions. But I won't bore you with the details. I entered this alternate, took control of the Iron Brotherhood, found the locally stationed Librarian, questioned him, and assumed his skin. Simple enough. Speaking of that, do you still have it?'

Irene abruptly wanted to be sick. She'd maintained some control during werewolf attacks, zeppelin near-crashes and silverfish fatalities, but this was different. *Questioned him. Assumed his skin.* 'It was you, wasn't it? The first time?'

He understood her question, ill-formed as it was. 'Oh yes. I was the one who met you and your student when you first came through. To be honest, you've been rather a surprise to me.'

'Flattery will get you nowhere,' Irene said primly, counting seconds in her head.

Something else was clearly ticking over behind Alberich's eyes too. 'If you'd found the book in the Natural History Museum, you could have gone straight back to the Library by forcing a portal elsewhere. You wouldn't have needed to come *here*. And you've admitted Wyndham knew that Aubrey was a Librarian. Answer me, Ray. Did Wyndham send the book *to* Aubrey?'

'Yes,' Irene said. The word came grating from her mouth in response to his question and his use of her name before she could waltz around the subject any further.

A high colour showed on Alberich's cheeks. It must be some sort of anger-reaction transmuted by the skin he was wearing. 'Are you telling me that the book came *here*?'

Irene could feel the response dragging at her throat, trying to say itself. Vale's eyes met hers for a moment, as she weighed the benefit of distracting Alberich further against the risk of his cutting Vale's throat if he lost his temper. 'Yes,' she said quickly, giving in and letting the word out, before Alberich felt the need to make good on his threats.

'And it's the book on the desk?'

Irene opened her mouth to deny it, but couldn't. The word dragged itself from her lips. 'Yes.'

Alberich exploded. 'You pitiful little idiot! Do you have any idea how much effort I've had to put in here over the last few days?' He was shrieking like a harridan, and though the knife at Vale's throat was steady, his face was *wrong* – his mouth open a little too wide, his eyes staring furiously, spittle spraying the side of Vale's face. 'I shift skins twice. I take my attention away from very important projects. And because you have been running around hiding this book, my efforts have been wasted. Do you think that's funny, Ray? Do you?'

The room began to shift and crawl around him. The papers on the desk ran into liquid and dripped away, running down to splash against the floor. Dead silverfish dissolved into vapour that blew outwards in widening curls, as though Alberich and Vale stood at the centre of a whirlwind. The panes of glass in the display cases began to vibrate, thrumming as if someone was singing at an impossibly high pitch. And now Irene could feel it pulsing at the back of her skull, humming in her ears. 'Stop it!' she cried out.

'No,' Alberich said. He smiled at her, abruptly calm. 'No, it isn't funny. I'll take that book. You will give it to me.'

'Or you'll cut your hostage's throat?' Irene said. She was still shaken from the sudden flux. Everything about it had been *wrong*. The Fae were bad enough, but this softening of reality had been much worse. She'd been ready to face death, even, but that – no.

'Be reasonable,' Alberich said. 'I'll need a new skin soon. Another Librarian's skin would suit me quite well. So would Vale's position in society. Don't give me any excuses, Ray. Don't give me any more reasons to slit this man's throat and then rip your skin off. Be very polite, be very helpful, and listen to what I'm about to tell you.'

Irene simply jerked her head in a nod. She was afraid of touching off that anger again, afraid for Vale's sake – and, more honestly, terrified for herself.

'Where was I?' For a moment he reminded her of Dominic Aubrey, making her wonder how much of that charade had been imitation and how much had been genuine Alberich, filtered through a dead man's skin. She'd *liked* Aubrey. 'Ah yes. Motivations. Tell me, Ray, what is the purpose of the Library?'

'To preserve,' Irene said automatically.

Alberich nodded as though he'd expected that answer.

'Now tell me – tell me honestly and sincerely – that you've never thought about using the knowledge you've helped preserve. To change the worlds around you for the better. Or do you think that they're already perfect?' His voice dripped sarcasm.

Irene felt as if she was having to run through a minefield blindfolded, with no idea what the correct answers were. 'Of course I've thought about it. But you know that they don't send us – ' For a moment she wished she hadn't used the word *us*. It brought them onto the same level. – 'out on missions unless they're certain that they can trust us.'

'And you accept that so readily?'

'It's the price I chose to pay to get what I wanted.' She'd never wanted anything else.

'Don't think I make this sort of offer to just any Librarian,' Alberich went on. 'You've shown a degree of intelligence which has impressed me. Not all Librarians know when and how to break the rules.'

'Excuse me a moment,' Vale said politely, while Irene wondered if Alberich gave the *normally I wouldn't spare your life, but you're special* spiel to every Librarian he met. 'Might I ask what happened to the original Miss Mooney?'

'Who?' Alberich said blankly.

'The woman whose body you are occupying.' Vale's tone dripped with cold disdain. 'Jennifer Mooney, one of the more influential figures in the Iron Brotherhood. I recollect the face from one of Singh's photographs. I wish I had remembered it earlier.'

'Oh.' Alberich smiled. 'Ah, Ms Mooney – I had to take her identity in quite a hurry, in order to use the Brotherhood as a diversion.'

Irene could have kicked herself. Of *course*. The alligator attack on the Embassy, to distract Silver. She clearly remembered him dashing off to protect 'a book'. And Alberich had

298

been right on the scene afterwards, leading to their almost-drowning. Then there was the assault on the Natural History Museum – all of it made sense now. That was what he'd meant earlier when he'd said that he had taken control of the Brotherhood. She saw Vale's face twitch in mortified humiliation. He must be having the same chain of thought, and blaming himself for not deducing it earlier.

'And they have the most baroque ideas about false names and false identities. You'd think that a pro-technology group would be more efficient about record-keeping, wouldn't you? Now if only you'd said "Damocles", I'd have known precisely whom you meant.'

He didn't even know her name. For some reason, that utterly chilled Irene through and through. And Alberich must have seen it in her face, for he went on, '**And now, Mr Vale, no more words; your vocal cords are locked shut.**'

Irene saw the sudden flare of panic in Vale's eyes and saw his mouth move, but he made no sound.

I don't think he copes well with being helpless.

Anger fought with the fear that held her still too, its heat against the cold. *And I don't think I cope well, either.*

'Let us assume that you have three options, Ray,' Alberich said, dropping back to his conversational tone. 'The first is that you agree to help me. Give me the book, swear your loyalty by certain oaths which I shall dictate to you, and join me. The Library was never meant to be just a storehouse for books and a school for the obsessive. It could change worlds. It could *unite* alternate worlds. It has potential, *you* have potential, and that potential is being wasted. I would swear my protection to you, just as you would swear your loyalty to me, and you would be safe. You could learn to use Fae powers, just as I have done. Perhaps in time you would challenge me, but together we would do terrible and wonderful things. You know that some key books can change the worlds to which they are linked. Help me, and we will change them for the better. You'll have the power to *make* things better. If you refuse that power, then that's a choice in itself, isn't it?'

All the worlds for her own. Of course she wasn't going to take the bargain. Of course she could never be his minion and slave. But the thought of the pure irresponsibility of doing precisely as she wanted, with the power to do it . . .

'The second choice is for you to put the book down and walk away.' He was watching her closely through the stolen eyes of the woman whom he'd killed. 'Your elders won't blame you. They know my quality, my power. They'll consider that you did the sensible thing. I might even agree with them.'

She gave a little jerk of her head in acknowledgement.

'And the third choice . . .' Alberich shrugged. 'You would regret putting me to that trouble.'

Irene swallowed. Her imagination was functional, and thus troublesome. It was now giving her unpleasant ideas about what Alberich might do if he actually exerted himself. If he viewed killing and skinning someone as merely regular business, what would he consider extra effort? Half-formed images nauseated her, and she swallowed back bile. She barely managed to keep her voice steady. 'I think that's only two choices, though.'

'Is it?' Alberich murmured.

'I have the suspicion that there's only one way I walk out of here alive.'

'Well, true,' Alberich admitted, 'but the second option would be comparatively painless for you. My word on it.'

'Can I ask—'

'No.' His eyes narrowed. 'I think you're playing for time, Ray. I need your decision now. I'll throw your friend in as a signing bonus, but I want your decision in five seconds.'

Four.

Three.

If she swore herself to him in the Language, she'd be bound for life. He wasn't stupid. He was the sort of person who'd have prepared the wording in advance. There would be no loopholes.

Two.

Perhaps people said he'd killed Librarians because nobody had ever come back. But maybe they'd all joined him. She could be joining a secret group who were going to change reality and make the universe a better place.

One.

Maybe someone who went round skinning and killing people (order as yet unspecified) was not concerned with making the universe a better place. Just a thought.

Zero.

'Ray . . .' Alberich said. He had a hopeful sort of smile on his face, as if he genuinely wanted her to say yes.

He probably did.

She was about to die.

What she needed was a miracle.

What she got was a dragon.

CHAPTER TWENTY-TWO

Irene had always assumed, when she'd read about dragons roaring, that the descriptions were figurative or at least hyperbolic. She'd thought that phrases like 'shook the earth' referred to the awe in which dragons were held. Naturally the world around them would be sundered by their fury. What else should one expect from dragons?

But the physical world wasn't shaken by a dragon's roar. Reality itself trembled.

'What the devil!' Alberich swore, the words at odds with his prim female persona. His hand visibly tensed on the knife at Vale's neck, and Irene knew with a sickening dread that he was about to slash the detective's throat open purely on reflex. Then his eyes narrowed in thought. 'Too simple. Ray. By my will and by your name, you can neither speak nor move.'

It wasn't the Language, it had nothing of the Language's command, but his words had their own power, and Fae magic hung in them like chains. Irene was pinned in place like a butterfly, her brand burning on her back as the Library's power fought his command. She was conscious of everything around her – the crushed insects, her hurried breathing, the trickle of blood on Vale's neck, Alberich's calculating eyes – and none of it was any use. There hadn't been time to invoke the Library and force him out of the room as she'd planned. She'd been as shaken as he was by Kai's roar, he'd just recovered faster. It made her feel stupidly embarrassed, but she had to remind herself that this wasn't a marks-will-be-awarded situation, it was a he's-about-to-kill-you situation.

But for all her fury, she couldn't move a muscle.

'A pity,' Alberich said. 'I was really quite impressed with you. Bradamant was efficient, but not remotely as perceptive. I'm afraid you've run out of time to decide, if there's a dragon in the picture, but rest assured that I will remember you fondly.'

The door slammed open, and Alberich's eyes widened as he saw who it was. He opened his mouth to speak, but three bullets in rapid succession hit him in the centre of the forehead. It was as neat and quick as a sewing machine's needle rapping down again and again. He staggered back from Vale, arms flailing as his skirts churned around his legs. He grasped weakly at the table, but no blood ran from the open wounds.

'**Vale and Irene, move freely!**' Bradamant shouted in the Language. 'And get away from him!' she added in English. 'I don't know if that's killed him.'

'It hasn't,' Alberich said. '**Gun, explode.**'

Bradamant threw the gun aside just in time. It came apart in mid-air in a burst of metal and fire. She ducked at the same moment, moving for cover. Vale threw himself to one side as Alberich gestured. But a ripple of air tore into Vale and flung him into one of the display cases, which shattered in a burst of glass. There was an ugly cracking noise.

Vale didn't get up again.

'I really shouldn't give people so much time to decide,'

Alberich said. He ignored Irene as she stood, frozen. His Fae magic still held her, wrapped in chains around her name and spirit. 'Bradamant, my dear, would you like to make a deal for the lives of your friends?'

'Only a fool would make a deal with you,' Bradamant snapped. She'd taken cover behind a large free-standing cabinet.

'Accurate but impertinent.' The holes in Alberich's forehead were bloodless, and unnaturally dark, with neither flesh nor bone visible. He raised his hand, palm towards Bradamant. 'The greater lords of the Fae don't manifest in their true form in the physical worlds. Do you know why?'

'Their chaos is too great,' Bradamant answered, her tone as sharp as if she was being questioned in class. 'They would unmake a world.'

'*Exactly*,' Alberich purred. 'And you wouldn't want that.' The very air began to shudder around his hand. It smoked as if his flesh was liquid nitrogen, cold enough to burn a hole in reality. 'And to prevent that manifestation, I only need one of you with your skin intact . . .'

Irene breathed. He hadn't forbidden her to do that. And she was not going to accept the binding he had set on her. She was a Librarian, and while that made her the Library's servant, it was also a protection. The Language was her freedom. Bradamant had told her to move freely. She could not allow . . .

and her brand was a weight across her back, a heavy burden, trying to force her to her knees

. . . she would not . . .

white hot iron, searing into her

. . . permit him to do this. She refused to submit. Even if he was a monster, something that had killed greater Librarians than herself, *she was not going to accept his binding.*

Irene opened her mouth. The tiny movement of parting

her lips seemed to take years as she watched dark fire blossom around Alberich's hand. She sought for something to distract him, to give her time to invoke the Library. And it came to her in a burst of inspiration. **'Jennifer Mooney's skin! Get off that body now!'**

And it did. In rags and tatters, like a piece of clothing being ripped apart along the seams. The flame around Alberich's hand died, and he opened his mouth wide in a howl of pain. The dress disintegrated, falling apart like the pale fragments of skin. What lay behind it was so painful to Irene's eyes that she had to turn and shield them with her hand. Behind the stolen skin, Alberich was a living hole into some place or universe that should not exist on any human plane. In that brief moment she had seen living muscle, tendon and blood – but also colours and masses that left burning spaces on her retinas. She'd seen things moving which bent the light around them and shifting structures which made no sense. All her reality suddenly seemed as fragile as a curtain which someone was about to rip through at any moment. Irene was aware that she was screaming, and she could hear Bradamant crying out as well. Yet behind it all was Alberich, his voice higher than any human's normal pitch, screaming in pure rage and pain.

So that's why he has to wear a skin, her thoughts rattled, as though the words could form a chain to sanity, link by link. *So that's why he has to wear a skin . . .*

Alberich turned and pointed at her, and reality warped in the wake of his gesture. The wooden floor rotted under her feet, and mouths opened in it to gulp at dead silverfish and bite at her ankles. Thick knots of webbing dropped from the ceiling, full of spiders and drifting ash.

'They'll come for you,' Alberich whispered. His voice had changed again; no longer female, or the voice of

Aubrey, but something else. Something that hummed like the keys of an out-of-tune piano, just missing normal human harmonies to strike out a more painful music. 'You've hurt me and I'll hurt you in turn, I'll give you to the White Singers and the Fallen Towers . . .'

A fold of spiderweb fell across Irene's face, and the sheer horror of having to drag it away, feeling the spiders begin to crawl into her hair, somehow yanked her back into sanity. Her horror turned from something alien and bone deep, into more mundane human disgust. She needed a moment to speak the Library's name and so invoke it. That had been the plan. Minimal and pitiful as it was, that had been the plan. But Alberich would know it the moment she began, and she had his full attention. She'd never get the word out.

Bradamant was screaming. No help from that quarter. And Vale was unconscious. She hoped. Better unconscious than dead.

Glass cracked and splinters from another display case ripped into her dress, distorting into glass singing birds with bright claws and edged beaks. She flung her arm up to shield her face, and a glass bird lashed at her hand, thrashing wings leaving deep scratches. Blood ran like ink down her arm.

Of course. A Language was far more than the spoken word, after all.

She clamped her hands shut around the squirming bird, and fell to her knees. She could hear herself screaming in agony as the thing sliced into her palm and fingers, but it seemed somehow distant. The impossibilities around her were far more real and visceral than the pain. She dimly wondered if she was destroying her hand. Again. But set against her life, or her sanity, then the choice was clear.

Through her tangled, cobwebbed hair she saw Alberich

raise his hand, perhaps to call up more horrors or deliver the death-blow.

Alberich could have stopped her if she'd tried to speak. He ignored it when she drove the squirming bird into the soupy wood of the floor, as she scraped it along to create a long, blood-filled cut. He merely laughed as more debris came raining down on her shoulders from the now-unstable ceiling. But she needed an excuse to explain her actions. Something he would expect her to try.

Irene raised both hands, pointing the bloody glass bird at him. '**Floor!**' she screamed in the Language. '**Swallow Alberich!**'

The heaving mass of rotten wood surged round his feet, but he remained above it as if walking on water. 'Let's try that the other way around, shall we?' he laughed at her. 'Go down and *drown* in it!'

She was already on her knees. She felt the wood slurp upwards around her legs like thick mud, sliding up to her thighs. It didn't soak through the skirts of her gown like water, but pressed against her like hungry lips. She had a moment of panic – what would happen if her idea didn't work? She let herself scream and, driven by the energy of that terror, sliced the glass bird into the remaining floor. And again and again, as she sank further into the wood, as if she were trying to save herself. Her blood spattered onto the scored lines, as the wood closed around her waist. The bird's marks stood clear in the slowly oozing floor. Maybe because it was written in the Language, or just because it *had* to work or she was worse than dead.

'Beg me and I'll save you,' Alberich said gleefully. 'Beg me and I'll make you my favoured student, my own sweet child – '

The cobwebbing covered her eyes now. She was working blind.

But some things she knew even in the dark.

'No,' she said, and cut the final line into place. The symbol representing the Library itself showed clearly in the rippling wood between them.

The Library didn't arrive like a roaring dragon or waves of chaos. But there was a light in the room that hadn't been there before, more penetrating and clearer than the fluttering gaslamps. The spiderwebs that had clung to her face and shoulders flaked away as fine dust. The Library's authority pulsed through the room in a steady whisper, like pages turned in slow motion, and stability followed. The floor was now firm where Irene knelt on it, and the glass in her hand was sharp, but it wasn't a living bird. The light even muted the horror of Alberich's form, turning it to something seen as if through dull glass, retreating further and further away . . .

He *was* actually slowly withdrawing. The Library's presence was driving him back, and though its touch felt welcoming to her, like a feeling of *home*, it was forcing Alberich away. And if the sounds he was making were any judge, his expulsion was pure agony.

He hadn't quite finished with her yet, though. Blackness flared in his eyes and his open mouth. 'You call this a victory, Ray?'

And then his back touched the wall, and he started moving through it. The wall thinned to translucency around him as he struggled, partly immersed, like amber around a prehistoric insect.

Then, as they watched, Alberich's back arched, and he screamed – but this was on a different scale than anything they'd heard so far. Irene felt her heart lurch in unwanted sympathy as she saw the punishment that he was suffering – Alberich was crucified between the reality of the Library and the barrier that Kai had created outside, a squirming *thing* of chaos trapped between two surfaces of reality.

Irene realized that she hadn't the remotest idea what would happen next. She didn't know. She didn't *care* as long as it got him away from here. There was no place for that sort of unreality in this world. It was abhorrent. What had he done to himself to become this? What sort of bargains had he struck?

'Release me . . .' Alberich choked out. Blood drooled from his mouth. 'You can't trust the dragons – they'll turn on you as well – release me and I'll tell you.'

'Don't be an idiot,' Bradamant spat. She was pulling herself up off the floor, her gown in shreds, leaning on the wreckage of a chair to support herself. 'Do you really think we'd let you go now?'

Thank you for so helpfully stating the obvious, Irene thought, but managed to keep it to herself. She simply shook her head. A slow-burning flame of something that might be hope was kindling inside her. What they'd done had hurt Alberich. It had *frightened* him.

They might actually win.

She hadn't realized how much she'd assumed they'd already lost.

'You'll regret this,' Alberich whispered in the Language.

The light increased, and he decreased in proportion, fading back and away from them like a disappearing stain. His last scream rang through the room, shattering the remaining glass and throwing books from the shelves.

Irene caught a last glimpse of his face, a human face livid with rage, as he vanished.

'Irene!' Bradamant was suddenly there and she'd lost a few moments of time. She'd been watching Alberich vanish and now Bradamant had an arm round her shoulder and was making her sit down. Vale – hadn't Vale been unconscious? – was fussing over her hands. 'Irene, listen, I promise I won't take it,' Bradamant was saying. 'I will give you my word in the Language right now, if you like, and Vale is here too as witness. If you let go of that book it will make it a lot easier for us to take care of your hands. Irene, please, *listen* to me, say something to me here . . .'

The door burst open. Again. 'Irene!' That was Kai shouting. Irene could only hope that no civilians were close enough to hear it. 'Bradamant! What have you done to her?'

Plus ten for genuine concern for my welfare, Irene decided, *minus several thousand for perception.*

'Please,' Vale said wearily. 'It was that Alberich person. Your plan worked perfectly, but I'm afraid that Miss Winters is in shock. If you would just help us persuade her to relax, so that we can bandage her hands – I have some brandy here.'

'Don't waste that on my hands,' Irene mumbled. She hadn't even realized that she'd picked the book up. She let Bradamant ease the book out from under her arm. 'I need a drink.'

'Miss Winters!' Vale exclaimed.

'Make that two healthy drinks. I'm in shock. Give me brandy.'

'But your hands,' Vale protested. 'They need immediate care.'

Irene didn't want to look, but she forced herself. There were deep cuts across both palms and the insides of her fingers. Flaps of skin hung loose, and she thought she could see bone. She looked away before she embarrassed herself by throwing up. The skirt of her dress was wet with her blood. She must be in shock, or it would be hurting even more than it already did. She'd never hurt herself this badly. She wasn't even sure if it could be fixed. 'There are people in the Library who can deal with this,' she said firmly, desperately praying that she wasn't lying to herself.

Her words came spilling out, quick and professional, a distraction from the reality of her hands. She could hear the forced lightness of her tone. Her speech sounded as if it was coming to her from a great distance, like the chirping of little birds very far away. 'Mr Vale, thank you for your assistance, and I'm sorry that you were dragged into this. Bradamant, please can you check the door – the inner door, the Library ingress – for any traps?'

'I don't think there could be any alien influences, after you invoked the Library inside this place,' Bradamant said gently.

'Oh.' She must be more in shock than she'd thought. 'All right, then. Kai, please help me stand.'

Kai slipped an arm around her, helping her to her feet. Under other circumstances she might have been more careful about leaning on him, but at the moment it really didn't seem that important. So she was leaning on him. She was injured. He was her colleague. It was only sensible.

His clothing was disarranged, but still there. So turning into a dragon didn't mean that you lost all your clothing. This seemed unduly significant, and she filed it away so she could ask questions later. 'Are you sure about this?' he asked in an undertone.

'I think it's best that we're out of here before any questions need answering.' *That* piece of wisdom was drilled into all Librarians very early on.

'Ahem.' Vale brushed at the trickle of blood on his collar, rather pointlessly, considering his generally dishevelled state. 'While I am willing to abet Singh in, well, covering this up, I would also be interested in finding out more about this. Before you go, Miss Winters, all of you . . . can you tell me about the last story in that book?'

Bradamant opened her mouth, and the first word was obviously going to be *No*, and so were all the rest of them.

Irene held up one hand to stop her. 'Mr Vale, are you sure that you want us reporting to our superiors that you read it? Whatever it is?'

'I find it hard to believe that they will assume I didn't read it,' Vale said drily.

That was true enough. 'I suppose there's no reason why you shouldn't look over our shoulders as we check that it's the right book,' Irene said slowly. She cast a quick glance at Kai, but he had enough sense to keep his mouth shut and not mention they'd already done so. 'Bradamant, you said to check the eighty-seventh story, correct?' She indicated the book, now in Bradamant's possession. 'I would open it myself, but my hands – '

Bradamant pursed her lips, then nodded. Perhaps she sympathized. Or perhaps she intended to blame every last bit of unauthorized exposure on Irene. She wiped her hands clean of dust and blood on the battered skirts of her dress and flipped the book open. 'The eighty-seventh story, yes. The Story of the Stone from the Tower of Babel.'

She breathed a deep sigh. 'It's here. Eighty-seventh of . . . eighty-eight?'

The silence hung in the room as they all considered that point. If it was unusual that an eighty-seventh story should exist, Irene thought, then what was the eighty-eighth doing there? Could Bradamant have been given a mere indicator, as opposed to the true reason why the book was so important . . . ?

'My German's not very good,' Kai said plaintively.

Bradamant gave a put-upon sigh. '*Once upon a time,*' she began to translate, '*there lived a brother and a sister who both belonged to the same Library. Now this was a strange library, for it held books from a thousand worlds, but lay outside all of them. And the brother and sister loved each other and worked together to find new books for their Library . . .*'

'No wonder your people didn't want this one getting loose,' Vale said with satisfaction.

Bradamant paused to raise her eyebrows at him before continuing. '*One day, the brother said to his sister, "Since this Library contains all books, does it contain the story of its own founding?"*'

'No,' Irene said.

'Surely it must,' Kai said. 'We probably just don't have access to it yet.'

'*If* you don't mind,' Bradamant said.

'I beg your pardon,' Kai said. Bradamant nodded coldly, and went on. '*"I suppose so," the sister said. "But it would be unwise to seek it." "Why?" the brother asked. "Because of the nature of the Library's secret," the sister answered, "that we both wear branded upon our backs."*'

'It has the proper cadence for a Brothers Grimm story,' Vale said helpfully. Irene felt her back itch.

'*Now the brother had never troubled to look at the mark upon his back,*' Bradamant went on. '*But that night he sought a mirror and read the writing on his skin, and what he read there sent him mad. He left the Library then and he colluded with its enemies against it. But most of all he swore vengeance against his sister, for she had spoken the words that set him on this path. A hundred years later, his sister returned to the Library following a quest that she had been set, and she was with child.*'

'A hundred years?' Vale said.

'It can happen,' Irene said. 'If she'd been in an alternate where there was some way to slow ageing – high technology, or high sorcery. But the pregnancy would be the problem—'

'Yes, exactly,' Bradamant said. '*And this caused great trouble, for there could be no birth nor death within the Library. Yet she feared to set foot outside it lest her brother should find her. So in pain she begged them to cut open her belly and take the child*' *out and they did so, and she was delivered of a child. They sewed up her belly with silver thread and hid her among the deepest vaults for fear that her brother should seek her again.'*

Irene could feel her stomach clench inside her in cold fear, very slowly and deliberately. 'So that's why he wanted this book,' she whispered. 'It wasn't because he could use it to gain power over this world. It was because . . .' She wasn't sure how to say it. Because someone knew this about his secrets? If this was Grimm, then it would have been written centuries ago. But time meant nothing in the depths of the Library, as long as someone stayed there. And Alberich was . . . well, nobody knew how old Alberich was. But how old would his sister be? And was she still there?

'A sister,' Kai muttered. His eyes narrowed in thought. 'And his sister's child. How does it finish?'

'That *is* how it finishes.' Bradamant slapped the book shut, hesitated, then slid it back under Irene's arm again. 'There. Now we must be out of here at once. Mr Vale, I hope we can rely on you . . .'

'I don't think it would do any good to make the matter public,' Vale said wryly. 'I am sure I can find someone to blame for all this – the Iron Brotherhood, perhaps, or Lord Silver. He will be most unhappy to find himself without book, conclusion, or enemy.' The thought made him smile. 'But I would value the chance to speak with you all again most highly.'

Irene pulled herself together. 'That depends on our superiors.' A nagging honesty pulled at her. 'But . . . if we get the opportunity, I would like that too. But for the moment – '

'Quite,' Bradamant said. She walked across to the far door. 'Kai, carry her if she can't walk.'

'Some brandy would have helped,' Irene complained as Kai steered her across the slippery floor. She hoped that

Vale wouldn't get any stupid ideas about trying to pursue them through the entrance. 'And I'm quite capable of walking without being dragged.'

'Allow me this small service,' Kai growled in her ear. 'After throwing me out and denying me the chance to protect you, and getting yourself quite this badly hurt, I must *insist* on it.'

Bradamant laid her hand on the door handle, murmuring in the Language, and the air shivered. The door swung open to show rows of shelves beyond.

'They do tell us not to get into arguments that we can't win,' Irene whispered. She was weary now, and her hands were alive with pain.

They stepped through, and the door to the Library closed behind them.

CHAPTER TWENTY-THREE

The door swung shut behind them with a clang, iron-bound and solid. Someone had upgraded the warning posters in the Library room. They were all red ink and Gothic font now, and, as her thoughts drifted, Irene wondered if they had been printed or hand-lettered.

'Sit her down here,' Bradamant instructed Kai, pulling command around her like a cloak. 'I'll go and fetch some help.'

'Just a moment,' Irene interrupted. She suspected that once Bradamant was out of here, she wouldn't be back for quite a while, and there was something very important that she wanted to say to her first.

'You can barely stand,' Bradamant said dismissively. 'You need help.'

Kai looked round for a chair, found none, and carefully lowered her until she was sitting on the floor. 'Irene, Bradamant's right,' he said in the patient tones that sympathetic men use to hysterical women. 'You're hurt.'

'Shut up,' Irene said, and watched his mouth drop open at her rudeness. She was dizzy, and her hands felt as if she'd dipped them in molten barbed wire. But she had to get this said before she lost the will to say it. 'Bradamant.

You cut in on my mission, drugged me and tried to steal my book, and generally broke quite a number of unwritten rules. True or not?'

Bradamant looked down at her. As usual, even in tattered clothing, her posture was effortlessly elegant, and Irene felt even scruffier than usual, sprawled on the floor as she was. For a moment Bradamant was silent. Then, finally, she said, 'True enough.'

'And?'

Bradamant shrugged. 'I can apologize, but I hope you don't expect me to say that I'm sorry.'

'I expect nothing of the sort,' Irene said carefully. 'What I want . . .'

'Yes?'

'What I want is for us to stop despising each other quite so much. It's a waste of time and effort.'

Bradamant raised her eyebrows. 'My dear Irene, for me to despise you, I would have to bother to—'

'Oh, please,' Irene cut in. 'You told me all about it, remember? You think I'm a spoilt brat and you'd be quite happy to have me fail publicly and obviously, even if you'd rather not see me dead for it. You wouldn't bother putting an insult like that together if you didn't want it to sting.' She saw the colour rising in Bradamant's cheeks. Kai's supporting arm behind her was a comfort that helped her hold herself together. 'I think what you want – what we both want – is to genuinely serve the Library.'

'Split infinitive,' Bradamant spat.

'Put it in your report,' Irene said, tiredness dragging her down. 'Just don't waste time hating me any more, all right? And I'll try to stop doing the same. Because I don't think it's helping. I don't think it's helping either of us.'

'Get that help now,' Kai said sharply to Bradamant.

'Please?' Irene forced herself to look up and meet Bradamant's eyes. 'Think about it?'

'I thought you wanted us to stop thinking about each other so much,' Bradamant said coldly. She turned on her heel and walked away, skirts swishing.

Irene's vision was narrowing, as Bradamant faded from view. 'Think about it,' she mumbled, the words thick and heavy in her mouth.

Kai's fingers bit into her shoulder hard enough to make her refocus. 'If you pass out on me now, I'm going to kill you,' he said conversationally.

'A bit counter-productive,' Irene said.

'It'd cheer me up like nothing else.' He leaned in closer, his face inches away from hers. 'You sent me away, you *sent me away* and you nearly got yourself killed. Do you have any idea how stupid that was?'

Perhaps his control was slipping, because his skin was like blue-veined alabaster, and his hair seemed dark blue as well, so dark that it was nearly black. There was a deep fury in his eyes that was a long way from human anger. It was about possessiveness, pride and a sort of ownership as well.

'It worked,' Irene said, managing to return his stare. His pupils weren't human any longer either. They were slit like a snake's, like that other dragon she'd met. But the person behind them was more real to her than Silver and his apparent humanity. Or whatever had looked out at her from Alberich's stolen skin. She wanted to find the words to tell him as much. 'We drove him out. Thank you.'

'He endangered you!' he broke in. 'I shouldn't have left any human alive in there!'

She could have thanked him for obeying or trusting her, or maybe because she could trust him. But for some reason, perhaps to divert him, she said, 'For helping me save Vale's life. I like him.'

To her surprise, that made Kai turn aside and duck his head, a scarlet flush blossoming on those pale high-boned cheeks. The fingers digging into her shoulder relaxed their grip, and there was something more human about his face. 'He is a man to be valued,' he muttered. 'I am glad you approve of him as well.'

It might be a major concession for a dragon to admit he liked any human at all. 'Right,' she muttered. 'Definitely. Could you get me some cotton?' She realized that she'd used the wrong word. 'Coffee. I mean coffee. Bit dizzy.'

'Stay still.' How stupid of him; did he really think she was going to go running off somewhere? 'Bradamant will get help.'

'It's just a flesh wound,' she murmured, then darkness came down over her eyes and swallowed her up.

Light came back grudgingly, filtered through long window blinds. Irene was lying on a couch, her heavily bandaged hands neatly arranged in her lap. She was in one of the rooms that overlooked the unknown city outside the Library walls. Someone had taken off her shoes and arranged the folds of her dress so that they covered her stockinged feet. That small thing, petty as it was, allowed her to relax. There was only one person who'd go to that trouble.

'Coppelia,' she said, raising her head to look for her supervisor. The tension inside her uncurled a little. Coppelia had always been fair. She was other things as well, such as sarcastic. And her level of expectations would challenge an Olympic high-jumper. But she could rely on Coppelia.

'Clever girl.' Coppelia was sitting in a high-backed chair near the couch. A portable desk covered her lap, stacked with hand-copied sheets of paper thick with the Language. She was sitting so the light fell across her desk, but left her face and shoulders in shadow. She shifted, and her joints creaked. 'Do you think you're strong enough to give me a report?'

Irene rubbed at her eyes with her forearm. 'Could we have a little more light in here?' The fluorescent panels in the ceiling were unlit, and the only meagre illumination came through the blinds. It left the whole room feeling dim and unreal, like a black and white film, where bleakness was a deliberate part of the artistry.

'Not quite yet,' Coppelia said. There was something guarded about her voice, although her face was as bland and unreadable as always. Her bright white hair was braided back under a navy cap, showing in stark contrast to her dark skin. In the dim light, it formed a pattern of brightness and darkness to Irene's weary eyes. The artificial carved-wood fingers of her left hand tapped on the edge of her desk, something Irene found comfortingly familiar. 'You've put stress on your body in a number of ways that you don't even understand. We've been bleeding off some of the excess energies, but for the moment you need to be strictly under-exposed to any sort of stimulation.'

Irene raised her eyebrows. 'You don't think that telling you my story is going to be stimulating?'

Coppelia chuckled a wheezing little laugh. 'To me, perhaps. To you, it will merely be desensitization.'

'How dull,' Irene said. Then she sensed the gap at her side, the empty space between arm and ribs where she had been clasping the book. She flailed around with her bandaged hands, trying to find it. 'The book – the Grimm – '

'Only seven out of ten for immediate reactions, I'm afraid,' Coppelia said happily. 'Yes, we have it safe, and Wyndham's letter as well. I suppose it would be too much to hope that you didn't read it? Of course it would. What on earth would anyone do under those circumstances?'

'Well, ah, yes,' Irene said, hoping that sympathy would translate into lenience. 'Of course I had to check that it was the right one.'

Coppelia's voice stayed merry, but her eyes hardened. 'And you knew to check that it was the right one *how*, precisely?'

This was where she decided how much she wanted to sell Bradamant down the river. *Well, Bradamant was trying to steal the book. Before I could bring it back, she poisoned me and left me in what she admittedly thought was a safe place. But she despises me and I don't like her much either . . .*

'I met Bradamant there,' she said, grateful that they were talking in English rather than the Language. She wasn't actually going to lie, but there was . . . well, there might be an element of flexibility. She knew it, and Coppelia probably knew it, but that was best left unsaid. 'When she discovered my mission, she provided some additional information that helped us identify the book. She helped us fight Alberich too.'

'Demerit for using the verb "helped" twice in succession,' Coppelia said. 'And then? I take it she also read it?'

'Only as much as I did,' Irene said, feeling on metaphorically thin ice.

'Which was?' Coppelia pressed.

'The eighty-eighth story.'

She genuinely liked Coppelia, and she thought it was reciprocated. Not just the sort of friendship that could flourish between any mentor and student, but a real, honest affection. It caused her to bring books back from assignment merely because Coppelia might enjoy them. It saw her oiling Coppelia's clockwork joints, or just spending hours talking with her in the timeless Library, where there were neither days nor nights. There was companionship under those constantly burning lights, as they observed the changing windows on the strange world beyond. She thought of all that, and felt a barrier rise between them as Coppelia's eyes narrowed.

'And your conclusions?' Coppelia said, entirely neutrally.

'Alberich had a sister,' Irene said. This was not the time or place to pretend to stupidity. 'The sister had a child. And Alberich either wants to hide the information, or he's looking for them, or both. Or perhaps it was just because the book was linked to the fate of that world, and so it could bring Alberich power. The story about the siblings and the child could be pure coincidence. But I don't think that. And you wouldn't believe me if I told you I did.'

'And that's all you think?' Coppelia pushed. The dry twist at the corner of her mouth showed tacit agreement with Irene's last statement.

'That's all I can be sure of.' There was a spike of pain in Irene's temple, and she raised a bandaged hand to rub at it. 'I can't see why Alberich would have gone to so much trouble to find the book, if it had just been some kind of diversionary tactic to distract from some larger plot. And he'd gone to such efforts merely for some scheme relating to that alternate – but hunting the book seemed so very personal to him . . . But if Kai hadn't been with me, I'd have died.' She did her best to give Coppelia a reproachful glance. 'You knew about Kai.'

'What you can work out in a few days, I have at least a sporting chance of noticing over several years,' Coppelia said smugly. But there was still that edge of caution behind her eyes. 'Does he know I'm aware of his nature?'

'I don't know,' Irene said. 'He knows I know.'

'Well, clearly,' Coppelia said. 'And does he know that you'll tell me what you know?'

'He'd find it astonishing if I didn't,' Irene said, after a

moment's thought. 'His views on loyalty are very definite.' She noticed that Coppelia wasn't asking whether or not she *liked* Kai. And seeing that she did, she felt it was best kept to herself. If they were looking for an excuse to assign him elsewhere, which was the last thing she wanted, acknowledging that she was less than objective about him would certainly do it. Which would be bad. So she would avoid subjectivity, or at least being caught at it.

'Well, he *is* a dragon.' Coppelia nodded. 'Kindly don't speculate too much to him about how much we already comprehend about him, unless the situation requires it. You'll know when. For the moment, we'll have to assume he understands that we know all.'

'All?'

'We are the Library,' Coppelia pointed out. 'What we don't know, we research. Now tell me the rest.'

Irene gave a brief, factual report of the details . . . *and then there was Alberich.* Alberich took up a great deal of the report. Even then, Irene found it not only easier, but essential to her sanity, to be minimalist in her descriptions.

Probably her current urge to grab everyone she met and check that they weren't Alberich in disguise would eventually go away. She hoped so.

Finally she trailed off. It seemed that they had slipped back into the casual banter of previous assignments. Everything had been simpler then, and arrogance had made it easy for Irene to talk glibly about secrets, about how elder Librarians could use her as a pawn. Now that that had probably happened, it was much less intriguing. It was like a splinter in her mind, which ached when she considered it. 'Could you have given me more information?' she finally asked.

'You were warned about Alberich as soon as we were

certain he was within that alternate,' Coppelia said gently. 'Before that, you might have been able to complete the mission on the information given. Do you actually feel any safer, with your current knowledge, understanding he suspects that you have it?'

She was about to reply, *No, not really,* but there was more to the question than that. 'I feel better able to handle matters now I've an idea about what's going on,' she said. 'People having nervous breakdowns due to knowledge that man isn't meant to know – that happens in horror literature. Not real life.'

'Yes.' Coppelia sighed. 'And yes, I know you prefer crime literature.'

'Detective stories,' Irene corrected her.

Coppelia raised an eyebrow. 'And is there anything else?'

Irene tried to guess her meaning, then gave up. 'Like what?'

'This from someone who claims to be an investigator.'

'But I didn't ever claim—' Irene tried to put in.

'I must say that I think you could have done a better job as an undercover agent.'

'But it was a very complex scenario, with limited information,' Irene blurted out. This was like an examination from her nightmares. She could feel herself cringing back against the couch.

'Oh?' Coppelia folded her arms in a manner that practically telegraphed stern judgement. 'Young woman, even though you're my student, you have overstepped a number of lines on this occasion. You've revealed facts about the Library to at least two uninvolved parties.'

Irene decided to just give up.

'You encouraged the manifestation of a dragon in public.'

'Excuse *me*.' That was a bit too much. 'I wasn't aware that was an offence against Library rules, and the Library sent him with me in the first place!'

'Your comments have been noted,' Coppelia said. She was sounding almost bored, but there was a spark of amusement in her eyes. 'Naturally I shall give them full consideration. I will also try to present them in a proper and reasonable light to the elder Librarians, should I need to justify your actions. Rather than treating them as a pitiful string of excuses.'

Irene glared at her. This was beyond unfair. This was outright unreasonable.

'I had expected better. Such a pity.' Coppelia tapped her fingers against each other. They clicked like death-watch beetles. 'Fortunately, as your mentor, I am competent to deal with this matter and there is no need to refer it up higher.' Now the message in her eyes was clearer. It was a warning. Irene just wished she had a better idea what it meant. 'As I said earlier, we are Librarians. What we don't know, we research. And you, my dear Irene, have a great deal to research.'

'I do?' Irene said, feeling her way carefully. 'I suppose that perhaps I do.'

Coppelia nodded. 'Yes. Exactly. In fact, I believe I am within my rights to place you on location duty in that alternate. That is until you've cleared up a few loose ends in the investigation. Your apprentice will stay with you, of course.'

Irene had an extraordinary sense of being on a lift in free-fall. 'But – I – Alberich – '

'Him at least you don't need to worry about,' Coppelia said. 'Quite without any sort of proper training, you've actually managed to banish him from that alternate. I'm impressed. Nine out of ten for inductive reasoning. What you have done will have set up a resonance in the inter-world barriers which will stop him from entering it again via chaos-linked magic. And of course he can't use the Library itself. It will also cause serious inconvenience to local Fae, but I don't consider that particularly important. At least, not to the Library.'

'You're wanting me to go back?' Irene squeaked. She took a deep breath, and forced her voice lower. 'That is, you want me to go back there on detached duty?'

'Precisely,' Coppelia said. She smiled warmly, in much the same way that an alligator, cyborg or otherwise, might smile after a full meal of whatever alligators ate. Librarians, maybe. 'I think that, at this moment, it's the best possible place for you. There is also a Librarian-in-Residence position vacant and you are familiar with the world.'

'That could almost sound as if you think it safer than the Library,' Irene said tentatively.

'You might very well think so,' Coppelia said. 'I couldn't possibly comment.'

Freefall had given way to an enormous vertiginous drop, but it wasn't actually that frightening any more. It was even exciting. 'I'll need an expense account to support myself and Kai, of course, and identity papers.'

'Irene,' Coppelia said severely, 'I expect you to manage your own identity papers. Really. Here.' She reached for a small leather briefcase, and offered it to Irene. 'This contains Dominic Aubrey's full particulars, including his bank accounts. See about getting the money transferred. Have Kai pose as his long-lost cousin or something. I'm sure your friend Vale will be glad to help.'

Irene flushed. 'You think so?'

'He sounds a practical man. I think he'll prefer to have you on his side.' She paused for thought. 'You probably won't get Aubrey's office, so you must notify us once you have lodgings. That way any future visitors to the alternate will know where to find you. You will be the Librarian-in-Residence, after all.'

'I will?' Irene said, and blushed again, this time out of genuine humility rather than simple embarrassment. Librarian-in-Residence was a post of some responsibility. It was something she hadn't even thought about handling for decades yet. Excitement began to give way to panic. 'I don't know what to say – '

'Thank you and goodbye should cover it,' Coppelia said briskly. 'Come now. Here you are, sitting around, with Kai fretting over you and worrying himself. A word of advice. Don't get yourself hurt if there's a possibility of him throwing himself in the way. He'll be far more upset about it than you will.'

'Coppelia.' Irene took a deep breath. 'Why?'

The old woman closed her eyes for a moment. She was frail, even for the Library, and her wooden arm and legs were the only solid things about her. The rest was all fragile flesh, spiderweb white hair and eyes as cold as black stars. 'Don't ask,' she said, her voice tired. 'Don't say anything, then I won't need to reply. And then later on, we can both answer truthfully that nothing was shared. You've always avoided asking questions in the past, but we've run out of time for that. It's true that we need to know more. You know the questions. Go and find answers, and let me report back that I sent you to investigate. It's true that you'll be safe there from Alberich. He's got bigger fish to hunt, that one. Let him do it. Let the rest of us throw ourselves in the way this time. Go and play detective, Irene, and do a good job of it. Make me proud of you.'

There was a rustle at the door, then a brisk rapping.

'That will be Kai,' Coppelia said. She opened her eyes

327

again. 'You'd better be going. He knows the way from here to the alternate's entrance.'

Irene swung her feet down from the couch, and stood up. 'Thank you,' she said. It came out grudgingly, and she tried again. 'Thank you, Coppelia. I do appreciate it. That is, I am grateful.'

'You don't, but you will,' Coppelia said. She sighed again. 'Your hands have been pieced together – I dragged old Wormius away from his runes to reattach all the bits and pieces. Another reason for you to be out in real time. They're not going to heal here in the Library.'

Irene realized that was true. Her hands might be stitched up and bandaged, but unless she left the Library, they'd never actually heal. 'Thank you again.'

Coppelia waited until Irene was almost at the door, before saying, 'Your shoes are under the couch.'

'Couldn't you have said that earlier?' Irene snapped, losing a lot of her gratitude. 'Just a moment!' she called to the door, then trotted back to the couch to sit down and put the shoes on.

'I'll be expecting regular reports,' Coppelia said, watching Irene fumble at the bootlaces with her bandaged fingers. 'And don't get too involved. Remember who you are.'

'I'm not likely to forget that,' Irene said. She finished knotting the laces and sat back. 'I'm a Librarian.'

'So you are,' Coppelia said. She didn't speak again, but nodded in dismissal, and Irene could feel her eyes on her with every step that she took towards the door.

Kai was waiting on the other side.

Irene managed a few confident paces down the corridor, once the door had been safely shut between them and Coppelia, before her purposeful walk slowed to a halting stumble. Kai frowned, and offered her his arm. Maybe he really thought she was that badly injured. Or possibly possessiveness was a characteristic of draconic affection. They were supposed to be hoarders, after all. Not so different from Librarians.

But just for the moment – just for this single moment, on their way back to this alternate that was now her home – she could relax and appreciate what she'd been given. It was all hers. Her territory, her open treasure-box of new books to read. A new world of great detectives, zeppelins, Fae and dragons. She wasn't going to complain.

And she certainly wasn't going to run away. She had questions to ask, and answers to find. She just hoped she lived long enough to enjoy it.